The Reed Warbler

The Reed Warbler

Ian Wedde

Victoria University of Wellington Press

Victoria University of Wellington Press
PO Box 600, Wellington
New Zealand
vup.wgtn.ac.nz

First published 2020

A catalogue record is available from the National Library of New Zealand.

ISBN 9781776563005

Published with the assistance of a grant from

Arts Council of New Zealand *Toi Aotearoa*

Printed by
Markono Print Media Pte Ltd

To my children Carlos, Conrad, Mischa,
Penn and Jack, and grandchildren Sebo, Stella,
Bella, Cara, Lenny and Banjo;
Gute Reisen!

Contents

Part 1
'a mind of her own'
11

Part 2
'what choice do we have?'
229

Part 3
'the fresh airs of time to come'
397

Afterword
621

Descendants of Josephina Hansen

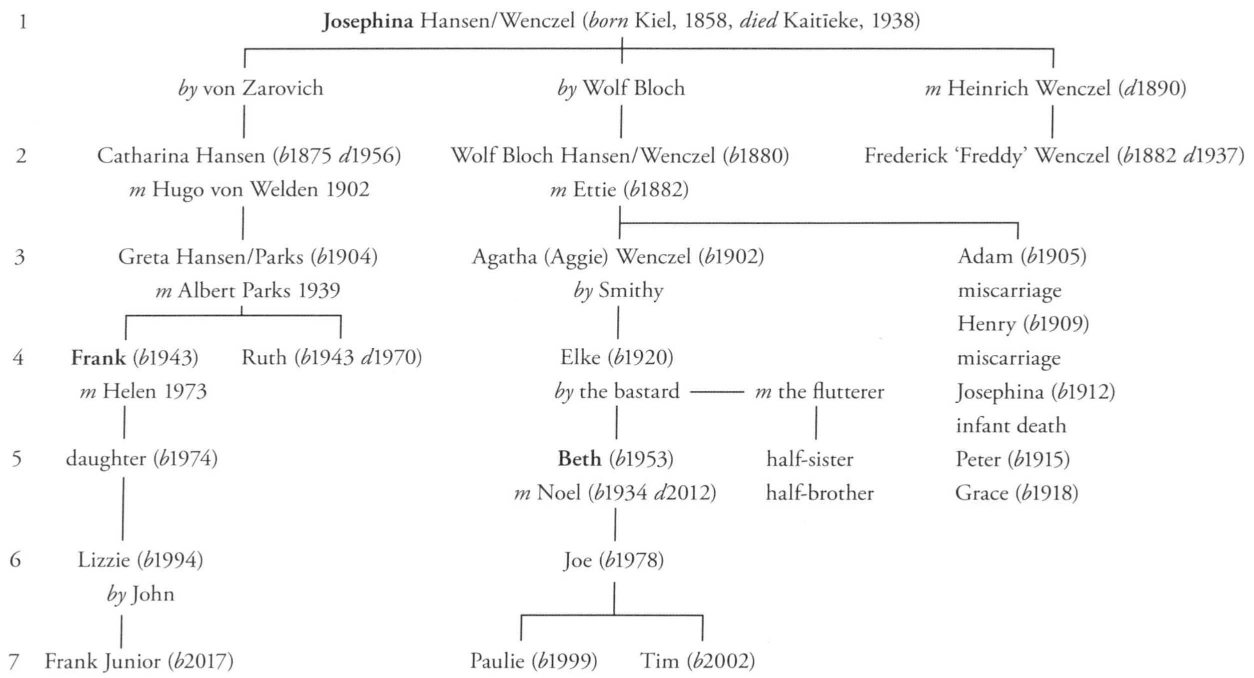

Part 1

'a mind of her own'

Beth and Frank

On the far distant horizon, down the long parched view shaft of the Kaitīeke valley and across the grey-blue ranges, shimmering and ghostly with heat and distance, almost indistinct, was the tiny, remote cone shape of Mount Taranaki.

'Can't you see it?' asked Beth.

Frank was squinting. 'Nah, you're imagining it.' He'd made an ironic point of pushing his glasses up on his forehead. 'Like much else just lately.'

'Great-grandad Wolf reckoned he could still see it without his glasses when he was eighty.'

'Your great-grandfather was full of shit.'

'Yeah, but it was Wolf shit.'

At the reunion, the sensational exploits of Great-grandfather Wolf had been much repeated.

A mob of panting sheep was sweltering in the yard by the shearing shed up the hill from the graveyard.

'Hope they've got some water,' said Beth.

'Hope there's still a pub down there.' Frank took Beth's elbow to help her over the roadside drop. 'Why would anyone still bother running sheep here, look at it, talk about shit country.'

'Old man Wolf flagged it, so not all that full of shit, maybe?' Beth lifted the latch to the cemetery gate, which swung open on one rusty hinge. Someone had driven a mower among the graves when the grass was long, and swathes of yellowing stalks and dry seed-heads lay across some of the concrete slabs. A slapdash spraying of weedkiller around the edges of the graves had given them all a dead-grass border.

They recognised Josephina Wenczel's grave by the wrought-iron railing around it. As well as everything else he was famous for being good at, including his decision not to run sheep on the shit hills he'd cleared of forest, her son Wolf had been a competent blacksmith. His decorative wrought iron featured a pyramidal tip on top of each twisted stanchion, with bent eyelet wings below, and the top horizontal was a chain braided in three strands like the trim on some kind of uniform cuff. It looked carefully planned, even coded, the work of a thoughtful, methodical mind. But the grave was in a terrible state of disrepair – the concrete slab was cracked in two places and covered in a thick reddish moss through which the river-worn gravel in the concrete showed here and there, and the plain granite headstone had fallen over so that its inscription faced upwards and had become waterstained and lichened. Weeds were growing in the cracks of the slab, including a couple of stalky ragworts like those on the nearby hillsides. Frank yanked them out.

'Never once came up here when we were kids, disgraceful, or did you?'

'Never,' said Beth, though she thought she might have. If so it was the bleating sheep she remembered, not the grave.

He gave her a sceptical look and used the ragwort stalks to scrub at lichens on the headstone. 'Josephina Christian Wenczel 1858 to 1938. Hello old girl.' Then his scrubbing uncovered some German words. 'Okay, help me out here, genius.'

'Wie traulich war das Fleckchen, Wo meine Wiege ging,' read Beth. 'How cosy was the little spot where my cradle went, or rocked, or something like that.' Her eyes flooded suddenly with tears. 'Christ, Mum used to sing that. She learned it from her grandad Wolf, and he learned it from . . .' She got a tissue and gave her nose a good honk. Wolf, of course, had learned it from the woman whose decrepit grave they were looking at. 'Mum and her grandad used to sing it. Nice baritone, old man Wolf, and Mum played the piano accompaniment. Brahms, apparently.'

But there was a second inscription below it that didn't ring a bell: *Zum Gedächtnis.* There were two initials on the line below: WB. *Zum Gedächtnis* in italics, like a quote, but WB not italics. It was a careful detail, like the wrought iron.

'The first bit's from that German song, was it called "Zum Gedächtnis"? Can't remember,' said Beth to her cousin's back – he was staring moodily down the valley in the direction they planned to go next, to where her great-grandfather Wolf had established his orchards and beehives, where he'd left the bush to regenerate, where Beth's and Frank's families had sometimes gone for summer holidays when they were kids, where Josephina Wenczel had ended her days. 'And I don't get the initials.'

Frank was pretending to be bored by her commentary – he tossed his ragwort brush over his shoulder. 'Auf Wiedersehen,' he said.

Then he was walking to the car. A couple of magpies were making a racket in the scruffy macrocarpa at the edge of the graveyard – one of them dive-bombed Frank at the cemetery gate and his yell caused a jostle among the sheep in the yard.

As he opened the driver's door, Frank looked back at the graveyard. 'When Tom and Elizabeth took the farm, Elizabeth's lips were red, and quardle oodle ardle wardle doodle the magpies said. Someone should fix the poor woman's grave up,' he said. 'Imagine coming all this way and ending up here. What a tragedy.'

'*Zum Gedächtnis* means something like "in memoriam". Could be the title of the song? But then "WB" should be "JB", Johannes Brahms?' Beth was fishing but Frank didn't respond. He was driving carefully down the steep, winding incline. The verges and scruffy overhanging scrub on the passenger side were grey with dust, and the eroded, clay-scarred pasture fell away on Frank's side. 'Can you even imagine what this was like when Great-grandad Wolf first came in? And Great-granny Ettie?'

'Different,' said Frank. 'And no, I can't imagine it, Beth.' He said 'imagine' with the hint of scorn she remembered from way back, when they were kids, when his scorn was part of the game they played, of him being the big cousin who knew stuff. But was he playing, now? He couldn't really look at her because he was concentrating on the twisty road, but she caught his quick sideways glance. 'But what if "WB" is short for Wolf Bloch Wenczel?'

'Great-grandad Wolf?'

'Don't be obtuse, Beth. You're the one who's been reconstructing. Use your imagination.'

Everybody at the reunion knew, or knew now, that Josephina arrived in Wellington a widow, with a five-year-old daughter, Catharina Hansen, who would be Frank's grandmother, and a new baby boy who would be Beth's Great-grandad Wolf.

'Everybody knew that Wenczel was the married name she took in Wellington, and that the boy she christened Wolf Bloch Wenczel was born on the way over.' Beth knew that phrases like 'everybody knew' would provoke her cousin, but what other way was there to describe the speculative chatter of the reunion?

'So poor old Heinrich Wenczel wasn't the wolf child's

father. Next?' Frank's hands on the steering wheel were speckled and dark from years of Queensland sun. She and Frank had written letters to each other for a few years after he left, and he'd always included a bad Aussie joke. She remembered the one about why so many Australian men suffer premature ejaculation (because they have to rush back to the pub to tell their mates what happened). She hadn't understood it at the time, but her mother had laughed a lot, without explaining the joke except by saying it was 'inappropriate'. Beth would have been about fifteen, her big bad cousin about twenty-five. She liked 'inappropriate' because her cousin was including her in something secret, and she liked it even more once she found out what the joke was about.

'Are you suggesting that a bloke called Wolf Bloch was Great-grandad Wolf Wenczel's father?'

'My grandmother Catharina née Hansen never explained why she had her mother's maiden name. And why the fuck would you call one of your kids Wolf Bloch dot dot dot name of stepfather? You should have heard them going on at the reunion. Talk about string theory. Woman of mystery, your great-great-grandmother Josephina Hansen Bloch Wenczel Whatever.' Frank's hand reached across and gave hers a squeeze. 'Didn't your mum ever tell you anything?'

'She told me what a premature ejaculation was. Eventually.'

Frank gave a bark of appreciation. Perhaps he remembered the joke.

If 'WB' was Josephina Wenczel Whatever's way of commemorating Great-grandad Wolf's real father, why had Beth's mum never told that story? After all, she was named after one of Josephina's sisters called Elke back in Germany – Great-great-grandmother Josephina had 'requested' it. And

Frank's mother was named after another of Josephina's sisters, Greta. Clearly, a 'request' by Josephina was not to be ignored, and so Elke and Greta it was for those granddaughters. Beth has seen only one photograph of her great-great-grandmother: straight back, nice trim on her blouse collar, direct gaze staring down speculation about the fathers of her children before she became Mrs Wenczel.

Frank was driving carefully down the winding hill road but Beth felt a bit sick from the winding around of names. She opened the window to let some air in despite the dust.

'Do you mind?' said Frank.

'Does it ever occur to you,' asked Beth, ignoring his pretend rudeness, 'that some of this same dust may have been blowing around when Josephina was here, when her son Wolf was cutting the road?'

'Are you telling me he did that as well as everything else?' Frank was kidding. Of course he knew about Wolf's famous one-man-band reputation, his homemade Peloton-wheel generator in the feeder creek, the wooden body he made for a Model-T truck chassis, his concrete-slab honey house.

'He built the bridge, Mum told me.'

'I know almost nothing about them,' said Frank. 'And I hardly knew a soul at the reunion. Bit late now.'

'And here's me pushing sixty,' said Beth, 'and what do I know? Just the oft-repeated, memorable DIY bits. It's sad. Mum was always vague about the old stuff. But then she was pretty vague about most stuff. I didn't know about the ancestral sewing-sampler thingie that was there at the reunion – it was pretty amazing I thought. That woman who brought it said she'd heard Mum say that Josephina was reciting poetry in German or Danish or trying to sing on her deathbed – I'd never heard that story before, maybe that's why that little song verse is there on her headstone – but Mum was only about eight or something when the old girl died.'

Frank's silence suggested he didn't want to talk about the sampler, nor about the headstone verse, nor the improbable memory of Josephina singing in either Danish or German or even both on her deathbed.

They crossed a one-lane bridge at the bottom of a long incline.

'That one,' said Beth. 'He built it, he surveyed the incline so the road would get to the river at the right height, and he built the damn thing. Imagine that. And then his mother Josephina came across it in a buggy or something to the house he'd built for her, from the timber he'd cut and milled. She'd have been just a bit younger than me, probably. Imagine that.'

'Please stop saying imagine that,' said her best cousin Frank. 'Especially since you've just told me you know sweet fuck all.' When they were kids down the Kaitīeke for the summer camping holidays he used to like chucking her into the river near the old Wolf homestead, and she loved him doing it, which is mostly why he did. 'Please, I beseech you, Beth. It's beyond me. All the imagining.'

But then neither of them had come back down the valley, all those years, until now.

Josephina

A little weak evening sunshine splashed across the flagstones. Josephina stopped mopping and listened. Yes – this time it was true. The birds had gone. She stepped outside and looked towards the town. The warblers weren't swirling around in crowds over the fjord. Their fussy little songs weren't coming from the reeds at the bottom of the slope by the river mouth. All she could hear was the whispering sound of wind in the dry stalks. The whispering sound had a swirling rhythm because of gusts blowing down the fjord towards the sea. The reed stalks had a rhythm, too, a ripple that went along the shore and repeated itself, over and over. In the pale blue sky above the fjord, also, it was as though the streaky clouds moving away in the direction of the sea at Laboe were making a whispering sound, like the wind. They made the blue-green Nikolaikirche steeple over the other side of the fjord seem to be toppling across the sky. A score of small coasters were anchored along the channel, along with two broad larger vessels waiting for lighters. They were all pointing up into the wind, and the small ones were nodding a little together as the waves pushed their bows up and down. What would it feel like, one day, to turn with the wind and the tide and go easily down the fjord, almost silently, once the sails were set and had stopped snapping at the clouds beyond Laboe?

She wiped away the loose strand of hair that had blown across her cheek, and with it the tears. The little Rohrsänger had gone, the twittery songs of their hundreds had stopped; they weren't there in the sky swooping about in formations, they weren't in the reeds by the marsh, their songs had gone away with them for the winter.

'They practise,' her mother had told her. 'They come and go for a while. Then, one day, they don't return and so you know that winter's coming certainly.'

'Where do they go?'

'Somewhere nice and warm, so the sailors say.'

'But where?'

'How should I know?'

'Do oranges come from there?'

'So they say.'

That was when she was a child.

Now Mutti was standing in the doorway, narrowing her eyes against the late sunlight so that her expression said, But now you're not a child anymore. 'So, have you finished?' Mutti said. She had on the faded blue cotton cap she liked to wear when washing new linens; her hair was all drawn back, and her face looked pale and severe.

Josephina could tell that her mother had seen she'd been crying. She still had the salty taste of the tears in the corners of her mouth and perhaps their snail-trails were still on her cheeks. But why should she hide them? When they were true?

'Yes, finished,' she said, and turned back to the view across the fjord. Finished what, exactly? Mutti's silence was stiff, like the freshly washed linens that would freeze if you left them out too late in the coming months.

Below the meadow the evening train tooted three times as it slowly approached the mill station. Its smoke was blowing away in a long streamer in the same direction as the clouds. The stationmaster would already be getting important and putting his official cap on. This he did three times a day. He had his whistle, of course, and his flag.

*

Yesterday as usual there was time for her to run down the hill to catch the morning train before it went back to the town. She'd passed her sister milking the cow, her face red with displeasure.

'Spoiled brat!' shouted Elke. Really, she didn't mean it, only the other cow was waiting with its bulging udder. It lifted its tail and, with a flopping sound, released a pile of shit. Josephina's mother had allowed her to wash with the lavender soap, and she was wearing the blouse with Bohemian buttonhole stitching at the neck. The pattern was of a vine with leaves and flowers, and it went all the way around. Josephina didn't mind that it was a little scratchy because it reminded her to hold her neck up straight, and so her hair too, under her 'town bonnet'. As well as that, it was her own work. She held her bonnet straight with one hand and in the other gripped the bag with her finished work for Junkfrau. The nightgown had a high neck with the same Bohemian pattern as her own blouse, long sleeves with cuffs embroidered in pink silk thread, and a button-up front scalloped like a waterfall. The cloth was fine white cotton but the buttons were stitched over with the same pink silk thread as the cuffs. When she'd wondered how anyone could sleep in it, Elke made the scornful clucking sound that meant, What do you know? But what Josephina meant was, How could anyone sleep in something that fine?

The stationmaster had his cap on, and his blue uniform jacket as well, and was standing in his best cavalry manner, his legs bowed as if he had just dismounted from a horse; he had his furled flag resting on his right shoulder like a sabre.

'Good morning, Lieutenant,' said Josephina, knowing he liked to be called that.

'Good morning, Miss Josephina,' said the stationmaster,

clicking his heels. 'And what is the purpose of Fräulein's town visit today?' His smile was false as usual because, she supposed, he was jealous of her visiting the wives of 'die adelige Preussen Offizieren' over there by Kieler Schloss, as he liked to say in his best 'proper' German. Also, she was standing too far away for him to bow and kiss her hand, as he rather liked to, pretending she was still a child.

'It's something for Junkfrau von Zarovich.' Josephina was looking past the stationmaster's red ear where it stuck out under his cap. Over by the station gate the mill owner's portly wife was advancing along the platform. She, too, had her 'town hat' on, but hers was black with a fancy lace trim around the front, some ostrich spads angled backwards and a great pile of black chiffon cascading past her shoulders from the crown. Behind her came one of the mill-hands pushing her trunk on a squeaky barrow. Frau Tiesel was out of breath and Josephina knew better than to delay her meeting with the stationmaster. Also, she would look at Josephina's embroidered collar with her sour expression that meant, And who do you think you are? 'Just into town,' said Josephina, so the stationmaster would know what ticket to put on her father's account, as her mother had instructed her. Also, here she was, going to town by herself, for the first time – the stationmaster had surely noticed that. She was going to stay the night with her aunt and come back with her papa in the sprung cart in the morning. She liked staying with Tante Elizabeth because they would all sing together after supper and then she would sleep with her little cousin Mathilde who said she loved her 'more than stars' but that she also loved the stories about Puck Puck the special chicken, could Josie please tell her one?

'Ah,' said the stationmaster in a knowing tone, 'one of

those new young ones, that Zarovich.' He knew all about the Prussian officers 'over there'. He touched his fingers to the brim of his cap for Josephina, but he was already preparing himself for Frau Tiesel – stiffening his back and so forth. Josephina saw that he'd carefully flicked his cigar stub away. Its nasty smell lingered, though, and a wisp of smoke came out from the dark space between the carriage and the edge of the platform.

She climbed up and took a seat facing the way the train would go when it returned to the town, on the side facing the water. Sometimes they would ask her to sing 'Wie traulich war das Fleckchen' by the strange poet called Groth who lived over on Schwanenweg. Tante Elizabeth said the melody was by the famous composer Brahms from Hamburg who was 'one of us' even though he lived in Vienna, and what's more his wife was a seamstress 'just like you', but Josephina had seen the poet in a long flapping coat in the Schlossgarten and thought he was too odd for such a famous composer. Mathilde liked the song about a cosy spot, though, and sometimes Josephina would sing it to her very quietly once they were in bed, instead of a Puck Puck story. Then Mathilde's breathing would begin to slow and soon she would be asleep.

Josephina's face was reflected in the carriage window with a glimpse of flickering water beyond, and she mouthed the words of the song about the cosy spot surrounded by leaves and flowers, thinking how nice she looked. Then Frau Tiesel heaved herself into the carriage and lowered herself with a grunt into a seat at the back. Josephina stopped mouthing the song and sat up straight, turning her profile to the miller's wife. Beyond her nice window reflection some little Rohrsänger were flitting about in sunshine above the embankment – surely they'd be going soon? Some boys from the mill jumped on at the last minute, shouting noisily, but then began to whisper. The stationmaster blew his whistle at last, the train tooted, and the birds all fled across the fjord in a crowd. They must be happy, surely, to be going soon to the warm place that smelled of oranges and not of the stationmaster's nasty cigar stub.

But now they really had gone; it was almost evening and beginning to get chilly, the pretty little twittering birds hadn't returned to the reeds along the river bank. When the evening train tooted to signal that it was leaving for town for the last time there were no crowds of birds fleeing away across the darkening water; all that remained from yesterday morning was the cigar smell, not of the stationmaster's stub flicked away into the horrible dark gap by the platform, but of the fresh cigar Hauptmann von Zarovich was getting alight over by the tall window with tasseled drapes and pink stained glass at the top, so that his enthusiastic puffing blew a cloud of smoke across the shaft of rosy sunshine coming into the room.

'Ah! Our little seamstress.'

Her mother had gone back inside but Josephina didn't want to follow her, as she was perhaps expected to. Yes, she was 'finished', but there would be more to do, though not sewing.

There would be no more sewing, her father shouted at Tante Elizabeth. Not that sort. Who did the girl think she was? Look what she did.

'And what did *she* do?' Tante's face was red, and little Mathilde was pulling at her dress and crying. Josephina wished very much she could have stayed at their house, but that morning she sat up on the sprung cart's seat as ordered to by her papa, while he and his sister argued right there in the street. 'She wouldn't even sing,' hissed Tante, pushing her face close to Papa's, 'can you imagine that? Our precious songbird. Yes, of course there was something wrong. What do you think I am? Stupid?' She was trying to keep their argument quiet because the neighbourhood children were beginning to notice. 'She won't talk to me,' said Tante in a loud whisper, so Josephina would hear. 'She won't tell me what's wrong, but something is. This isn't our Josie.' High up on the sprung cart's seat, where everybody could see her, Josephina sat very still with her hands in her lap.

'Yes, Elizabeth,' hissed Papa, also trying to keep the argument quiet. 'I do think you're stupid, because what if your precious songbird costs me my business?'

'Ah, so that's it,' said her aunt, stepping back. '*Meister* Hansen!' Then she spat right at his feet and used the bad word Josephina had heard the mill boys call each other, 'Meister Scheisskopf!'

Her father and Tante Elizabeth just stood there with their faces quite close together. Josephina could see them out of the corner of her eye. Then one of the neighbourhood boys let out a loud guffaw and shouted something – Josephina couldn't hear what he said and she didn't want to turn around and look for who he was. But then with a clatter of clogs a dozen of the children ran yelling past the sprung cart where she sat looking straight ahead. They didn't stop where Papa and Tante were glaring at each other, because just up the hill a horse had lost its footing and the carter had jumped down to put blocks behind the wheels. The horse stood with its head down, its flanks heaving and flecked with froth and streaks of blood from the carter's whip. It was defeated, it just wanted to stop, to be free of the cart's weight. The cart was overloaded with barrels, it wasn't the horse's fault, but the carter was cursing it anyway.

Then they were rattling along. Papa had loaded some fresh poplar planks and he would use them to make plain coffins, not the special ones that cost a lot.

'Stupid,' he said, looking over old Gunnar's nodding mane and the wilted bunch of wildflowers under his collar. Did he mean Tante Elizabeth or the carter? Or Mutti, for not coming with her? Or did he mean her? What had happened wasn't her fault. What happened on the hill by Tante's house wasn't the horse's fault, and what happened in Junkfrau von Zarovich's house on Faulstrasse wasn't her fault. She wanted to lean her head on Papa's hard shoulder and breathe in his neck-smell and the nice smell of sawn timber in his coat, and with her right hand reach around his shoulders and hold the big lobe of his ear between her finger and thumb, which would make him growl down in his chest without opening his mouth. But he sat looking straight ahead, as did she, while Gunnar clopped along as usual, as if only the horse knew how things should be and the proper way to ride home in the cart. What Josephina knew was gone; she sat there with her pain on the cart's hard wooden seat in an awful hollow space with nothing familiar in it, and the world went past her straight-ahead gaze like a shadow play.

'Did he pay you?' said Papa, adding 'von Zarovich' after a cough.

Inside her hollow space she was all at once both freezing and burning. Pay her for what? But she couldn't say it.

'For the needlework,' said her father as if he'd heard what she didn't have words for. And then he roared the words again, lurching forward on his seat. 'For the needlework, girl, for your precious goddamn needlework!' And then he did turn towards her, and she saw that her papa's eyes were completely red and his lips were shaking. 'Did the bastard pay you?'

But still he couldn't reach for her and for her misery, as if the happy loveliness she'd felt in herself the day before, and seen in the stationmaster's eyes, and in the morning train's carriage window, and in Frau Tiesel's spiteful look, and in the housemaid Clara's head-wobble and up-and-down smiling assessment of her at the servants' entrance to Junkfrau's house – as if the loveliness and happiness she'd felt that morning had been impregnated by a filthy smell, like a stale cigar, that everyone would notice.

Josephina reached into the bag in which she'd delivered the fine nightgown with her best Bohemian embroidery work, and brought out her little purse with the coins in it. She put the clinking purse on the seat between herself and her father without looking at him, without moving her eyes out of the strangely echoing tunnel in which Gunnar's nodding head was pushing forward past noisy huddles of buildings and then past silent trees and meadows that she seemed not to be among.

'Hmm-hmm,' said the housemaid Clara. Her eyes went up and down Josephina's dress and blouse. She leaned with one arm across the doorway and wobbled her head from side to side, taunting a little. She was a big, strong girl with dark hair and thick eyebrows – she made her eyebrows go up and down as she did her inspection of Josephina's appearance.

It was chilly at the back of the house, which was not one of the grand ones, since Hauptmann von Zarovich was a junior; it was a narrow four floors in a row of others curving around on Faulstrasse, with a shared yard and stables that you entered through an alleyway. That morning there was fresh horseshit in the alley and Josephina worried about getting some on her shoes. It was a good place to start, her mother had said when they came the first time; word would soon go 'upstairs' to the rich senior officers; best to start with clean shoes.

Josephina liked Clara's admiring look and even the teasing head-wobble and eyebrows, but the *hmm-hmm* was annoying. But then Clara stood aside with a mock curtsey and Josephina went into the kitchen. There was an appetising, strong smell of coffee and hot bread, and the cook was filling a basket with freshly baked Rundstück. A plate of sausage and cheese stood ready on the broad table.

'Good morning Josephina where is your mother?' said the cook in a joined-up way, and then, 'Get a move on girl!' She meant Clara, who was putting the breakfast on a tray.

'Junkfrau isn't here,' said Clara. 'She's visiting.'

'She's away,' said the cook.

Then they were both staring at Josephina.

The cook was a very tall, thin, peevish woman with a pointy nose at the top, strangely wide hips halfway down and, at the bottom, long, turned-out feet in felt slippers with bunion bumps – Josephina's mother called her 'the Stork'. On their first visit, she and Mutti had a whispering talk in a corner of the kitchen before showing Josephina's samples to Junkfrau upstairs in her bedroom, and Josephina heard the Stork say that Junkfrau was very young and very vain and that she liked to stay in bed while Herr Hauptmann was out at morning parade, and also that she liked to go to her family in Vienna quite often, which put her husband in a bad mood, because, you know.

But now the Stork's mouth wasn't in that thin, peevish line. Instead, she was trying to smile at Josephina, her mouth making different shape attempts, until she gave up and waved her big red bony hand at the breakfast tray.

'What are you waiting for take the man his breakfast.'

'But I've got the work for Junkfrau,' said Josephina, adding, 'the nightgown she asked for specially.'

'Not you what are you dreaming?' snapped the Stork.

Clara made a show of straightening her apron and bodice, and of pushing her hair up under her cap. Then she picked up the breakfast tray. 'Why don't I ask Hauptmann von Zarovich if it would please him to see, hmm-hmm, the nightgown,' she said, with an unkind emphasis on 'the nightgown', making her thick eyebrows go up and down.

'Please, Clara, thank you,' said Josephina. She was hot with blushing, but what was she supposed to do? This was her first time on her own. What would they say at home if she came back without showing the nightgown and without the money for it? This was her chance to be known 'upstairs'. And perhaps she'd be able to tell them, after she'd told Tante Elizabeth, that she'd shown the nightgown to Hauptmann von Zarovich himself, because his wife was away, far away in Vienna perhaps, so she just had to go ahead and do it all by herself.

The maid hooked the door shut behind her with her foot. The Stork was looking at Josephina with her lips in that peeved line. Then, with a deep sigh, she said, 'Sit down girl have some coffee you'll have to go soon.'

But a shaft of bright, clear light came suddenly into the kitchen from a window high in the back wall – the sun must now be in the stable yard. It was already late morning, then; the morning muster over by Kieler Schloss was finished, the fresh horseshit in the alley meant that Hauptmann's horse had been stabled, he was now having his breakfast – and here she was, in the warm kitchen with its nice smell of freshly baked rolls and coffee, with a cup in front of her that the cook was about to fill. Surely she would be allowed to show her work? Surely, after the parade, he would be in a good mood, and he'd be thinking about his beautiful young wife, and missing her, and thinking what a nice surprise it would be to have the nightgown ready for her when she came home from Vienna, tired after her long journey, glad to see her husband, grateful for his thoughtfulness, and loving the Bohemian needlework and the pink silk thread on the buttons? 'So this is all your own work, Fräulein?' he would say to Josephina, noticing also her own collar with its vine and leaves. 'So beautiful, your mother and father must be very proud of you!'

Josephina could see that the Stork was making a show of looking at how her hand trembled as she brought the coffee cup to her lips – her peevish mouth turned into a V-shaped grin in which her large top front teeth stuck out.

'Now you listen to me girl,' she began, but then the kitchen door banged open and Clara hurried in.

'Another cup for the seamstress, and please to bring the work.'

Then neither of them said another word. Their silence pressed in on Josephina like the narrow dark stairway she and Clara were going up, Clara in front with the fresh cup and saucer, and Josephina following behind with the nightgown in a bag. Clara's smell was quite strong, from her morning's work, no doubt, and Josephina was glad Mutti had allowed her to use the lavender soap that morning.

Then Clara opened the door to a large bright drawing room into which rosy light was coming through the stained-glass panes at the top of tall bay windows, where Hauptmann von Zarovich stood puffing a cloud of cigar smoke across the shaft of sunlight.

'Ah! Our little seamstress.'

Her face was pressed into Elke's strong, breathing back. Her sister heaved and made an annoyed groaning sound, almost words but not quite. In Josephina's dream there had been a loud shout that woke her up – had she shouted or had someone else? She'd been trying to push through darkness that was thick with a moire shimmer. It was like a narrow alleyway or passage. Her face pressed into it. It was hard to breathe or make words. Then, suddenly, the loud shout. Then she was awake and trying to speak. There was Elke's nice strong warm back. She could feel the vibration of Elke's words on her cheek, and the hum of her steady breathing.

'A bad dream, Josie?' Elke was waiting for Josephina to say what the dream was about. Usually they would do this, taking turns. Last time was Elke's turn; her dream was about a crowd of sausages marching along being soldiers while a wolf followed behind, snapping them up one by one and singing *eins zwei drei!* What a boring dream, Josephina had said, it just means you're hungry.

Early morning sunshine came into their room through the trembling leaves of the aspen – pale light flickered on the ceiling, the fluttering leaf shapes were like the signalling flags and bunting on ships coming into harbour, the flags and leaves were words the wind spoke, but in a few more weeks the yellowed leaves would be gone and the low winter sunlight would be still and silent and the ships without their talking flags would have sailed away down the fjord and then the loud shout of her dream would be gone as well.

Soon she'd have to get up and stoke the stove fire and the one in the fireplace, and Elke would have to milk the cows. 'We have to get up,' she said.

'What about your dream?'

'It was nothing,' said Josephina.

Elke turned over with an angry heave. 'Why don't you talk to us?' Josephina could hear that her sister was about to cry – her voice was wobbly. Then Elke grabbed her by the hair and gave her a shake. 'Why don't you talk to *me*, to *me*. I'm your sister, Josie, what's the matter with you?'

'I told Mathilde a story when I was at Tante Elizabeth's,' said Josephina, taking Elke's hands out of her hair. 'But I didn't want to sing. That's why Tante got annoyed.'

Elke sat up in bed and shook her fists in the air. It was what she did when she was fed up. 'Tilde's five,' said Elke, taking big breaths. 'And you're my little sister. My Schwesterchen. My *bébé*! I used to sing to you. I told you stories.' Now she was crying – some big tears ran down beside her nose and she licked them off her lips with a quick, impatient flick of her tongue. 'All right, then, get up. If you can't trust me. If you're so high and mighty now.'

Mathilde's little head was against her shoulder. They had a candle, and Josephina was making a Puck Puck the chicken shadow with it. Puck Puck walked across the wall and then faded away into darkness. 'All right, now,' said Mathilde. 'Now you can sing it.'

'*Wie traulich war das Fleckchen, Wo meine Wiege ging,*' began Josephina very quietly, but then her voice just stopped. A big lump rose up in her throat and choked the words. Mathilde poked her with a sharp, bony little elbow and then gave her a kick. But she couldn't do it.

'I'll tell you a story,' she said. 'You love me more than stars, remember?' The child was quiet. 'How shall we begin?' whispered Josephina. The story was there in her mind, all joined up in a pattern, like the cascade of vines and flowers down the front of Junkfrau's nightgown. 'Once upon a time there was a cosy spot where a child lay sleeping in her cradle. By day, the trees and flowers and vines sheltered the child from the rays of the sun. Beautiful songbirds perched in the branches of the trees and sang to each other about the child who was laughing with pleasure to hear their songs. Beautiful butterflies . . .'

'You've already used that word,' said Mathilde, but she was almost asleep.

'. . . colourful butterflies alighted on the flowers and vines and fanned their wings above the child in the warm breezes. In the evening, when the stars began to appear in the sky and a big yellow moon floated up out of the sea, dragging her shining sleeve across the water, the child would sometimes spend an hour before bedtime looking up at the stars and the heroes and animals twinkling in the heavens.'

'Tell me a hero,' murmured Mathilde, 'or a Puck Puck story,' but then her voice turned into some lip-smacks and she began to snore.

One night, as the child lay looking up at the stars, a hero with a sword came down from the sky. He chopped away the vines and branches that were protecting the child and pushed his way into the cosy spot. And then he shouted in a terrible voice, *Ah . . .*

Elke was pulling her clothes on in a huff. 'Please yourself,' she said. 'But he did something, that Junker, otherwise why all the fuss and bother?'

'He told me not to come back,' said Josephina.

Now Elke was giving her that big-sister look. 'But why? Why would he do that? If he liked the work?'

Josephina wanted to say, Why don't you go into town all by yourself and drink a coffee with Hauptmann von Zarovich and ask him why he said that, but she didn't. She turned her back on Elke and put her bare feet on the chilly floor.

From the kitchen their mother called out angrily that they were late. Josephina knew Mutti blamed her for spoiling their chance to go 'upstairs', but did she also feel bad about not going with her to the von Zarovich house? Well, if Mutti wouldn't say so, why should Josephina talk? She'd gone into town on the train by herself, she'd walked from the top of the harbour all the way over to the Hauptmann's house in Faulstrasse, she'd shown him the nightgown, she'd got the money, she'd gone all the way back to Tante Elizabeth's house over towards Gaarden, now she was home again. That was all.

Josephina put her chilly feet and legs back under the eiderdown. *So, are you finished?* Yes, she was. Now she was finished. When her mother didn't call her again, or come angrily to the bottom of the loft ladder – or come up the ladder to say she was sorry and give her a hug – Josephina closed her eyes.

Finished.

*

The ships lined up out in the harbour roadstead all had long cords stretched fore and aft from their masts, with dozens of pretty flags strung along them. Josephina went fast along the harbourside where the lighters came in to unload at the jetties – it was rough and noisy, but couples were promenading there and looking at things some of the sailors were offering for sale. One of the sailors was about Josephina's age; he looked as though he'd been baked, his hair was almost as white as Mutti's sun-bleached linens, and his face and arms were as dark as coffee. On a dirty blue neckerchief by his feet was an enormous trumpet-shaped shell with whorls going around it. When he saw her look at it, he picked the great shell up and held it out to her. His smile was terrible, with only a few black teeth left.

'Hold it to your ear, Fräulein,' he said in thick Lübsch dialect. 'This one can talk. It can tell you where it came from.' He put it to his ear and stood with his head on one side and his eyes closed. The fourth finger of his right hand was missing and so was the lobe of his ear not covered by the shell. 'Ah, what a place,' he said, opening his eyes again. 'So beautiful. Like you, Fräulein.' He held the shell out again.

Josephina hurried on. She'd have liked to listen to the wonderful shell but the young sailor frightened her – he looked half crazy. What would he do when she told him she had no money to buy his treasure?

Some of the well-dressed townsfolk were exclaiming over a new three-masted steam-yacht with two slender funnels on top and mighty paddle-wheels on either side, like hips. It was just launched, people were saying, it was for the King of Portugal. It was steaming slowly down harbour as if being displayed. The crew, dressed in white uniforms, were lined up along the deck facing the town. One of the well-dressed spectators watching the King of Portugal's steam-yacht with its well-turned-out crew would surely buy the young sailor's beautiful shell. And one day they would surely want to buy her embroidery, which they would have heard about from Junkfrau von Zarovich, or seen, perhaps, when Junkfrau was looking at a royal steam-yacht while wearing an outdoor promenading outfit with a high-collared blouse embroidered in the Bohemian manner by Fräulein Josephina Hansen.

Josephina looked back as she turned away from the harbour towards Rathausstrasse and Nikolaikirche and the streets that led on down to Kieler Schloss and the garrison houses, but she couldn't see the young sailor. The old church sat weightily on the ground and it was hard to imagine how its tall green spire could seem to fall so lightly across the sky as the clouds went past. It was like a signal, and Josephina sent a message through the open door asking that Junkfrau would please admire her work on the nightgown, adding could someone please buy the poor young sailor's wonderful shell. Then she closed her eyes and imagined the tall steeple pointing to heaven and waving her message.

It was as if she then opened her eyes again to find that the Nikolaikirche steeple had indeed sent her message, because there was Hauptmann von Zarovich smiling at her with his big teeth stained from cigars, in his shirtsleeves and riding breeches and, which gave her a shock, on his feet a pair of embroidered green tapestry-cloth house-slippers with red and white roses done in cross-stitch – she saw the slippers as, following Clara's hand signal behind her back, she bent to curtsey, and as she straightened and met the officer's examining stare she saw the ends of his moustache twitch and knew that he'd seen her noticing his slippers. Her heart was beating quickly, at first because she was nervous, but next because the Hauptmann's unexpected embroidered slippers were like another encouraging sign from the steeple.

He had thick fair hair and a moustache turned up at the ends Hussar-style; when he showed his big teeth in a grin the waxed ends of the moustache stood to attention.

'Very comfortable slippers from *Gujarat*,' he said, barking the strange place-name. 'Do you know where that is, Fräulein?'

'No sir,' she said, feeling the blush rise up out of her collar.

'Nor do I, Fräulein!' He was laughing at his joke and waving for Clara to leave the room. There was a careful clatter as she put the extra cup on the tray with the Hauptmann's unfinished breakfast, and then an equally careful click as she closed the door behind her. 'Nor do I,' repeated the man, 'my wife chose them as a present, she loves that sort of thing,' adding 'Gu-ja-rat' with exaggerated movements of his lips. 'But then,' he said, continuing to stare at Josephina, 'everything beautiful comes to Kielerhafen in the end, wouldn't you say, Fräulein?'

Josephina thought of the poor young sailor's great whorled shell that could speak where it came from, but instead she said, 'I like the sweet oranges, sir.'

'Ah, the sweet oranges! I too like them.' There was a silence while he continued to look at her. What was she expected to do? Then, inclining his head at a chair by his breakfast table, he said, 'And the stupid girl didn't even pour our coffee – would you mind, Fräulein?'

Outside by the main door, Papa's journeyman Franz was planing coffin planks. The regular panting sound of the plane came into the house and as far as the back where Josephina and her mother sat at opposite ends of the big table with the shroud between them. It was one of the fresh new linens and smelled of sunlight. They were doing a border of blue crosses. Because they were not talking to each other anymore, the sound of Franz planing was like words going back and forth, mixed up with the clucking of hens looking for grains near the fodder stall. Mathilde now had Josephina's old linen scrap treasure with the picture of Puck Puck the special chicken she'd embroidered on it, but Josephina sometimes told herself Puck Puck stories in the silence of her work with Mutti, and remembered the warmth of her special chicken against her chest when she was little, and its occasional pecks. When Mutti wanted to move her section of the border she rapped with her knuckles on the table. Soon it would snow, and Papa and Franz would keep their work inside for winter. Then they would all be there together: the two cows and old Gunnar in their stalls, the chickens, Franz or whichever worker stayed long enough, Josephina and Elke in their little loft, the trestles with unfinished coffins and tabletops on them in the space between the stalls, and Papa and Mutti by the fire arguing about how to get established in the town.

But 'the Oma' wasn't there – her grandmother's sampler that was Josephina's now, covered all over with stitches making pictures of flowers and houses and animals in different coloured threads, and a snowy mountain with a little deer on top, that spoke the names of the stitches and also had Oma's voice in them, in the stories that each stitch told – little words for big stories that Oma told over and over and especially in winter, starting when Josephina was too small for sewing anything but Strikkelise, and when the birds made footprints that were like stitches on the snow by the big door and told the stories of the birds' songs, how they were cold now, not like those lucky ones that knew how to fly away somewhere nice and warm. Oma died after her husband was killed in the Danish war at Dybbøl Mill – he was buried over there by the marshes, along with the other 'fools', including two of his sons who thought it was a great thing to shoot at Danes with wonderful Prussian rifles because otherwise they would take all the farms and smallholdings like theirs. Josephina was seven when Oma fell down dead after making a sweep of her arm to scatter grain for the hens outside in the yard – she heard the old lady shout 'Hein!', which is what she called her husband, and then she fell down flat on her face like a plank. She was too angry was what Mutti thought, angry with the 'fools' who marched off to get blown to pieces for the Prussians, it was anger that killed her. But Josephina could remember Oma's stories, which were not angry; and when she was twelve Mutti gave her 'the Oma' to look after so she could properly learn the stitches that told the stories that told the stitches and that, after a while, began telling Josephina who she was: that she was a young woman now, that she could be proud of her skill, that she had value. But now the Oma was locked away in the big dark chest in her papa's and mutti's room, and Josephina couldn't have it back until she began to talk again.

Mutti rapped her knuckles on the table and then gave the shroud cloth a yank. Josephina was snipping a thread and the yank made her hand slip; the scissors pierced her thumb and some blood flicked on to the white linen.

It wasn't her fault, and when her mother said, 'Now look what you've done you stupid girl,' Josephina stood up and walked down between the stalls and out the big door past Franz who stopped planing to smile at her and make a little bow – it was going to rain, he'd be coming inside, he said – and down the hill as far as the gate. An inky black storm cloud quivering with lightning was stalled out over the sea. She stopped and let the great sobs burst out.

When as requested she came back into the Hauptmann's breakfast room with the nightgown on over her shift 'to show off your handiwork' – was it wrong to do that, it wasn't proper, she was ashamed, but perhaps it was what was expected? – she didn't know he would at once open the front of his breeches where his hand was already busy inside to make his big thing jump out, that he would push her face into the back of a sofa and tear at her undergarments, thrusting himself against her and then with a loud *Ah!* into her. There was blood on the nightgown when she changed back into her street dress; she left it on the floor and went out by the front door as ordered to. *And don't come back you little whore* – he threw some coins on the breakfast tray and left the room, and she just went out and walked. First she walked the wrong way over towards Ratsdienergarten, but there weren't enough people and voices to hide her, the lake was full of glaring light like a mirror and the hissing swans had left their filth all along the bank, so Josephina walked back across the town to the harbour. It was crowded and noisy so she stood near the place where the young sailor had been, she could buy his shell with the Hauptmann's money, but he'd gone, and so had the King of Portugal's grand wide-hipped steam-yacht. When a man came and stood too close to her for a while and then said, 'So, Fräulein?' she walked away quickly and kept going all the way until she got to Tante Elizabeth's place and the huddle of houses, workshops and gardens there at the edge of Gaarden. This was where her papa planned to be 'established', but Josephina wanted him to come with good old Gunnar and take her away back down to the Schwentine where the town looked small and distant across the other side of the fjord and where the sky spread out and was almost white like silence above the sea beyond Laboe.

Mutti was excited and happy the day she and Josephina went to show samples of needlework to Junkfrau von Zarovich; she was imagining when they'd all move into a proper house in the town or at Gaarden – maybe even a house like the one on Faulstrasse where the Hauptmann lived, it wasn't so grand after all. The housemaid Clara didn't go *hmm-hmm* or make her thick eyebrows go up and down that time, because she was respectful of Josephina's mother – but, before opening the door to Junkfrau's bedroom, she put a finger on her lips and whispered that the Hauptmann's wife was not feeling well this morning, she'd had peppermint tea but nothing to eat for breakfast. Mutti nodded as if she understood the significance of the peppermint tea. Then they went in.

The large bed had a canopy supported on dark wood-turned spiral columns that Josephina thought her papa would very much like to see, and perhaps he would, one day soon; and there was a fine chaise longue with a lion's head carving on the back and tapestry covers depicting colourful birds where Junkfrau von Zarovich lay shielding her face from the windows. She was wearing a loose, long-sleeved dressing gown in a lightweight material the colour of pale milk-coffee; it had ruffles down the front and pale-blue bows at the cuffs. A pair of embroidered slippers peeped out from the hem. She had a childish triangular mauve crochet shawl with slip-stitch edging around her shoulders and some strands of fair hair hung below her small white lace cap. She didn't get up to greet them, not even Josephina's mother, who spoke to her in her best German, calling her 'gnädige Frau' even though she was not much older than Josephina. She liked looking at the samples, though, running one finger over the stitches while looking at Josephina; but she didn't talk to her, only to Mutti. She especially liked the Bohemian vines and flowers, and she held out the ruffled cascade on the front of her dressing gown for Josephina to look at. Then she lay back and turned her face away; she hadn't once spoken to Josephina.

Clara was waiting outside the door and Mutti said nothing to her but in the kitchen she proudly told the cook that Junkfrau liked Josephina's work very much and wanted her to make a special 'lie-in' nightgown. The Stork was busy and in an irritated tone told Clara to show them the door.

'Old vinegar-face,' said Mutti once they were outside, but she and Josephina sang on the way home from Tante Elizabeth's with Papa in the cart; she'd told Tante how much the very beautiful young Frau von Zarovich (Mutti was no longer calling her Junkfrau) had loved Josephina's work and how she'd asked for a special lie-in nightgown to be made with a cascading ruffle front, which meant she was probably going to have a baby and there would no doubt be special baby clothes and comforters to make, and word would get around when other officers' wives saw what Josephina had made, they'd be jealous of Frau von Zarovich, and they'd also certainly hear about the fine wood-craft work of Meister Hansen – and that night at home everyone was so happy, even Elke, who still had to get up and milk the cows after

Papa said Josephina could leave the coffin cloth work for a while and make the special 'lie-in nightgown' for Junkfrau von Zarovich. He was smiling at her and his eyes had filled up with tears – from too much brandy perhaps but also because he was proud of his youngest daughter; he was very proud, very proud, he said so several times before it was time to go to bed, and he kissed her on both cheeks before she went up there with Elke. Then Elke was snoring a little; it was nice and warm; there was an owl.

Beth and Frank

There was no one around at the river bank by Great-grandad Wolf's old abandoned slab-concrete honey house, so they took their clothes off and hung them over a mānuka branch. Little dark native bees were busy around flowers higher up in the tree. The river flowed quietly along in a deep section before the pebbly shoal at the bend where their families had camped on the grassy flat a few times in the summer. There used to be a rope swing by the pool beyond the bend, and Frank would do his 'Ayiiiyah!' Tarzan-ape-yell when he swung out and splashed into the water.

'Couple of scrawny bloody old ragworts,' he said before doing his Tarzan yell and jumping. When he came up again and spouted a mouthful of water, it was the same Frank-grin Beth had known meant mischief a bit over fifty years ago. Then she was six and the big cousin she worshipped was the magic age of sixteen, which meant he could make his Tarzan voice do a kind of yodelling thing when he mimed Elvis Presley singing 'You ain't nothin' but a hound dog'.

Then she jumped. The delight of the cool water wasn't even a memory, it was as though her skin had gone on being in the same present as when she was six. She floated downstream a little inside her delight, and there was her cousin Frank drifting headfirst beside her. They floated together for a bit. Then she turned and swam back against the gentle current. She could sense Frank trying to catch her feet but she didn't let him.

There'd been no pub in Kaitīeke, so they shared the last of Beth's bottles of 'pretentious fizzy water' by the honey house. He blamed foreign '*Lord of the Rings* tourists' for contaminating the rivers with Giardia. He reckoned that back in the day they'd practically drunk the river dry on a daily basis, and then pissed it all back in again, no trouble.

'Kind of you-could-not-piss-twice-into-the-same-river,' Beth said.

'Here we go again,' said her cousin.

'Feels like time doesn't flow, it just waits for the now to make space for it.'

'Holy hell,' said Frank. 'What happened to good old you're born, they rip out your tonsils, most of your teeth, your spleen, your man's foo-foo valve, and then you die?'

'You left out the bit where they cut off your tits,' said Beth.

'Old-fashioned good manners. I was raised proper.' Frank tipped up his bottle of fizzy water and she watched his Adam's apple go up and down in his skinny neck with its folds and creases.

She put her finger on it. 'You used to chase me with that lumpy thing when it was brand new. You said it was your dragon tongue coming out to get me.'

'I always swallowed it, though,' said Frank, who seemed sad all at once. 'Always did, eh.'

And the melancholy river, too. 'Wolf Bloch' circling back in that eddy by the far bank. The river's placid surface below the shallows silent, like Great-great-grandmother Josephina on the subject of the time-eddy.

'Always did, Frank. I'll give you that.'

Josephina

Catharina was asleep on her breast and Josephina had been asleep, too, perhaps, for a while – her neck ached. The baby's warm mouth still made weak sucking movements. Josephina put her finger in a corner of the little mouth and removed her nipple. Please let the child not cry. And she didn't – her face clenched in annoyance and a thimbleful of sour milk spilled down her chin, and then she slept on against Josephina's chest. Perhaps in a while she would move the baby to her crib and make shoosh-shoosh sounds like waves sloshing against the harbour wall where the fishing boats were knocking on each other's hulls just across the quay, and this would soothe Catharina, like the rocking of a little boat, and then she wouldn't wake the others. The small room at the top of the house was too warm and there wasn't even enough breeze through the window to flutter the candle flame; the creases in little Catharina's neck were moist. Josephina liked how the air smelled by the window when a breeze came up off the fishing boats and she could unravel the threads of fish, sea and tar, and sometimes the delicious tang of the Bückling smoking-yard further along the quay; but tonight there was only the sour stink of the baby's little puke and of her own sweat.

She lifted Catharina into her crib below the window – perhaps a breeze would come down along the harbour later – keeping the baby's body close to her own until the last minute, keeping her face and breath against the moist little head, making the shoosh-shoosh wave sounds and rocking the little boat with her foot, and when the baby didn't wake up, stepping back until her calves met the edge of the narrow bed and then folding herself down across its coverlet. The salt cart rattled past on the cobbles below; so, it would soon be dawn.

It was cool outside under the pear tree that didn't have any leaves yet; the sunshine came down on Oma's cap that looked like one of the big brown mushrooms she found where the old trees grew on the hills above the river and where Papa, in his growly voice, said there were wolves. But if there are wolves, why does Oma go there? Ha! said Oma, I have a trick, see? She turned her back on Josephina and bent over, holding her skirts out to make herself huge and jumping backwards, which made Josephina scream where she was sitting on the pinewood stool Papa had made for her with the big skein of rough grey woollen yarn across her held-out hands while Oma wound it into a ball. Papa's stool had pictures of deer on it made with a hot poker; they had antlers that were like Josephina's hands held up with the yarn across them. When you wound the yarn around the nails at the top of the Strikkelise it came out the bottom as a tube. If you make yourself very small, said Oma, that tube becomes a tunnel you can crawl into. And what happens then? said Josephina, knowing the answer already. You come out where everybody has funny little faces, they all have two blue dots for eyes and another red dot for a mouth. And do they have arms and legs? No, the poor things have no arms or legs, instead they have round bodies like the legs of your stool, only hollow, they have a little grey wooden scarf around their neck and a little red wooden belt around their tummy where their legs should start, only they don't. But how do they move around?

Ah, said Oma, they move around by doing a little dance, they hop around each other like this, they go around this way and then around that way, they turn themselves around and around. The skein of grey wool danced back and forth between Josephina's antler-hands and went across the space between her and Oma, who was winding and winding the wool into a big ball. When the ball was big enough it would roll away from the pear tree across the cow meadow and down the hill to the sea where a giant herring would snatch it up and swim away unspooling all the way to where the little Strikkelise people were waiting to wind it into a tunnel for Josephina to come home through.

Danne was laughing and shouting loudly at his wagoner in the street, his voice booming and hoarse – '*Fuck dig!*' The man whistled and the horse clopped away. The front door slammed and Danne's voice was vibrating in the room below. Then her sister was laughing and telling him to keep his hands to himself. There was a long streak of sunshine across the wall, it seemed to be slowly widening, but perhaps that was just the effect of waking up and coming out of sleep. Oma was there, not quite in the dream but not quite out of it either. The baby was still asleep in her crib, but Josephina hadn't even got properly into her own bed or taken her day clothes off. If she hurried now she'd be able to go to the outside privy and also have a wash before Catharina woke up.

Greta and Danne were sitting at the table having coffee and talking in Danish with their heads close together – when she came in there was a little pause before they smiled at her. Finn had his beak-clacking wooden duck on the floor and was pulling it around on its string. When he saw Josephina he said, 'Catha, Catha?'

'She's still asleep,' Josephina said, as much to her sister and Danne as to the boy. Then she went quickly out to the yard. Greta had already hung out some washing – that was Josephina's job now the maid had gone. Big glittery flies were buzzing in the light that came through the fish-shaped opening Danne had cut in the privy door, and when she clapped her hands the pitch of their buzzing rose shrilly as if they were terrified of the light-fish. The bucket of ash by the lavatory seat was full – that was her job too. She washed at the pump and dried herself with one of Catharina's damp napkins on the line. It smelled of the yellow laundry soap and the verbena leaves that Greta liked Josephina to throw into the copper, only she hadn't done that this morning, Greta had. We were getting short of napkins for Catha, Greta told her, so, well, little sister . . .

'Danne's just gone off to Flensburg to talk to the Germans.' Greta said this with a smirk; it was the joke she and Josephina liked to share, since the smoked herring Danne took south came back north as the rum he tested diligently for quality before selling it to the good Danish citizens of Sønderborg. Now the baby was crying upstairs. 'Go on, go on, bring her down,' said Greta impatiently.

'I'll feed her first,' said Josephina. 'And change my clothes.'

She was filling a jug with warm water from the kettle to wash the baby when she felt the huff of Greta's breath on her cheek as her sister's hand reached past and took the jug from her.

'Bring her down, Josie, for the love of God, please,' said Greta. She was standing the way she more often did these days, a little lopsided, one hand on her stomach. The other hand holding the jug she waved at the room without her big booming husband in it – some water splashed out on the table. 'Nice and quiet,' she said. 'For a week, imagine that.'

The hand that Mutti put on Josephina's where it rested on the packet-boat's rail wasn't like the hard bony one that had struck her on the face. Mutti had taken her glove off and Josephina thought her thin white hand was like one of the little terns that were chasing behind the ship as the sails began to fill and stop snapping at the pale sunrise where the fjord flowed out at Laboe. It was foggy and the place where the sea began and the sky stopped was blurry and pink – you couldn't really see what was water and what was air. The little terns were catching the breeze that had begun to spill from the sails, they were playing joyfully in the gusts, turning and dipping and skimming the ship's wake, but Mutti's hand just rested quietly on Josephina's. She began to feel its warmth through her glove, and the tapping of Mutti's fingers that meant she wanted to comfort her but couldn't make the tapping obvious like a pat, or even put her arms around her, because there were other people from Kiel on the Flensburg coaster, successful men, they knew Herr Mayer certainly and Tante Elizabeth as well perhaps, some might also be going on from Flensburg through the Bugt to Sønderborg, and they would notice. They would notice something and then the purpose of the voyage would be spoiled and wasted. *We're going to visit my daughter in Sønderborg*, was what she had been telling people and, depending on who she was talking to, *Her husband's doing very well, they have a house right next to the harbour, he comes down often to Flensburg.*

That was perhaps why Mutti suddenly began to sing the

song that had always meant they were having fun when Josephina and her sisters were children: *Backe backe Kuchen, Der Bäcker hat gerufen.* Her voice was a bit strained and squeaky, and what did baking cakes have to do with being on the ship, and the lines about *Eggs and lard, sugar and salt, milk and flour* made Josephina feel sick. But when Mutti sang the last line about *Push it into the oven* Josephina began to laugh, she was laughing and laughing but almost crying.

'But I'm not a child, what do you think you're doing, Mutti?' She wasn't going to cry, even though her heart was breaking in half in her chest as the ship slowly approached the Schwentine and the mill that was there above the estuary, and the railway station, and the hillside where Elke might even then be going down through fog-dewy grass to milk the two cows, and her home among the apple and pear trees that had only just got their first pale-green leaves – she couldn't really see any of it because the ship was on the far side of the fjord and there was fog. But also she could see it, she could see all of it, the picture in her mind saw right through the fog. There was Elke walking past Oma's old pear tree with her milking stool in one hand and a milk bucket in the other, she was calling *Bossy Bossy*, and the two cows were running to get their handful of oats from the bucket, the fog was coming in clouds from their grassy mouths, it was their sweet breath.

But then it was Mutti who was crying, she was doing it very carefully and quietly with her face turned away towards the pink sky above Laboe so that the other passengers on the packet-boat wouldn't see her tears. But what did they care, they didn't know Mutti. When Josephina put her arm around her mother's shoulders she didn't pull away, but Josephina could feel how hard she was trying not to shake with her sobs. She seemed to have become smaller suddenly, or else Josephina hadn't noticed her getting smaller and thinner during winter, and the little tern-hand on the rail was so thin and bony that Josephina put hers on top of it.

'We used to sing it all the time when you and Elke and Greta were little, really when you were just a baby, and Greta used to sing it to you, you liked it, you liked it when Greta sang to you.' Mutti's shoulders were firm again, so Josephina took her arm away. 'You liked it then,' Mutti said. Then she took her hand from under Josephina's and felt in her sleeve for a handkerchief. She had steadied herself. 'I was just remembering,' she said. 'Because we're going to Greta's, after all, are we not?'

Remembering what? Everything to be remembered began before Hauptmann von Zarovich. Even before Mutti's first daughter, clever Greta, left to live with her new husband, a big Dane from Sønderborg? He was becoming rich, said Mutti sometimes, as if that was a cause for complaint; they had a maid. Tante Elizabeth had a maid, too, after all, in Gaarden, they didn't spend the winter like peasants in a Bauernhaus with the animals inside and their piss running down the slope-floor, didn't they deserve to have a maid?

It was snowing outside; Mutti had come in from the pump with a bucket of water to sluice the slope-floor and seen Josephina being sick inside old Gunnar's stall. She was holding herself steady with one hand on the horse's warm flank – Gunnar didn't notice what was happening, he just kept grinding away at his feed of oats, she could feel the vibration of his grinding teeth under her hand. That was when Mutti struck Josephina on the face and Gunnar lifted his head suddenly and stamped one hoof when she cried out.

No, indeed, it was true, she hadn't bled for two months, she said, and Mutti hit her on the mouth with the bony back of her hand. Papa and Franz were there, they were cleaning out the stalls, and Elke was pushing water down the slope-floor with a big willow broom. Everyone stopped what they were doing when Josephina cried out and Gunnar blew a startled gasp from his nostrils.

What was the matter with her, Elke wanted to know – she was wringing out the rags in their 'blood bucket'. Because, you know, they always went together, in the same week, but now, twice, no little sister with her in the bucket? Elke was looking at her with that expression that meant she thought she knew more than Josephina did. There was a nasty smell of chlorine coming from the bucket but that didn't explain why Elke was wrinkling her nose; it was Josephina's silence that made her do that. The silence hid Hauptmann von Zarovich shouting 'Ah!' and then pushing her away sideways across the back of the sofa. 'Get out of here you little whore' – wasn't that enough? His face was crimson and he was wiping snot from his whiskered lip with the back of one hand. No, she wouldn't talk about it, not to Tante Elizabeth who was the kindest person she knew, not to her mutti because she was already angry, not even to Elke who thought she knew everything but she didn't.

Yes, it is true, she said to Mutti, holding herself steady against Gunnar's warm flank, no bleed for two months, yes, now I feel sick when I wake up. That was when Mutti hit her on the mouth, as if she wanted Josephina to shut up, as if she preferred her silence of the past weeks. Josephina's lip was cut, she had the taste of blood in her mouth, and when she shouted right into Mutti's face that *yes, Hauptmann von Zarovich stuck his big thing in me*, it was as though the words tasted of blood, as though the little sprays of blood and spit that landed on Mutti's cheek were the words Josephina had not spoken from the moment she walked back across the town from the hissing swans at Ratsdienergarten and couldn't make herself sing 'Wie traulich war das Fleckchen' at Tante Elizabeth's house – as if at that moment when she shouted the bloody words into her mutti's white face the Strikkelise tunnel opened before her and she went through it and came out in the Bauernhaus with Mutti and her papa and Elke and Franz all staring at her while old Gunnar ground away at his oats. And then Elke put her big strong arms around her and walked her away from the slope-floor to where the fire was burning in the living space and it was warm, and held on to her until her papa and mutti got there.

'I knew it,' said Papa, putting out his hand to touch her but from a distance, 'that bastard shithead Junker!' But if that was true, if it was true that he knew it, why didn't he do anything the day he came to get her from Tante Elizabeth's, why didn't Tante Elizabeth say, 'I knew it, that shithead bastard,' and make her papa do something, why did Mutti agree to be silent when she, Josephina, decided to stop talking? And anyway, it was her big warm sister Elke who said it first when they got to the fireplace – 'I knew it, Josie, I always knew it!' – even if it wasn't true that she always knew it, how could she have always known it? But her strong arms and the warm smell of her working body and her tears that smeared together with Josephina's on their pressed-together cheeks were true; and then the others were there, and they all started to talk at once, all saying they knew it, all except poor Franz who went out into the snowy morning and didn't come back until evening to get his things from his crib next to Gunnar's and leave for ever without talking to anyone.

How beautiful her big sister was – Greta's cheeks were flushed with anger or impatience, but that just made her more beautiful. No wonder Danne couldn't keep his hands to himself, he especially liked to rest one open palm on Greta's stomach just where it was starting to swell out below her apron bib. Little Finn noticed that his mutti was talking in an angry voice; he pulled his clacking duck across the floor towards her, calling 'Mor, mor,' and for just a moment it was as though Josephina didn't know where she was – of course this was his dänisch home and Greta was Mor, not Mutti.

Then Josephina put her arms around her beautiful *mor* sister and said, 'I'm sorry, I was tired,' into her hot cheek.

'Mor!' Finn was tugging at Greta's skirt and preparing to cry.

'We're all tired, Josie,' Greta said. 'It's normal.' She picked the child up and jerked her head at Josephina: it meant go upstairs and get the baby, right now.

When she came down again Greta had made some chamomile tea and they sat outside in the back yard while Josephina fed the baby. The day was hot so they sat in the patchy shade of the napkins on the clothesline. Bees were humming in the purple verbena flower-heads along the wall by the privy and there were big slow flies to wave off the baby's face. With one hand Greta wiped at a line of sweat above her top lip and with the other she tried to restrain Finn. Danne was looking for new opportunities, she said. He wanted to sell the Bückling smoke-yard because the fisheries were not so good anymore. She thought that if her new child was a girl she'd call her Ayla after her oma back at Kiel and because it was an interesting name, but Danne wanted to call her after his mother who lived way up north in Skagen, God knows why. Now was a good time to dry the verbena for tea, they should hang some bunches. Most Danes thought the Germans in Sønderborg should have packed up and left after Dybbøl but after all her and Josie's opa was buried over there poor foolish man, and the two uncles as well. In November when it was getting cold Catharina would be able to eat a warm spoonful of stewed apple with honey.

She hoisted Finn into her lap and gave him a pretend shaking.

A big question waited in the space between her and Josephina but the space filled up with small-talk because Greta couldn't find a way to get started. The question had been there for weeks and Josephina sensed that Greta and Danne were discussing it when they spoke Danish and then stopped if she came into the room because now she could understand some of it. Perhaps they'd agreed that Greta would ask the question while Danne was away in Flensburg. That was why Greta got annoyed with her but then changed her mood to sweet and made some chamomile tea 'because it will help Catha to sleep'. Maybe she would ask the question when Catha did go back to sleep and when Finn had his nap after lunch. But now Finn was jealous of Catharina and wanted Josephina to take him across the quay to look at the boats and leave Catharina behind. It was a little drama in which the question Greta couldn't ask yet was being acted out. Greta gave Finn another playful shaking and looked at Josephina across his head while he writhed and pushed at her.

Are you going to leave? Or it could be, *When are you going to leave?* – which was really, *When are you going to leave Catharina here with us?* Because that was the plan.

'I'm not going to,' Josephina said.

'What, take Finn to look at the boats?' Now Greta was furious again.

'Leave without Catharina,' said Josephina. 'Come on, Finn, let's go to see the *baad*, maybe there will be some fishes.' Her sister's mouth was wide open above the boy's squirming. The question she hadn't asked was trapped in there. Her expression made Josephina laugh – it reminded her of the first time she went to the Sønderborg market where the loud, busy woman at the vegetable stall asked her in Danish if she wanted anything else and she said yes, thinking the woman had asked if that was all.

'So, what then?' the woman shouted, staring at Josephina with her hands on her hips. 'What more do you want?' She was red in the face from her exertions, but she was only pretending to be fierce. When Josephina's pregnancy became visible the woman would stuff one or two extra onions or the strippings of cabbage leaves into her bag.

'Nothing more, thank you.' That was what she'd learned to say to the market woman.

'What do you mean?' said Greta.

'What I said, nothing more.' Finn was tugging at Josephina's leg, so she took the baby from her breast and put her in Greta's arms. 'When I go, I'll take her.'

Then she and Finn were on the quay. The morning bustle was over, some of the fishermen were tidying their boats, and the sea glittered so much that Josephina and Finn had to squint their eyes. Squinting at each other made Finn laugh. He laughed with all his heart and soul, it came from the place of joy inside him, and then he got the hiccups, which made him laugh even more.

No, little Finn-and-Catharina cousins, you probably won't see each other again after Catharina and I go. The thought should have made Josephina terribly sad, but it didn't. Danne was a kind man despite his noise, but really he was doing what Greta wanted him to agree with, which was keeping Catharina in Sønderborg after Josephina went home. Greta would surely love Catharina and make her happy, and no one could ever tell her what to do, but even so she was really doing what Mutti and Papa had asked her to, which was to send Josephina back without Catharina.

What do you want? I want Catharina. *Anything else?* No, nothing. The thought was very clear and simple. So was the thought that she wouldn't be going back to the place where the Strikkelise tunnel opened into her childhood, where the Oma resided in her mutti's dark wooden chest, where old Gunnar knew the way back home from Tante Elizabeth's house in Gaarden and could go there without being made to, and where Elke's warm back would be breathing at the same speed as Josephina's chest when they slept together near the owl that lived up under the roof. These were sad thoughts but they were now also completely clear in her mind. Not having them clearly there had been making her tired – not the baby, not the housework, not the difficulty of trying to speak Danish, not trying to sew enough things for Danne to sell in the Flensburg market, just not knowing certainly and simply what she wanted. But now she did.

So they went along the quay little by little while Finn's hiccups and choke-laughing died down. Josephina was singing to him in German, *Backe backe Kuchen, Der Bäcker hat gerufen*, it was a skipping rhythm, they skipped along holding hands.

There were still a few big baskets of herring on the quay that the squawking seagulls were interested in, and Finn wanted to poke the fishes' little shiny eyes but Josephina wouldn't let him. Then, at the far end where the quay turned out into the breakwater, there was a gigantic halibut the length of a man that people were admiring – Why both eyes on one side, Finn wanted to know, why bumpy skin, did it eat children? No, Josephina told him while his hand tightened on hers and he pressed against her leg, it doesn't eat children, it eats crabs, you can find them in its tummy. He put his free hand up to his face, he was checking where his own eyes were – it was the halibut's eyes that terrified him, and its ugly skin and gaping mouth. Then Finn began to whimper, which made the proud fisherman laugh. He was standing very upright next to the huge creature and holding a gaff hook-upwards like a soldier; he used the gaff's hook to prise open the halibut's enormous mouth, which made Finn cling on to Josephina and cry, so they went quickly back along the quay.

He cheered up when Josephina showed him the swallows flying in and out from their mud and straw nests under the eaves of the harbourside houses. They go away in the winter, she told him, they go to warm places where oranges grow. Their babies have to practise for a while but then they all go too; probably they have to learn to speak another language where the oranges are, but they all do it.

'And then they all come back,' Josephina said past the big swelling in her throat. 'They come home again – look how happy they are, dancing together in the sky!'

Finn flitted along the quay towards home with his arms outstretched. He'd forgotten all about the monster. Then his little legs got in a tangle and he fell over, so Josephina carried him the rest of the way piggyback.

The lump in her throat was her mother – Josephina had to speak around Mutti when she saw Greta draping a muslin shawl over Catharina's bassinet on the shady side of the yard.

'We saw a big fish, didn't we, Finn?' She pulled her lower eyelids down with two fingers and gaped her mouth. But Finn was trying to take the muslin off the bassinet. Greta was pulling his hands away while looking at Josephina with an *Are we going to talk?* expression. Or perhaps it was *What more do you want?*

I want the Oma. These thoughts were coming to her in an orderly way. The thought about the Oma came to her so simply while she and Finn were looking at the swallows because they reminded her of what Mutti had told her about the Rohrsänger. But the swallows were singing that she, Josephina, would not be coming home. She would have to find a way to say that. She and Greta had to find a way to ask their mother to give the Oma to her before she left Sønderborg – and that would mean she wasn't coming home. They had to find a way to tell Mutti that Josephina was taking Catharina with her, she didn't know where, and that she had to have the Oma. She had to have Catharina and the Oma, and that was that.

Are we going to talk? What more do you want? Greta had one hand on her stomach and was holding on to the back of Finn's shirt with the other; she had the kind of smile on her face that could mean she was amused or could be angry again any minute but she wasn't going to be the first one to speak. She stuck her bottom lip out and puffed at the sweat on her top lip. Then she tipped her head on one side.

'And I want the Oma,' said Josephina. 'We have to ask Mutti for the Oma.'

'Monstrom,' said Finn, goggling his eyes.

Greta's smile was back. It was almost angry but not quite. 'No, Finn,' she said while looking at Josephina, 'your Oma isn't a monster, what do you mean?'

'He means the big fish we saw, don't you, Finn?' Josephina pulled her eyelids down again and made a gaping halibut mouth. Then she pretended to chase him. 'I'm going to gobble you up like a tasty crab!'

Finn shrieked and hid his face in Greta's apron. She was shaking her head at Josephina – the smile was a straight line. 'Ah yes,' she said. 'Clearly, the precious Oma. Well, we shall see, let's wait and see, Josephina Hansen.'

Josephina knew when Greta's smile wasn't one anymore because there were no wrinkles at the corners of her eyes. She'd seen that not-smile many times; she used to call it 'the look'. 'The look' frightened her when she was small, but now it didn't. She lifted a corner of the muslin cover on Catharina's bassinet; it was one of those she made for the market, with all-round blanket-stitch borders to hold the edges together – this one used the thick blue yarn that Danne had brought back for her from Flensburg, and she'd done different-length vertical stitches to make a pattern like writing. Catharina's eyes were closed but just for a moment, when Josephina lifted the cover, it was as though the baby was lying there peacefully reading the patterned edging.

Josephina knew the Oma's stitch-writing better than the letters she and Elke had copied over and over in the smelly dusty schoolroom with Pastor Köhler and his wooden smacking spoon, and she knew the Oma's stitch-stories and songs better than the ones in Sunday's *Psalter und Harfe* – but then the Pastor's lessons had come to an end when she was twelve and was given the Oma to work with and could still remember the songs and stories from when she was only old enough to make Strikkelise tubes out of the balls of coloured wool offcuts her grandmother gave her. Every stitch had a name and a story and a little picture of a flower or an animal or a red house with a window on either side of its green door and people in the windows; there was an owl of course, and yellow ducks on a blue lake, a snowy mountain with a little deer on top, and an alphabet in different colours around the border. The Oma was half the size of a bedspread and couldn't ever be washed because the different threads and dyes would get mixed up, and it had a secret smell that it exhaled when it was unrolled. Her grandmother would close her eyes and breathe in deeply whenever she unrolled the sampler, and she would always tell the story or sing the song of the stitch she was using that day. And it wasn't long before she gave Josephina a scrap of linen and Josephina embroidered a picture of Puck Puck the special chicken on it, and carried it around with her, and made up stories.

But now she would have to make Finn his bowl of soup with bread and then she would have to sew until Catharina woke up. Today it was going to be cabbage and potato with a little cut-up sausage in it – Finn enjoyed 'fishing' for the round bits of sausage in his soup bowl while Josephina mopped the floor. There was a mangy cat that sometimes came over the wall into the yard, so Josephina kept a lookout for it in case it jumped up on the bassinet. Then she persuaded Finn to have a pee at the end of the yard where there were some weeds in a patch of dirt, which was his special place. He made his pee go as far over the weeds as possible. Then she took him up to have a sleep on Greta and Danne's bed. The window was open and she could hear Greta talking in Danish to some women in the street below. Sometimes lately Greta had a nap at the same time as Finn but not today. Josephina hurried downstairs and out to the baby in the yard, but the mangy cat hadn't come to visit. She lifted the muslin shawl to look at Catharina who was starting to wriggle before waking up. The blanket-stitched border with longer and shorter stitches was like writing but not quite. There was an old bible in the Bauernhaus above the Schwentine and, once she'd learned how to do it, Josephina had carefully written her name in it just below Greta's and Elke's. Josephina Christian Hansen. Like that. Mutti's name wasn't there because she'd never learned how to write it.

There was still the yoghurt to drain into curds and hang up in a muslin bag, and her sewing, but before them the baby. She needed to chop some kindling now that Danne was away in Flensburg, and to bring the napkins in from the yard, especially as Greta had washed a lot of them that morning when Josephina should have. Then, when Catharina and Finn were asleep again, Greta would be waiting for her. *And so, what more do you want now, little sister?*

Josephina had already answered the question to herself while she did her jobs, and Greta didn't ask it when they had their supper. Danne had left some fresh soles before going off to Flensburg, and they ate them with pickles and bread. They were behaving as though everything was normal. They drank some verbena tea. Then Josephina sat upstairs by the window and sewed in the pale, clear late light, rocking Catharina's crib with her foot. The baby was calm, twitching her arms around. The crib, which had been Finn's and before long would have Greta's new baby in it, had paintings on both sides, of ships at sea with smooth blue waves and white sails bulging with wind next to islands with green palm trees. Sometimes the paintings made her think of the young sailor by the harbour in Kiel with his wonderful great talking shell.

She made the sewing and the rocking have the same rhythm because it was good for thinking.

Finn was chattering away downstairs, then he and Greta went out to the quay so he could play with the neighbour's children – they ran up and down squawking like seagulls. Then he had his drink of milk and complained for a while when Greta put him to bed. Then Greta was standing in the doorway of Josephina's little room. Josephina was feeding Catharina again.

'What, are you hiding?' Greta said.

No, not hiding, thinking. Then and then and then. Moving the big simple thoughts along a road over and over, from now until then, until she knew the way, until it was as if she'd already done the journey many times, like Gunnar returning from Tante Elizabeth's to the Bauernhaus above the Schwentine, which he'd already done when Greta still lived there and even before that. So when she and Greta finally took chairs outside in the cool of the sea breeze where people were enjoying their last evening walk along the quay, she didn't wait for her big sister to ask, she just said that yes she did want something else, she also wanted to get better at reading and writing because she'd need to be able to do that, wouldn't she. She was holding Catharina on her lap so the baby could kick her legs and burp.

'Able to do that after you leave, you mean,' said Greta. 'That's what you mean. After you *leave*.' The way she said *leave* was a little sarcastic. Then she leaned across and put her arm around Josephina and rested her head on her shoulder and kissed her on the neck. 'Josie, Josie, sweet little Josie,' she whispered, keeping her lips there so they tickled. 'You always were *that one*.' She picked up Josephina's hand and put it on her almost-big stomach. 'But you'll have to wait just a little longer, won't you, Schwesterchen? Just a little bit?'

Josephina was looking down past Catharina's wiggling feet – how long before those funny little feet would be tripping on the cobblestones? A year? It was impossible to imagine she and Catharina would still be here in another summer; her then-and-then-and-then thoughts had already gone away into the story she was telling herself and knew so well, like Gunnar's nodding head and mane moving forward along a view between houses or trees that kept on narrowing until it opened . . . not to the Bauernhaus and Oma's pear tree – but of course, of course.

'Of course,' Josephina said.

'Of course.' Greta's hair smelled a little of cloves, her stomach was firm and warm where she was pressing Josephina's hand against it, and then she gave a sudden start and sat up straight.

Josephina recognised fru Jepsen who greeted them in Danish-sounding German. She had visited soon after Mutti left to go home that time, her husband was the pastor at Saincte Marie Church; its red brick tower with a big clock and a dark steeple stuck up above the houses at the end of the quay and reminded Josephina of the Nikolaikirche on the far side of Kieler Förde and how its steeple always seemed to be falling across the sky. Fru Jepsen was wearing a dark, high-necked dress with a white lace collar, and her grey hair was drawn back in a tight bun under a simple white cotton cap – Josephina at once felt disreputable and untidy.

'So, your husband is away in Flensburg?' The question must have been for Greta, surely, but fru Jepsen was looking at Josephina and the baby. 'And how is the little one?' She stood with her hands folded in front of her and her head on one side. She had a gentle, kindly way of talking, but Greta's hand gripped Josephina's where it rested on her stomach.

'My sister's husband was a soldier, fru Jepsen, did we not tell you?' said Greta. She was still hugging Josephina and now she pulled her even closer. 'But sadly he is no longer with us.' She gave Josephina's hand a squeeze and took her arm away from the hug and sat up rather straight. 'But we are lucky, as you can see, fru Jepsen, we have this beautiful child.' She put her hand on Catharina's forehead. 'A gift from God.'

The pastor's wife held Greta's look for a while, shaking her head in sympathy. 'I am so sorry to hear that,' she said finally, extending her hand to Josephina. It was warm and dry and slightly rough, as if accustomed to doing at least some housework. Josephina allowed the woman to hold her hand for a while – it seemed she was expected to say something in response to fru Jepsen's gentle clasp and her calm, direct gaze, but Josephina preferred *to look her square in the eye* as Oma used to instruct her when she was little and perhaps a bit nervous, *direkt in die Augen schauen!* Show that you are not afraid and also show respect.

The pastor's wife released Josephina's hand and smiled with her mouth but not her eyes. 'Perhaps we can expect to see the beautiful child baptised before too long?' She didn't wait for Josephina to reply. 'And my respects to your husband when he returns from Flensburg, Frau Andersen, I'm sure his transactions will have been profitable.'

'As if she didn't know what she was doing,' Greta whispered as the pastor's wife walked away, nodding her greetings to others along the quay. Then they were very quickly back inside and laughing so hard that Catharina was startled and began to cry. Greta went to the big cupboard at the back of the room and took out a bottle of Danne's brandy from Flensburg. 'Time for a profitable transaction,' she said.

Josephina had never drunk spirits before but after the searing sensation in her throat stopped she took another sip and felt a pleasant warmth in her stomach and behind her eyes. Greta was standing by the table with a glass in one hand and the other resting on the unfolded pile of freshly washed napkins. She was giving Josephina her best *direkt in die Augen schauen!*

'Perhaps we can expect to see the beautiful child baptised before too long?' Greta was mimicking fru Jepsen, but without mockery. She took a swallow of her brandy, and her laugh turned into the sweet smile Josephina loved. 'What do you think, Josie? We could do that?'

Catharina had stopped mewing and was looking up at Josephina's face with a silly baby grin – was it a real grin or did she have the tummy ache that so often started in the evening?

What did she think? 'Not at home,' Josephina said. 'Not back there.' It was another of those clear thoughts, like the road opening out into well-lit space beyond a clutter of houses – not a destination but a way ahead. She was gazing at Catharina's grin, so she didn't see her sister's expression, only heard the sound of her glass being put down firmly on the table. 'Because they sent Catharina away,' said Josephina, looking up into Greta's chest-heave sigh. 'They were ashamed of her.'

Greta began to fold the freshly washed napkins. After the first one she said, 'This one was stillborn.' The next one: 'This one is me.' Then she did two more. 'But these died, a girl and then a boy.' Then another: 'This one miscarried.' Another: 'Elke.' Another: 'The winter chest fever, it was a boy.' Another napkin, carefully and quickly folded and added to the pile. 'She miscarried.' Another: 'The special one, but not a boy, it was you, Josephina. And you were the last one. The *special one.*'

'I know,' said Josephina. 'I was told, too.'

Greta poured herself a second glass of brandy. She was looking at Josephina with the smile that could mean this or could mean that. Then she folded another napkin on to the neat pile. 'And this one miscarried late, it was a girl, she was almost complete, she was mine, you didn't know that. She was mine and Danne's – Mutti and Papa knew but they didn't tell you and Elke because I asked them not to. But she was another one, for them she was another one.' She folded another napkin very slowly. 'Finn. Our Finn. The boy at last.' She took a swallow of brandy but didn't offer to pour another for Josephina. 'In case you should wonder why Mutti is so sad sometimes and wants to go and live in a proper house. In case you should wonder why you are Papa's *special one.*'

'I can't do it,' said Josephina.

And what did that mean, *special one*? For weeks now she had lived in a kind of thought-fog – it was a fog of love. No one had ever told her it would be like this, that the sight and smell and warmth of her baby would utterly overcome her with bliss, even when she was tired and sore and wanted to sleep more than anything in the world, even when she would be falling asleep with Catharina on her breast. No one told her she would go about her tasks in a daze that was part tiredness but also the bliss-fog, that the sensation of Catharina suckling would occupy every part of her body and being, including her thoughts or the part of her that could think separately from the sensation of that determined little mouth. But now quite suddenly today it was as though she had emerged from the love-fog of *special one* – it began after she came down late this morning and saw that Greta and Danne were talking about what was going to happen next, what was she, Josephina, going to do next? And now her thoughts moved clearly along a *way ahead.*

Greta had pulled a chair close and was sitting directly in front of her. 'What do you mean, *can't*? You mean don't want to, you don't want to give them that, that's what you mean, isn't it, Josie? Don't want to.' She said *don't want to* in a mocking, childish voice, the teasing voice she'd sometimes used when they were both children, but now she was looking at her little sister as though she'd never seen her before. She took another swallow of her brandy.

'No, I don't mean *don't want to*, it's not the same. Because of course I want to. Why wouldn't I want to take Catharina home, why wouldn't I want her to be a joy? But they're ashamed of her and they sent us away, they sent her away before she was even born. So I can't.' *Direkt in die Augen schauen!* Josephina would not, she would not look away from Greta's face and her eyes that were a bit glassy. Her own face was burning, but not from a blush and not from anger, it was as though her new clear thoughts had caught fire inside her and her whole body was glowing.

Greta leaned in and kissed her with brandy breath. She held Josephina's cheeks between her hands that were warm and dry from the napkins. 'Then we can do it with fru Jepsen's Pastor-mann who very much likes Danne's Bückling but especially with a good glass of profitable transaction from this house my darling.'

Greta's sentence was very confused but of course doing what it said would keep the shame away from *this house*. 'Yes, of course we could do that,' said Josephina.

'And perhaps they will come,' said Greta.

No, they won't come. Now Catharina had fallen asleep, so Josephina took two freshly folded napkins from the table, kissed her sister, and carried her sweetly sleeping special one upstairs.

Dearest Papa and Mutti

And naturally my beloved sister Elke whom I miss more than it is possible to speak about but she will understand won't you Elke.

I am sorry if my writing is poor but I am practising every day and also reading and copying from a book that Greta has in the house here in Sønderborg. It is called *The Swiss Family Robinson* do you know it? Sometimes I feel as if I am lost on a desert island like that family but that is not why I am writing. I am writing to tell you some important news but first to say I am well and Catharina yes that is her name she is also well and the joy in my life every day. Also that Greta and Danne are kind to me and to Catharina and their boy Finn your grandson is Catharina's friend at all times.

I am writing to tell you that the baby you do not want to have at home has been baptised and christened here in Sønderborg and so you are spared the trouble of doing it at home with Pastor Köhler. That would have been difficult for you I am sure because you are ashamed of the baby. Her God Mother and God Father are Greta and Danne your daughter and son-in-law they wished to spare you the trouble of coming here I hope you understand.

It is hard for me to have the baby away from home but better now she has been baptised and christened by Pastor Jepsen here in Sønderborg. He and Frau Jepsen speak German and so it is done and Catharina can be here without it being a trouble for her God Father and God Mother your daughter and son-in-law.

The baby's name is Catharina Elke Lange Hansen you will understand what the parts of the name mean. Catharina was my Oma's name she taught me everything about sewing and more besides and she gave me her sampler as you know when I was old enough to deserve it. I have more to write about that but not yet.

Elke you have to be there in the name I am sorry I could not ask you but you know why you are there. Please be happy for Catharina you will see her one day I know and you will love her.

Lange you will know was Oma's name before she married Opa and I want to remember that name because I will never be married to the father of my child thank God for that. There are names that need to be remembered and others that are best forgotten.

Hansen is my name and the name of the family into which I was born and so it is also the baby's name even though you do not want to have her in the family. That should make me sad but it does not because it is her right. Now I see there is a path for us in life without the family that was ashamed of my baby Catharina Greta Lange Hansen and so what I also have to tell you is that she and I will not be coming home to where I was born and grew up. I will not be coming home without my baby and so I will not be coming home again ever. There will be another path for us in life.

I am sorry this is a long letter and full of mistakes. I had to write down everything you need to know and now I have almost finished but there is one more thing I need to write. That is I must have Oma's sampler the one we call the Oma that you Mutti took away from me after the trouble with that house in Faulstrasse that I pray to God I will forget one day.

You must send the Oma sampler to me here in Sønderborg because I cannot come to get it without Catharina and you will not allow me to come with her. My oma gave the sampler to me because she began to teach me everything in the sampler when I was only old enough to make Strikkelise and she always said one day this will be yours Josephina Hansen. She could not say my middle name Christian because it was Opa's but she said as much as she could. It was complete and it was clear what she meant.

Please send the sampler with Danne when he comes to Kiel or even to Flensburg. You know he has business there he says he can arrange it. Or you can send the sampler with Tante's husband Herr Mayer or his man who comes to Denmark with their ship the one I came here to Sønderborg on with Mutti. You will not have forgotten that voyage Mutti. I wish I could. In any case it will not be difficult to do this and you must it is right.

I will finish by saying what you know already that what happened to me in Faulstrasse was the worst thing that will ever happen to me in my life please God. But now it is in the past and what matters is what will happen next in the life I will have with my baby who will one day be a woman as I am now and please God in a place where she can be Catharina Elke Lange Hansen and not a shame that had to be sent away as if to a desert island where no one could find her.

Your daughter Josephina

Elke I hug you and kiss you I know we will see each other again.

Daughter

You have turned this family against itself through your actions, and so even though we loved you once, that is no longer of consequence and is as if it never was so. We could not attend the christening of Greta's child in February. We can no longer speak to your Tante Elizabeth. These are the results of your actions that have caused us much grief and trouble. Now you have turned your back on us as we grow old and need the help of our children that we cared for without stint, and so you can expect nothing from us. You had no right to take those names for your child, but that too is no longer of consequence as you will not bring that child here ever, as you write, but that is because we forbid it, not because you wish it. You have been a vain girl, and the airs you gave yourself have been your downfall. You have no right to claim your grandmother's favour. The thing you call the Oma belongs to the family and will remain here with the family of which you are no longer a part. We are glad for the child's sake that you have had it baptised and we commend your sister Greta and her husband Danne for that. No doubt it was their good sense that made this happen. You were once our special one and it has broken our hearts to lose you. For the sake of that special one we loved once we hope you will prosper and that the child will too.

Your Papa and Mutti

Beth and Frank

'Authorised version,' said Frank, wiping beer froth off his top lip. 'My Grandma Cath was the eldest of my great-grandmother and your great-great-grandmother Josephina's kids. Then came your Great-grandad Wolf. Then another boy that went awol.'

The 'lodge' units at the back of the hotel were pretty basic, with budget skiers in mind. They had thin walls, tatty candlewick bedspreads, and cheap plastic fittings in the bathroom. Beth longed for the candlewick and the pull-down blind with a faded pattern of leaves on it – once green, the leaves were now autumnal, which was how she felt after her day down the Kaitīeke with Frank. But he was bent on having a beer on the hotel patio that looked out over the highway towards Ngāuruhoe.

Of course he knew that stuff, what was he on about? She sipped her beer and said nothing. All day he'd pretended he wasn't really interested in the family story, but now he just wanted her to stick around.

'One born in Germany . . .'

'Denmark,' said Beth. She couldn't help it.

'I stand corrected,' said her cousin, who was subjecting her to his piercing look. 'One born in Denmark, and the question of why Denmark arises; one born on board the ship coming out here – why, again – and one born in Wellington, the father a sailor who jumped ship and married Josephina a year later here in our little corner of the Pacific, a very long way from Germany, or Denmark for that matter.'

There was a dog on a chain at the back of the hotel. It set

up a mournful, half-hearted barking until someone yelled at it.

'So unless our sailor boy . . .'

'Heinrich Wenczel. Polish.'

'Thank you. Heinrich Wenczel, of course. So unless sailor-boy Heinrich pole-vaulted around the Baltic region and across the sea to New Zealand, impregnating our great-grandmother at intervals along the way, we have an intriguing story on our hands.'

Pole-vaulting Wenczel struck Beth as intriguing enough. But she was tired – not of the story and its intrigue, nor of her cousin's attempts at humour, but of his veering moods and of the way her day had gone on sliding between a then and a now, as if the modest distances they'd covered on their expedition down the Kaitīeke had been stretched out by time. She'd travelled a lot further than down the hill to Great-grandad Wolf's patch and back.

'Sorry, Frank,' she said. 'I'm pretty buggered, going to have a lie-down. You go ahead and get dinner when you feel like it, I'll come and find you, don't wait for me.'

Frank pretended to be staring across the road at the distant pyramid of Ngāuruhoe, and she knew his silence was a rebuke of sorts, but she gave him a kiss on the wrinkly back of his neck and walked through the bar to the yard behind the hotel, where the dog barked at her in a half-hearted way. It went on yelping intermittently after she pulled down the brown-leafed blind and lay on the candlewick bedspread. The shawl she pulled over herself was the old one she'd got from her mother Elke, who said it came from her Great-grandma Josephina back in the day. You weren't meant to wash it more than once a year, if that, and only by hand, in tepid water. She'd only washed it once, after Elke's cat threw up on it. That was about ten years ago, not long after Elke died, and the cat followed soon after – he never forgave her for not being her mother.

Dim light entered her room through the leafy blind. The dog's doleful yelps kept her from sleep for a while but then followed her into a dream. The barks came from trees on the far side of a river. The surface of the river was placid and the trees were reflected there, waving about a little in the slow current. She couldn't see the dog. Then her mother Elke emerged from the trees – it was she who was barking. Beth understood perfectly well what her mother was saying, and continued to understand for a while after she woke up. She lay thinking about what Elke had said. But then it was gone. That, too, was familiar.

The Sisters

They came along the quay with Danne's man pushing the things in a barrow, and there was Elke, there she was. When she saw Josephina with Finn and Catharina further down by the fishing boats she made a shrill squawking noise like a seagull, and though Josephina already knew it was her, now she was certain. Then she smelled like Elke and her strong body felt like Elke and how she grabbed Josephina by the hair was Elke. Danne's man stood there with a shy silly smile on his face – he was really just a boy with some fluff on his cheeks, but then he asked in a best manly voice whether he should take the things to herre Andersen's house now?

'They're old,' said Elke into Josephina's ear. She was panting a little after running along the quay. 'They don't know what anger is for.'

Danne's man was looking at them with a helpless expression. Catharina had just learned to walk and had staggered to him; she was holding herself upright on his leg. Now Elke swooped on her and snatched her up, which made her cry. So then they were walking along the quay towards Greta's house while Danne's man followed behind with Finn and Catharina hanging on tight in the barrow. As well as Finn and Catharina there were some bundles in the barrow including a long rolled-up object wrapped in oilcloth, and an old Reisetasche – the battered bag Mutti had brought on the voyage last spring – but that wasn't what Josephina was looking at over her shoulder, making Danne's man blush. She knew what the rolled-up object wrapped in oilcloth was, she knew what it was but couldn't believe it: how could it be the Oma after Papa's letter only two months ago?

But then Elke noticed Josephina glancing over her shoulder. 'Oh yes, such a good-looking boy,' she said, teasing him. Of course she was pretending. So they stopped just by the door of the house and Elke held Josephina's head against her chest. 'Yes, naturally,' she said. 'What did you think? I would come without your precious sewing thing?' Catharina began to shriek jealously in the barrow but Josephina could not lift her head from Elke's chest or stop the sobs.

Yes, this was her little Josephina with the knobby shoulders and that long neck with fair goose-down peeping under her cap at the back, and weeping with hiccups the way she always did, only now she was the mother of that beautiful child in the barrow who was looking at Josephina's shaking shoulders with a woeful expression and inventing different shrieks that she was quite enjoying (Finn was copying them, only louder, and laughing), which her mother used to do at that age and even older. But this was her little Josie, and the child would have to wait a while. Elke rested her chin on the top of Josephina's head and made silly faces at Catharina, and then felt the hiccupping sobs stop and her sister's voice say, 'Shit,' quite emphatically. Josephina had lifted her head and was looking over Elke's shoulder.

Greta was there in the doorway, holding baby Otto. Her mouth had opened to ask what was all the noise about, but then she saw Elke with Josephina and Danne's man with the barrow and no words came out. Oh God, there they were, the two of them, *die Bande*, the gang, the little one whose smile opens doors and the big one who then goes through them, the *special one* and *Papa's helper*, God in heaven, here they were, here we are.

'Well, here I am, so it would seem,' said Elke. 'And here we all are. Amazing, isn't it?'

Danne's man wanted to know if he should bring the things in. Yes, yes, said Greta, as if she was waking up. So he lifted Finn out of the barrow and then handed Catharina to Josephina as if she was a dangerous parcel. Elke took the rolled-up Oma, and Danne's man the old Reisetasche and some other bundles, and then they all followed Greta inside, first Finn proudly leading the way and then Josephina with Catharina triumphantly on her hip, then Elke with the Oma under her arm, and last Danne's man with the bag and other things. He was leaving as fast as he could when Danne pushed past him into the room.

'A minute,' he said, looking hard at Greta, and they went out into the yard.

Elke had that expression that Josephina knew well, it was both guilty and smug, the one that used to make Pastor Köhler reach for his wooden spoon all those years ago. 'Well, while we're waiting,' said Elke, 'you should know a few things.' She still had the rolled-up Oma under her arm. Then, pretending she'd only just thought of it, she held the object out to Josephina in a mock-ceremonial way, across both hands, and bowed.

'What things?' Josephina was holding the familiar weight of the Oma against herself in a space that wasn't the ground-floor room in Greta's house – the conversation with Elke was happening in that room but at the same time as Josephina was somewhere else.

'You're being crazy,' said Elke. 'Why don't you put that thing down?' She was looking around. 'It's a nice house,' she said. 'Must have been pretty nice staying here?'

'Greta and Danne have been kind to me,' said Josephina,

but she didn't put the Oma down.

'Greta needs to know this too, but all right, why wait?' Elke was looking at the door to the yard. 'You need to know that Mutti is sick, it's the cough, that's why I can't stay very long. And old Gunnar died.'

His jaunty mane, the wildflowers Josephina would tuck under his horse-collar that was shiny inside with his smell. This had happened somewhere else in another time, but now it was here and she was back in the room with the sound of the quay just outside and her sister Elke looking at her with a sorrowful expression. She put the rolled-up Oma on the table and sat down.

Elke sat down too. Yes, well, it was true, from the time Gunnar first arrived they would find Josephina standing on an upturned wooden chaff bucket to reach the horse's nose, and he would let her – he didn't shake his head and knock her over, that funny little thing. 'He just stopped on the road back from Gaarden. Papa took some milk to Tante Elizabeth but she refused it, they were always arguing, so he was bringing it home again, and he said Gunnar just stopped and then sank down, the milk tipped out of the cart, it was his heart, it burst. Papa sent him to the knackers for some money but it wasn't enough for a good one – it's only got one eye so it can't go straight, it's a lot of trouble.'

Well, no more sobbing – across the table her little sister, Gunnar's favourite (he would snort love-breaths at her), sat calmly with the fingers of one hand lightly stroking her precious Oma-thing and her pale eyes looking steadily into the present moment.

When Josephina and the children were first out on the quay that afternoon, big black spring clouds were boiling over in the sky and people were saying there was going to be a storm. Now, gusty rattles of rain struck the windows and Greta and Danne hurried inside with the baby, followed by a draught of cold air.

'So, Elke,' said Greta, 'do you have something to tell us?'

'I just told Josie,' said Elke. 'Old Gunnar died.'

Danne was going out in his greatcoat – he said something angry in Danish and slammed the front door. Finn had helped Catharina to climb up on the window seat and they were pretending to lick rain off the panes, which would usually have annoyed Greta but she ignored them. She gave baby Otto to Josephina and sat down opposite Elke. *Die Bande*, so help me.

'And Mutti has the cough.'

'Don't make me angry,' said Greta. 'What would be the point?'

'And Papa sold one of the cows. And all the new poplar planks. And he doesn't have a journeyman anymore, just a stupid boy who keeps hurting himself with a saw or a hammer or something and he cries at night in the stall.' Elke reached for Greta's hand across the table. 'And I didn't tell them I was coming here.'

'And?' said Greta, letting Elke hold her hand.

'And I took the special sewing thing, Oma's sampler, it's Josephina's, they were wrong to keep it from her.' She was holding Greta's hand in both of hers and beating it gently on the table. 'They are old. They don't know what anger is for.' Then she said it again. 'They are old. They don't know what anger is for,' and Greta repeated it with her, so that it was hard to tell whether Elke was saying it again or whether she was echoing Greta.

Josephina was listening to them talk *about her* and about *anger* as if she wasn't completely there, and at the same time she was watching the children licking pretend rain off the windowpane. The rain wasn't there, but also it was, and the anger?

'So, what does that mean, *They don't know what anger is for*?' Greta allowed her sister to keep beating her hand on the table while Elke didn't answer, but then she withdrew it quite gently and went to make tea. When she turned around from the stove with the teapot, Elke and Josephina were both looking at her – neither had spoken. The two children were still pretending to lick rain off the windowpane and Catharina was laughing loudly, a hearty laugh like her aunt Elke's. Josephina was holding Otto over her shoulder and patting his back.

Greta put the teapot and three mugs on the table and it was as though what was happening in the room was now arranged in an orderly way around the tea – her sisters, the children, even the troublesome bundle on the table that Josephina was looking at while patting the baby's back. The one thing that didn't find its place was the word *anger*. Where did it belong? Danne was angry because Elke had tricked him and because now, God damn it, he had all three sisters under his roof. Greta was angry because Elke had made Danne angry. Elke was angry because she thought Mutti and Papa were wrong to be angry with Josephina and not let her have Oma's old sampler, who could argue with that. And Josephina? Josephina was looking at her across the Oma on the table in that steady way, hardly blinking, *direkt in die Augen schauen* – well, of course, everyone knew now why Josephina was angry. Tante Elizabeth back in Gaarden knew, Mutti and Papa knew, but where did their anger fit? No one except Josephina could make it fit properly anywhere. But everyone was angry with her as well, in one way or another, for one reason or another. Except maybe Elke, because here she was. But even so.

The tea was verbena, Greta told them, looking back at Josephina's stare (*Where do you keep your anger now?*), same as the one Mutti always likes at home, from that bush at the back. Near the juniper. The old one. She should drink it for the cough, it's good, you should tell her. And nettles.

Josephina was now holding the baby on her lap and stroking the Oma bundle, and at any moment she expected the bundle to begin to squirm a little, while Greta's voice went on about the tea. But then Elke butted in because of course she knew better, after all she'd just come from that old Bauernhaus above the Schwentine with the strange new one-eyed horse in poor Gunnar's stall. It probably wore Gunnar's collar now, but who collected the flowers for the horse's bouquet, the one that would dry and fall out on to the road? No one, probably.

Papa gets Mutti laudanum from the apothecary over by Ellerbek, Elke was telling them while looking hard at Greta over her cup of *verbena* tea – the fat, boring Apothek with bad breath who talks too much. It's good, makes her sleepy though.

So what does that mean? Greta wanted to know. So Mutti can't work? Much? Is that what you're saying?

Elke paused and blew on her cup of tea. Her hand was trembling, she wasn't going to risk a sip, not yet. 'She stopped. She doesn't.' So, now, the weak flavour of the sip. And I know where this is going, big sister, so all right: 'She can't.'

'Can't.'

'She says she's too angry. But you know she just can't. Anymore.' And now Greta will surely say: 'What are you doing here then? If Mutti *can't*?'

Well, anyway, baby Otto was now asleep, he'd fallen asleep while those two went on at each other, so Josephina took him upstairs and put a blanket over him on Greta and Danne's bed, a nice grey woollen one she'd edged with a border of round-eyed blue owls. Rainy squalls were beating on the bedroom window and for a while she watched the agitated masts along the quay tossing about in the dim light.

Then she went down again. Her sisters were sitting closer together and holding hands, only now Elke wasn't beating Greta's on the table. The two children were playing with Finn's duck on the floor, Finn was making it quack its way around Catharina while she snatched at it and laughed. It was clear that soon Finn's teasing would frustrate her and she would cry – so, as usual, there wasn't long to say what had to be said.

Josephina stood behind her sisters and put a hand on each of their necks. They looked around at her with happy expressions on their faces, Elke's that broad smile with her brow furrowed up towards her hair, Greta's her sweet sickle-shaped one with the dimples in her cheeks. She was looking so fine, Elke told her, being a mother suited her, who could have imagined it? Yes, who, agreed Greta, our little Josie? And she's been such a help. Then Josephina quite gently pushed their faces down towards the table and held them there with her hands as far around their necks as they would go.

'He pushed my face down into the back of a sofa and squeezed my neck with one hand so I could hardly breathe, then he pulled my clothes out of the way with his other hand and stuck his cock between my legs right up there and pushed it to and fro, then after a while he pushed it all the way in and squeezed my neck so hard I couldn't breathe at all, it really hurt, then he called me a whore and told me to never come back.' She let the sisters go then, and stepped back against the big cupboard so the plates and mugs rattled inside. 'I know what anger is for. It means someone should have cut the shithead's throat.' Josephina wiped with her sleeve at the heat in her face; a trickle of sweat ran down between her shoulder blades. The children had noticed something was happening, and they were both staring as Elke and Greta stood up and went to Josephina and put their arms around her, which is when Danne banged in out of the storm and saw the three sisters standing in a close huddle while the children gaped up at them from the floor.

Elke

It was sunny in Faulstrasse and everywhere the autumn sunshine came down through the trees making nice shadow patterns on the cobblestones and the dry brown leaves, the kind of thing that Josie would have noticed and exclaimed happily about making pictures with her hands, and that Elke was noticing because of Josie restless in her thoughts that were like a small black growling cloud that hovered above her head, it was moving with Elke towards 'the house on Faulstrasse' and there it was, the house, the windows upstairs were flashing with sunlight and the place looked cosy and fine, not too grand, the kind of place Mutti and Papa dreamed of living in with a housekeeper and a maid perhaps to empty the chamber pots, imagine that, even a cook and a place at the back for the workshop and for horses and for Papa's journeyman and a stable boy.

Her 'empty, lifeless heart' was how Josie had described what she felt like, not so much after 'what happened in Faulstrasse' as she called what the 'shithead' officer had done to her at that address but after everyone got angry, and what was at the bottom of that? – for Mutti and Papa it was not being able to live now and perhaps never in something like 'the house on Faulstrasse' or over in Gaarden perhaps where Tante Elizabeth and the 'very successful' Herr Mayer had already been for some years and who Papa said now thought themselves too fine for milk from 'the family farm', but of course that wasn't what the feud was about, it was because Mutti and Papa blamed Josie and Tante Elizabeth blamed them and Herr Mayer blamed his wife for making a fuss that everyone was talking about now, and where was the family's reputation going to end up? – on the dungheap out at 'the family farm' said Herr Mayer according to Tante Elizabeth who was also angry about the bad feeling between herself and her husband now, or even in 'the paupers' graveyard' as Mutti feared, making herself sick with the worry of it – but where was Josie, where was she in this swarm of flies buzzing over a single turd, the turd was Hauptmann von Zarovich but no one could see it, could see him, the great shithead turd anymore, they couldn't see past the ends of their noses and they certainly couldn't see little Josie, growled the angry black thought-cloud above Elke's head.

She had stopped across the road from 'the house on Faulstrasse' and was looking at its cheerful windows – Josie's 'empty, lifeless heart' had filled up again and come to life when Catharina was born she said, she no longer cared what happened to Hauptmann von Zarovich, there was a time when something should have happened to him but who could have spoken on her behalf, she'd put on the nightgown meant for Junkfrau von Zarovich and she'd taken the Hauptmann's money so what did she expect? – well, she expected nothing anymore she said in that new calm voice she had since getting Catharina, and that clear firm look in her Kornblume eyes blue like the flowers she used to tie together and tuck under old Gunnar's collar, her heart was full again, she had a path ahead said that little Josie and who knew where it might lead finally? – not back to the reedy marsh by the Schwentine where the little Rohrsänger practised flying away to a nice warm place she said where oranges came from, and one day they did it, off they went, and she had done it and now she had to keep going, and she would said grown-up Josephina that time back in Sønderborg at Greta's place the day she and Josie and Greta went on an outing with the two older children on the little ferry across Alsund to Dybbøl and walked up to the rebuilt mill destroyed in the battle where Opa and his two sons 'the fools' were killed fighting for the Prussians, well they didn't get far said Josie but not laughing – it was a good long walk and they took turns piggybacking Catharina, and Greta was fretting because she'd left baby Otto with the neighbour, they had a drink of water and ate some bread and apples on the higher ground by the patched-up ruin looking back at Sønderborg across the water.

Elke was leaving the next day to go back, *die Suppe auslöffeln* she laughed, to spoon up the soup she'd cooked for herself and take care of Mutti. When will I see you again she said to Josie, not laughing anymore, I don't know said Josie. I don't know maybe never. Because I have to keep going I can't stay at Greta's place much longer and I won't take Catharina 'back there' – it was the word 'home' that sank out of sight under 'back there' as if into the choppy blue-white Alsund sea or into one of the boggy collapsed trenches below the hill they'd just walked up where Opa and the uncles were, since they didn't go 'back there' either, they were here somewhere under the wet turf.

It was easier walking back down the slope, and then before she knew it after one last night hardly sleeping not wanting to sleep and waste any of her last time squashed together with her little Josie lightly breathing through her Josie nose with small murmurs like always in their life before 'the house on Faulstrasse', there she was by herself again with the old Reisetasche on the boat to Flensburg waving to Josie and Greta and the children and her heart didn't break or become 'empty and lifeless' like Josie's had before Catharina because now here she was crossing the road to 'the house on Faulstrasse' and her heart, Elke's very own heart, was beating like a drum.

She cried a lot on the way to Flensburg and was a bit sick too, the passage into the harbour was long and twisty with wind-shifts so the boat swayed this way and that, she wasn't the only one being sick over the rail but it was as much about her heart as her stomach, her heart was sick but not broken or 'empty and lifeless', and it was better up there in the wind with the rude sailor who wanted her out of the way than down in the sick-smelly cabin.

Then Danne's man who was impatient and rude helped her to find Herr Mayer's man who was also impatient but looked at the letter from Danne and so knew she'd been visiting her sisters in Sønderborg at Herr Andersen's house and needed to get a boat the rest of the way to Kielerhafen. Both Tante Elizabeth's husband Herr Mayer and Herr Andersen Greta's husband were important and successful unlike Papa and so she stayed for two nights in the house of Herr Mayer's man in Flensburg until there was a boat going the rest of the way to Kielerhafen – she could tell that Frau Lande the wife of Herr Mayer's man Herr Lande wanted to ask her questions about her sisters in Sønderborg but she didn't ask them she just left gaps in her conversation that were like missing cobblestones in the street that you might trip up in—yes the journey was difficult, more difficult than the one going up to Sønderborg to see Josie and Greta and the children because she had to stop on the way back at Flensburg this time but also because as well as the twists and turns of the boat coming into Flensburg and the complication of stopping on the way home to Kielerhafen she had to find her way past the unasked questions and also past the questions that *were* asked by Frau Lande the wife of Herr Mayer's man Herr *Steuerer* Lande.

Steuerer was a new strange word that Frau Lande had to say twice before Elke felt confident enough to say it herself, it meant the man who looked after all Herr Mayer's cargoes coming into or going out of Flensburg, and there were a great many of them said Frau Lande who clearly thought her husband was an important man and perhaps he was, 'a great many cargoes' mostly cloth and fine craftsmanship – questions such as why don't we see your papa Meister Hansen's fine work coming here anymore, the coffins for example and the fine cloth-work? – which was really a missing-cobble question and so Elke walked around it carefully and didn't trip up and now here she was approaching 'the house on Faulstrasse' and it was as though the twists and turns and missing-cobble-traps of her voyage home from Sønderborg were about to come to an end because here was her destination, this was where she was always certainly going from the moment she and Josie and Greta and the children looked down from the rise at Dybbøl above Alsund and Sønderborg and the boats going south down the Bugt towards 'the house on Faulstrasse' as she imagined they all were with their sails set firmly in that direction on that happy sad day of the picnic at Dybbøl when she knew she might not see Josie again or Catharina who had her little mama's blue Kornblume eyes.

When will I see you again she said to Josie back on the hill at Dybbøl, I don't know said Josie. I don't know maybe never. Because I have to keep going, I can't stay at Greta's place much longer and I won't take Catharina 'back there'. The word 'because' and the word 'and' were so clear and sure in what Josie said, like the determined straight line of her mouth, different from what Elke was used to which was Josie making those pictures with words that mixed up how things looked and how they smelled or tasted or moved like the bees in their summer flights back and forth from their hive in the old hollow elm on the hill down to the meadow flowers and wild grasses, flights that Josie said were streaky mare's-tail clouds of honey in the sky that you could taste if you closed your eyes and listened to the flavour of the bee-sound – yes she was almost crazy sometimes that was what Mutti and Papa thought but they were also proud of their 'special one' at first, until she learned with having Catharina how to make 'because' mark the exact path of her thought while 'and' marked the place where her thought changed the way everything had always been, as if one day the bees decided no we can't go back to the elm anymore and so all disappeared into the woods.

But what would be their 'because', *because why?* – or *because what?* – the bees? But Josephina had a 'because', the 'because' was 'the house on Faulstrasse', the front door was painted shiny green with some chips around the hinges and a heavy polished brass doorknocker, it was up six steps from the street and you could see that the steps had been washed that morning and the bucket of water thrown across the cobbles – should she go up the six steps and knock at the green door with the heavy brass knocker that was a lion's head showing its teeth, no perhaps it would be wrong to trample the mud and horseshit from the street across those six freshly washed steps, no of course that is what she should do, go in the door Josie said she was sent out of, but would she meet shithead Hauptmann von Zarovich or his 'Junkfrau' wife that way? – no they wouldn't open the door, the maid would, so perhaps she should go through the alley and around the back where the kitchen door would be or the door where things got taken into the house, the firewood and the things a house like that needed, what would they be? – the things that Mutti wanted, no not the milk, they had that *so long as Elke was there* and not the firewood *so long as Papa's stupid boy was there*, they had plenty of vegetables and fruit *so long as she was there* screeched poor Mutti, *so long as she Mutti was there to do all the garden work*, not even the flour and meat, they already had those things even if not enough of them anymore.

What Mutti wanted was in her eyes that were red from coughing and anger, she wanted to live somewhere like 'the house on Faulstrasse' the one where Junkfrau von Zarovich liked very much the work she brought to show her, Mutti couldn't say Josephina's name, it was as though Josie was no longer there and had never done the work when they went to 'the house on Faulstrasse' – Mutti wanted not to live in the Bauernhaus with animal piss running down the slope-floor in winter she shouted at Elke, her eyes all red and the screeching cough like a rooster, she didn't want to be bleaching the linens anymore, how could Elke run away like that didn't she know that her mother was not well and strong anymore she couldn't work anymore, 'I can't, Elke!' – it was Josephina's fault, she didn't say it but her eyes did and her crow-cough and the way she talked about 'the house on Faulstrasse', the door they were meant to go through to the life she deserved and that her husband, Elke's papa, *Meister* Hansen, deserved, but now her other daughter Elke was a thief how could she? – how could she take the Oma sampler to the – but not saying that her youngest daughter was what, a whore? That Josephina her youngest daughter was a whore?

The girl who opened the door at the back was staring at Elke with a fierce 'what do you want?' expression from her heavy eyebrows pushed together in a frown and her hand on the doorframe as if Elke would try to push past into a kitchen with a big table and a big black stove in three parts – *What did she want?* Who are you, the frowning girl was saying, what do you want? What did she want, why was she there, *what was she going to do* – she didn't know, all she'd thought about all the way to 'the house on Faulstrasse' was Mutti's red eyes and crow-cough and Josie's mouth in a straight *because and* line – *What was she going to do when she got to 'the house on Faulstrasse'?* What are we going to do? Mutti wanted to know, how can we go on, I can't anymore, I can't Elke, I can't.

She was Josephina Hansen's sister, Elke told the fiercely frowning girl who'd been sieving flour, it was on her hands and apron and there was some on her cheek as well, do you remember her, she brought the special lie-in nightgown for Junkfrau von Zarovich, my sister made it, it was a while ago, nearly two years, two autumns, do you remember her, my sister Josephina, quite small and fair, a pretty one, you'll remember her I think, she came in the autumn and she was by herself, Elke was telling the floury girl – is Hauptmann von Zarovich at home she asked the girl who then quickly shut the door to the kitchen and jumped with a thump down to the step Elke was standing on and pulled her strongly by the arm around into the alleyway at the side of the house.

Yes I remember your little sister said the big girl with thick eyebrows only she wasn't frowning now, she was still holding Elke's arm with her strong hand, I remember her, she went up to show Herr Hauptmann the thing she'd made for Junkfrau, we didn't see her again, how is she? Oh yes Josephina was fine, Elke told the girl, she had a baby, a beautiful little girl, her name is Catharina Elke Lange Hansen, that's my name, Elke, Catharina has it too now, I'm her aunt. I'm her aunt,

I'm Catharina's aunt and I want to talk to Hauptmann von Zarovich – the floury girl with thick eyebrows let go of Elke's arm – I want to talk to Hauptmann von Zarovich, Elke told the girl, because he is Catharina's father the fucking shithead and I have to tell him.

Dearest little sister Josie and my darling Catharina

I hope you are well I think of you all the time and also of Greta and the children, kiss them for me. Well it is nearly winter so you will not be travelling yet thank god. Tante Elizabeth is helping me to write this letter but this is my writing not too bad I hope you agree. First of all I have to tell you some important news about von Zarovich. I know you said you did not care anymore but I think you need to know what has happened so forgive me Josie. I went to that house on Faulstrasse because I wanted to tell the Hauptmann what he had done. Tante Elizabeth thinks that was stupid and she is right but I had to Josie. I met the maid who works there her name is Clara she remembered you. She told me that the Hauptmann is dead, his horse fell on him during exercises at Schlossgarten. They brought him back to the house that you remember I am sure but he died after a few days. You also need to know that his wife had a baby, Clara told me it was a boy, but they are gone now, her family is in Vienna. The house is a garrison one and now there is another Prussian army family living there, Clara does not like them. Josie I also have to tell you that Clara found the nightgown you made for the Zarovich wife, she said it was spoiled so she burned it. Tante Elizabeth thinks that closes a door and perhaps you will think so too. Of course life goes on here and thank god at the moment Herr Mayer has sent one of his men to help Papa's boy with the firewood for winter. Papa is quite well but his business is not so good anymore, he only does repairs or makes plain things and not much money. Mutti is not strong and so I worry about the winter. I have to ask you Josie, and Tante Elizabeth is asking too, will you please change your mind and come back here? You could do it before the snow and ice. Then Mutti and Papa could see Catharina and they would love her I am sure and so would Tante Elizabeth and of course Mathilde who says you are her favourite and that she loves you more than stars but also loves Puck Puck. These are their kisses on the end of this paper and this one X is mine, your sister Elke.

Beth and Frank

What was it about those old things like the Danish shawl she'd got from her mother Elke who'd got it from her grandmother Ettie who'd got it from her mother-in-law Josephina? And that sewing-sampler thingie that was at the reunion, that had been Great-great-grandmother Josephina's and someone else's before her – her own grandmother's perhaps? Nobody really knew about these things, and they could mostly only go ooh-ahh because they were so old, imagine that, what was life like back then? They were ghosts but material ones – they had substance and texture, they smelled of what they were; the shawl could still keep you cosy and the sampler could still show you how to make stitches. They still had agency, they were still what they could do, right now, in the present – many, many people had died while the sampler and the shawl just went on being what they did in the here and now, including amaze us with their ability to make nonsense of time, and one day someone would just chuck them away and that would be that.

Over by the hotel proper the dog was making awful anxious sounds that were a cross between a half-hearted bark, a whine and a growl. It was rattling its chain, and she wished someone would give the poor bloody thing a bone or something. So Frank would probably be having his dinner by now, and probably getting stuck into a bottle of wine – she'd better get over there. He was so moody, something was bothering him, but first.

First she had to have a quick go at checking out *Zum Gedächtnis* WB.

But first the hotel's Wi-Fi. The slip of paper in the folder with the attractions of the 'Central Plateau Land of Legends' had the password '100pcp'.

Zum Gedächtnis WB drew a blank, but then Frank's hunch, Wolf Bloch.

And there he was.

Wolf Bloch!

Born 15 Januar 1843 in Brno, Hauptstadt von Moravia, nachdem der Vater seine Firma nicht halten konnte, siedelte die Familie nach Hannover und 1851 nach Hamburg über, father's firm went bust & moved to Hannover and then to Hamburg. Ab 1872 war Bloch Mitglied der Sozialistischen deutschen Arbeiterpartei, den sog. Eisenachern, after 1872 got involved with the German socialist workers' party, die Hamburger Bürgerzeitung zu gründen und als Redakteur zu leiten, he founded the Hamburger Bürgerzeitung and was its editor. Blah blah blah, not our man, no way, whoa!

Zum Gedächtnis!

In dem Gedicht *Zum Gedächtnis* (1875) würdigte er die Pariser Kommune von 1871, in the poem *Zum Gedächtnis* he celebrated the Paris Commune of 1871.

She looked away from the screen for a moment and closed her eyes while she attended to the constriction in her chest and the sensation that it had filled suddenly with something, time perhaps, that pressed on her heart and made it thump. When that stopped she looked back at the screen.

There was a photo of this Wolf Bloch from 1878, little chap with an asthmatic's hunched shoulders, a pair of rimless glasses, a bit scruffy in a dandyish sort of way, with a rather wicked look about him and an eccentric boutonnière of what was probably wild tree blossom.

Her great-great-grandfather?

There was plenty more – there were references in Das Elektronische Arkiv to correspondence with Friedrich Engels in England – but that would do, that would do for now, in the here and now!

As she rushed out with her iPad, the old shawl got caught in the door of her unit and she only just resisted the urge to give it a yank. She went back in and carefully folded the shawl on the bed with its manky candlewick bedspread. There was something appropriate about the arrangement, the worn old and the faded new folded together, but that was a bit precious.

And besides, there was a ridiculous full moon in absolutely clear sky above the hotel. It made her heart thump again – that moon and her ridiculous WB risen brightly into view.

Greta

Well, yes of course Josephina should. But of course she would not.

These were Greta's views on the matter.

Then Danne's beard was against her ear and his voice was rumbling into it.

Her family needs her more than we do. We can get a maid. We had one before. Or don't you remember? And she didn't have a child to look after.

This was what Danne thought.

But Finn and Catharina are playmates, was Greta's argument.

So are we, was the beard's. Saying, *Feinsliebchen*, in best German, into her ear.

What difference does that make, Greta wanted to know. And please stop doing that, because we have to talk about this.

She required.

To no avail.

And anyway, Greta resumed after a satisfactory while, not only did her sister, who had become stubborn, not wish to go back to the farm, she also did not wish to stay there in Sønderborg.

Because she's a crazy little bitch and you have to talk to her, was the opinion Danne offered the wall beside their bed, but gently, without anger. Then he began to snore.

But she had. Over and over, many times. Josie, think about it. What will you do? What will Catharina do? How will you live? Where will you live?

It was impossible.

So then the 'crazy little bitch' held up the blue-owl border on the nice grey blanket that was around Otto, who was blowing milky bubbles on Greta's lap.

She would sew. Now that she had 'the Oma', for God's sake. As if that old offcut of shroud-linen with its little pictures of yellow ducks on a blue lake, a red house with a window on either side of its green door and grey wool smoke coming from its chimney, the mountain with its little deer, and the owls, of course the favourite blue owls, and the rest of it, including the crooked alphabet in many colours – see, she knew it too? But what was the use of arguing? Josie would take the little pictures and the soiled old linen to a bigger town, and she would earn her living.

A very young woman with a child and no man.

Have you learned nothing, Josie?

So then that new direct look.

Yes. She had. She had learned much. She didn't need to say so.

So, Danne, what about your uncle in Hamburg, Greta wanted to know, having lost the first part of the argument with her husband. The part that suggested Josephina could stay because Finn and Catharina were playmates. And cousins.

She and Danne were walking along to the Slot on a day when he wasn't away or working, while Josephina minded the children and washed salt off the window-glass. Of course they'd all get wet, that was how she did it.

The part of the argument Greta hadn't lost was that 'the crazy little bitch' wouldn't go home to her family on the 'family farm' by the Schwentine at Kiel.

Because she wouldn't. That was that. She *would not.*

My uncle? Danne stopped and repeated the question – his *uncle*? He was using his whiskers to comic effect, to exaggerate his expression of disbelief and scorn.

Do you know what that's called, he wanted to know.

Ah, 'selling the debt'. Of course, Greta had heard that expression already, on several occasions lately, usually to do with the Bückling yard.

But was her sister a bad debt, she wanted to know.

Like the . . . ?

Like the Bückling smoking-yard, Danne suggested.

They were having a nice walk, it was sunny, they could have a drink and a bite over by the Slot, talk to some friends, how often did they have the chance? But no, of course he wasn't suggesting Josephina was a 'bad debt'. Just a crazy little bitch. Why would he wish a crazy little bitch on his uncle in Hamburg?

Because she's a clever crazy little bitch, suggested his wife. And she's my sister. And your sister-in-law. And she got fucked by a Prussian.

So then they were walking back, too quickly. Danne was a man who got angry with good reason.

What was the good reason? This time?

The last time was when her other sister stole that stupid sewing-thing and tricked his business partner's shipmaster into bringing her to their house. For a couple of months, remember? Another clever one.

Best not be saying anything more about my sisters in that tone, was what Greta was composing in a sentence that would stop short of 'making the beard catch fire', because what would be the use of that?

This time, there was the little clever one, with a mop and a bucket, washing spray-salt off the glass. It was something people along the quay did before winter. Finn and Catharina were getting wet in the puddles, as expected. Really, that was more important than washing the windows, even though the days were now chilly. Otto was on the owl blanket in a patch of sunshine on the stoop.

Everyone was astonished, of course.

Why were they back? Why were Greta and Danne back, wondered Josephina. *Mor* and *far*, back, asked Finn.

We just wanted to make sure you were all, were all . . .

Of course they all were, Josephina reassured Danne while looking at her sister.

Warm enough, he suggested.

So, they would talk later, promised Danne. He was making *hrrm hrrm* noises in his beard and showing his teeth in a false smile.

They turned around and went back towards the old Slot again. Josephina had ordered them to have a nice time and not hurry. She and the children were all fine and happy.

As anyone could see.

But despite this, Josephina would not stay, as anyone could also see.

They were walking along nicely, like many of the other couples. They knew quite a few of them. It was perhaps 'the last day before winter', as many people agreed. Danne had his good warm coat on, the one that smelled a little of the increasingly unsuccessful Bückling yard. He was also wearing a nice red woollen scarf that Josephina had tasselled. Greta's arm was through Danne's and they were both looking straight ahead. They were greeting people and smiling.

Oh yes, what a nice day it was.

'The last day before winter.'

They agreed.

Yes, probably!

So nice!

However, 'God damn it!' was the expression Danne chose as they stopped for a warming brandy by the wall of the Slot. There was an accordion being played rather badly, and a stall with pretzels and meatballs.

He wasn't referring to the brandy or the meatballs, nor even to the accordion player.

So, you agree, suggested Greta. My darling man?

Then she put her arms around him in a manner that wasn't quite proper, probably, in the eyes of many there at the Slot, in public, on 'the last day before winter'.

Agree what a nice day it was? That it was indeed 'the last day before winter'? Danne's response was thickened by the meatball in his mouth, but by something else as well.

Indeed, he agreed, and pointed out to her that everybody in the town thought so too, clearly.

He wasn't returning his wife's embrace and his tone was sarcastic.

To the uncle, persisted Greta. You agree?

She wiped some sauce from his beard with her glove. It wasn't just the brandy that was heating her.

Danne's big grey-blue eyes didn't leave hers alone while he finished his meatball and took a swallow of the brandy, which was probably the 'profitable transaction' he brought up from Flensburg, not a bad-debt aspect of his 'business interests'.

His tongue explored the possibilities of brandy in his moustache.

The teeth she saw after the swallow of good Flensburg brandy didn't resemble the ones Danne had revealed in his hopeless smile back at the house on the quay, where his crazy bitch sister-in-law was making the children happy and cleaning salt off the windows in the fresh sunshine of winter just beginning.

Now the teeth were biting off the ends of his words.

He had been going to tell that crazy selfish little bitch, Greta's sister, that there was nothing to argue about, she would go back to Kiel and help her sister Elke with the farm and their sick mother, that was that.

He would arrange it.

He was sick of arguing about it.

But then.

Greta didn't try to re-engage her arm through his. They stood to one side of the crowd, facing each other. When she unlocked her eyes from Danne's, she was looking over his shoulder with Josie's red tasselled scarf across it, and across the harbour basin and the breeze-ruffled water to the quay and their house. She couldn't see Josephina and the children, of course, but she could picture them in her mind. She could even hear them laughing, and Josie as well, with her hiccups. But the breeze was getting up, it was a bit nippy, as was usual in the late afternoon.

The words Danne was biting the ends off were a bit nippy as well.

They nipped in and out of the thoughts she had, about the need to take the children back inside and dry them now that it was the chilly part of the afternoon.

But of course Josie would be taking good care of them, she knew.

Danne's thoughts were as follows.

Whatever else you might say about her, Josephina was very good with the children.

Clearly, he couldn't help but notice that.

Whatever else you might say about her?

He was confident she could be trusted.

You've just noticed?

And, as mentioned, he'd been going to tell her to go home and do what was proper.

But then.

But then, again.

Her expression was patient.

The teeth in the beard were making hard work of it.

But then he'd seen how good she was with the children. How she could be trusted. Of course he'd seen this before.

How determined she was. He'd seen this before, too.

If she had to go, if she was determined to.

Rather, *since* she was determined to go, whether home to Kiel or somewhere else, he corrected himself.

Not to Kiel, obviously, he amended his correction.

Since she was determined to go somewhere else, she would have to wait until spring. She could stay and help with the children until then, he suggested, confidently.

For at least four more months, he estimated.

She was a good, trustworthy girl, he judged.

The words *who'd been fucked by a Prussian* almost escaped Greta's mouth, but she kept it shut while Danne continued.

Enough time to make some arrangements.

Yes, perhaps the best thing.

(He was thinking about it.)

Yes, perhaps the most *responsible* thing, was the way to look at it.

She is your sister, after all.

And she's been fucked by a Prussian, Greta reminded him. As everyone in Kiel will know by now.

Her trump card.

Knowing very well herself that there was no love lost between Danne's family of Danes and 'those Prussians'.

Yes, perhaps the most responsible thing, persisted Danne, registering 'a Prussian' by drawing his eyebrows together, would be to use the winter months to make some arrangements.

With your uncle in Hamburg, suggested Greta.

That was an option, agreed Danne.

Greta understood that it was asking a lot. Of the uncle but also of him, Danne. Times were a bit hard, after all, with the Bückling yard.

His look was a little suspicious. He knew his wife.

But yes, it was asking a lot. He gave her that much.

But they could try. He was confident of that much as well.

They went back to the brandy stall and had another one each 'because it was getting a bit chilly'. Greta put her arm through Danne's, and he permitted it a squeeze.

Yes, they could give it a try.

Those teeth at last, through his beard.

The smile she loved.

And that huff of breath, somewhat like a horse, that she also loved.

Her own smile she restrained, in case it appeared triumphant.

It was that warm huff of breath up into his moustache that was the signal, the sign that she recognised as meaning something was resolved in her Danne's mind.

That, and the teeth.

He was happy now. He'd ordered his thoughts the way she'd seen him order his crew to trim the sails on the sturdy packet-boat he owned with Herr Mayer.

Who held the majority share.

As did she in the 'Hamburg uncle' idea, but she knew better than to assert her majority.

Danne had 'trimmed his sails' and 'set his course' and now all would be well. There was a destination and they would get to it.

Yes, all would be well.

And what hazards would this course avoid?

Not, of course, the hazards that lay ahead for Josephina in Hamburg after four or five months, in spring next year.

There was one hazard the 'Hamburg uncle' course would avoid, that neither of them had spoken about, and perhaps they wouldn't, though the hazard was her aunt's husband, the very successful Herr Mayer, the majority shareholder in the packet-boat.

Which was named *Elizabeth* after his wife, the younger sister of Meister Hansen who was the father of the disgraced girl.

Yes, the sea was full of hazardous rocks and shoals in close proximity.

Without doubt, Herr Mayer wouldn't welcome the return to the family circle at Kiel of his wife's niece, the mother of an illegitimate child by one of 'die adelige Preussen Offizieren' with money to spare.

Herr Mayer with the majority share in the *Elizabeth*, the 'very successful' Herr Mayer who might also not be displeased to see that foolish girl leave the house of his business partner in Sønderborg, that girl whose story had already circulated in Flensburg on account of her delinquent sister Elke, who was a chatterbox.

His business partner whose reputation was suffering from the Bückling yard.

Greta rebuked herself for imagining thoughts in her husband's head that might never have been there. But she didn't rebuke herself for having them, because they were there in her own head and she trusted her ability to think them and to think with them.

But also because this wasn't the first time Danne's teeth and huff had signalled both his satisfaction and her own.

There was the time, for example, when her papa said yes.

Yes, this man could marry his daughter.

Even though he was a Dane.

But obviously a respectable man. And trusted by Herr Mayer. His brother-in-law. Who was a good judge of character, of character and enterprise. And of the market value of fine craftsmanship, including his own, the fine craftsmanship of *Meister* Hansen, that is.

And of course there was the time before that, when she said yes to the 'respectable and enterprising Danish man', under the pear tree's white blossom above the Schwentine, and saw his happy teeth inside the beard, and then felt the huff, respectfully restrained at this time, on the back of her hand, with his kiss.

The enterprising alliance of Danes and Germans was toasted around the big table they had carried out under the pear tree, while Mutti wept at the imminent departure of her eldest daughter to the place where her own father and brothers lay under the turf, declaring her tears to be 'of joy', and while Greta's two sisters looked at her with eyes round like an owl's.

And of course the less respectfully restrained huff and the teeth quite a few times subsequently, in the pale light of the long summer nights, when the sound of waves against the quay turned their bed into a rocking boat.

They looked happy, Josephina declared, when Greta and Danne came in. It must have been nice, down by the Slot, with people.

The children looked happy too, and Danne thanked Josephina for that.

Perhaps they could all have a drink and a talk, once the children were asleep?

Josephina's eyes went quickly to her sister, but then returned to Danne, and firmly stayed there.

Of course, that would be a good thing to do after such a lovely day.

Yes, they should do that, agreed Greta, waiting for her sister's eyes to return.

Which they did.

Those Kornblume eyes.

Direkt in die Augen schauen!

Dearest Papa and Mutti
And also of course my dear sister Elke, we miss you and so do the children, they often ask where is Tante Elke?

I am writing to tell you the news about Josephina and her daughter, Catharina Elke Lange Hansen, your granddaughter and the niece of Elke and myself. Papa and Mutti, perhaps it will make you angry that I have used the child's full name, the one that Josephina gave her, and the one that Danne and I also gave her as her godparents. But that is her name, the name by which she was baptised and christened by Pastor Jepsen here in Saincte Marie church, which is also where our children Finn and Otto have been baptised and christened. We were sad that you would not come here to Sønderborg for Otto's baptism and christening on account of Josephina being here with our goddaughter Catharina, and we hope that one day the love of God will heal this painful wound in our family. When he baptised Catharina, Pastor Jepsen used a text from the Bible that said, 'Believe in the Lord Jesus, and you will be saved – you and your household.' We are a household that has known grief in the deaths of men who went to war, Mutti, your father and your brothers who lie under the ground just across the Alsund from where we now live, and in the deaths of children, yours Mutti, and as you know mine also. But one day I hope we will rejoice in the whole household of those who are alive, including Tante Elizabeth and Herr Mayer and of course their dear little Mathilde, but also our beloved sister Josephina and her daughter Catharina.

This is the place for me to say that it was wrong of Elke to leave without telling you, and to take Oma's sampler to bring here to Sønderborg without asking you, Papa and Mutti. Both Danne and I were angry with you, Elke, for the trouble you caused Herr Mayer and the worry you caused Mutti when she was not well and strong, but we forgive you because we know you did what you did out of love, and in the good spirit of Pastor Jepsen's words about the household.

We are sad also that Josephina would not take the advice you wrote in your letter, Elke, and has steadfastly refused to go back to Kiel and her home there, even though we believe all of you there including Herr Mayer and Tante Elizabeth would love her child Catharina and welcome her to the household of our family. But Josephina has her own strong will, I can tell you that certainly, because I have lived with her strength for nearly two years, and I believe the wrong that was done to her has made her stronger. I mean the wrong that was done to her by the Prussian officer, but also the wrong she felt in the judgement of her family. It was also her strong will that decided her not to stay with us here in Sønderborg once winter was past, as it now is. One reason she gave for this decision was that she did not wish to be a burden on us at a time when Danne's business is having some difficulty with the Bückling yard. It is not true that Josie and Catharina would be a burden, but there are some problems with the Bückling and she would not allow us to deny it.

I can tell you, and Danne will agree with his whole heart, that Josephina has been a blessing to us in this house and a constant help with the work to be done, and especially with the care of our children. Her own daughter Catharina was born in this house and it will always be her home for ever. We had a hard winter this year, with thick ice in the Alsund and no fish, but now that is past and we have had to say goodbye with heavy hearts to our beloved sister Josephina and goddaughter Catharina. We will miss them very much, and Finn especially will miss the stories he was told by Tante Josie, and also the story of the Swiss Family Robinson which she was reading him.

You will know from our marriage agreement that the house we live in here at Sønderborg was once the home of Danne's uncle herre Aksel Andersen before he went with his family to Hamburg. It is an old house in a row where most people pay rent, but herre Andersen had begun to buy the house and he gave his share to Danne as a wedding gift. One day perhaps Danne will be a householder if all goes well and he can increase the share begun by the generous man he calls Farbror Aksel.

Farbror Aksel's generosity has now been extended to Josephina and Catharina, as he has agreed to be Josie's protector in Hamburg. He has seen some samples of her work and admires it very much. He has a colleague who owns a sewing room where fine garments and military uniforms are made, and he has promised to speak to this man on Josephina's behalf. As you can imagine this was not an easy decision for Danne to make as he did not wish to place a burden of responsibility on his uncle, especially since Josephina's situation is the cause of trouble on our Hansen and Mayer side of the family. But now it is done and Josephina has gone to Hamburg with Danne's and my blessing and with the kind protection of herre Aksel Andersen, the uncle who helped Danne's family after his father drowned up in Kattegat. He is a kind and Christian man and I am sure he will do what he can to take care of Josephina and her daughter Catharina.

I will finish this long letter by saying I hope the news of Josephina going to Hamburg will soothe some of the anxiety I hear Herr Mayer has about the effect of Josephina's misfortune on the family's reputation. Now our sister will be away from the places where that reputation and the family's interests may be affected, and this will be a relief to him I am sure.

Papa and Mutti, I hope that now you will agree to come to Sønderborg to meet your new grandson Otto.

Elke, I kiss you and hope that you will also come back to see us and also Finn and Otto, who will always grow faster than your memories of them.

Your daughter and sister Greta

Greta, daughter

You are the eldest of our daughters and the one we trusted with the wisdom to manage the situation of your younger, foolish and disobedient sister Josephina. We were glad that you and your husband Herr Andersen agreed to take Josephina into your care, and we respected your decision to manage her child's baptism and christening, even though the manner in which that was done was arrogant and disrespectful to the family, as we have come to expect from that girl. But now you have betrayed the trust we had in you, you have allowed that vain disobedient girl to command your decisions. Now the family of your husband Herr Andersen has been set against that of our Hansens and that of your aunt Elizabeth's husband Herr Mayer. How do you think your conspiracy to make your husband's uncle the protector of your wicked sister will be talked about here? How do you think the associates of Herr Aksel Andersen in Hamburg and elsewhere will speak about the family of that girl and her bastard child? You say that Herr Aksel Andersen is a kind and Christian man as if we are to understand that our family and that of your aunt Elizabeth's husband Herr Mayer are without those qualities. Do those qualities belong only to Danes? Do not hope that I and your mother will come to Sønderborg. Besides, as you know already, your mother is sick and not able to do much.

Your father and mother

They are turning the whole thing into a Danish–German war; what's more Elke was right, 'they don't know what anger is for', was Greta's response to the letter that had come from her papa and mutti at Kiel.

Otto was only just then asleep after a long period of coughing – it was the late-spring pollens, and especially the flowering elder tree at the back. She was exhausted, they had as yet no maid to replace Josephina, and even Danne was fed up with the supper she'd prepared, he was bone tired as well, and he looked at his plate of bread and boiled salt cod with an expression that was no expression, a blank unsmilingness that wasn't even going to bother with a complaint.

Not even some carrots or potatoes. But he didn't say it.

And what did they mean, 'conspiracy'? Greta wished to know Danne's opinion. And would Finn please stop making that noise with his nose, what did he think he was, a pig?

Yes, he did think he was, he was a pig! Oink oink! So Danne took him by the collar and dragged him oinking up to the top room where Josephina and Catharina had been only a month ago.

Of course Josie would have found a way to keep Finn quiet and get him to eat some of his supper. She'd have been a little fellow pig and Danne would have smiled secretly into his beard. She could picture that.

But now he was back at supper and looking at Greta across the table.

They'd better not try and start a German–Danish war with Farbror Aksel, was his opinion, as frugal in its way as his supper.

But behind his frugal opinion Greta could detect a dark cloud of circumstances: they had allowed themselves to be persuaded to take in Greta's little sister because her parents were afraid of scandal and the loss of business opportunity, they had bowed to little sister Josephina's refusal to leave without Catharina and also her refusal to go back to Kiel, which had resulted in Danne agreeing to petition Farbror Aksel on her behalf, which had now evidently resulted in a rift between him, Danne, and his majority-holding business partner Herr Mayer, and how did she think he, Danne, felt about that? Was he going to say anything about all that? Did he have an opinion?

Of course she herself didn't feel good about any of it.

It was Greta who ticked these circumstances off on her fingers while Danne looked at her with his unsmiling expression.

And yes, she was very sorry that it had come to this.

But what else was there?

But did he remember the day that Josephina and Catharina left? The day he wept? And kissed Catharina on the crown of her head?

And walked with her, Greta, and with Finn running ahead in circles and Otto on his shoulders all the way along to the Slot and home again, and drank a generous brandy back at their house?

She herself remembered the blue sky and the shimmer of early-morning sun on the calm Alsund. There was a very light offshore breeze with a hint of woodsmoke in it. This was the kind of day that happened in late spring and early summer. Oh yes, they were lucky to live where they did, in the house that Farbror Aksel had made possible for them.

Yes, they were. She often thought so.

She remembered Josephina's shoulder blades like brittle little wings under her hands, and the brisk way she then left her big sister's embrace and was lifted by a sailor down into the packet-boat's lighter, and Catharina after her with a squeal. Then the lighter's stern oar dipping ripples in the surface of the water as it went out towards the packet.

Was Josephina looking back at them? Was that Catharina's hand waving? It was hard to tell, there were several passengers crowded into the lighter.

Yes, that was Josephina's pale face turned to look back, and yes, of course, that was Catharina's hand waving, Josephina was holding her hand and they were waving together.

Finn didn't really understand what was happening. But then they were walking along to the Slot because Danne had begun to cry and didn't want to be there at the quay with people looking at him. So they walked all the way there and back, and then he had a brandy but she didn't.

But what else was there?

Now she was looking at Danne across the supper table.

Did he remember that?

He was putting a spoonful of fish in his mouth – she saw the gleam of his teeth, but not of his eyes.

Then it was as though she didn't ask the question, rather the question used her to ask itself.

Had he, Danne, been in love with her sister Josephina? Was that why he'd wept? Was that why he'd known Josephina had to go away? Was that why he'd agreed to organise something with the generous Farbror Aksel?

Had he been? Was it?

Then the gleam of Danne's big eyes and the clatter of his spoon.

Yes, yes, he had. Of course he had. But as if Josephina was his daughter or his little sister. Like that. For God's sake. And it was not as if she hadn't made up her own mind to go, for God's sake. Her own mind.

He emphasised *Her own mind* as if Greta had never thought of that.

So then Greta got up and went around to his side of the table and stood behind him and put her face in Danne's thick hair with the nice smell of his old oilskin hat.

And yes, there was the tremor of a sob he held in and stopped with a spoonful of salt fish.

Yes, there it was, a sob, inside him.

And his head tipping back to press against her breasts, and his upside-down eyes looking up at her, and the thick flake of salt cod that had to be lifted from his beard by her forefinger and popped into his mouth.

Josephina

Josephina heard and then saw a long room with grey light coming in through tall, sooty windows. The light was the colour of the city, which was also the colour of the sky and of fog. In addition, there were gas lamps suspended from the ceiling so that their yellowish light fell on the bent heads of the ten or twelve women sitting on either side of four long work tables – about ninety in all. Dust was floating in the shafts of light. There was a continuous hum in the room, like a hive, but muffled, as though it was the sound of words trapped and beating themselves against the cool grey windows. It was the sound of the women murmuring, but they didn't seem to be talking to each other, as their attention was on the work in front of them. Each of them had a small wicker basket with sewing materials in it, and many wore calico aprons with padded bibs for pins.

At one of the tables on the far side of the room some of the women were using sewing machines, and the swift chattering sounds of the needle foot and the whirr of the belt were like another language, so that it was hard to tell which sound was speech and which was machines. Mutti had always wanted a sewing machine – of course Tante Elizabeth had one in Gaarden with a richly decorated body and a large shining hand-wheel that Mathilde was allowed to turn to make the needle foot chatter up and down. Josephina had tried it to do a hem – it was fast but didn't feel like sewing and she didn't like it. There were some other sounds in the big grey-lit room as well, the tap of a thimble on the tabletop, the clatter of scissors being quickly put down, all multiplied many times by the number of women at work.

The effect of all the sounds and the light mixed up together was not of busyness but more like the thick fog of those dreams in which she was unable to move her arms and legs fast enough to go somewhere or escape something – dreams from which she used to wake up to find Elke's strong arm across her face, but now it was Catharina's little arm that would sometimes wake her in their narrow cot behind the kitchen of Herr Aksel Andersen's house. In the morning, the cot folded away to clear access to the kitchen. The house was in a terrace with others; they were old houses that had survived a great fire, Herr Andersen had told her. There was a river or canal at the back, and supplies for the house often came from a little barge that stopped at the landing. It was one of the smallest houses, very narrow, the rooms stacked up one on top of the other. The walls at the back by the river were rather cool and Josephina worried that the atmosphere might be unhealthy for Catharina, but she didn't want to complain.

But now Catharina was holding Josephina's hand very tight and looking with big eyes at the humming sewing room. It was certainly the biggest room either of them had ever seen. There were two men standing at the end of one of the long tables, looking at the work being done. One was a tall man with grey hair; he was wearing a good coat of dark worsted material and shiny black boots. The other was a short man with a pigeon chest and high, narrow shoulders, wearing a rather worn, low-crown wool top hat and a pale gabardine trenchcoat with a black velvet collar. His coat had damp patches on it and his brown boots were quite muddy, so it was clear he'd been walking outside in the rain. Both turned to look at Josephina and Catharina, and at Herr

Andersen. One of the women at the table where the men were standing also looked at them – she smiled and gave Catharina a little wave – but all the other heads remained bent over the sewing work. Perhaps that was because the two men had been watching them. A woman in a green velvet street coat with its hood thrown back was walking slowly along between the rows. Perhaps she too was watching the sewers at work.

The tall man came over and shook Herr Andersen by the hand, but he didn't look at Josephina or Catharina. The short man with the hunched shoulders and pigeon chest remained over by the work table but was looking hard at her – he had big black eyes and was really staring quite rudely, and then to her surprise lifted his hat and smiled. And then, disconcertingly, he tilted his head on one side and hunched up his shoulders, as if to say, why are you here?

Yes, this was the sewing room, the tall man was saying to Herr Andersen, and the young lady could try for a while, they would see how suitable she was for the work. He'd seen some of hers, it was certainly fine, but what was needed here was speed, it was all about getting the work done, the buttons and buttonholes, for example, and the braids, insignia and piping, you understand, the hems, the uniforms.

Then he was looking down at Catharina, who hid behind Josephina's skirt. Ah yes, some of the women had children. There was a Kita nursery, but the cost of that came from their wages, did the young lady understand that? And then, finally, he was looking at Josephina. He was very sorry to hear about her misfortune, he said, keeping his hands clasped behind his back. The loss of her husband. A misfortune, indeed a tragedy.

Josephina was unsure about his sincerity. He spoke

plainly and looked at her without condescension, but his tone was cool. 'Yes, a misfortune,' she agreed, because what else could she say – pausing because she didn't know how to address him, and he hadn't offered to shake her hand and introduce himself. He noticed her looking over his shoulder at the little man in the damp trenchcoat – now the man was standing with his head on one side and one fist on his hip, as if making a show of waiting. He'd been joined by the woman in the green coat. She was leaning close to him and talking in a confidential manner.

'Wolf Bloch,' said the owner of the sewing room, so Josephina held her hand out, glad to be able to thank him properly and introduce herself. But he ignored her and returned his attention to Herr Andersen. 'The editor of the *Bürger Zeitung*.'

'I know him,' said Herr Andersen. 'And what he writes.' He was looking over at the little man. 'And his sister also, I see.'

Then Josephina realised that she'd nearly made a mistake.

'The young lady may come in tomorrow,' said the anonymous owner of the sewing room. 'She can bring the child.'

Then Herr Andersen was thanking him and they were preparing to leave. Over by the long table of women working, the little man called Wolf Bloch and the woman in the green coat were still talking with their heads close together.

Yes of course she was grateful for Herr Andersen's support and the agreement of his wife Frau Andersen whose given name she, Josephina, was not allowed to use. But she could not make the hot blush that had risen up out of her blouse collar go back again out of sight as she and Herr Andersen went down the stairs from the sewing room, and it was still there when he lifted Catharina up to her in the waiting cab. He had business to attend to, he said, the cab would take her back to the house, they should enjoy the ride. Then he gave the driver some money and walked away quickly.

The young lady. The child.

No doubt the owner of the sewing room, the man with the good coat and the fine black boots, meant well, as did Herr Andersen, and meanwhile Catharina liked riding in the cab as it bumped along over the cobbles. She already knew the word for horse and kept repeating it – yes, it was a nice horsie, Josephina agreed, while the blush turned from embarrassment into anger and then sank back inside her collar.

She had a name, it was Josephina Hansen – the sewing-room owner didn't even want to know that, nor the name of 'the child', which was Catharina Hansen, and clearly Herr Andersen didn't want to ride back with them in the cab, he had his business to attend to and no time to ask Josephina what she thought about the sewing room, or to explain about the Kita nursery. And how would she and Catharina go to and from the sewing room once she started to work there? Not in a cab, certainly – she would have to find out about the horse-trams. And how was the nursery organised, and where was it, was it close to the sewing room, did they give the children food? Herr Andersen's manner towards her and Catharina had changed since he first met them on the platform at the Altona railway station; now he seemed impatient to leave them, and she still didn't know the name of the man in the good coat at the sewing room.

Though it was a warm day after the morning's showers, and the cab's windows were open, Josephina felt stifled because the air was grey and dull and her mind was like that, too.

Leaving Sønderborg only one week ago the air had been so fresh, and the fear she felt about going to Hamburg was also a kind of joy, because here she and Catharina were, they were going away on their new life's path, and this had been her decision, no one else owned it. When the packet-boat's sails were hoisted with a clatter and the canvas flapped and they began to move down the Alsund, it was as though her future filled the sails and moved the boat forward with little nods. She looked back to see if Greta and Danne were still there on the quay, but they'd gone. There was a space of clear sunlight and water-dazzle between her and the row of quayside houses with glinting windows, the same windows she'd washed the salt off before winter. The light was a splash of fresh cold water across her thoughts, it made her breath tighten high up in her chest – she was blinking not tears but freshness. Behind one of the windows was where she and Catharina had slept and where Catharina had grown to be almost two years old, but now the houses were getting smaller and smaller, as if time not distance was shrinking them, because it was her and Catharina's future that was urging them onward, and it was their future not anyone else's.

She guessed that the man with the thin, tired face was Danne's uncle Herr Aksel Andersen, whom Danne called Farbror Aksel, because, although he wasn't a big man like Danne, he had the same kind of measuring look and a similar way of pushing his chin out as he peered around the station. It was a big space with light coming in through a sooty arched window over the way out, and everyone seemed to know where to go except her, so she stood in one place near the train that was still hissing steam across the platform from its boiler, while other passengers hurried towards the way out or to greet people they knew. Also, the man was searching for someone he didn't know, that was clear – his search went past Josephina and Catharina a few times, but came back to them and then stayed. Should she go towards him? How could she be sure? The platform was so loud and busy, and the man whose gaze had fastened on her and Catharina might be one of those that Danne and Greta had warned her about, the ones who took advantage of young women arriving at the station. Don't believe them if they say they can help you, or when they ask if you need help, or if you're lost, or if you need a place to stay, Danne and Greta said several times in a kind of chorus, don't trust them, or the women who ask you questions like that either, it's a wicked and dangerous place, Hamburg, because of the port there are many sailors coming and going, and many brothels, just wait for Herr Andersen, you'll know him, he's a tall thin Andersen, and his head sometimes jerks around a bit. Danne did an impersonation of his uncle's jerking head but became huffy when Greta laughed. It was an old war wound, he said, show some respect, don't be so German.

And indeed, the man who was looking at them and starting to come towards them did have a nervous twitch to his head, but also a careful smile inside a thick beard like Danne's. Josephina and Catharina were standing to one side of the shouting and busyness; Catharina was clinging to Josephina's leg but wasn't frightened, just overwhelmed, and she didn't mind when, after he'd shaken Josephina's hand and introduced himself – familiarly calling them both by their first names – Herr Andersen bent and gave Catharina a friendly kiss, and then picked her up. It was very nice to make her acquaintance, he said to her, and would she like to go for a ride in a tram, it had two horsies to pull it along, it could take them into the town and she could have some nice soup, what was her favourite, his was cauliflower with a little cream and some speck, did she know what speck was?

It was strange that he found it easier to talk to her through Catharina; perhaps it was because that way he didn't have to ask serious questions? All Danne had written in his letter was that his sister-in-law was the widow of a soldier killed in an accident and that she hoped to find a way to support herself in the city and not be a burden on her family. So they talked about soup, and then about Catharina's cousins Finn and Otto back in Sønderborg. Herr Andersen looked forward to meeting Otto soon, and every so often when his head twitched as they rode along in the horse-tram Catharina reached up from Josephina's lap and put her hand against his beard. A beautiful child, he observed to Josephina several times, how lucky you are, how very lucky!

The streets beyond the station were dirty and badly paved, with houses crowded together, some were six or seven storeys high, with many broken windows boarded up or covered in oiled paper. Most open windows had people in them, as if they were getting fresh air, and the streets were also crowded with people and with little stalls and barrows of food and goods. The air was smoky and smelled of sewage and rotting rubbish. Josephina was used to the smell of the cow shit and piss, and of course that of old Gunnar back at the Bauernhaus, and she was used to cleaning it out, but the muck in the drains in these streets hadn't been washed away, it stank, and it was from people.

This was where many of the city's workers lived – Herr Andersen told Josephina this through Catharina, who of course didn't know what he was talking about and was falling asleep against Josephina's chest – but soon they would come to a better part of the city and then they could go on a little canal boat to the house, to his and Frau Andersen's house, they would go on the canal so he could show her the waterway, it was in a good part of the city, often there were ducks.

'I know you'll like it,' said Herr Andersen to the sleeping Catharina, and he looked at Josephina with a sideways twitch of his head, and the smile inside his beard seemed to get stuck there. Then he closed the smile and turned away while Josephina was thanking him again for meeting them and saying that yes, she was sure she and Catharina would like Herr Andersen's house, she looked forward to seeing it and also to meeting Frau Andersen.

She was about to say, 'And the children,' but stopped herself, because Danne and Greta had never mentioned any children at Herr Andersen's house.

The buildings became grander with large shop windows, and the street wider and well paved; there was no longer such a smell of shit and rubbish. Josephina held Catharina close to stop her from slipping from her lap, and looked around from the tram window. There were boys and men sitting on the seats on the tram's roof, they were shouting and singing, perhaps they were drunk? They all climbed down at a quay with a landing for small river craft, where gypsies were playing a violin and a drum – they had a monkey on a rope, it was dancing, and the drunk boys pretended to dance for a while and then went off singing along the quay. Herr Andersen hadn't spoken again since Catharina had fallen asleep, and now he simply lifted up his arms for Josephina to pass her out of the tram. Then he was holding her quite easily as though he was used to doing it.

There was a boy waiting for the tram and he held a bucket of water for each of the horses to drink from. Herr Andersen made a sad face as if to say what a shame Catharina couldn't see the horsies getting their drink, but he still didn't speak, not until he shouted down to a boatman that they needed to go around to Deichstrasse. Then she climbed down into the boat, and Herr Andersen passed sleeping Catharina to her, and her bag to the boatman, and off they went, again without speaking.

But then, 'He's like a son to me,' said Herr Andersen abruptly as thc boatman rowed through a long dark bridge underpass – his voice echoed under the stone vault, it was mixed up with the splash of the oars, it was as though he was talking through water, and his face was submerged in rippling shadow. Then they nudged out into the grey, cloudy light. 'My nephew,' he said. 'My nephew Danne. A good boy.' Clear of the dim underpass, his gaze was fixed so intently on her that at first she was unable to respond that yes, Danne was a kind man, he'd been kind to her and to Catharina, she was grateful that he'd agreed to be Catharina's godfather, and her sister Greta of course Catharina's godmother, they were good people, she was grateful.

Still he kept his eyes fixed on her – he wasn't smiling or frowning, his face was quite impassive, he didn't even seem to be expecting a response. And then the tic jerked his shoulder and head and it was almost as though he woke up. Yes, he agreed, they were good people, he was so happy that their little family was growing, the times were not easy but Danne was prospering, he was a good provider, a hard worker, he had a wise head on his shoulders.

And then he said, 'And your papa and mutti? How are they? They still have the smallholding? Meister Hansen is still making those fine things, the furniture and so forth?' His fixed look. 'Of course they will miss their beautiful new granddaughter.'

'Yes, I'm sure they will,' said Josephina, smiling very calmly, hearing another meaning in her words. Then, as if she was sitting beside a puppet of herself, she made the puppet tell the story she'd rehearsed for this moment. 'Mutti is not well and can't do much anymore, and so Papa has to look after her and do some of the work she used to do, the gardens and so forth, and even the linens, but they have my sister Elke to help them, and also Tante Elizabeth over in Gaarden, not so far away, so they will manage.'

Still he kept his direct gaze on her, and still she returned it. Perhaps this was impolite of her.

Then, finally, he smiled again – the smile-in-his-beard that was very like Danne's, a nice one, though now she didn't quite believe it. 'You are a very brave young woman then – Josephina Hansen, isn't it? – to go out on your own, to not overburden your family in their hard times, to trust the talents that God has given you.'

Josephina was facing the stern of the boat where Herr Andersen was sitting. Behind her, the oars creaked rhythmically in their rowlocks, and past Herr Andersen's smile she could see the oar-dip ripples receding on the surface of the dirty water – like days and months, perhaps, or like the events in her life that kept moving her on to where she was going. She kept on watching them, and him, waiting for Herr Andersen's smile to close and for him to say something more, but the smile stayed there and he said nothing until they reached the landing below his house.

'Here we are, at last,' he said. And then, 'Danne was right, you are a determined young woman, Fräulein *Hansen*.'

He used 'Fräulein' not 'Frau' and emphasised 'Hansen', and she easily guessed what he was doing, and that it might not be simple, after all, living in the protection of Herr Aksel Andersen, who'd made it clear that, although he thought Catharina a beautiful child, and Josephina lucky to have her, and determined as well as lucky, he was, in respect of *Fräulein Hansen*, only doing a favour for the nephew he thought of as his son. And so it was once again the consequence of her past that arrived first at the threshold of the future that kept moving her on, and when would she overtake that past, she and Catharina, and go beyond it?

The rain was falling steadily and almost straight down through a thick sea fog when the packet reached the entrance to Kieler Förde. It was now dark, and because there was so little wind and visibility was bad the boat dropped anchor below the lighthouse across the water from Laboe. So, they would go on when the tide turned and when there was a breeze, perhaps in the morning – the young sailor who shouted this down into the cabin was soaking wet, he had the meagre beginnings of a beard and water was dripping from it. They'd been sailing for twelve hours and it seemed as though the boat had gone backwards from morning into night.

It would surely be nicer up on the deck where the air was fresh, but Josephina didn't want Catharina to get wet, so she played piggy-toes with her and gave her the last of Greta's stewed fruit and the last drink of milk with a little honey in it. The elderly woman called Olga who was going to her grandson's wedding in Kiel, and who had made herself very comfortable in a large woollen shawl, offered Catharina a piece of her cake, but Catharina turned her face against Josephina's chest. Earlier the woman had asked Josephina if she was going to Kiel because she had family there, and Josephina had said that she was continuing on the train from Kiel to Hamburg to introduce Catharina to her uncle, which was partly true and partly the story she needed to be confident of in order to tell it. She was glad the woman was there, because she rebuked one of the men in the cabin for lighting his cigar – the place was too close, he should take his smoke outside, didn't he think, like a gentleman?

When the woman first introduced herself in Danish, and said that Josephina should call her Olga, that was enough for a short trip, and when Josephina replied that her name was Josephina Hansen, the woman knew at once from her accent that she was Holsteine, and so they spoke in German. Of course, said the woman, Josephina's name, Hansen, could also be Danish, it was common enough in the north. It was possible that at some time her family had come down from Denmark to Hamburg? Yes, it was of course possible, Josephina agreed, feeling the names Hansen, Andersen and Mayer shift about anxiously in her mind as if trying to evade the pleasant conversation she was having.

And what does that tell us about the wars, the woman wanted to know. 'When a lot of the time, for all our differences, we can hardly tell each other apart? And now, look, here you are living in Sønderborg with your family? You see what I mean?'

Josephina knew that a gentle investigation was under way. No, she corrected the woman, she was only visiting a sister in Sønderborg, but sadly she agreed about the wars – her opa and two uncles were buried at Dybbøl.

The woman tut-tutted and took Josephina's hand. 'Men

go to war, we bear children,' she said. 'That is their power, this is ours.'

Two men in respectable merchants' coats on the other side of the cramped cabin then began a mocking conversation in Danish about the nonsense the woman had spoken and what they thought of Germans. That was when Olga asked one of them to take his nasty cigar outside at the same moment the memory of von Zarovich's 'Ah!' and the rope of yellow snot on his moustache returned suddenly to Josephina's thoughts – something she didn't ever want to see again and had successfully banished from her recollections of that day on Faulstrasse, but there it was, the sound of his loud 'Ah!' and the shameful and disgusting sight of the Hauptmann's snot on his fine adelige Preussen Offizier moustache with its ends turned up and still wet with his coffee, but also there again was his scorn and the way he threw some coins in a scatter across the breakfast tray. If she could have shown the two smartly dressed Danish merchants this picture she would have done so, but instead she calmly thanked the woman for banishing the man who wanted to smoke, because it would have made Catharina cough.

Her memory of Hauptmann von Zarovich and even of his name had made her shiver, the shivering was perhaps connected to her going backwards from morning to night and backwards in returning however briefly to the place she had left behind her. But then she felt completely exhausted and, after helping an unwilling Catharina to use the stinky latrine, went suddenly to sleep curled with the child on a banquette, and when she woke to the sound of the packet's anchor being rattled up at dawn she found the woman's wide shawl across her and Catharina. It had a Danish pattern in its weave, a widely spaced knit of good heavy grey-blue wool, with pyramid-peaks around the border and a broad-leaf motif in the body.

She went up on deck and found the elderly Danish woman called simply Olga standing at the rail somewhat away from the other five or six passengers, including the two scornful Danish merchants who were smoking cigars and talking as if sharing secrets. The little packet was once again following the filling-up of its sails with a good breeze into the long defile of Kieler Förde. Josephina tried to give Olga back the fine warm shawl, but the kind woman told her to keep it, she suggested that Josephina and Catharina had a long way to travel yet – yes, they had that look about them, they would be needing a good warm shawl more than her, much more than her, after all she was going to a wedding, the wedding of one of her favourite grandchildren, such a good young man, she was the lucky one, she wished Josephina well and her child also, she hoped that the child's father was a kind man and not one who would hastily go off to war, but meanwhile would they like to share what was left of her cake, it was a special one for travelling, it had six eggs in it, could you believe that?

Then, two or three hours later, as the early mist lifted and bright sunlight struck through the clouds that were already blowing away from the shoreline that was steaming on the Schwentine side of the fjord, where Elke might even then be taking her two buckets down through the wet grass to the impatient cows – if she, Josephina, could only see her, somewhat grumpy probably, but good with the cows who also knew her and the familiar tug of her hands – the packet easily, with its sails once again full of her future, passed the place where Josephina had been born and that she was now about to leave for ever, perhaps; and as she wept the elderly

Danish woman whose name was Olga pulled the shawl with its peaked, pyramidal border more closely around her and Catharina, and said, in her not-quite-right Holsteine German, that Josephina should take good care of this little girl, because she would be the future, not those men who thought only of whom they should overcome.

And there waiting for them at the familiar wharf, where the young sailor with a piece bitten from his ear had shown her his wonderful whorled shell, were Tante Elizabeth and Mathilde, who was now a big girl – they had come back when the packet didn't make harbour the night before. Elke would come to the house later, when she'd done her work, Mathilde told them with a serious expression because this was important information. Catharina was looking at her with shy hope and was happy when Mathilde took her hand and walked with her to the little buggy where Herr Mayer's stable-boy was waiting. And no, Tante Elizabeth informed Josephina without being asked, her papa and mutti would not come to see her, they 'didn't wish to know', and Herr Mayer was, as it so happened, 'away on business'. But Elke would come later, she repeated.

So Josephina was both there and not there, she was both 'back' and in the future that was pausing while Elke's kisses drove her down into a chair; she was watching Mathilde help Catharina to eat her special supper as if this little cousin 'who loved her more than stars' wasn't really the same one who'd jabbed her with a sharp elbow when she wouldn't sing 'Wie traulich war das Fleckchen' or tell her a Puck Puck the brave chicken story – only this time, in this 'now' that wasn't securely fixed, she was indeed happily singing the song about a cosy spot written by the poet in the flapping coat from over in Schwanenweg, a place that already sounded foreign, and Mathilde was clapping like a little grown-up, not like the querulous child Josephina had cuddled in bed on that night three years ago while trying not to shiver and wake her up, the shivering that wasn't on account of the cold, because Mathilde's warm little body had been there close to her, as well as her warm breath that smelled sweet from her bedtime cup of elderflower dreaming-milk.

And then, before she was really awake in the moment when time moved forward again, they were rattling along through early-morning noises of people shouting, squashed together in the buggy with Catharina on Tante Elizabeth's knee and Mathilde on Josephina's. And soon Tante Elizabeth was weeping and Mathilde also because her mother was. The train to Hamburg tooted three times just like the smaller one that came to the mill on the Schwentine and went back to the station at Kiel that you walked from along the harbourside to Nikolaikirche and the streets around Kieler Schloss, such as Faulstrasse, only this time it was a different train. It was beginning to speed away from those places and the times they were stuck in. Josephina and Catharina couldn't see Tante Elizabeth and Mathilde anymore, so Josephina lifted her daughter down from the window. She would soon be almost a big girl like Mathilde, but in that moment she was still too young to understand that a moment had passed, and so she began to wail, because she liked waving goodbye and didn't want to stop.

Beth and Frank

Yes, Frank could see the mountain 'perfectly well, thank you Beth, yes, amazing!' – looking east past the three-quarters-empty bottle of 'pretty average Aussie red', rather than west down what he called 'the bleating wilderness of the Kaitīeke place-that-time-forgot, god, Beth, doesn't it depress you just a little, could hardly miss the famous cone shape of Ngāuruhoe, and the full moon, nothing like a full moon viewed through claret, and those wind-bashed trees leaning away from the prevailing?'

'Feeling a bit poetic this evening?' suggested Beth. She put her iPad down on the table next to his plate.

He'd gone ahead without her as instructed and the remains of his dinner were pushed aside on the trestle table. The restaurant patio was dimly lit, but she could see that he'd barely picked at his lamb shanks. He filled the glass she'd brought with her from the bar, and his own. The bottle was now empty.

'Poetic, no,' he said, 'but I'd rather have a bottle in front of me than a frontal lobotomy, who said that? Tom Waits?' He stood up and walked steadily back in to the restaurant.

Was he going to tell her what was bothering him? Or rather, when was he going to do that? Because even though they hadn't seen each other for such a long time, she still knew him well enough to read those mood dips, from sardonic fun to melancholy, and his silences – he'd always done them, those silences, even as the sometimes glum hero of her childhood, sitting on the riverbank in a 'don't talk to me' cloud – but now they seemed to conceal stuff that was getting closer and closer to the surface where words would break through. But until they did she'd just have to wait – so long as he got around to telling her what was up with him before they finished their trip and he went back to whatever his life was about these days over there in Queensland, something obscure to do with soil.

He came back with a fresh bottle of wine and a plate of bread and dips for her: 'Remember when a dip was what grown-ups did in the river?'

'Your mum always said, *I'm just going for a little dip, nur ein kleines Bad*, and then she'd immerse and sit on the bottom, waving her hands about to frighten imaginary fish away. *Nur ein kleines Bad* was what your Grandma Cath used to say, evidently.'

Frank lifted his glass to his lips and waited, looking at her. Then he took a good swallow. The 'dragon tongue' rose and fell back. 'Your point?' he said. He tapped her iPad. 'Been dipping again?' He leaned close and pushed his glasses down to the end of his nose.

Beth opened the screen – on it, backlit as if by moonlight, like the dark glyph of Ngāuruhoe to the east, as if portents were being highlighted everywhere she looked, was a blocky column of blackletter text.

'You can read that stuff?' Frank's breath was a bit winey.

'It's blackletter Gothic. The Germans kept using it after everyone else had stopped. Typical. But it was standard in the nineteenth century. This text was printed in Hamburg in about 1876.' Then Beth stopped, not because she anticipated her cousin mocking her little lecture, but because she had a lump in her throat and because the typography on the screen had bled out into the nightscape, into what Frank had called the 'wind-bashed trees', the askew signage for the restaurant lit from time to time by speeding cars on the highway, the big moon, hauntings.

'So what is it, professor?'

'It's ghosty, is what it is.' Beth pointed at the heading on the screen. 'Just for the hell of it I looked up "Zum Gedächtnis WB" and got this. Remember it was on the headstone?'

Of course he remembered, but once again he looked away from the moment – he even winced. But she would not get annoyed.

'Turns out there was a poet called Wolf Bloch in Hamburg in the 1870s who wrote this long poem called "Zum Gedächtnis" in memory of the Paris Commune of 1871 – it's about the final battle between the revolutionaries and the regular army in Père-Lachaise cemetery in Paris on "Fiertletzter Tag im Monat Mai", fourth to last day in the month of May. How about that?'

'How about what?'

'Zum Gedächtnis, WB, Wolf Bloch, Grandad Wolf Bloch Wenczel, Jesus Christ, Frank.'

'Steady on, my dear Beth,' said her cousin, slopping wine into his glass. 'What are me and Jesus doing on that dance card together?'

'You can put Friedrich Engels on there as well, if you like. According to Google, Wolf Bloch was corresponding with him. The guy was all over the place.'

'Fuck's sake, Beth. The conclusion I hear you racing hastily towards is that the guy was all over our ancestress Josephina Hansen as well. And let's leave poor old Engels out of it for the time being, that's getting way too racy.'

'You want racy? Our respected ancestress arrived in Wellington with an infant son born en route who was christened Wenczel when she remarried here, and a daughter, your grandmother Catharina, whose maiden name, Hansen, was also her mother's birth name – a little anomaly that no one at the reunion could quite get their heads around, though there was a fair bit of idle chatter.'

But of course Frank knew all that.

He was poking at one of the dips. 'But really, it's like this shit,' he said, sucking the goo off his finger with a grimace. 'Whizz a whole lot of stuff up together and hey presto! – it's become a thing.'

The waitress came out to collect Frank's plate, but then hesitated.

'Nothing wrong with the food,' said Frank. 'Excellent in fact, compliments to the chef and indeed to the lamb, just my appetite, I'm sure the dog will enjoy it, so long as it's not a huntaway.'

The waitress gave him a look – it was obvious from his tone that he knew the dog out the back by the accommodation units was a huntaway. Why couldn't he resist doing that kind of thing?

'That was a bit mean,' said Beth. She leaned across Frank and brought up the photo of Wolf Bloch.

'No it wasn't,' he said. 'That was vintage Wolf-wisdom, passed down through the generations. Never feed your working dogs bits of the flock. It's got a ring to it, that does, at the metaphorical level, you have to admit. Your mum used to quote him. Wolf-man.' He took a swallow. 'Am I getting shickered? I can't tell anymore.' He was peering at the image of Wolf Bloch. 'Who's this funny little chap?'

The 'funny little chap' seemed to be peering back at them.

Was now as good a time as any? 'What's up with you, Frank? Ever since we left the reunion on our little trip you've been going all moody.' When she took his hand he didn't remove it – in fact he put his other one on top of hers. He'd always had big paws; now they were a bit gnarly, with knobby knuckles, and liver spots on their backs. But his cheek-kiss was as gentle as ever.

'Remember when we were down the valley earlier?' He gave her hand a squeeze. 'We were looking across the river at the hill your Grandad Wolf had cleared for pasture? You could see where he'd left the big stuff alone, in the gullies, and the odd patch here and there. Then there was this big triangular section of regrowth, almost the whole side of the hill, where he'd let the bush come back. It's tall stuff now, but you can still see the difference from the original bush in the gullies. The big timber he felled turned into the houses and bridges and fence posts down there, the stockyards and what-have-you, and the rest got burned. Then the topsoil fell into the river and fucked it up.' He removed his hand to pick up the wine glass and take a drink. 'It's all very well to go poking around to see which house or which bridge was once those trees, or digging up vintage photos for that matter, but they're all fucking corpses as far as I'm concerned, and the part I like is where the bush has just come back and covered up the place where all that shit happened. I like to look at that new stuff. It's doing the opposite of fucking everything else up. It gives me hope.' He put his hand back on top of hers. 'And Lizzie's pregnant.' Lizzie was his granddaughter. He was going to be a great-grandfather.

A couple of cars tore past on the highway. 'One-forty k at least,' he said. 'You'd think they wanted to kill themselves.' His look, a bit glassy but steady. 'And yes, I hope I can see you thinking, why indeed would anyone put a reference to the Paris Commune on a headstone in the Kaitīeke valley?'

Josephina

They were going up the stairs in Herr Andersen's house, she and Catharina, they pretended to be climbing a big mountain like the snowy one with a little antlered deer and pointy pine trees on the Oma they often looked at in the evenings before Catharina went to sleep. The story Catharina liked was somewhat like the one her oma used to tell, but in Josephina's version the little deer wasn't lost and looking for its mother. Oma made it climb back down the side of the mountain on the two-step stitches and find its mother waiting at the bottom. In Josephina's version of the story, the deer was looking around at the world from the top of the mountain to see where to go, and then it went back down the stepping-stitches one by one to what it had seen, a warm place where oranges grew.

There was a fruit cart by the tram stop near the sewing room, and they would sometimes share an orange that Josephina bought from the impatient woman there, and peeled for them to eat before taking Catharina to the nursery. They would pretend to be little deer, making antlers with their fingers.

Yes, they would go there, she said to Catharina, to where the oranges came from, but not today, and first we have to climb the mountain, up we go!

Up they went. This was the first time they'd been past the floor above the Andersens' kitchen, the one with the street door to the tram stop. She could have the place downstairs and food in the kitchen, she was not to talk familiarly to Frau Andersen if they met – Herr Andersen hoped this arrangement would help her 'in her situation'. But now they were going up. Catharina was doing a two-step ascent of the stairs, pushing up with one foot and then following with the other to the same step, and then repeating, two-feet-by-two-feet-by-two, step-stitching.

There was just a curtain that pulled across her and Catharina's little space with its foldaway cot, and she'd heard the housekeeper and the cook, both of whom were called Frau Schmidt, talking about her and Catharina without even trying to whisper. In their opinion she was 'trouble'. It seemed that was what they'd been told and they agreed that it must be so, because why else was a member of Herr Andersen's family not allowed to go upstairs? – was it perhaps because of, you know, Frau Andersen? – but they were kind to Catharina and let her play with wooden spoons and a big bowl under the table. Josephina called them Schmidt One and Schmidt Two in her thoughts but Frau Schmidt when she spoke to either of them, which was seldom.

Was she grateful to Danne's uncle, Herr Aksel Andersen? There were other ways to ask the question. For example: What did she expect? How could she, now, tell Danne that it was quite difficult being in his uncle's house? A better question was: How could she now move forward from her 'situation' in Herr Andersen's house? *That* question made the issue of gratitude irrelevant. But she could never tell Danne or Greta that Herr Andersen had been merely convenient.

And what was the meaning of, *you know, Frau Andersen*?

And besides, how was she to move beyond the convenience of her 'situation'? As yet, the answer to that question remained in the realm of the story she told Catharina at bedtime when she was a little deer whose eyelids were fluttering on the edge of sleep.

And in any case, she herself had organised her 'situation': she was in Hamburg, she was working in the sewing room, she was able to keep a little of her money, she understood the tram that took her and Catharina to and from work, Catharina was in the nursery where she had soup and a sleep at midday, on Sundays they could go for a walk over to the big bridge where there was a stall with jellied fruits, and sometimes the gypsies with the dancing monkey, and Catharina had learned quite a lot of new words, including some foreign ones from her playmate Alex at the nursery, including *pane*, which was Italian for bread.

Schmidt Two came earliest in the morning and prepared the breakfast. She was a tall, fine-looking young woman with a dark complexion who kept her aprons very clean and crisp and wore her black hair gathered up under a floral embroidered cap. Josephina would have liked to know where the cap came from, but the young cook didn't talk to Josephina, only to herself – 'Now, now, now, where did I put that buttermilk? Where, where? Now, pancakes, pancakes!' Josephina and Catharina took their hard-boiled eggs wrapped in pancakes out to the horse-tram before Herr Andersen came down. Catharina ate hers on the tram, or as much of it as she could manage, and Josephina kept hers and what was left of Catharina's to eat later, when the women in the sewing room had lunch.

Schmidt One was still there when they came back from the sewing room in the evening, and they all had supper together in the kitchen. She was an older woman who had been with the Andersens since they arrived in Hamburg and so, she told Josephina, she had better mind how she behaved. Schmidt One usually had a glass or two of wine with her supper. Then she would always go out to the privy on the landing above the river. Her expression was, 'Time to feed the fish.' When she came back, the two Frau Schmidts would wish 'Sweet dreams' to Catharina under the table, and tall, dark Schmidt Two would often give Catharina what she called a 'Genuss' made with honey syrup. They would say good night to *Fräulein* Hansen, Schmidt One would say remember not to disturb Herr and Frau Andersen, and then they'd go up one flight to the street door.

There were no servants in the house at night – the household of Danne's uncle Farbror Aksel was in reality a modest one, more so perhaps than Danne himself knew. Josephina would wash Catharina and herself with a basin of warm water on the kitchen floor, and she would wash their undergarments with the same piece of yellow soap that Schmidt One left out for them, and hang them by the stove. Sometimes she could hear other people talking upstairs, but the household was mostly very simple and frugal, and there were seldom visitors.

The room where Herr and Frau Andersen and occasionally their visitors had their meals was off a narrow passage that led to the street door. The stairs to the upper rooms were also off the passage. Thus, there was a simple way up through the house to the very top, and opening along the way would be rooms with closed doors. The house was the shape of a secret or even forbidden narrative, with questions opening off it. There were three questions, and it wasn't as though she asked them, it was more as if the questions asked her. Why had she put the nightgown on? Why had she taken the Hauptmann's money? Why hadn't she immediately told Tante Elizabeth what had happened in Faulstrasse? These were the questions that repeated themselves to her every day since arriving in Herr Andersen's house with its closed rooms and 'her situation'. Nor had she yet seen Frau Andersen, whom she was forbidden to address 'familiarly' if she did meet her. Schmidt One had suggested by the important expression on her face that Frau Andersen would be easily upset.

But tonight, as recounted approvingly by the two Schmidts at supper, Herr and Frau Andersen had gone to the opera, they'd drunk some champagne and eaten some snacks with friends in the room upstairs and then gone off to the Stadt-Theater looking very fine, and 'about time, too'. Frau Andersen had on her pale milk-coffee-coloured evening dress with pearls and silk flowers, and her husband his best tails and white waistcoat, it was too bad about his twitch, it always got worse in company. They were going to an opera by Wagner called *Tristan und Isolde*, and during their champagne and the Schnitzen that Schmidt One took up, they and their guests were discussing the scandal of a review of the opera by the radical editor called Wolf Bloch. He wrote in the *Bürger Zeitung*, and it was sensational, the guests all agreed, and of course they were clever people, Schmidt One was confident they knew what they were talking about, this Wolf Bloch had better mind himself, he'd end up in chains.

'What did he write?' asked Josephina, feeling a little shock like a pin-prick in her heart – she was reaching down to stop Catharina from bumping her head as she emerged from under the table where she'd been playing with her wooden spoons, all of which had names now, the names of children at the nursery, including Alex, and so Josephina was looking up at the Schmidts from under her eyebrows, awkwardly and perhaps somewhat disrespectfully, especially as she seldom spoke to them. Of course Wolf Bloch was the name of the strange little man in the sewing room, in the rather shabby clothes, with the pigeon chest and the somewhat insolent stare, when she'd almost made a fool of herself in front of the owner and Herr Andersen.

'"The curse of nationalism",' quoted Schmidt One in a satirical tone for Josephina's benefit, and, simultaneously, 'What do you care?' said Schmidt Two scornfully.

'I saw him,' said Josephina. 'I saw Wolf Bloch.' She clearly remembered the quizzical tilt of the man's head, her sense that he was asking, why was she there? Catharina was climbing into her lap, so she stood up to stop her making a nuisance of herself at the table. 'He was at the sewing room with his sister the day Herr Andersen took me there.'

'He's a Jew and an agitator,' said Schmidt One, as if that explained something. Then she went out 'to feed the fish', and the two Schmidts left soon afterwards, leaving Josephina to clean up the kitchen. This she did very quickly, and next, without waiting to think about it, or about the excitement she felt all at once in what was usually the weary end of the day, she lit a candle and went to the stairs with Catharina and began to go up a two-stitch step at a time, towards the rooms she'd imagined with closed doors like unanswered questions.

But the first three doors weren't closed after all. The first was the room where the Andersens and their guests had been drinking their champagne, and there was still a single table lamp burning in one corner. In the gloom, the furnishings looked plain and comfortable and there were a few small pictures on the walls. Catharina wanted to go in, but Josephina wouldn't let her. There was also a bathroom on this floor, but they went on up to the next room. This, too, had its door open and a single lamp in a yellow shade beside a large bed. It was very plain, without any pictures or ornaments; it smelled just a little of tobacco, and Josephina felt sure that Herr Andersen slept there – but perhaps not his wife? Then there was another bedroom on the next floor, with its door slightly ajar but no lit lamp inside. The room's aroma by the open door was of gardenias and Josephina recognised the perfume because it was Tante Elizabeth's favourite, especially in summer. They didn't look into the dim room, but went on up to the last floor, slowly, because little-deer Catharina had to be coaxed up the mountain.

The stairs were unlit up there, but enough light came from the landing below and from the candle for them to see a closed door. By now Catharina was very tired and was beginning to complain, so Josephina told her to sit on the top step while she tried the door handle. The door opened with a little creak and a musty smell came out. There was just enough light from the candle to see what was in the room, and Josephina knew at once what it was. It was a child's room, but an unused one. She stepped across the threshold and crossed to a small bed with some dolls on it and, just visible in the candlelight, a string of paper cut-out animals suspended across the window, below which was a rocking horse with a large staring eye.

She stood there for a while. There was a roaring sound in her ears.

The room's musty air filled her chest painfully. She hurried back on to the landing and closed the door, because all at once she felt strange.

But where was Catharina?

A woman was standing four or five steps below the landing. She had on a pale evening dress, with silk flowers that Josephina could see parts of on either side of the child. The woman was holding Catharina against herself and looking up at Josephina over her head. Catharina's arms were around the woman's neck and her cheek rested on her shoulder – she looked quite peaceful and contented.

'A beautiful child,' said the woman. 'Just sitting there.'

Her name is Catharina Elke Lange Hansen. This was what Josephina then said to the woman, but it was only the thought of saying it, as Frau Andersen turned her back and walked carefully down the stairs, holding Catharina close. Catharina shifted her head on Frau Andersen's shoulder and looked back up at Josephina, who began to follow her down with a cold, giddy sensation of stepping into a void that was silent because her anger and her fear were cancelling each other out and she couldn't speak, she could only keep her eyes fixed on Catharina's that were blinking slowly as the woman in the beautiful dress went carefully down the stairs, very carefully, because she was holding Catharina with both arms and couldn't use one hand to steady herself on the bannister.

It was hard to leave Catharina at the Kita nursery the first time because she shrieked loudly and held her arms up to be lifted and held tight. But it was not after all the only time she'd done that – she'd cried and cried when left with Elke for the first time while Josephina went to the market back in Sønderborg, but then she was just one year old and, besides, when Josephina got back, Catharina was no longer interested in her, it was Elke she loved best. So Josephina went quickly out of the nursery, leaving Catharina writhing and shrieking in the arms of a young woman about Josephina's own age, and up the stairs to the sewing room.

The young woman's name was Maria. They had met her the day before when they came to see the nursery and make arrangements. Maria was from quite far away in Magdeborn, her husband had died in a mining accident, now she was living with her sister and husband in Dovenfleet, their child was also at the nursery, her sister was upstairs in the sewing room – it was all right, she said, the children were all right there. Maria was wearing a plain pinny, it looked quite clean, and although she talked very fast and seemed jittery, Josephina was comforted to know that her sister's child was also at the nursery because that surely meant she would take care of Catharina.

An older woman asked only if Catharina knew how to relieve herself. Then she went back to a corner with a stove in it and a table where she was chopping vegetables. There were about a dozen children in the room and, on the side away from the grimy windows, some cots for babies. A boy was riding a horse-trolley fiercely towards other children who seemed to like running away from him – Josephina hoped he wasn't too rough – and in one corner some girls about four years old were sitting on the floor in a cluster, playing with something she couldn't see that was making a clattering sound. And then one of the girls stood and ran with the thing in both hands while the others chased her. She was the winner – she was holding up a large painted wooden farm-girl doll, like the old one at Greta's place with brightly painted girls that went one inside the other. Then the victorious girl was caught over by a stack of little pallets, and they all sat down in a circle and started again.

The room was warm but not too stifling or smelly, and there was a comforting aroma of the soup that the older woman was preparing – Josephina could smell kohlrabi, and she hoped there might be a meatball in it for each child as well. The stack of little pallets was pushed against the wall near the cots, for the children's midday sleep, said the young woman called Maria – usually it was quite peaceful then, did Catharina like to have a nap? Yes, usually she does, Josephina told her, and she likes this special shawl, as you can see it's got a sucky corner, may I leave it here for her? When we come back tomorrow? And an orange?

And now they had done it, she and Catharina, and she was going up the next flight of stairs while Catharina continued to shriek on the floor below.

The sewing room was up two more flights from the nursery, which was one above the street. Each step up took her further from Catharina, but at the same time closer to where they were going together, it was a place but it was also the future and she had its fresh smell on her fingers, it was the smell of an orange.

But no, she had to go back – how could she leave Catharina there?

But then Catharina's shrieks stopped, and Josephina went on quickly, before her dread of what had caused the shrieks to stop made her turn and run back down and snatch her away from the young woman with the nervous, babbling manner. It was her 'situation' that she was inside as she climbed the stairs; it was her 'situation' that made her attentive and polite as her day's task was explained to her. She was inside her 'situation' like the painted toy Bauernhaus farm-girls inside versions of themselves as she began, with downcast eyes, to sew buttonholes on a man's four-button twill jacket.

There was a stack of twelve jackets in a basket on the floor beside her, she should finish them before going home – it was piece-work, yes, but there was a quota she was expected to complete, if she was unable to there would soon be another young woman in her place, did she understand that? Was that clear?

Yes, she told the supervisor, who leaned in close to her and had obviously had a smoked herring with pickle for his breakfast, and who watched the workroom from a raised platform where he made notes in a book and picked at his teeth – yes, she understood perfectly well, thank you, the nature of her situation, it was quite clear. And then, when she'd finally finished the jackets, she and Catharina went two-stitch-stepping down the mountain from the nursery where the little deer had a new friend called Alex, who talked funny.

Josephina's back and sewing fingers were very sore, she was hungry and thirsty, the street was dirty, it was a long walk to the horse-tram, and Catharina had to be carried the last half of it. But now she was happy – it was as though she'd caught up with the future, and that was even what she saw when she and Catharina entered the kitchen at Herr Andersen's house, and Catharina told Schmidt One that she had a new friend called Alex and the old grump smiled at them both.

Why had she wanted to go into that room, why had she, why that room? This was what the woman who Josephina knew to be Frau Andersen was asking. Not who was she or what was the beautiful child's name. They were now in the gardenia bedroom and Catharina was sitting on Josephina's lap in a comfortable chair with padded arms. They were both looking across at Frau Andersen in another nice chair.

'Why?' asked Frau Andersen. 'Tell me.'

Was she angry? Her tone was calm, and her face, dimly

lit by the lamp, seemed also barely lit by any clear emotion from within. Her hands were folded in her lap – she'd taken off her gloves, and her entwined fingers were white and thin. Josephina had yet to speak, she was holding Catharina close and breathing in the warm smell of her hair. The woman had handed Catharina to her on the landing and then gone into the room and lit a lamp, trimming the wick to a soft glow, and then, while Josephina stood hesitating outside on the landing, had called out, 'Come!' and pointed to the chair.

My name is Josephina Christian Hansen and my daughter is Catharina Hansen, my sister is Greta Andersen and her husband is Herr Andersen's nephew, Danne Andersen. Even so, we are forbidden to go upstairs in this house. Why does what happened to me in the past continue to close the doors to my future? Do you want to know what happened? The Junker made me put on the nightgown I'd sewn for his wife, he stuck his cock in me, he threw some money on the breakfast tray and said Don't come back you little whore.

But Josephina didn't say any of these things. She looked across the dim room at Frau Andersen and saw that she already knew all about it, so why should she say everything again and again, since every time she did it, those things – the nightgown, the Ah! and the snot, the money, her own silence – every time she said them again, to herself or somebody else, they just pushed her future further away, they closed the doors to it? And what was going to happen then, would she become like Mutti, always longing unhappily for a future that had a house in Gaarden or even in a street like Faulstrasse in the town, without animal piss running down the slope-floor, and with the respect that was due to Meister Hansen?

'You don't want to talk to me, Fräulein Hansen,' said Frau Andersen, whose fingers were now twisting themselves together in her lap. 'That's a pity.'

'I'm very sorry indeed to have offended you, Frau Andersen,' said Josephina as politely as she possibly could, wanting now more than anything to be out of the room with its sad perfume of gardenias and the woman whose fingers were knotting and unknotting in her lap. 'And now, if you don't mind, I should put Catharina to bed.'

Because if she stayed any longer, how could she stop herself from asking the woman whose emotions were hidden in the dim shadows of her face but whose hands were restlessly signalling them why she and Catharina couldn't have used the room at the top of the stairs? But of course she knew the answer, because it was her 'situation' and she was familiar with that.

'I can see that you're a good young mother,' said Frau Andersen, 'and of course the child must get her sleep. But first there is something you should know.'

Josephina had begun to stand up from the comfortable chair with Catharina whose weight was now that of a sleeping child – her arms hung down and her head was lolling against Josephina's shoulder.

But she sat down again and listened as Frau Andersen's almost monotonous voice explained that Fräulein Hansen may have thought that she had left the opera because the music was bad, but that wasn't the case. The music was excellent. No, she had left because she couldn't endure the sympathy of the people she met there. Even when they only gossiped the sympathy was present, the sympathy was always there, in what they didn't say. When would it end?

Now Josephina was sitting very still within Frau

Andersen's gaze, because she was hearing what her own anger and resentment had almost pushed to the side of that look at once without emotion and yet pitiful.

Their only daughter was seven years old when the cholera killed many in the city, Frau Andersen told her. That was almost ten years ago. Did Josephina know what cholera did? It emptied the body and burned it up with fever. That was something you didn't forget. And now Herr Andersen would not permit anyone to enter the room that had been their daughter's. Her name was Isolde. Did Fräulein Hansen think it had been easy to go to an opera with that name in its story? Did she think it had been possible for people at the opera to be unaware of her situation? Their friends? To conceal their unspoken sympathy? But her husband, Herr Andersen, had insisted.

And now, of course, Fräulein Hansen should take her beautiful child off to bed.

But Josephina knew clearly, as she went carefully down the three flights of stairs to the kitchen with the breathing weight of Catharina in her arms, that it had not been Herr Andersen who had forbidden anyone to use Isolde's room at the top of the house, it had been his wife, and what could he do but try to protect her?

Now Josephina remembered the tenderness with which Herr Andersen had picked up Catharina at the train station, how he'd held up his arms to her as they got down from the horse-tram, and the care with which he'd handed her down to Josephina in the boat that took them under the dark arch of the bridge and along the river to the back of the house on Deichstrasse, which was the way to enter the house at the bottom level without going in through the front door. Because the front door was the entrance to the story that Danne's uncle Farbror Aksel didn't want Josephina and Catharina to be in.

And what had it been like for poor Frau Andersen to come home alone from the opera with her dead daughter's name in it and go up the stairs and see, above her, a sleepy little girl sitting on the top step next to her daughter's room?

And now, how could she and Catharina stay a moment longer in this house?

Friedrich Engels

My dear Pasquale, or let me rather say Dear Citizen Martignetti

I'm glad to tell you that my efforts in your matter have not gone without success. Wolf Bloch, editor of the 'Bürger Zeitung' in Hamburg, writes to me that a local businessman (in the cotton business and also runs a sewing room for young ladies in distressed circumstances), a personal friend of mine, political without prejudice, perhaps has a task for Martignetti, if at first just a modest one. It is however desired that M first send his photograph. It's funny, this – my friend himself finds it so – but necessary for practical reasons. It would be good if M could even send the photograph to the gentleman with a letter of recommendation. His name is Johannes Paul, in Paul & Steinberg Company, Alterwall 58.

If you want to find out if a position can be found here you would do well to send Herr Paul your photograph. From my side I will provide you with the outline of a letter of recommendation to the same gentleman, such as is commonly used in commercial situations in Germany. In this matter, I draw your attention to the need to keep away from ostensible political activity in Hamburg, as you will otherwise absolutely be expelled. The situation of Socialists in Germany gets worse by the day, and new coercive laws are in view. On the other hand, you have been offered an opportunity to take on a commercial activity and through that enter into a new carriera as you say in Italian.

My eyes are recovering finally, so it seems. But I cannot as yet think about serious work, and so the manuscript of your Italian translation of Marx's essay 'Outwork and Capital' is still resting.

I attach my draft letter from you to Herr Johannes Paul in Hamburg and wish you success.

With best wishes
Yours, F. Engels

To Herr Johannes Paul in Hamburg

Through Herr Wolf Bloch I learn with pleasure that there is a prospect for me to find employment with your worthy company, but that you first require my photograph. I will provide you with this, and note that I have worked here for [insert number of years] years in the royal Notary Office. If you would have the goodness to inform me as to the nature of the activity and the other conditions I can expect, I will be deeply grateful and in your debt. Should the opportunity on offer be realised, I will gladly do everything to fulfil my new obligations in accordance with your wishes, and sign with sincere thanks for your sympathetic approach
Respectful and devoted P.M.
And the external address:
To Herr Johannes Paul
Herren Paul & Steinberg
Alterwall 58
Hamburg
Germany

Beth and Frank

Frank was groaning in the next unit – should she check if he was okay? Then he was talking loudly on his cellphone. He'd always shouted on the phone back when they still did their 'cooee' calls.

'The Great Galah here, how's my favourite Kiwi?'

Ages ago.

Then he was laughing. He laughed for a long time, with joy and abandonment. What would it be like to hear him laughing like that from far away in Townsville or somewhere like that perhaps? If it was pregnant granddaughter Lizzie who was listening? Or her mum, whose name was? Who lived where? How could she be expected to remember? If she'd ever known? Then it sounded as if he was saying goodbye. Then his door shut firmly and his footsteps crunched away on the gravel path.

Then Beth closed the door in her mind that had opened for her to go outside to keep an eye on her pissed great-grandfather cousin. At the top of a fresh page in the A4 notebook she'd girly-swottishly named Reunion Notes, she wrote, *Wolf Bloch (1843–?1880): Zum Gedächtnis. A (very) rough translation.*

> It was in the churchyard Père Lachaise/ On the fourth last day in the month of May/ There fell the last Kämpfertrupp [?fighter squad?]/ Crushed by fire, steel and lead/ The last proud Kämpfertrupp/ That ~~these hordes resisted~~ resisted these hordes/ The [?Die=plural?] Mac Mahon, the [?singular?] hero of his order/ Bloodhound equal, out of Bolt [?placename? family name?] sent.

If that opening stanza was anything to go by, Wolf Bloch's memorial poem was going to be a long retreat across the rubble of historical cliché. But inside this stuff, like a ghost summoned up by scraping lichens off Great-grandma Josephina's headstone, was a German man whose inspiration had been the French Commune and its martyrs. The same mystery German who *may* have been Grandad Wolf's father.

She rather hoped so.

No sound from next door. Frank was still out there somewhere.

One down, twenty-five verses to go.

> And as banged, echoed now was/ The shotgun [?musket?] noise, the fury shouting/ And as the place of graves did/ From the swarm of soldiers become free/ There one heard from afar still/ The long [adjective], dismal streets long [adverb]/ Always duller, further, dying/ The battalion seriously went.

'The battalion seriously went.' Laboriously? Heavily? When Marx and Engels wrote about the Commune in their introduction to *The Communist Manifesto* they didn't say 'The battalion seriously went'. Professor Schreiber gave the Introduction as a translation exercise back in the day – he got covered in red paint at the anti-Vietnam War demo in Auckland in 1971 and was a bit of a long-haired radical sex symbol, but then got busted for inappropriate relations with students and went back to Germany. She'd given the opportunity some thought herself, but nah. And now Prof Schreiber was just another ghost out here on the margin of State Highway 3 with moonlit Ngāuruhoe like a white-faced spook. Maybe he'd meet Frank wandering around laughing his head off in the headlights of speeding cars – they were both mad buggers, they'd probably get on fine.

Clearly, WB was a mad bugger too, in his day, maybe even a sexy radical firebrand. What he seemed to be saying in verse two was that it was all over for the Communards, the Mac Mahon Kämpfertrupp, the echoing noise of muskets and furious shouting was gone, the swarm of soldiers had left the graveyard and, in the distance, for a long time along the long, dismal streets, the sound of the departing battalion could be heard as it seriously/laboriously/heavily went.

Yes, true, she had somewhat fancied Schreiber, quite a lot actually, before he seriously went, the way his nice teeth bit off the words of Brecht's 'Five Theatre Poems', especially the 'Zeigen' and the 'gezeigt' of *Das Zeigen muss gezeigt werden*: 'The showing has to be shown!'

'Das Zeigen muss gezeigt werden!' she said to the ghosts in the room, the old shawl, the garbled text, her old body with no tits. Wouldn't it be nice to have someone to talk to on the phone at night about those times, to have some of that back – now would be good, to have a laugh about it, to show the showing.

The Great Galah and his bad Aussie jokes?

No, probably not the Great Galah.

Josephina

Would she and Catharina like to ride to work with him in the cab this morning – it was a long time since he'd seen them or spoken to them, it would be nice to have a chat?

Tall dark Schmidt Two was surprised on the other side of the kitchen; she'd been grinding some coffee and telling herself what to do about the oven pancake mix that needed to be ready in ten minutes, was the oven hot enough, and so forth? And now Herr Andersen, who never came down to the kitchen, had come there before breakfast was even ready. Schmidt One, whose manner towards Josephina had warmed somewhat over the past weeks, hadn't yet arrived at the house, and it was still too early for Josephina and Catharina to take their breakfasts up to the street door and along Deichstrasse to the horse-tram.

And how was Catharina, he wanted to know. Was she enjoying her days in the nursery? Did she have some little friends? Catharina was drinking her milk and she looked with wide eyes over the cup's rim at Herr Andersen, whose head gave a twitch and whose hand that had reached out to touch her curls returned quickly to his coat pocket.

'Alex,' said Catharina. She had a milk-moustache and that was what seemed to make Herr Andersen smile, since he made a playful show of licking his own moustache.

'That's her friend's name,' said Josephina, 'it's Alexandra,' and then stopped before saying that sometimes the friend was called Alessa, because she couldn't organise what words were best to push through the confusion that Herr Andersen's appearance in the kitchen had suddenly caused. She had an armful of dry clothes from the rack by the stove – was she supposed, now, to hurry? And Catharina's hair still had to be plaited, she had to have her hands and face washed, and be encouraged to go unwillingly to the privy on the landing, a small drama every morning – was Herr Andersen to witness that? And Josephina herself, how could she, now, move so quickly from her memory of what had happened the night before, and the image still in her mind of Frau Andersen's face unlit from within by emotion but her white hands knotting themselves together in her lap? And as well as that image of Frau Andersen, the thought that she, Josephina, had lain awake with for a long time next to the breathing and dream-whimpers of her own daughter, listening to the slapping sound of water on the landing's piles and the shrill cries of the birds that flew about over the river at night – the thought that she could no longer stay in Danne's Farbror Aksel Andersen's house, and in addition, over and over in her thoughts that were more like counting and recounting a list of things she'd forgotten to do, her realisation while listening to Frau Andersen's cold, unlit voice that she'd misunderstood Herr Andersen's odd behaviour on the day she and Catharina had arrived in Hamburg, and the knowledge that she had put herself at the centre of her 'situation' as the one who was continually wronged, when it was in fact likely that Herr Andersen had done his Christian best to help her as requested by the nephew he thought of as his son, while also making an arrangement that would protect his wife who was clearly, ten years after the death of her daughter from the cholera, still mad with grief.

Over and over again, the thoughts and the image of Frau Andersen's unhappy hands.

And then the sound of early traffic on the river woke her,

the clattering of oars and the shouting – she and Catharina had slept later than usual and Schmidt Two was shaking their curtain and insisting that soon some kitchen supplies would be arriving at the landing, would they please for the love of God get up? Would they please, at once? What was the matter with them?

Of course she knew what Herr Andersen would want to 'have a chat' about. He would want to know why she and Catharina had gone up to the closed child's room at the top of the house, why had she taken advantage of the house being empty? Was it any of her business what happened upstairs in the house that was her only refuge under the circumstances?

'But please, Josephina, do not hurry,' was what he said before leaving the kitchen, noting before he did so that Frau Schmidt's coffee smelled especially good this morning, and he hoped that Josephina would enjoy hers, and her breakfast, and Catharina also, did she like pancakes? – and he would let them know when he was ready for the cab.

Josephina?

She stood there holding the warm, wrinkly dry washing against her chest which had begun to pant a little with the shock of hearing Herr Andersen call her 'Josephina' and not 'Fräulein Hansen'. Schmidt Two was also surprised and stood with her mouth open like the bowl with pancake mix in it. It was as though the meaning of who and what she was had suddenly been shifted from the story of her 'situation', the story in which she and Catharina were characters who kept being concealed from themselves in their 'situation', like the brightly coloured farm-girl dolls at the nursery – as if they had now emerged as themselves.

'Well, well,' said Schmidt Two with a bewildered smile, 'so now it's *Josephina*, what next?' And she began vigorously to mix the pancake batter, as if she needed, now, to show *Josephina*, a member of the household family after all, who was about to ride with Herr Andersen in his cab, that she could apply herself to her tasks.

But, after all, Herr Andersen had hoped that Josephina would enjoy her breakfast in the kitchen – and he would let her know when it was time to join him in the cab, once he had finished his own breakfast, upstairs with his wife, no doubt.

But still, there was a kind of lightness or breath-held sensation in her chest – it was happiness, perhaps it was hope?

So then they ate their pancakes and eggs at the kitchen table while Schmidt Two went upstairs with the breakfast and coffee on a tray but only one cup and only one plate.

What was the name of the man in the dark coat and boots who was there in the sewing room the first time she came to see the place with her sponsor Herr Andersen? She'd found out the name of the strange little man who was also there with his sister, it was Wolf Bloch, an unusual name that you wouldn't forget – but who was the other man, the owner of the sewing room, what was his name?

The woman working next to Josephina was called Wilhelmina, but she said to call her Willa. It was Willa who'd given Catharina a little wave when they came to see the sewing room the first time. Now, as they did most days, they were talking to each other in the low, murmuring voices the women used while keeping their attention on the stitches in front of them, under the gaze of the supervisor on his platform. Willa was also doing buttonholes on the four-button twill jackets; she was a very quick sewer, and also spoke quickly, as if what she was doing made her speech keep pace. She also spoke in the rhythms of the stitch, with a little tug at the ends of certain words and phrases.

'The man's name is Herr Johannes Paul sometimes you'll see his business partner who's called Steinberg they're cotton merchants but some people say that he and Steinberg' – Willa spoke in a whisper – 'are socialists but best not talk about that because they're banned.'

'Banned by whom, why?' Josephina whispered, but Willa's face had coloured up and she was shaking her head, so after that they murmured about other things, such as how Catharina was liking the nursery and what it had been like living in a Bauernhaus up north with animals and so forth, and why did she have to leave and did Josephina have to do maid's work at the house where she lived, but why not? – and where Willa was living now in a shared room with five other women, two were sisters from Russia who worked in a glove factory and stole offcuts of kid leather to sell in the street, there was an Italian chambermaid whose husband was in prison in Bolzano for counterfeiting and she'd had to cross the border at night and leave their child behind with her aunt, and there was an older widow who worked in a Jewish bakery and brought them onion rolls that wouldn't keep until the next day, they all had to share a privy with six other rooms on their floor in that building, Josephina was quite lucky by the sound of it – but she also made a point of telling Josephina that she was lucky to be working in this sewing room with its Kita for the children, because of the owners.

But then she stopped again and just repeated that they were lucky, both of them were, but you had to keep working hard, you had to finish your quota every day, you couldn't stop for long to eat or drink or go to the privy because a lot of other women would rather be working here than in most of the other places, she'd been in a couple of them herself, they were dirty, with rats and vermin, and often with men who bothered you.

Some of the pieces of her and Catharina's story were beginning to make a pattern, like a quilt, and Josephina was moving them around and rearranging them a little every day. She saw clearly the pieces of Herr Andersen agreeing to help her because of Danne but not wanting Fräulein Hansen upstairs. She saw that the two Schmidts understood this and that it gave them a licence to treat her as 'trouble'. It was because those pieces fitted together that she and Catharina had to sleep behind the curtain by the cool back wall beyond the kitchen. And now, after talking to Willa, she saw that Danne's uncle had done the best he could to find a place for her to work that was better than most of the others, which fitted in next to the piece about his duty to Danne, of course.

And in addition, also from Willa, but mysteriously, as if it were a dangerous secret, she had another piece to fit in next to those ones, which had to do with the word *socialists*, because that's what Willa said the owners of the good sewing room were. But what did that mean? Was it a guild, like the cabinetmaker one Papa belonged to? Were they charitable religious men? And why was it banned, if it was to do with making garments or being a cotton merchant? What was wrong with that? Papa's guild was why he was so proud to be a Meister and have an apprentice and sometimes a journeyman at his command, and why he and Mutti wanted to be 'upstairs' and not in a Bauernhaus with the animals.

But she didn't want to ask Willa about it, because it made her nervous. At supper a few days later, she carefully and politely pushed the annoying word across the table towards Schmidt One's munching cheeks and her ears that also munched away below her cap. But the cheeks and ears just stopped munching briefly while the housekeeper gave her a hard look and tut-tutted. So it was no use asking the Schmidts, since they already considered her 'trouble'.

So, very casually, as she and Catharina and the young woman Maria whose sister worked in the sewing room were leaving the Kita on a chilly, rainy day, she asked her if Herr Johannes Paul was a 'socialist', and what did that mean? They were waiting for a moment on the threshold of the building before jumping over a big dirty puddle below the step while each holding one of Catharina's hands, but Maria let go of the hand and jumped by herself. Then the supervisor from upstairs pushed past with a testy 'If you please!' – and as he hurried away along the street Maria jumped back to help with Catharina and muttered, very fast, 'He's a stool pigeon, a stool pigeon, for goodness sake, don't you know that?' But she never explained what a stool pigeon was or why that frightened her – after all the man with herring and pickles on his breath did just sit on a stool and peck away at his notebook – and Josephina didn't want to ask again what it meant if you said the owner of the sewing room was a 'socialist', because Maria began to pretend she hadn't noticed her when she came in with Catharina in the mornings.

So that piece of the story patchwork continued to be missing, and in the end what did it matter? What mattered was that Herr Andersen had bothered to find a good place for her to work in even though she was 'trouble'. And what also mattered was that the sewing room had a Kita attached, where Catharina had soup and a nap, and where she also had a new friend called Alex, from whom she was learning some Italian words. The newest word was *arancia*, which meant orange – she was sharing her arancia with Alex, Catharina told Schmidt One, who permitted Josephina a brief little smile, despite tut-tutting at her the week before.

Perhaps Catharina would like to ride up top with the driver, suggested Herr Andersen. Since it was nice and sunny, even though quite cool? Would she like his scarf? Up she went with a squeal, and then Herr Andersen was holding the cab door open for Josephina. Schmidt One was approaching along the street, usually they'd be gone before she arrived at the house, and Josephina saw her look of shock as they clip-clopped past with Catharina perched up top. The cab smelled of stale tobacco which made Josephina wrinkle her nose. Herr Andersen noticed and pulled the window down. The air was chilly, with a coal-smoky tang because it was autumn, and the sunlight was misty and yellow.

Then he was looking at her very directly. 'Do you like the autumn?' he asked.

Of course, now she and Catharina had been at Herr Andersen's house since late spring, was this his meaning? 'Yes,' she said, 'I like the autumn very much, the colour of the trees, and thank you for your kindness, Herr Andersen, but perhaps now is the time for us to leave before it gets cold?'

Because the memory of last autumn was suddenly vivid in her mind but also because she couldn't think what else to say about leaving, she told Herr Andersen that last autumn she'd washed salt off the windows of the house at Sønderborg, how pleasant that had been, with the children playing and getting wet, and baby Otto in sunshine on the front step of the house.

Then, startling her so that she gave a jump on the seat,

he leaned forward and took both her hands and held them between his. He was wearing grey kid gloves, they were old and soft and, because she was surprised and looking down at their hands, she noticed a little tear between the thumb and forefinger of his left-hand glove.

'Let me tell you what I know, Josephina,' he said.

Was he going to talk about what happened last night, about Frau Andersen, about their daughter who died of the cholera? Was he going to reprimand her?

'I'm very sorry,' she said. 'I meant no harm.'

'Please, look at me, Josephina,' he said. 'I have seen that you can do that, you have a clear mind, you see clearly.'

His neck and shoulder were making small jerks, and these travelled down into his hands – and his eyes, when she looked at them, were blinking rather quickly, which was unexpected, as she remembered both his way of talking to her through Catharina but then his direct gaze.

'In one house I read about there was a basement room with a family of twelve people living in it, they slept in their work clothes on bags of wood shavings, they had torn up one of the floorboards to make a privy. There are lodging houses with five or six beds in a room and each bed will have four or five people in it. Such places are full of vermin. Of course, you will have seen people living where they can hide by the streets. In England there are those who call this social murder, and here there are some who would agree.'

Outside, on the driver's seat, Catharina was shouting, 'Giddy up!'

She'd learned that at the Kita.

The cobbles were getting bumpier on the rough streets away from Deichstrasse.

'We need to take care of Catharina,' said Herr Andersen.

He gave her hands a gentle squeeze and then folded his own in his lap. 'I shall talk to Herr Paul, whom you met, the owner of the sewing room.'

Then he was looking out the cab's open window – but at what, exactly, through his blinking?

He hadn't disagreed with Josephina that 'now is the time for us to leave before it gets cold.'

Dear Danne, and of course my darling sister Greta and my little nephews Finn and Otto

I miss you all very much, Catharina and I kiss you all many times, I know that writing this letter will make me cry.

Danne I hope you are not annoyed that I call you by your familiar name, it is strange for me to have been living for some months in the house of someone with the same name as you, of course I mean your kind uncle Herr Andersen. The truth is that I have seen very little of Herr Andersen and his wife only once, this has been different from the way we lived together in Sønderborg as a family thanks to your kindness, and so I think of you as my sister's dear man Danne, I hope you don't mind.

And so Danne I have to thank you from the bottom of my heart and from the bottom of Catharina's heart also, you should see her now, she knows so many words including Italian ones and has nice little friends at the Kita. The work in the sewing room has been fine, I had no difficulty with it, they say that it is a better room to work in than some others, it was your uncle Herr Andersen who arranged that, perhaps he has told you already. It has not been hard going to and from the sewing room, perhaps a little at first but we got used to it, Catharina likes the horsies at the tram and she usually has a nap so she isn't tired at the end of the day.

But now I have to tell you that Catharina and I have left Herr Andersen's house. This is not because we have been treated badly, of course I will always be grateful for Herr Andersen's help. It is because of something I didn't know when we came here and that you and Greta didn't tell me about, I think you had a good reason for respecting Herr Andersen's wishes. But now I know that Herr and Frau Andersen's daughter called Isolde died of the cholera ten years ago, she was seven years old so now she would be only a little younger than me. Frau Andersen told me this, it was the only time I saw her and the only time she spoke to me, we met by accident upstairs in the house where Catharina and I were not allowed to go, it was my fault. At first I didn't understand why we had to stay below by the kitchen, I thought it was because Herr Andersen knew what had happened with the Hauptmann and so once again what happened to me had spoiled what could happen next. But now I think Herr Andersen knew Frau Andersen could not live with a girl nearly the same age as her lost daughter, nor with a girl child as sweet as Catharina, because her grief has never healed, I saw that very clearly and will never forget how that poor mother looked at Catharina.

Herr Andersen did not tell us to go but he agreed once again to help when I said we would, that it was time. This was because I could no longer keep Catharina in that house where a mother was still grieving so much after ten years that after she saw my beautiful daughter and your niece she could not leave her room for many days and may not have left it yet even though we have been away from that house for some weeks now. Greta you know what it means to lose a child, and Mutti also of course, but I could not have imagined such terrible grief as Frau Andersen's. Danne, your good uncle loves you like a son, he gladly did what you asked for on my behalf, but now the situation at his house is too hard for him to continue with your request.

This is a very long letter with not much happy interest in it, I will write another one soon and tell you more about our life here in Hamburg. But for now I will tell you that I have moved on by my own wish, it is my own future that I want. I am now living with Catharina as the maid in a house known to the owner of the sewing room, Herr Johannes Paul. Herr Paul is well known in Hamburg as a businessman who believes in treating his workers well. Herr Andersen knows him and what he does and once again he spoke to Herr Paul for me. The house where we are now living and where I am working is called the Bloch House and is quite well known so it would seem, it is the house of Herr Wolf Bloch and his sister Fräulein Theodora Bloch, it is very different from Herr Andersen's house because a lot of people come here all the time for talking and dinner, and sometimes for early breakfast as well. They call me Josephina, and Fräulein Bloch asked me to call her Theodora, which I am getting used to, but for now I will write Fräulein Bloch.

Now I must also tell you that surely providence has brought me to the Bloch House, since I saw Herr Bloch and Fräulein Bloch at the sewing room on the day Danne's good uncle Herr Aksel Andersen took Catharina and me there for the first time. Now I know that they were looking at the sewing room to see how Herr Paul had organised it. Herr Bloch is the editor of a newspaper called Bürger Zeitung, where the conditions of places such as sewing rooms are reported, that is what they were doing. The Bloch House is by the lake in the middle of Hamburg, there are some large houses there but the Bloch one is quite small, however it has a nice little garden where Catharina can play. Sometimes she plays with her friend Alexandra whose mother and father quite often come to visit Herr Bloch and join the gatherings that happen here, now let me write it without hesitation, in the house of Theodora and Wolf Bloch.

It is a very busy life that I have here now, and different from life at Herr Andersen's, there is only a laundry woman who comes every week, a man who brings the coal and a cook who comes when there are large dinners, so I am doing most of the work. But I am glad to be here and I know I will learn a lot from what happens in this house especially what visitors are talking about.

Now I must stop because it is late and the nights are cold, the house has to be warm for Herr Bloch who has a weak chest. I need to feed the big stove and another one by the bedrooms.

I kiss you all, yes I did cry a little but please believe me when I say that Catharina and I are happy in our new situation.

Your sister and goddaughter Josephina and Catharina, this space is for Catharina's kiss when she wakes up in the morning.
Josephina

Elke

The clever cat that lived in the fodder stall next to the horse and killed mice and rats was sick it didn't have kittens even once this year so she didn't have to put all the kittens except a female in an oats sack and drown them in the stream below the cow meadow. Once she'd opened the sack and put it to dry on the gate the dead kittens would get caught in the reed stalks by the bank and in a day or two the eels would arrive and begin to eat them, it had to be done, in a few weeks the horse and the cow and her heifer would be coming inside for winter and there was the cat, it was the only one left this year, it was making a coughing sound and trying to retch up something, it was thin and there were those worm-seeds by its tail, really in winter they needed it and a couple more because mice and rats came in from outside, but it was useless now, its eyes were gummy and it didn't even try to get away from her when she hit it with the back of the dung shovel. Then she took it outside by the tail and threw it as far as she could into the furze beyond the orchard and when she turned around Johannes was there, he was grinning at her, my God he said, let that be a warning to me!

So then of course Elke who was quite glad that Johannes had seen her kill the cat because after all it showed that she could make a decision and do something about it, so then she demanded to know what her – he hoped! – future husband was thinking if he could even think which she doubted. He'd never seen the cats that came before this one, they just couldn't resist those wild tomcats from the woods could they? And all her pretty kitty daughters had run away after those wild boys in the woods and who could blame them? – though they tried to sneak back when it got cold but then their mother would fight them, and he thought his life was too complicated did he, Johannes, the fool? Well, he had some learning to do and she was willing to teach him, was he ready, was he really?

Then Johannes who was still grinning at her made his serious stop now face and she heard the cart with Lefty coming around the corner from the road and soon there it was with Papa. Of course its head was turned a bit to the left because of its missing eye and Papa dragging the reins across its neck as if Lefty needed to be told how to get to the grass in the meadow, but first the cart had to be unhitched and Johannes hurried to do that and tipped his cap at Papa who was giving Elke a look rather like Lefty's with his face turned half away from her as he hurried inside to see Mutti, he'd been to the fat apothecary at Ellerbeck and always came back in a bad mood. She'd wait until he'd had his supper and a glass of brandy before telling him she'd had to kill the cat, they'd need to find a new one or maybe a couple before the mice and rats took over, she could walk over and have a talk to the mill people in the morning. They always had some, they were hard to catch but if she got one she'd have to keep it inside and feed it plenty of milk and fish for a week otherwise it would just run back to the mill and the other cats over there. But she wouldn't add run back *not like some people* meaning Greta and Josephina, and wasn't that why Papa said Mutti needed more of that laudanum from Ellerbeck? Even though they all knew that wasn't the reason?

But soon she'd have to start drying off the last cow in her stall and feeding her heifer that would be ready for the bull next spring, there had to be enough dry hay feed for them.

She could measure how much was needed against the old marks on the wall of the feed bay, they had enough from cutting the orchard grass and half the fenced meadow, that was the other thing half the fence poles were falling down, and Johannes knew how to swing a scythe considering he was a cabinetmaker's apprentice and was supposed to be doing apprentice work, he had that nice step-forward and turn of his shoulder, it could get Papa into trouble making him do that but there was only just enough grain in the byre silo or perhaps not enough and how could they afford to buy more? And Johannes would have to fix the leaky fodder-stall roof soon or the hay would get mouldy, he'd already split the shingles for it.

But these were normal concerns and she was used to them, what she wasn't used to was the dull soft thickness of the shovel hitting the sick cat's body, it kept being there in her mind as she thought about the practical things, and the sound of it, not of the cat because it didn't make any sound at all which was also horrible in a way but the dull thud of the shovel not like the sound of metal hitting something but a different kind of sound, no hard ring to it just that dead thud.

Papa had gone inside to tend to Mutti and she should too but first she took hold of Johannes's thick strong arm and pulled it in close against herself for a moment and breathed the smell of work on his shirt and then walked quickly away from his expression that didn't know whether to be pleased or surprised, her husband-to-be, and he'd better have the balls on him to ask Papa soon, he'd better do that soon, remembering Papa's Lefty horse sideways look, he might be half blind to what was going on but he could see what he could see! But where would they be the three of them without her Johannes now that Mutti couldn't work at all and Papa had sold off all the good poplar coffin planks and was mostly doing piecework like fixing broken chairs brought home from the town, at least the silly crying boy had left and they had Johannes.

What, so you're back daughter you've come running back *not like some people*? was what Mutti's expression said the first time after she came back from Sønderborg towards the end of last summer but she didn't say it because Tante Elizabeth was with her. She'd driven Herr Mayer's new gig and brought a gift of three freshly plucked and drawn young cockerels out to the Bauernhaus – the cook was cleaning out their little flock before winter said Tante Elizabeth rather carefully – so Mutti had firstly to ignore the new gig and secondly thank Tante Elizabeth for the chickens because to notice the gig would have meant admitting how well Herr Mayer was doing compared to the Hansens, and not to have thanked Tante Elizabeth for the leggy cockerels would have suggested she resented the hint that their own fowl run was no good even though it was in the country and four times or more bigger than the Andersens' one over in Gaarden, and besides it would be Mutti who would make soup with the chickens, not 'the cook'. So then her mother's quick dry kiss and after it the quick rattle of a cough that she hid in her handkerchief. She didn't ask about Greta and Danne and her grandchildren in front of Tante Elizabeth as they drank verbena tea by the sunny north-west wall of the house looking down Kieler Förde the way Elke had just come home. Mutti might as well have been pretending her daughter had never left, she didn't ask about Josephina and Catharina and of course she didn't mention the Oma – she peeled an apple with the old bone-handled clasp knife she carried in her apron pocket and passed some slices around, she threw a peel over her shoulder for luck and laughed scornfully, the apples had been very good this year she said, looking past Elke who hadn't been there to pick them, unfortunately there were a lot of windfalls but this was a good one for eating, would Tante Elizabeth like some? Elke could fill a basket for her? Papa wasn't there, he'd gone with the boy to collect some furniture from the town, that's what he was mostly doing. There were people who appreciated the quality of his workmanship in the town of course.

Tante Elizabeth said yes she'd like to have some apples thank you, she might use them to make some sweet onion jam. She was trying not to show that she was noticing how Mutti was scratching herself and Mutti was trying not to show that she was doing it, and everything they were doing or saying including drinking their tea and looking down past the Schwentine but not at her, not at Elke who'd just come back the day before from seeing her sisters and their children and had slept that night with her cousin Mathilde, everything they were saying and doing including denying the scratching, and that she had just spent three months away in Sønderborg, everything they were doing and saying was hiding what was really happening and what really had to be spoken about. If she stayed there by the sunny wall a moment longer drinking verbena tea and talking about nothing she would begin to scream and tear the grass up by its roots!

Yes her heart was breaking for her poor little Mutti who'd become so thin and whose cough threw her poor thin shoulders up around her ears, but she went to get a basket of apples for Tante Elizabeth who kissed her and thanked her and gave her a close look in the eyes before climbing up into the gig. And then Elke untethered the horse which was a fine young chestnut gelding with a white face and two nice big eyes, she gave it a pat on the nose and it shook its mane for her, and then Tante Elizabeth flicked it with the reins and it went off towards the road at an easy trot that was saying it was happy to be doing that, and there was Tante Elizabeth's straight back that wasn't saying anything.

But Herr Mayer and I, we can't have any more children, was what Tante Elizabeth had told her weeping the night before after Elke had walked from the port to the house in Gaarden and after Mathilde had gone unwillingly off to bed, doesn't your mutti know what a blessing it is to have her daughters and her grandchildren, why is she making herself sick with those thoughts she has, my God, she thinks we Mayers are lucky, why can't she see that she is blessed, she and my stupid brother both of them, how can we cleanse them of the bitter taste they walk around with in their mouths? Look at their expressions, they've forgotten how to rejoice and be happy, they and my husband as well for that matter, as if everything that has happened was that little Josephina's fault, well bravo to her, she has her own mind, who knows where she will end up that one, not in this pigsty of gossip in any case, and bravo to her! said Tante Elizabeth again, bravo! with a smile that was catching the tears she had to lick away, bravo! I think she is lucky that one and I think she will be happy too.

Well yes of course Elke hoped her little Schwesterchen would be happy, but she was lucky? After what happened to her? And was her kind Tante Elizabeth so unlucky that she measured her niece who'd been raped by the Junker to be luckier? And what about her, Elke, who had now to go back to the Bauernhaus *die Suppe auslöffeln* to swallow what her papa's and mutti's anger would put in front of her? There was a rattle of heavy rain against the windows and just at that moment Herr Mayer came in with a huff from the stable at the back of the house, he was beating his wet hat against his leg and exclaiming in a loud voice about the new gig what a fine thing it was and Elizabeth should take it for a drive in the morning so long as the rain had passed over and the new young gelding also was a good one with a calm nature! – and then he saw Elke. Well, well so you're back he said with a change in his enthusiastic tone, and Tante Elizabeth was quickly removing the traces of her tears of happiness for Josephina or sadness for herself, who could tell? So how was everything in Sønderborg Herr Mayer wanted to know, the new baby? By which he meant Danne's and Greta's Otto, not Josephina's Catharina, and perhaps Elke had met with Herr Steuerer Lande and Frau Lande in Flensburg or had she come directly to Kielerhafen? But of course he didn't have to ask that, he knew that she'd come by way of Flensburg because Danne had made the arrangements two weeks before she left Sønderborg on that day she would never forget after the picnic at Dybbøl that she would also never forget when Josephina had said 'I don't know when I'll see you again perhaps never because I have to keep going.' Yes she said to Herr Mayer, the family in Sønderborg are well they send their love to you and Tante Elizabeth and hope to see you and Mathilde before too long, and Josephina and Catharina are well too and they send you their love also – not wishing to be disrespectful but feeling some heat rising up her neck. Herr Mayer nodded and went to pour himself a schnapps, he had his back to her so that was that, but what she knew at that moment was she had to go to Faulstrasse to the house of Hauptmann von Zarovich because nobody else would do it, not Papa or Herr Mayer and even dear kind Tante Elizabeth had made what happened there into a story about Josephina's luck!

But now there was Mutti at the table by the fireplace with her arm raised and the big cleaver in her hand, she still had the strength or the anger to bring the blade down with a good whack on the cockerels, she quartered all three and threw them in the stockpot, get me an onion and some thyme daughter she said, what was she standing around like that for, hadn't she come home after all, wasn't she here now, and some carrots? So then she went outside to get a sprig of thyme from the bush at the end of the vegetable garden, it wasn't well kept and there were signs the hens had got into it, they'd scratched up around the carrots, that would be her morning's work tomorrow no doubt after milking the cow, and there weren't many bunches of onions hanging inside by the fodder stall, and so she 'had come home after all', she was 'here now' – but it was as though what she'd done by going to Sønderborg and taking the Oma to Josephina, and Mutti's anger at that and at her returning in the Mayers' new gig with her papa's sister who thought herself so high and mighty, and these three miserable cockerels that were good for nothing but the stockpot, and so on and so on, daughter! daughter this and daughter that! It was as though Mutti's anger as she stopped with the cockerels and sat in a chair breathing hard and waved her hand at 'daughter' to chop the onions, it was as though her anger had simply swept away the time between 'daughter' stealing away to Sønderborg with the Oma and her coming back, the whole three months! As though the sun had set and then risen and there was 'daughter' in the morning as usual to remind Mutti of all the reasons she didn't want to be where she was a day longer, but what could she do? – only of course she didn't say that, she didn't really say anything, she talked about the cockerels and the soup!

But nor had Mutti said anything nine months later when 'daughter' took Lefty and rode over to Tante Elizabeth's to say goodbye again to Josephina and Catharina the night before they were to catch the train to Hamburg, after which as Josephina said back at Dybbøl in the lovely summer above the Alsund that Elke would never forget, 'I don't know when I'll see you again perhaps never because I have to keep going', and yes she did, she just went, that little one whose laughter always brought on an attack of the hiccups, but first she sang 'Wie traulich war das Fleckchen' for Mathilde without stopping, not once, and no tears.

But after the return from Sønderborg and the preparation of the soup there came Papa with the boy, they unloaded some chairs from the sprung cart, they'd passed Tante Elizabeth in her new gig on the road but Papa didn't say any more than that, 'Passed my sister on the road,' looking at Elke.

'Yes,' she said, 'Tante Elizabeth brought me out.' And then, 'They are fine, Papa,' though he hadn't asked and just nodded.

But after the return from Faulstrasse, which was between coming back from Sønderborg after saying goodbye to Josephina and Catharina and from Tante Elizabeth's after saying goodbye to them all over again, *that* time when she told Papa what she'd done because she had to and he had to know what he should have known by going to the Hauptmann's house himself – how the maid Clara had burned the nightgown because it was spoiled with blood, his daughter Josephina's blood! – she thought at first he was about to bellow like the cow when her calf is taken away and perhaps he was, but what he bellowed to her face was that now there was no chance of compensation because the evidence . . . ! But she didn't want to ask, compensation for whom? Because it was enough that she'd seen him have the same thought himself and that he was even ashamed because he'd seen that she'd seen it, so she just added that the Junker was dead, his horse had fallen on him and crushed him to death with great pain so she'd been told, and his widow and baby had gone to Vienna – she didn't say you could have found this out for yourself, Papa, but she saw that he'd had that thought as well. So that was when he abandoned his authority over her and left her to run the farm and so never complained or rebuked her when she took Lefty and rode over to Gaarden to say goodbye to Josephina and Catharina perhaps for the last time, and after that the crybaby boy ran away, he was useless anyway said Papa.

And then Johannes came up from the mill where Papa had seen him doing woodturning work for Herr Tiesel. He kept his stall tidy and didn't hurt himself with the tools, he could swing a scythe as well, he was quiet-spoken and understood what a joke was, and Elke soon thought, well we shall see.

She was going to get a new cat or two she told Mutti in the morning when she took in her tea with honey, she'd had to kill the old one yesterday because it was too sick to take care of the mice and rats, she'd go down to the mill after milking and see if she could catch a couple, she'd take a little fresh milk to tempt the cats and some eggs for Frau Tiesel. Mind the fat old witch doesn't eat you up, said Mutti with a laugh that was also a cough, she was measuring the drops of laudanum into her tea, Elke counted fifteen. Then she took a swallow and looked at Elke – Killed the old cat, neh? Daughter? – but she was smiling when 'daughter' kissed her dry cheek. It's sunny, Mutti, she told her, you should sit outside in the nice sunshine.

There were some eggs in the usual places by the fodder stall inside and outside under the furze fence around the vegetable garden, and also in the hen shelter where there was a spread-out sullen broody hen with a clutch under her – a bit late sister it's getting cold hadn't you noticed? The self-important rooster advanced sideways towards her leg in a stupid aggressive manner so she gave it a good kick that made it flap off squawking, and then she put some straw in a big basket for the eggs and a sack to cover the cats when she'd caught them and the fresh milk in a corked bottle and a tin bowl to put it in – maybe she could talk to Herr Tiesel about getting some more oats, even some sweepings, she could come down with the sprung cart later? Outside in the sun by the big door to the Bauernhaus, Johannes was holding a blade to a length of wood on the lathe there, the shavings curling down on to the ground, she could see his knee going up and down above the treadle strap so steady the way it just kept on going it was nice to watch, but he couldn't look up at her, and there was Mutti in sunshine by the pear tree, was she asleep? She was going to catch a nice little cat she said to Johannes as she passed him, and then his eyes did lift to her under his thick dark eyebrows before he bent back to his work, Puss puss he said to the piece of wood. The morning train had gone some time ago so the bustle of loading up flour would be finished and the cats would be enjoying the sunshine undisturbed. The clouds were hardly moving beyond the trees down there, the leaves were almost all gone now and those big pale clouds with slowly rolling shapes would soon turn the colour of dirty tin and fill with snow, Johannes had better keep his promise to speak to Papa at supper or he'd be feeling the cold all alone in his stall!

The sweet young heifer trotted over from where she and the cow were grazing together down the bottom of the meadow, she liked Elke to rub the hard bone between her eyes. In spring when she came on season the bull would be walked over to her from the Webers' place at Wellingdorf and then after a while her calf would go to pay for the bull, she would bellow but then stop when she got used to Elke's hands milking her, season after season it was the same, just the same or nearly so regular and steady like Johannes's knee under the lathe, just the same or nearly so as long as she could remember, except for the knee of course and of course when Greta went to Sønderborg, and then Josephina to somewhere only she would know about when it happened but of course she would tell them. When Greta went to Sønderborg it was to expand the sameness and make it more profitable but when Josephina went that plan was spoiled just like the nightgown she'd made for the Junkfrau, or so most people thought so it seemed, but meanwhile here she was, here was Elke walking over to the mill to get a new cat and not for the first time, and there was the young heifer with her head down again enjoying the last of the fresh grass before winter, and that wasn't unusual either and Elke still liked it and also the coarse rub of the heifer's brow against her knuckles.

She'd brought some fresh eggs, Elke said to Frau Tiesel who was sitting outside under a wide hat by the house door next to the mill, would Frau Tiesel mind if she caught a nice young cat or two, theirs had got sick and she'd had to kill it, they needed a new one or perhaps two before winter drove the mice and rats inside. And she hoped Frau Tiesel was in good health, and her husband as well? And that business was good? Frau Tiesel was spread out on her chair rather like the broody hen back at the Bauernhaus and her expression was also sullen – So, she enquired, were they satisfied with that Johannes that her father had persuaded to leave the mill and go up to the house of Meister Hansen the esteemed cabinetmaker and master of coffins? Was that Johannes living up to their expectations and the expectations of Meister Hansen? And indeed of Frau Hansen, and how was she? She hoped so, and that Frau Hansen was better and recovering from the disappointment of her youngest daughter leaving the family, because they would know by now that Johannes was not to be trusted, he was a traveller with no family and no assets, he would be gone by next week, see how easily he was persuaded to go up the hill, did they wish to heap disappointments on poor Frau Hansen?

The mill wheel was sloshing and groaning away down at the race, the mill hands were shouting happy insults at each other while hoisting grain sacks, and for a moment Elke considered an insult of her own, for example didn't Frau Tiesel find herself overstuffed not just with cakes and flour dumplings but with 'uncharitable thoughts', the term old Pastor Köhler had liked to use in advance of the wooden smacking spoon, and too bad she didn't have a wooden smacking spoon or better still the heavy dung-shovel within reach at that moment as Frau Tiesel looked at her with a what-are-you-going-to-do-now expression? Well she wasn't going to let the fat old witch eat her up that was certain – she thanked Frau Tiesel kindly for her advice but 'as it happens' it had not been her papa Meister Hansen who had persuaded Johannes to come up to the Bauernhaus, he had persuaded himself and without finding it hard to do so it would seem, he was a steady man with a mind of his own and many useful skills if not assets as such and no doubt he would stay as long as he chose to as Frau Tiesel knew he was capable of, and where would Frau Tiesel like her to put the eggs? – not somewhere unmentionable was what she thought while Frau Tiesel adjusted her wide hat and said take them in to the maid, there had better not be any old ones and there were some cats living by the stable she could take as many as she wanted if she could catch any, they were a cunning lot those cats but then the Hansens were clever people also were they not?

Yes they were you old shit-sack witch, and it wasn't long before the two mill hands hoisting grain sacks had added some fresh mullet to the enticing milk and there were two young Katzen in the basket – they made a fuss at first but soon went quiet with only occasional humming moans and groans under the sack. And how is that Johannes, asked one of the mill hands, you'd better look out for him girl he's trouble that one! Ah said Elke, trouble, and what do you boys know about trouble? Your trouble is sitting over there like a great black toad, if she sees you helping me with the cats she'll leap over here and squash you! No but she was harmless that Frau Tiesel said the boys with sorrowful expressions, no fun to be had there, too bad she can't even catch blowflies with her tongue that one however much she waves it around.

Supper time, it had better be supper time, supper time today, she told Johannes as she walked past him with the humming basket of cats. He was holding up a freshly turned chair leg and looking at it with one eye shut – he kept the eye shut but swivelled his head to watch her go past and didn't change his expression, 'Genau,' he said. So it wouldn't just be her plan for cabbage soup with dumplings that would be 'on the table' later together with the mullet the mill boys had given her, they caught them in nets where the tide came up the Schwentine below the mill and she would poach them very fresh with some capers and parsley, Papa's favourite, and potatoes too – because Papa would have to be in a good mood when Johannes told his true story at supper, how he was 'a traveller with no family and no assets' according to Frau Tiesel, did Papa know that?, and what apprentice term had he and Johannes agreed on before that 'traveller' might indeed 'be gone by next week'? Along with the promise about what he was going to say to Papa 'when the time was right'? The cats were annoyed and so was Elke because she knew less than she thought she had about that man Johannes who'd only ever told her he was travelling not as a journeyman but simply because he liked to and because he learned about places and people and how to do different work. She put the tin dish with some fresh milk and the remains of the cut-up mullet from the mill in the boarded holding pen next to the fodder stall and then tipped the cats out of the basket and shut the gate, they flew about complaining and trying to climb the walls for a while but then sat still with the tips of their tails twitching, then finally went to the milk and fish, yes that's how it was – what looked like a prison at first might soon appear differently and indeed seem desirable after a day or two, but if she was to finish her jobs and then make the supper she would first have to unclench her fists which were gripping her annoyance as if there were buckets of it that she had to carry somewhere and do something with. She carried the buckets of annoyance out to the garden and made herself useful there for a while in the fresh autumn sunshine until it was time for her to begin supper.

And so then Johannes walked past the kitchen area twitching his nose at her, he'd washed at the pump and his black hair was dripping down the shirt on his back, 'Aha, supper time,' he said, 'is it not?'

Then they ate for a while, she'd got two nice little cats Elke told Mutti and Papa, and how was Frau Tiesel asked Mutti, she was glad to have the eggs said Elke, and Johannes was looking at her – *Meister Hansen*, she saw his lips beginning to shape her father's name just before he said it.

'Meister Hansen and Frau Hansen!' said Johannes boldly standing up and moving his chair back firmly, he had wiped his mouth and beard with his fingers, 'I want to thank you for your kindness and hospitality these past weeks, I don't believe I have said so before or if I have then not often enough.' Then he paused and Elke's heart shut but not in time to stop a cold draught entering her body – what, was he announcing his wish to 'be gone by next week'? They had trusted him, Johannes told them with one hand on his heart and the other holding the edge of the table, his voice was low and quiet now and he seemed certain about what he was telling them, he was an orphan with no family that he knew about since he had grown up by himself first in an orphanage in Göttingen in the south of Hanover where he was told that his father was a Frenchman as a result of which he was sometimes treated harshly, so he left the orphanage when he was about twelve years old and worked in stables in the town and then left Göttingen which was a nice enough town but one for which he had no love, and so it went for some years as they could see since he was no longer young and inexperienced and he considered himself a free man 'with diverse skills', a pause, including reading and writing and numbers.

He'd brought Lefty inside to his stall after Papa came back

from the town with a cartful of broken furniture, and the sound of the horse grinding steadily at his feed and stamping a hoof from time to time was what was happening in the silence before Johannes went on in his level voice to say to Papa and Mutti, who had both stopped chewing, that despite his circumstances he hoped that Meister and Frau Hansen and indeed Fräulein Hansen would think well of his service and abilities and indeed not think any less of him because he came with little besides his skills and his willingness to help them, not that he expected them to be grateful, it was he who was grateful for the opportunity they had given him to work for them and show them what he could do – the word 'help' had made Papa's mouth open indignantly but he shut it again before an objection came out of it because Johannes then said that he hoped he might respectfully ask for their daughter Fräulein Hansen's 'hand in marriage' – he said 'hand in marriage' with the first sign of discomfort since he'd begun as if its formality was awkward for him and didn't come easily from his planned words to his mouth and then out into speech.

Elke's heart opened again and a warm draught came in this time, it went up into her face that Mutti was looking at without smiling, she could feel that her face was red whereas Mutti's was very white, was it whiter than usual? It seemed as though Mutti was about to say something because her mouth opened and shut quickly many times with a little clapping sound of her lips but then she pushed her chair over on to the floor with a crash and hurried away out of sight into her and Papa's room – Go to your mother, Papa told her without taking his eyes off Johannes who was still standing with one hand holding the edge of the table. As she was opening the door to Mutti's room Johannes said in his even voice that it would be an honour to become a member of Meister Hansen's family and then with more warmth and quickly before she could shut the door again that he truly dearly loved Fräulein Hansen the daughter of Meister and Frau Hansen, she was strong and beautiful and a 'lily of the field'.

'A lily of the field' – it was dark but Elke found Mutti's body curled on the bed, and curled herself behind the thin wheezing back holding it close and also holding close what Johannes had said, 'truly dearly loved' and 'lily of the field' – 'Mutti', she said against her mother's little sharp shoulder blade, 'Mutti, I love that man, I love him.'

Dearest sister Greta and Herr Andersen and also Josephina, I don't know where you are now little sister in Hamburg somewhere, Greta please send this letter to my Schwesterchen if you know where she is residing she knows I miss her and of course also Finn Otto and Catharina I hope all those little lilies of the field are well and happy. This letter has bad and good news in it, the bad news first I am sorry. Our dear Mutti died she was so thin and not able to breathe or talk without coughing. The Apothek came from Ellerbeck and listened to her back he said her lungs were filled with poisonous liquid, what about the laudanum asked Papa, too late for that said the fat monster and Papa threw him out of the house I don't blame him, he has cost Papa a lot of money and we have very little of it. Mutti went to bed on an evening that I will tell you more about soon and she never got up again, she died a day and a morning later. I had to take her clothes off and make her put on a nice warm nightgown the one with roses embroidered on the front that you made for her Josie when you were quite young about twelve I think, she didn't speak again after that night except for saying your name when she saw the nightgown I'm sure you want to know that little sister because there was so much anger in this house after what happened on Faulstrasse and perhaps our Mutti had learned what anger is for at last and what it is not right for. I have to tell you that her body was a pitiful thing so thin and scratched all over its front, that was what the laudanum did to her Papa thinks. He is very sad mourning for his dear wife day and night and will not sleep in the room he and Mutti used for many years, he has made a bed for himself in one of the stalls just like an apprentice or a journeyman would, he goes there after supper and makes no sound at all but keeps working during the day just the same as he always did without any change but with no joy in his labour. Mutti is buried in the graveyard down at Pastor Köhler's Kapelle, of course it isn't Pastor Köhler's anymore but that's how we still think of the place, the new pastor is quite young with a nice little family of boys and girls, his wife looks after the school which will be a good thing but more about that soon. Mutti is buried next to her mother our oma, all three of us daughters as well of course as Papa are named as mourners on her headstone. Josephina I hope you will be happy to know that and forgive our mutti for her anger, I do believe it was what took her life in the end but now as Pastor Kolnick the new pastor said she is in a place of forgiveness where our sins are washed away. Tante Elizabeth and Herr Mayer and Mathilde and also the miller's family Tiesel came to the funeral and burial and the Weber family from over in Wellingdorf and also Johannes who has been working for Papa and was a very steady and able man in this time of need. It was a cold day but the sun was shining and the air was fresh I kept thinking it would be good for Mutti's health that is what happens when someone dies you can't believe it. Tante Elizabeth brought some food and wine over from Gaarden, we had a little Hinsicht by the pear tree where Mutti liked to sit after she got sick and where Oma liked to sit when she was alive and where Greta and Danne's marriage breakfast happened I'm sure you remember, also we planted a verbena by the grave I hope it lasts out the winter and grows strong next spring it was Mutti's favourite tea as you know. Now for the good news I hope you don't think it disrespectful to put them together like this but the bad and the good news touch each other on the evening that Mutti began to die quickly from her sickness. It was supper time when Johannes asked Papa if he could marry me, we two had talked about it but not to Papa or Mutti until then. I think it was a shock to Mutti who always hoped that my husband would be a successful man like Herr Danne Andersen or Herr Mayer over in Gaarden that would lift her out of her life of common toil as she said, but Johannes has no family and no assets other than the skills of which he is proud and rightly so in my opinion and I love him with all my heart for his honesty since he has never pretended to be more than he is that is an orphan who cannot know his family and whose assets in this hard world are what he can do which includes sitting with me his future wife to help with this letter. We will be married in the spring by Pastor Kolnick and I hope that my sisters and their families will come to our wedding we will send you a proper notice when the arrangements are done, we can also have a remembrance at Mutti's grave at the same time. And now I will finish my letter I am happy to end with the good news. Your sister Elke with love and from Papa also whose hand has pressed down on this page.

Greta

Dear sisters and also Papa
And also Catharina, perhaps we shall see you again before too long sweet child, I hope you remember your cousins Finn and Otto and your Tante Greta.

This is a short letter because I will write something like it twice and send one copy to Josie in Hamburg with your letter Elke and your bad and good news.

I have to start with the good news. Of course we are all grieving for the loss of our dear Mutti but we have to go forward with our lives and the lives of our children and now Elke has a path to happiness with this Johannes Somebody, please tell us his complete name! Elke I hope this man will make you happy, he had better do so or he will suffer the wrath of your sisters! I kiss you Elke and hold you close for a long time, you have borne much of the grief and work caused by our poor Mutti's sickness, but now that is over and you can begin another part of your life. Danne wishes you well also but he says that man Johannes Somebody had better know what he is doing because our sister Elke is like a squall, she will tip him over if he doesn't watch out.

I was very sad to hear of Mutti's death and that she is now buried down at the old graveyard, please kiss Papa for me and tell him we are very sorry for the rift that has come between us, it meant he and Mutti would not come to Otto's baptism and christening but also that Danne and I and our children were not near Mutti as her sickness got worse, and could not be at her side at the end or at her funeral, we didn't know until too late. Papa of course we will all come to your daughter Elke's wedding and to visit Mutti's grave, I hope that the wound between us will heal then, please do not forbid this, you cannot, we have lives to get on with and enjoy including the lives of all your grandchildren Papa.

Josie has written to say that she has left the house of Danne's uncle Herr Aksel Andersen in Hamburg and is now living at what is called the Bloch House also in Hamburg, she is happy there and so is Catharina, but she will write to you about her situation I am sure, and perhaps we will see her and Catharina at your and Johannes Somebody's wedding Elke, it's surely not hard for her to catch the train. It would be such a joy for us all to be together again. Josie's address in Hamburg is Haus Bloch, An der Alster, St Georg, she can tell us all about it when we meet God willing.

As for us here in our nice Sønderborg, we are all well thank God, no one got sick this winter past, it was a hard one again with too much ice in the Alsund. The Bückling yard has gone at last thank God I say but Danne is grieving for it, poor man, but other business is good enough, Finn is beginning to learn reading and writing over at fru Jepsen's, he doesn't like it but too bad!

And now I will stop and send this to my lucky sister Elke with many kisses, and will write another one like it to send to our little Josie in Hamburg, together with Elke's letter sent here just days ago. Elke kiss Papa for me and give my best wishes to Johannes Somebody, remind him that I am the eldest sister and he will have to answer truthfully the questions I am preparing for him!

Daughter and sister

Greta

Beth and Frank

None the worse for wear, Frank, and back in his last-night's possie with its view across the plateau to Ngāuruhoe, a well-cleared breakfast plate pushed to one side of the trestle table with flickering sunlight on it this morning because of clouds racing across the sky, and his sparse hair blowing about as well. The lips that he extended in a cautious, trembling tube towards his coffee were determined, nonetheless, as were the glasses halfway down his nose – he was trying to read a newspaper folded against the breeze and held down on the table with his saucer and free hand.

'Bloke here reckons all immigrants should be sent home, name of McGregor, couldn't agree more, bloody Celts!' He held his cheek up sideways for her kiss – he'd shaved, and there was a hint of classic aftershave, bit like the one Noel used to have – Tabac? 'Cona coffee,' he said, making a show of smacking his lips, 'god it's good, and plenty more where it came from, have you ordered? They do a bloody excellent mushroom omelette.'

Beth was having English Breakfast tea with some Vogel's toast and marmalade. 'Tea and toast,' she said. 'Creature of habit.'

'Did you know,' Frank said, sipping and swallowing with a lip-smack, 'that Cona coffee with a "c" comes from Kona coffee with a "k" which is an *arabica* from the slopes of the Big Island of Hawaii? Behold our multicultural immigrant breakfast, the humble Italian *frittata*, the *arabica* via Hawaii, and the Cona vacuum brewer from our always ingenious Germans, your tea from the imperialist British, your marmalade from a place where oranges grow – Portugal let's say, or the Mediterranean via Arabs, Islamists for sure – and your fermenty toast the bloody Germans again, Herr Vogel.' He made a show of folding the newspaper shut across McGregor's letter-to-the-editor. 'Back home where you came from, McGregor!'

Frank's mock-pedant routine was probably to wind her up because of her own tendencies, so she didn't bite.

But he'd spotted her notebook. 'Travel diary?' he said, creeping his fingers towards it. 'Give us a look?'

'Family reunion notes,' said Beth, and he withdrew his fingers as if from something red-hot. Then a cattle truck tore past on the highway, leaving a whiff of sheep shit in its wake.

'Off somewhere they hadn't counted on called lamb shanks. Bad karma,' Frank said, but then put his arm around her shoulders and gave her a hug. 'We can stop doing this now if you like.'

'Doing what?'

'Obsessing on about all that reunion stuff, families, who was what to whom, etcetera, you know. Guess what I did last night?'

'You went out more or less completely pissed, as I recall.'

'Yes, I did. I went and sat with the dog back there. He was glad. We shared the moon, and an occasional fart. We were just in the moment. He moved his nostrils and ears a bit. After a while I told him about Lizzie being pregnant and that she knew who the father was, young guy called John, she thought he'd be a good enough dad. Then we just sat there a bit more. Then I came back and had a damn good sleep. Your light was still on.'

'Good enough?'

'It doesn't matter. She's a smart girl, Lizzie, she'll love the kid and it'll have a great young mum for a long time, how lucky is that. Maybe young John will be in the picture and maybe not, let's hope things go well for him too.'

In the notebook by her elbow were the twenty-five stanzas of the German poet Wolf Bloch's *Zum Gedächtnis* memorial to the martyrs of the 1871 Paris Commune's final bloody paroxysm in the Père-Lachaise cemetery in Paris, a '(very) rough translation' filled with hyperbole and words like 'dismal', 'crazed', 'despair', 'place of death', 'sweat and blood', and 'longings of mankind are awakened/ In the fresh bosom of youth', as well as 'valiant courage' and 'ultimate beauty' and quite a bit of 'third estate' – stirring stuff but also, this morning, next to Frank's night with Hotel Dog, a bit dispiriting.

Beth left the notebook shut where it was.

'Heard you having a good laugh on the phone before you went out,' she said. 'Not that I could hear what you were saying or who to. But was that your granddaughter? Lizzie? Must be a hard case.'

Frank took a careful sip of his Cona from Kona and shook his head. His smile was careful and almost tender.

'I was talking to Helen.'

Helen was his wife of some forty years, a librarian in Rockhampton – Frank used to skite about her passion for native plants, she'd written an often-reprinted field guide to the northern end of the Great Dividing Range. They had three kids and one more each from previous marriages that went phut early; she'd died ten years ago, heavy smoker, lung cancer.

He wasn't kidding.

'I don't need a phone to talk to her, Beth.'

Josephina

'We zigzagged,' said Herr Bloch, making a zigzag movement with his palms joined together – his hands ended up to the left of his head, pointing at the ceiling. 'Like perverse Ostjuden, from east to west and a little bit north as well, zig-zag-zig-zag, from the stetl to the boulevard, as we say, from Moravia to Freiberg where our beloved Kinderfrau turned back. We never saw her again – my mother said I cried for weeks on end.' He took his spectacles off with a flourish to wipe imaginary tears from his eyes.

There were tall windows overlooking the little garden – Catharina and Alex ran past with muffled shrieks, and then Signora Martignetti, more slowly, with a parasol, as Josephina bent to take away Herr Bloch's soup plate. The signora paused and gave a wave at the window, and shrugged – surely she'd like to come inside again soon, for some more lunch?

'Then after a while rather suddenly to Leipzig,' Herr Bloch continued his story, 'where we learned proper German and in my case how to cough politely in company' – he coughed politely with a rattle into his napkin – 'then to Hanover where our dear papa lost all his money as usual, then to the charming unknown town of Uelzen where he began all over again as a clothier out of sight of his creditors.'

Signor Martignetti was a nice-looking man with grey hair at his temples and a neat beard that he held in one hand while listening to Herr Bloch's story, which he seemed to be enjoying. With his free hand he was crumbling a bread roll and making a pile of the pieces without looking at it. He'd told his and Signora Martignetti's story first, in strongly accented German with quite a lot of Italian words that he asked for help with, while they all ate their Schnitzen and drank a glass of white wine. He seemed to be a more serious man than Herr Bloch, who was telling his story as a series of self-mocking jokes – he kept his eyes on Martignetti, and Josephina already knew from experience that they were what Elke called 'laughing eyes' because he crinkled them up at the corners, the kind Elke always liked best – she always said never to trust a man whose eyes don't crinkle, little sister, never, it's the best rule, but what would she know.

'And Uelzen was where our mother decided, again perversely, that she would never speak German, only Yiddish, and where, in spite of that, Theodora and I finally finished our schooling, because our father had moved with the times as he said, being the son of an enlightened Haskalah and by learning about capital the hardest way, by bankrupting himself.'

Herr Bloch raised his glass to Theodora who was putting pieces of the cook's Sauerbraten on plates and passing them to Josephina to take around the table. There was also a potato casserole and some braised red cabbage with onion and apple which the guests could help themselves to – surely now she should go outside to mind the children while Signora Martignetti returned for her lunch?

'Fräulein Bloch was the top of her class,' said Herr Bloch. 'Her little brother, however, preferred the safety of mediocrity – also wise because, as you can see, whereas my sister is a beautiful woman, I am not *sportlich* and the Lutherans liked to draw attention to their superior health by pushing me over into puddles.'

'I was top in Latin,' Theodora said with a tsk tsk. 'Nobody

else was interested.' She wagged her finger across the table. 'It's not true that Wolf was mediocre, only that the Rektor would not permit a Jew to take first places.' She blew her brother a kiss. 'Also, he was disrespectful.'

Now Josephina was filling new glasses with the Italian red wine that Signor Martignetti had brought four bottles of – she thought she might try some later, with the cook, to see what it was like.

Herr Bloch took a sip and lifted his glass to Signor Martignetti this time. 'Il sole del sud!' Then they all raised their glasses and repeated what he'd said, it was Italian.

'Ai compagni!' said Signor Martignetti with enthusiasm, and they all repeated it, more Italian, and drank again, and then one more time as Signora Martignetti had come in and demanded to raise her own glass – the two little girls were having their lunch with the cook.

'And now,' said Herr Bloch, 'to finish my story, which has gone on too long, you must know that a famous poet was born in Uelzen, his name was Hermann Hölty, a Lutheran pastor – his terrible poems about nature were sticky like Schnecken with extra syrup. It was because of him, and being pushed into puddles, and my father's thorough researches into the pitfalls of capital, and my Haskalah grandfather's desire to go west and a bit north, that I became a socialist.'

Everybody except Josephina laughed heartily at Herr Bloch's story, especially the ending. Signor Martignetti drummed on the table with both hands, making the crockery rattle, but Theodora was looking at her with a little smile.

'Sit down, Josephina, please,' she said. 'Please have something to eat. And please, tell us your story.'

What do I know and how do I know it?

All the eyes around the table had been fixed on her. They were so clever, those people, their stories were the stories of clever people, they understood each other's stories and especially the jokes, and they had ways of knowing that she didn't know about. She knew that when she shut her eyes into Catharina's hair what she *saw* wasn't the hair but the song she sang about it and into it, 'Die Lorelei', the same one Papa had sung into her hair when she was a little girl – but how was it possible to see a song? What kind of knowing was that?

But that was where she'd begun her story back in Hamburg at the lunch table – begun with Papa singing into her hair, in the Bauernhaus, where it was warm by the fire in winter. That was where she'd begun to know. It was that place, with her papa's growly voice in it and the story of the girl with beautiful hair and the poor sailor on the river below, that she saw in her own hair when Papa sang, and now in Catharina's hair when she sang to her, with her eyes shut, about Die Lorelei.

But now her papa was kneeling in front of her and pressing his head against her. His arms hung down, and it was his thick grey hair she was looking down into – he'd washed it at the pump not long before but it still had some bits of straw in it and she picked them out while he wept against her.

'Get up, Papa,' she said. 'Here is your granddaughter, here is Catharina.'

Catharina was hiding behind her, and the others were all looking on. Elke had big tears rolling down her cheeks but a wide, quivering grin in the middle of them, Tante Elizabeth had a scornful expression for her brother even though she too was crying, Mathilde was holding Tante Elizabeth's hand tightly and looking serious and grown-up because she'd been taken out of school for the day, and the tall man with long black hair was standing somewhat away, looking at his feet, Johannes Somebody.

Yes, she knew everything here except Johannes Somebody – the gentle fall of the land away down to the marshy reeds by the Schwentine, the trees with fresh new green leaves further up where the mill was, the water of the fjord that had a quivering pattern on it, the pattern that seemed to be at once moving and without movement, a shimmer, always a wonder in her childhood, the high streaks of mare's-tail clouds in what was called a mackerel sky above the sea down beyond Laboe that meant it would get windy later, the nearby puck-puck of the hens picking around the yard, the people, the musty smoke smell of her papa's hair as he began unsteadily to stand up while holding on to her arm – she knew everything but as if it was a memory and not as if she was there inside the knowing, inside the now place of it.

Papa had wiped away his tears and now he was holding one of Catharina's hands between both of his – he was very pleased to meet her at last, he told her, did she know that this was where her mutti had lived when she was a little girl the same age as her, she had a favourite chicken that she liked to carry around and the chicken let her do it but sometimes it gave her a peck? Had her mutti told her about the chicken? Catharina shook her head, she was keeping a close watch on this man who had just been kneeling in front of her mutti with his head against her – Ah, he said to her, opening his red eyes very wide, you have a direct look just like your mutti's, and Kornblume eyes as well, the same as hers!

And then Tante Elke was scooping her up and telling her and her mutti that this was Johannes Franzose, and Herr

Franzose kissed her on the cheek and Mutti as well, and everybody began to clap – But where was Mutti's favourite chicken, Catharina wanted to know.

Had it been a happy childhood, Theodora had asked. Oh yes, she had two big sisters and an oma who showed her how to make Strikkelise, and she'd had a favourite chicken – when she'd learned the stitches well enough after she was older she'd embroidered a picture of the chicken on a linen scrap and kept it for a long time. She used to give the embroidered chicken roles in stories she made up for her little cousin Mathilde, the chicken was called Puck Puck, and then one day she gave Mathilde the embroidered chicken when she asked if she could have it – but she still thought about it sometimes, the embroidered chicken, it was one of those little things that you remember, yes? That was how her childhood seemed to her now, the story of many little things, they were how she began to *know*.

And school? Was there a school when she was a child back at the Bauernhaus, with all the animals, Signor Martignetti wanted to understand, struggling with the word *Bauernhaus*. Oh yes, there was a school she and her sisters went to, and some other children from around there, it was the school of Pastor Köhler, they learned to read and write, and numbers, and also about the Bible, but she stopped when she was twelve and had to work with Mutti on the linens. The linens? Yes, her papa was a Meister, a cabinetmaker, he made very fine coffins, and she and Mutti did the linens for them, as well as the special clothes.

It had become quiet in the lunch room, even though the children were clattering about with kitchen things nearby – had she said something strange? Or wrong? She took a swallow of the red wine from Signor Martignetti and then said aloud, quickly, the thought that had come suddenly into her head at the same time as the wine reached her stomach with a nice warm sensation – that the Bauernhaus was a good place to learn about many things, from Pastor Köhler's school of course but also from her papa, Meister Hansen, who knew everything about making fine furniture and about the trees the wood came from, from watching the animals and how the cows had their calves, from the garden that Mutti taught her to look after, and the orchard that was also Mutti's domain, and, of course, the chickens, but most of all from her oma who taught her a great many stitches, hundreds probably, she'd never counted them, but each one had a story that explained why it existed and what it was for.

So there was this special thing that she called the Oma, after her grandmother, she'd told the silent guests at the table, it was a sampler of all the stitches, it had come from her grandmother's mother and perhaps even from her mother before that, it was like a book of all the stitches that she could know.

'An encyclopedia!' exclaimed Herr Bloch, who was even quite excited.

Should she go and look after the children now, she asked – but not what is an encyclopedia?

Oh no, no! they had protested. Surely her story had only begun – how old was she now, at this time in her story, so interesting, working with her mother and father?

She was then about seventeen years old, Josephina told them, seeing as well as hearing their silence in which a question was waiting for her.

But now her papa wasn't looking at her as he would once have looked at a young daughter of seventeen who had never been further away than the town of Kiel, and who, only a little time ago, would walk around outside holding her Puck Puck the chicken that seemed to be asleep, talking to it. Now he was looking at her as the mother of the child who'd just run sturdily down towards the meadow where the cows and the chickweed were – his head was tilted slightly forward, not held stiffly upright to show his authority, and he was asking about the city of Hamburg where she now lived, he had been there himself once or twice when he was a young man, it was a noisy and confused place, surely, not easy for – his head dipped forward a little more – a young mother and her child?

Yes, she was then only just seventeen, she told them, she'd been working with her mutti and papa for four or five years, they were proud of her work, there were important people in the town who would be interested in it, they believed.

What kind of important people, Josephina, Theodora wanted to know.

She liked the taste of Signor Martignetti's wine – she took a sip after eating a morsel of the Sauerbraten, which was rather too rich for her. She wanted to tell the lunch guests that one of the most interesting and beautiful things she saw while living at the Bauernhaus was the wings of wild bees that she picked off the bodies of those that fell down below the hive in the old elm when the weather got colder – most of them stayed inside the tree, just like her family did in the Bauernhaus, to keep warm. When she held the little wings up to the light she could see that they had tiny bones in them – their delicacy made her throat feel funny. But she didn't tell the lunch guests about the bees, although she'd thought about the tiny bones in their wings the first time she saw Catharina after she was born, in Greta and Danne's big bed in Sønderborg. She was healthy but not a big girl, quite fine in her bones, just like you, little sister, Greta told her, and the baby didn't complain when Josephina unwrapped her to look at her ribs and fingers. Josephina was very tired and soon went to sleep, but when she woke up again she had another look at the baby's little bones and at her fingernails and toenails, and her silly ears that were a bit squashed.

What kind of important people? They were people like Catharina's father.

The guests were waiting for her to answer the question none of them had really asked, not even Theodora, who'd barely kept the question hidden in her *What kind of important people?*

'They were people like Catharina's father,' said Josephina, not expecting that she would. 'He was a Junker, Hauptmann von Zarovich. He was killed when his horse fell on him.' She took another nice swallow of the wine. Clearly, in the silence, the guests were now anticipating her answer to the very last piece of the question they hadn't asked. She looked at each of them in turn. 'And so, here we are, Catharina and me,' she said, and saw Herr Bloch's eyes crinkle at the corners, as if he enjoyed the way she had and had not told her story. But his sister's eyes hadn't crinkled at the corners as if Josephina had amused her – instead, her mouth was a little open as if she wanted to say something, but couldn't, and her eyes were blinking as if she couldn't cry but wanted to.

'And that is how I have become what I am,' she said, copying the way the others had finished their stories about how they had become 'socialists'. 'That is my story.'

There were lots of yellow and purple spring crocuses and blue grape hyacinths along the side of the path by the trees on the way to the graveyard, and Josephina, Catharina, Mathilde and Elke picked posies of them for Mutti's grave. Johannes Franzose was back at the Bauernhaus – they could still just hear him splitting firewood with regular, well-spaced cracks of his axe. He was 'Franzose' because he'd been told his father was a Frenchman, Elke explained with her face in a bunch of the spring flowers – her eyes were looking at Josephina over the flowers so that they, too, were like flowers, and she'd tucked a yellow crocus into her hair so that it peeped out crookedly from under her blue cap – but some of the people in the neighbourhood thought he must be a deserter from the war with Napoleon, which was stupid because he spoke good German and why would he call himself 'Franzose' if he was a deserter who was hiding up in the north? But that's how people are around here, Elke explained, as though her little sister was, now, a stranger from somewhere else. That fat old witch Frau Tiesel had been the worst of them at first, because she thought Papa had stolen Johannes away from the mill, but now Frau and Herr Tiesel were Papa's best friends because he allowed Johannes to do jobs at the mill and didn't ask for money. They were going to come to the wedding – they'd have to bring Frau Tiesel over in a cart! – and so was Herr Mayer, in fact he was going to ride over from Gaarden this evening to make sure the arrangements were in order, you know how he is. And the Webers from Wellingdorf, did Josie remember, with the bull, how they would walk it over with some flowers between its horns? They were coming, but without the bull of course, there would be no need for that! And there would be some others, but not too many, the new pastor and his wife of course, did Josie remember them? And a couple of their old friends from Pastor Köhler's, one of them was Anna, she'd married that crazy boy Eric from the mill, the one they watched jump from the top of the millwheel that time, with no clothes on, now they had a couple of kids?

It was as if she, Josephina, had left a very long time ago, and not just four and a bit years, but then the years didn't count the time, something else did, something like the measure of what she knew and how she knew it – but here was Papa opening the gate to the graveyard and making her and Catharina and Elke and Tante Elizabeth and Mathilde stop for a moment in a jostle while he made a short speech. This was where his dear wife and the mother of Josephina and Elke and Greta was now, he told them – their mutti and Catharina's oma, he said to Josephina and Catharina, did Catharina understand that? – while Elke and Tante Elizabeth and Mathilde stood waiting with lowered eyes. Well, she'd had a hard life at the end but now she was at peace, the things that had troubled her no longer mattered. Then he seemed to lose the thread of what he was planning to say, and just waved his arm towards Mutti's grave.

Well no, of course Catharina didn't 'understand that', she'd never met her oma, but Josephina didn't say this. The wild grasses and weeds had begun to grow up eagerly in the graveyard, cow parsleys and daisies and cornflowers, and there were lots of bees busy among them, there was a humming sound all around, and the bees kept flying at the crocuses and especially the blue hyacinths they'd picked on the way over, so they quickly put the posies by Mutti's grave near the verbena bush Elke had planted that was struggling to establish itself. The grave was quite simple, and the grasses had already grown up around the base of the headstone, which was a nice plain one with an arch shape on the top.

Papa's friend the one-eyed stonemason Herr Fischer had made it and cut the inscription – did Josie remember him, Elke wanted to know. The man who'd lost his left eye when a chip of stone flew into it? Who used to frighten them with the stitch marks where his eye was closed, and the sharp chip that he kept in a special pouch? And he pretended that the stain on the chip was blood? But perhaps it was?

Elke was babbling, but then she stopped as Josephina knelt down in the weeds to look at the inscription – she had to push some stalks away to see the last line. Yes, there was Mutti's name, she was Agatha Hansen, she was the beloved wife of Adam Hansen – the two A letters were cut with nice identical flourishes on their right feet – and she was the mother of Greta, Elke and Josephina and the grandmother of Finn, Otto and Catharina.

Yes, there she was, there was Catharina, her name peeping out among the stalks, but Elke hadn't put that in the letter Greta had sent on from Sønderborg. So it was meant as a surprise? And there was Elke kneeling on the other side of the grave, she was nodding and smiling that big Elke smile, the yellow crocus had slipped down from her cap across her forehead – Yes! she was mouthing, yes! but then pointing with her eyes towards Papa who was standing just to one side of her.

'Thank you, Papa,' said Josephina, 'and Catharina says thank you as well. One day she'll understand this.'

But that was all she was going to say to Papa, because she'd stopped grieving for Mutti somewhere in the time that months and years didn't measure – yes, she was glad that Catharina's name was there together with her cousins', she was glad that Papa had changed enough to allow that to happen, or that Elke had made him do it, or that Elke had changed him by her example, by taking the Oma and coming to Sønderborg, by bravely going to the house on Faulstrasse – or even that she, Josephina, had changed him by showing him that she was continuing to move her future forward towards where she was going, and that he could not change her course. He was now looking at her as if he expected her to say something more, or that she might give him a daughterly kiss – he was waving the bees away from his face, and seemed to be waiting – but then he turned and began to walk back towards the graveyard gate. Tante Elizabeth followed her brother with Mathilde holding her hand, and after a while Elke gave a little shrug and followed them. She'd taken the yellow flower from under her cap and she dropped it on Mutti's grave as she went.

Now Catharina was tugging at her hand – 'Come on, Mutti, they're going!' – and so she got up and gave the headstone a rub across its curved top, and ran her fingers over the names below, and pulled some leaves from the verbena shrub to get its smell on her fingers, and followed after Catharina who was running to catch up with the others. But no, she didn't have to forgive her father for being hard-hearted in the past, or thank him for now opening his heart again to her and to Catharina, because it no longer mattered. Now it was better to say little about the past, including those portions of the past that had crept back into this present that was filled with Elke's happiness. And she didn't have to thank him for allowing her to come back, to come 'home', to this place that she knew well, including the flowers between the bull's horns and the jokes about Frau Tiesel in a cart and all the rest of it, but now knew more as if 'home' was a memory that she recognised, so that her feelings were not as strong perhaps as Elke and Papa thought they should be.

But that was just how it was, and she couldn't do anything about it. And also, it was as though ever since she'd told the lunch guests at Herr and Theodora Bloch's house, where there were often lunches and dinners, and meetings with coffee in the mornings – ever since she'd told the Blochs, and Signora and Signor Martignetti, who were the mother and father of Catharina's best friend Alex, the story of where she came from and how she had become who she was – ever since she'd finished that story, it was as though it left her, and the place the story came from left her, so that now, having come back to that place, she couldn't really be there anymore.

Catharina had run after the others, and her opa had swung her up to sit on his shoulders with her legs hanging down in front. She was holding on to his ears and shouting Giddy up! And yes, Josephina remembered that as well, her Papa's rather bony shoulders, as she walked along behind them in the empty space they left for her.

Herr Mayer was there punctually as he'd promised he would be, in time for an early supper outside under the pear tree where they'd leave the table for the wedding lunch tomorrow, yes?, and to have a last discussion about the arrangements. His man and their cook would come out in the morning with plenty of beer and wine and the wedding food. But for supper they were just having some over-winter kale from the Bauernhaus garden, with white sauce, and smoked ham with bread? Herr Mayer thanked Elke for organising this. Tante Elizabeth had brought some beer and schnapps in the buggy that morning, squashed in together with Mathilde, Josephina and Catharina – Herr Mayer thanked his wife for seeing to this too, and greeted Josephina and Catharina quite formally, saying it was nice to see them again. She saw that the words *Fräulein* Hansen almost came out instead of *Josephina*, but then he busied himself with the thick bottles of beer – their tops opened with a bang that made Catharina hold her hands against her ears – and the thin one of schnapps. Elke had brought out the mugs and glasses, and Josephina and Tante Elizabeth filled them, the tall mugs with the beer and the little glasses with Herr Mayer's favourite Köm, 'the best in Holstein'! The two little girls had mugs of apple syrup with water. Then they all stood under the pear tree and drank a toast to Elke and Johannes, first a small swallow of Köm followed by a good swallow of the cool beer, and then, all together, a shout, good luck and happiness!

It was too bad Greta and Danne and the children hadn't got in to Kielerhafen yet, said Herr Mayer – he'd heard that the packet would be coming in at night on the tide, not too late. So they drank another toast to the eldest sister and 'the lucky Dane'. Then they all sat down to have some supper. Johannes had been banished to his stall inside the Bauernhaus after the first toast, because it was bad luck for him to be at the table on the eve of his wedding, but Elke gave the two little girls a bottle of beer and a plate of food to take in to him, and said they were allowed one kiss each, on his cheek.

Almost everything was familiar to Josephina, because she'd been to other weddings, including Greta's not long after she began to work with Mutti on the linens, and also to her friend Anna's – they'd shared a desk at Pastor Köhler's but Anna was the naughty one who knew well the end of the wooden spoon; she told Josephina that she and crazy Eric from the mill had already 'done it' before they got married. Of course everyone having supper under the pear tree had been to other weddings, even Mathilde, probably, who'd just returned giggling with Catharina from taking Johannes his supper – he'd pushed open the stopper on the beer and drunk most of it in one go, and did a big burp! – and was Mutti going to get married too, Catharina wanted to know, tomorrow, because she liked Franzose, as he said to call him. No, my darling, Elke told her, my little sister can't marry Franzose because he's mine! – but of course they can be good friends.

And then, perhaps because there was a silence, the tip of Papa's tongue carefully prised his lips open in a smile. Now that Josephina was no longer living in Hamburg at the house of Danne's uncle, Herr Aksel Andersen, would she like to tell them about her new circumstances?

She was now living at the house of Herr Wolf Bloch and his sister Fräulein Theodora Bloch, it was a nice house near the lake in the middle of the city, it had a small garden that Catharina and her friend Alex could play in. It was a very busy house because Herr Bloch and his sister entertained many people, there were often dinners and lunches, and also meetings with coffee in the mornings.

And what does this Herr Wolf Bloch do, Herr Mayer wanted to know. Since he seems to have a busy social life? Herr Mayer's mouth had opened and shut when Papa mentioned the house of Herr Aksel Andersen, but now he was looking at Josephina with a rather determined expression, as though he expected her to do some explaining. And is this Bloch married, he wanted to know.

The pleasure Josephina felt in meeting Herr Mayer's firm gaze was unexpected, because it emerged with such an enjoyable rush from her feeling of sadness about the familiar joy of weddings. No, she told everyone at the table, but especially Herr Mayer, though it should have been her papa because he'd begun the questions about her 'circumstances' – no, Herr Bloch wasn't married, and the many people who came to the house mostly came because of business.

'Ah!' said Papa and Herr Mayer in unison.

'Yes,' said Josephina, and moistened what she was saying with the last of the Köm in her glass. 'Yes, it's a place of discussions and talking, because Herr Bloch is the editor of a newspaper, the *Bürger Zeitung*. He also writes for it often, and so does Theodora, that's what she prefers to be called. In addition, Herr Bloch writes reviews of theatre and music, they are quite famous, and he is a poet. He and his sister often work together. They go together to look at the conditions and organisations of places of work, and they report on them.'

'And that is their business?' This time Herr Mayer spoke alone.

'Yes,' said Josephina. 'They are socialists.'

Her papa had no expression on his face, as if he hadn't heard her answering his question about her 'circumstances', Tante Elizabeth had a little smile in one corner of her mouth, Herr Mayer was putting his fork full of smoked ham down very carefully, and Elke was frowning severely as if her wedding supper had begun to be spoiled, as perhaps it had.

'They are very good people,' said Josephina. 'They are kind to me and to Catharina. They care about the circumstances of people working in places like the sewing room where I was, the one belonging to Herr Paul, who is Herr Aksel Andersen's friend. Herr Paul is also a socialist, his sewing room is well organised, and it has a Kita. That is their purpose, they call themselves social democrats, their purpose is to improve *circumstances*.' Josephina enjoyed saying *circumstances* with special emphasis. 'But this is Elke's party,' she said. 'This is my dear sister's wedding supper, here we are, so let's not talk about what I might be doing in Hamburg, because it's not important, it's not as important as Elke.'

The first owl of the evening hooted – there always had to be a first one, it was over in the woods somewhere, a little bit early – and there always had to be a first song, and almost always the person who started had to be Elke. The song she started by knocking her beer mug on the table was 'Du, du liegst mir im Herzen', You, you lie in my heart! – it used to be Mutti's favourite, of course Elke knew that, and soon they were all singing it, including Mathilde while Catharina looked at her with devotion, and Papa was wiping his eyes and nose with big swipes of his shirt sleeve, and taking good swallows of his beer between verses.

There was a half moon like a ghost in the sky over the fjord. They would go on singing more songs for a while until it was almost dark, and then Herr Mayer and his wife would return to Gaarden, with Tante Elizabeth and Mathilde in the buggy with a coach lamp and Herr Mayer riding ahead. The animals knew the way, and so did Josephina when she went inside to get lamps to hang in the pear tree, because she and Elke and Papa would sit out there for a while longer, with the moths, and Johannes would come sneaking out and sit down to have another beer now that the others had gone, and then she'd carry the sleeping Catharina in to Papa and Mutti's big bed where she and Catharina and Elke would be sleeping that night, where Elke and Johannes would be sleeping the night after their wedding, and perhaps if she left the lanterns lit in the pear tree Greta and Danne would see them as they came up the fjord later that night past the Schwentine towards Kielerhafen – Look, they'd say, I wonder if Josie and Catharina are there?

Wolf Bloch

To Friedrich Engels, in Primrose Hill, London

My dear Engels

I am writing first and foremost to send you my and Theodora's sincere condolences on the death of your beloved Lydia – your 'Lizzie'. We were saddened by the news, as were the friends and comrades who were assembled here at Bloch House when the post came. We drank a toast to Lydia's memory, and in your honour also, and on behalf of the Hamburg chapter of the Socialist Workers' Party. The Party's members hold you in high regard despite our colleague Marx's severe critique of Gotha, which they continue to discuss of course as I'm sure you can imagine, despite which I'm happy to report that our soireés at Bloch House remain congenial much like yours at Primrose Hill, so I am told. I hope that you will be able in time to enjoy again the good life you have so generously advocated for by your own hospitable example, and that you will continue to find joy in music and poetry, as we do. In the meantime, please allow us the honour of sharing your grief. Its dark clouds will disperse, I am sure, and the sun will once again shine on Primrose Hill.

I am sure, too, that we are both still mourning the recent death of our dear friend and inspiration Ferdinand Freiligrath, while taking comfort in the knowledge that his poems and the memory of his laughter will prevail over sadness.

I also hope that your eyes are better than they were last time we exchanged letters. That seems a long time ago, and now we need clear sight and indeed foresight more than ever before. At the time of our last communication we were preoccupied with our friend and comrade Pasquale Martignetti, whose situation here in Hamburg we were able to resolve, with your great kindness and generous advice, to his satisfaction and that of his excellent wife Signora Maria Martignetti and their charming daughter Alessandra. We have often enjoyed their company and indeed the bottled 'sole del sud' the Signor has kindly provided. Back then, despite the surveillance to which you have long been subjected in England, we were saying only, with professional caution, that the situation of socialists in Hamburg was becoming worse by the day! But now, as you will have heard, we have reached a threshold well beyond that understatement. Bismarck's laws, recently enacted, have come as no surprise given the unconcealed harassment and intimidation of socialists here in Hamburg as elsewhere in Germany since the establishment of the Empire. Clearly the Chancellor fears revolution, and he is not wrong, since efforts to improve the conditions of workers are now treated as sedition.

Poor Martignetti and his family have once again had to flee these oppressions. There were, and are, spies keeping watch over Herr Johannes Paul's businesses where, thanks to your intervention, our friend Pasquale was employed as a notary, and these stool pigeons had begun to take an interest in him. They had also begun to ask questions of others employed in the manufacturing and trading departments of the Paul & Steinberg enterprises, some of which, such as the sewing room, had become well known as models of good worker conditions. Theodora and I must take some responsibility for this, since we have published careful accounts of both the good and the bad in the *Bürger Zeitung*, as you well know.

Copies of your *Conditions* are treated as though they were infected with English cholera, and disposed of accordingly. It seems nothing has changed in thirty years. Paul & Steinberg have now forfeited their profitable military contracts, and the Martignettis have gone to Bremen and will almost certainly travel on from there to America, the 'land of the free'. And indeed of Freiligrath's comrade-poet, Henry Longfellow!

Our Bloch House soirées, while remaining congenial occasions for discussion, have now become furtive and take place behind closed curtains, which we find necessary but offensive and even shameful. Some of our most frequently welcomed guests have recently declined our invitations. Their reasons are simple: if they are perceived to be meeting regularly in the company of known 'subversives', they risk banishment or worse. Our discussions now focus more often than not on what it is both useful and prudent to publish in the *Bürger Z.*

And so I come at last to the news that I have remained unwilling to share with you, my dear comrade, overburdened as you are with your own unhappy circumstances. It is clear that we must close down the *Bürger Zeitung* before the state does that for us and seizes our few assets, and that Theodora and I must anticipate the order to leave Hamburg, and go by our own volition to Bremen, where we may have some time to take stock. The evil that is happening now may be short-lived, we can only hope so. However, my old Ostjuden instincts tell me that this is unlikely to happen in the near future, and in fact I fear there will be worse to come. And so my own inclination is to keep on going, not 'west and a bit north', as we used to say, but rather across the ocean to a place that has not yet begun to rot under the weight of its corrupt history.

Forgive my vehemence, dear Engels, and let me finish by saying our work, and yours especially, will not be wasted. But we must survive, after all, as you have done under constant duress, but always with hope and belief in our capacities to do good.

Theodora, my dear older sister and companion in good and bad times, and a true warrior for our cause, asks to be respectfully remembered to you.

And so, until the next letter, from who knows where

I remain
Your admiring and devoted friend and comrade
Wolf Bloch

Josephina

Theodora's very friendly kiss surprised her and ended with a little warm huff that had the smell of coffee on it – would Josephina like some? She'd missed her so much, she said, *so much!* – and of course Catharina too, and she looked forward to hearing all about her sister's wedding, it must have been an 'emotional experience' for her to go back to the place where she'd grown up 'and everything', and she hoped it had all gone well for 'the happy couple' – but here in Hamburg things were not so good, Josephina probably hadn't heard about any of that up there by Kiel?

No, she hadn't – any of what? – but, she told Theodora, she'd heard from her big sister Greta about her little nephew Finn being told not to speak German at school and how her brother-in-law Danne had an argument with the Rektor about that, and she overheard from Danne while he was talking to Herr Mayer that his uncle Farbror Aksel's business in Hamburg was failing and that he and Frau Andersen might go to America – Ah, yes, Theodora and Wolf knew Herr Andersen, Theodora had heard about that. Josephina had heard from her friend Anna that she was going to have another baby – probably Theodora hadn't heard about that – and that her man Eric was 'a steam engine'. She'd heard from Herr Mayer while he was talking to Papa that he thought it unwise to entitle the Bauernhaus and the land to Elke who was now called Frau Franzose, and she'd heard Papa's reply, which made Herr Mayer walk away and good riddance – Theodora was impressed by Elke's 'entitlement'. She'd heard from Tante Elizabeth that she envied her having a new life in Hamburg that must be different 'from this'? Theodora must think it probably was? Quite different?

The food and drink provided by Tante Elizabeth and Herr Mayer had been enjoyed and praised. The pastor who'd spoken so nicely at the wedding, and who'd specially mentioned the beautiful chaplets of spring flowers on Mathilde's and Catharina's hair, seemed to get a little tipsy at the lunch and left earlier than expected with his wife and a row of children following behind – everyone saw him sit down suddenly in the chickweed by the gate, and how Frau Kolnick kept going with her from-tall-to-small ducklings following behind her – and yes, of course it was different from life at the Bloch House, it was very different, and probably not very interesting for Theodora?

But perhaps Theodora would be interested in what her sister's new husband Johannes Franzose had said to her, having heard about the talk at supper the night before? And what talk was that, Theodora wanted to know, seeming even more interested. It was about the important work that she and Herr Bloch did to improve the circumstances of people such as the women in the sewing room where she and Theodora had first seen each other, and how Theodora and Herr Bloch and many of their visitors were socialists, social democrats, in fact.

'You told them that?' Theodora put her coffee cup down with a startling clash.

Why, yes, naturally her papa had asked her about where she was living now in Hamburg, and what her employers did, and so she'd told him and also the others at supper, what Theodora had explained to her so kindly when they were telling their stories at lunch with Signor and Signora

Martignetti, and when she'd felt so ignorant and had talked about such stupid things, like seeing a song in her hair. But they weren't stupid things, Theodora told her in a warm tone, putting her hand on top of Josephina's – she'd said it already and she'd say it again now, Josephina was a very special young woman – but please, what was it that her sister's new husband had said, at the wedding lunch, that might be interesting? That she might find interesting?

Catharina was becoming restless and had already wondered when she would see Alex, and there was certainly plenty of work to do, despite the coffee with Theodora, so Josephina hurried her answer while making Catharina come out from under the table where she was mumbling 'I want Alex' just loud enough to be heard.

Johannes had said, Ah, so now his sister-in-law was consorting with social democrats, so he'd been informed by Herr Mayer, and had these social democrats in Hamburg told her about the revolutions of 1848, or the uprising of the Paris Commune just a few years ago?

And no, they hadn't, Herr Bloch and Theodora hadn't told her about those things, but what were those things, what was he talking about?

And then she was startled by Theodora's laughter, and by her warm palms pressing against her cheeks – her story was amusing, but why? And why did everything she thought she knew immediately make a fresh space for something she didn't?

Meanwhile, the cook would be there in an hour or two, said Theodora in her quick, practical tone, and without answering Josephina's question about 'those things', could Josephina please help her get ready for some guests? Catharina could play with some toys in the kitchen? Because Hamburg had become agitated these past weeks, Josephina would soon be hearing about it.

And indeed, the table in the back room overlooking the garden at the Bloch House was now even busier than before, and sometimes Josephina had to bring in more lamps at night so the visitors could look at the pages they were discussing. They were usually smoking, which made Herr Bloch cough, but they had to keep the curtains drawn over the windows, though the weather was now quite warm.

And Catharina's friend Alex had gone away with her mother and father to Bremen. But why? Catharina was inconsolable and sat sobbing over the two dolls they'd often played with – she called one Alex, and talked to her and had to sleep with her at night. And also, when could she see Mathilde again? And why not? But Josephina also wanted to know why Signor and Signora Martignetti and Alessandra had to go so suddenly to Bremen, what was the matter? Because the authorities had found out about him. But what had they found out? His activities. But which 'activities'? And meanwhile Catharina began to tip over her drink of milk and say Alex did it, and then sometimes the cook smacked her.

And how could she explain about Alex to Catharina if she herself didn't know the answer? And how could she go on living between two worlds, one she knew and understood but could no longer be in, and another that she was in but was not permitted to know?

It was very late, but at last everyone had gone. Josephina had taken several pots of coffee into the room where some of the men had been shouting, and also some brandy and glasses, though she had to keep running up to the bedroom from time to time because lately Catharina had begun to come out and sit on the stairs in her nightie. Once, from the kitchen, she heard Theodora's voice above the others, angry and clear, biting the words, and then Theodora had come in to the kitchen cursing under her breath and stood stiffly with her back turned over by the pantry. Then she'd gone back to the meeting again, but she said nothing to Josephina, who was becoming impatient and even 'nettled', as Elke would say, with Fräulein Theodora Bloch, as she might as well call her, and with her sometimes warmth and affection, because what was the use of her pats and smiles if she wouldn't tell her why there was 'agitation' in Hamburg, and why it obviously upset her so much – why, indeed, was *Fräulein Bloch* treating her no differently from the way she, Josephina, was now forced to treat Catharina, by not explaining to her why her friend Alex had gone away to a place called Bremen without even saying goodbye, or how they could go there and visit her? And why couldn't they, why not?

Herr Bloch came slowly into the kitchen and filled a jug with warm water from the stove kettle – It was all right, thank you, Josephina, he could manage, thank you – and went upstairs to his bedroom. Josephina went into the room where the meeting had been going on for some hours; she opened the curtains and then the windows to air the tobacco smoke. The evening was rather cool, and perhaps she could go outside for a while and sit at the far end of the garden where a breeze sometimes came off the lake – the smell of the fresh water was quite mellow, unlike the salty tang of Kieler Förde, perhaps some of that sharp northern air would do those anxious people sitting in their fug of tobacco smoke some good! Then she began to assemble the used cups and glasses and the ashtrays and the plates on which she'd served some hard cheese and pickles, she would get them all washed before she closed up the windows again, and with luck Catharina would have remained asleep.

And then, 'Ah, Josephina!' she heard, a sigh rather than speech. Theodora was sitting back from the table in the shadows. 'What would we do without you?'

It was a laugh but also a growl or snarl that then startled Theodora as Josephina sat down and poured herself a glass of brandy from the open bottle on the table. 'What indeed?' she said, and drank. And now perhaps Fräulein Bloch could explain to her what was going on in this room night after night and why it was not possible to tell her so that she could understand, and also so Catharina could understand why her friend Alex had been taken away from her, surely Fräulein Bloch could see how affected the child was by that?

'I told you and only you that I was raped by the Junker,' said Josephina, 'though of course you already thought you knew. Do you think that was easy for me? So how hard can it be for you to tell me why "things are not good here in Hamburg", why in fact the place is "agitated", as you say? How bad is "agitated"? Does "agitated" mean sitting around drinking coffee and brandy and arguing?'

How good it felt to sit down and sip brandy, and then feel her anger drift out the window like stale smoke. She saw that Theodora heard her own words repeated – she made a little pfff sound of appreciation.

'You're angry, Josephina,' she said. 'And so am I, but not with you. May I too have a brandy, please?' She came over to the table and sat down. Would she now do what she had begun to do more frequently, give her hand a pat? Or even her cheek? But she didn't.

'Hamburg is now part of the German Empire. The social democrats are banned. Our members are being persecuted.

Soon, the *Bürger Zeitung* will have to cease publication. Wolf and I will have to leave Hamburg. We will be banished, certainly. We might be killed. This is now clear finally, tonight, and so I can tell you.' Now the hand on Josephina's cheek, trembling a little. 'I am truly, truly sorry that I didn't explain how things are until now. I didn't want to frighten you.' She sipped her brandy but put the glass aside with a shudder. 'Wolf thinks we should leave Germany. We don't agree about that. In the meantime, once again, west and a little bit north. But you, Josephina?'

Yes, she would go outside and down to where the cool, freshwater breeze came up off the lake, and then she would come back to wash the cups and things before going up to bed.

And yes, it was rather cool, down there, near the lake.

But you, Josephina?

Perhaps because she felt sorry, Theodora had washed the cups and glasses from the meeting and was no longer downstairs. Josephina closed the windows – the room was much fresher now, certainly – and she put the last lamps out. Perhaps it would even be chilly upstairs? Perhaps she should light the little stove on the landing by the bedrooms? She had set it that morning, as usual, because Herr Bloch was susceptible to chills and sometimes had the stove lit even in mild weather.

The door to his bedroom was ajar and she could see Herr Bloch sitting up in bed reading a book. He had a shawl over his shoulders.

'Are you cold, Herr Bloch?'

'Wolf,' he said, with a little cough past his teeth that Josephina could see in the lamplight. 'Please, just Wolf, would you mind? Josephina?'

Part 2

'what choice do we have?'

Theodora

Friday, 31 October, 1879, Bremerhaven

This is my first journal entry on a momentous day. I will write it with as firm a hand as possible, though my body and my thoughts are unsteady.

Now the days are shorter and quite cold, but that is not the cause of my unsteadiness. Nor is it because the ship's movement is unsettling. We are told it will be some time before the ship is untethered (is that the correct word?) and begins its passage towards the open sea. Then unsteadiness will be a euphemism. I dread this moment as I'm sure do those in the cheapest accommodation. They sleep three or four in bunks stacked two high, an undesirable condition emphasised to us as we enquired after costs. No doubt we seemed good prospects. It's easy to say that I don't regret our privilege, just as it's easy to say I feel for those I saw jostling at the entrance to their quarters below. A 'familiar diagram of class and conscience' of course, as Wolf pointed out to Josephina, whose silence was accompanied by a little smile best described as wry.

But after all, thanks to those who contributed to our subscription, we are sharing intermediate-class quarters with a family from Denmark. Their name is Frederiksen and their children are two boys and a girl. The boys are about eight and ten years old, and the girl a little older than Catharina, perhaps seven. They are all 'on deck'. No doubt we will be on first-name terms soon enough since our sleeping compartments adjoin with four bunks in each and a shared bathroom and stateroom that we will also share with the other intermediate passengers on our side of the ship, whom I am yet to meet. Need I say more. Josephina, Wolf and Catharina are also on deck. They are very excited, and so I have this hour or two in which to begin my account of what Wolf calls 'our great adventure'.

I can't remember who wrote: 'To live in the body is to die.' Perhaps the same who noticed 'my watchful self'? I am living in a body that cannot question what it knows, a helpless longing. At the same time I am living in a mind that watches that helplessness and despises it. Does it make sense to say that to live in the body is to die trapped in the body but that to live in the mind is to die liberated into the world? Wolf's 'great adventure' is to go to a new world as a man filled with the naive joy of being reconciled in mind and body. I, however, cannot reconcile what I desire and what I think. And I fear we are going to a world that will soon be like the old one.

The indelicacy of what my body knew the first time I saw Josephina in the sewing room now has another image superimposed on it, like the reflection in a window behind which an interior has become indistinct. That indistinct image is of a young woman who could almost still be a girl except for the child holding her hand. The girl-mother was slight and fair, with a piercing gaze that I will never forget. I saw it again many times. It always seemed to be looking past the present moment. The child who was holding her hand had the same intense stare, though she was only about two or three years old. The combination of the girl-mother's delicacy and forthright look, and the pathos of her hand holding the child's, pierced me to my body's core. The sewing room was filled with a murmuration of voices, like a hive. For me it was the internal hum of disordered thoughts. Wolf was watching Andersen and Paul discussing the terms of the girl's engagement. The 'supervisor' was perched on his dais. 'Quota, quota, quota,' said Wolf, and also, 'I pity that child.' What 'child' did he mean, the mother or her daughter? Now this dim interior is overmantled by an image of the young woman and her grown child and Wolf together on the wharf at the moment of their embarkation on the 'great adventure'. This time both Wolf and Josephina are holding hands with Catharina, who is between them. It is this superimposition that unsteadies me.

The oddness of their tableau vivant should have been lost in the crush of people on the wharf where all sorts and sizes and ages were converging. But for me the crush highlighted the poignancy of my 'little brother' with his crooked back and pigeon chest, the young woman with the straight back and upright head, and the lovely child between them. Most onlookers would think the child was theirs. They would also guess the young woman's loose cloak concealed another.

Josephina's only experience of sex had been brutal, and Wolf's improbable. They came to each other as distorted innocents. Perhaps they were well matched. Wolf's kindness comes from his experience of being pushed into puddles. I doubt Josephina could be attracted to brutes who do the pushing.

And now I can hear the happy Frederiksens returning. They are like a pretty painted toy crèche of a wholesome family and I can see there will be praying. I must steady myself, because we have a long way to go.

Beth and Frank

'Feel a bit funny, leaving?' It was Beth's turn to drive, so she was talking at the road unspooling towards them through scrappy, bedraggled forest and at the rear-view mirror where what had gone was constantly replenished. There were long straights on the road, with perplexing dips and rises – the kinds of articulated trucks they had seen from the National Park hotel patio at breakfast loomed suddenly over crests and accelerated with dirty squirts of diesel smoke from their exhaust chimneys. The highway crossed the railway line, and there was the turn-off to Raurimu and the world-famous Raurimu railway-line spiral, not finished when Great-grandad Wolf went into the back country down the Kaitīeke valley to the west of the line about 1908, and immediately after it the turn-off to Kaitīeke, and just down there was his mother Josephina's grave in the Raurimu cemetery with its doleful chorus of parched sheep. 'Think we'll ever come back?'

'Helen hasn't, nor did Ruth.'

'Can't you stop doing that? It was a perfectly simple question. Because I do.'

'You do what?'

'Feel a bit funny.'

'Want me to drive?'

'I want you to engage in civil conversation. Because we've got a long way to go.'

'We've got a long way to go, but our love will grow,' sang Frank in a raspy voice. 'Really bad seventies band that Ruth liked, bless her hippy heart.'

After a while there was a place called Manson's Siding with a turn-off across the railway line that Beth took with cursory sideways glances for trains and Frank's hand suddenly clutching her arm, then a bit of nondescript farmland, and then the road petered out in a grassy area on the edge of big forest. She got out of the car and walked fast to where the trees began at the edge of the grassy flat. Suddenly it was very quiet, there were no trucks, just a few birds in the trees – could that be a korimako? – yes, there was a pair, they were warbling to each other that she and Frank had arrived, better look out, trouble.

There was a stile over the fence and a track that disappeared into the trees – should she go there? Into the coolness? The dim light? But she sat down on a bench next to a slab-timber picnic table with empty beer cans scattered around it and looked over at Frank's head dimly visible in the car window. He was staring towards her, his face a pale motionless oval partly obscured by the reflected fragments of trees.

Then the window wound down. 'Are we coming or going?' he shouted.

How the fuck should I know? But she didn't say it.

Then he opened his car door and ambled towards her with a bottle of water swinging from one hand. The korimako lifted the urgency of their conversation but their calls seemed to be belling in her head; Frank's tall lean frame was swaying as he approached, but as though in a mirage, indistinct and unsteady and shimmering, and then she knew she was falling off the slab-timber bench and down to the ground among the half-crushed beer cans.

There was that fresh aroma again, like dear Noel's Tabac. She was propped against Frank's chest, and when he spoke she felt the vibration of his voice against the back of her head.

'Count to ten,' he said. 'Aloud. Don't think it.'

'One two three four five . . . why am I doing this?' Her tongue felt flannelly and dry but the words came out okay.

'You haven't had a stroke,' said Frank's vibration against her head. 'Lift this arm and grab my hand.' He wiggled her left arm and then waved his own within reach. She seized his hand and held it. 'Good as gold,' he said. He was gripping her hand quite tightly, she could feel his bony fingers. He'd propped himself up against the bench with his legs outstretched; she was lying between them and looking past the toes of his nice brown shoes – he had on grey and red argyle socks with that lozengy pattern, his pants were khaki, what Noel used to call dockers, he could never explain why. So now she was noticing that he'd dressed quite smartly for their trip back up to Auckland, as though the holiday part of it was over. The day before when they went down the Kaitīeke and had a swim by Grandad Wolf's old concrete honey-house he'd worn a pair of grungy shorts and well-worn sandals, as if he'd purposely dressed like the scruffy sixteen-year-old cousin who went away to Australia three or four years later with his twin sister and his mum, and kind of broke her child's heart, except that he wrote her letters with snapshots of him and Ruth at a billabong, on a long beach with huge tangled trees behind, and snaps of road signs or Australian animals, a koala hanging on tight to a tree, a dead snake draped over a veranda rail, distant kangaroos in a red-dirt landscape with termite mounds, and the jokes, what do you call a lazy baby kangaroo? – a pouch potato! – but nearly always his twin sister in there somewhere, which she'd hardly ever been when they were camped by the river down from the old homestead. Ruth, the quiet one.

Nor did Ruth.

'Sorry I was grumpy back there,' she said, and felt his big sigh lift her head.

'Got a sore chest?'

'Nothing wrong with the ticker, just the packaging.'

'Reckon you could stand up now? My back's killing me.'

The korimako started warning each other again, bell-ringing melodiously as she got up, waiting for the little surges of dizziness to pass, and sat on the bench by the picnic table, feeling a bit sick. The trees beyond the fence were mostly beech with some big tree ferns among them, and some straggly makomako along the forest edge – it was nice to be looking in that direction and not across the manky picnic ground towards the car.

'You weren't grumpy, Beth, my old mate.' Frank had sat down facing her across the table and was holding the bottle of water out to her. 'You were feeling funny.' He had an expression on his face like the one she'd seen years ago when they were kids and he knew she was pushing the risk, jumping off the rope swing into the river and going in over her depth – maybe it was so he'd have to fish her out and tell her off. 'So was I,' he said, pushing the water bottle into her hand. 'Feeling a bit funny. Go on, have a good swallow.'

She did, but the water was hardly there, there was nothing to it, not like the river you never ever forgot the taste of.

'Washed quartzy gravel, a hint of forest leaf mould, sunshine,' she said. Frank still had that remembered expression on his face, at once solicitous and amused. 'Not this crap,' she said. 'The river. The beautiful old river.'

'A river runs through you.' His big smile was still pretty much the same, he'd always saved it for something special – teeth not so flash anymore but there it was. 'Nice mineral finish,' he said. 'A good palate-cleanser.'

'You never forget it. Nothing is ever as good again.'

'So, all right then, why were you feeling funny?' He reached across the table and took the tips of her fingers in his hands. 'You go first.'

She couldn't work out which her was where when. A kind of déjà vu on repeat. And those strange alternative times and places leaning in or folding themselves over what and where she was, like the WB on Josephina Wenczel's headstone, her mother Elke barking like a dog from the trees across the river, the old shawl that refused to come with her out of the National Park hotel room, Frank talking to his dead wife.

The simple version, for Frank. 'I had the feeling that I wouldn't be back. That I was leaving more than just the old places we visited.' Frank was stroking the backs of her fingers with his thumbs. 'That I was leaving my life back there down the valley but I didn't even know what most of it had consisted of or what it meant.'

'Crikey,' he said. 'Me, I was just remembering my sis Ruth down at the river, and feeling a bit sad.' Then he grimaced, as if at the effort to continue his story, or to stop it. 'Last time I heard from Ruth was June 1970, she was working as a stringer in Jordan when the strife between the fedayeen and Hussein's mob broke out. She rang me from a phone at a joint called the Red Lion Tavern in Amman, she said it was where the correspondents gathered. I could hear them in the background, a rowdy lot – she told me they started drinking about eleven in the morning, were pissed by three in the afternoon which was when their informants arrived, they used the phones at the pub to file their stories rather than going back to their offices. She was killed the next day in crossfire in a press convoy near Wehdat refugee camp – she was one of the few who got out of the pub long enough to do her job. That was her.' Frank had tucked his hands in his armpits. 'She was twenty-four. We were. I've always remembered the names. Wehdat. Djebel Amman, where the pub was.' He had that special smile on his face again, only this time it was wincing. 'No need to say you're sorry,' he said. 'I know you are.'

'We just heard she'd had an accident,' said Beth. 'First I've heard about all that other stuff. Fucking hell.'

'She used to beat me over the head with an essay by Hannah Arendt called "We Refugees". Refugees were the vanguard of their people, she reckoned, Arendt did, back in the 1940s. I was thinking about that down there at the river, and in that sad little graveyard – you have to admit it's pretty sad. Josephina Wenczel, the vanguard of her people.' He was listening. 'Are those bellbirds?'

'Yes, they are – korimako.'

'I didn't know that,' said Frank. 'That's their real name? Christ, aren't they lovely? Aren't they just? Haven't heard anything that lovely for years.'

Beth thought his eyes might be tearing up, but he was just squinting at her.

'And what about dear old Noel?'

Bit patronising, but never mind. 'Dear old Noel was gone quite some time before he went, I'd have to say.'

Frank turned away to look at the trees where the 'bellbirds' were.

Let's leave it at that, then. 'Shall we go?' she said.

'Yeah, let's.' Frank turned back from the birdsong. His expression said, Please don't make me fish you out of the deep bit again. But I will.

Theodora

Sunday, 9 November, 1879, Bay of Biscay

So now at last the storm is abating and I can write again with a pen that is steady and a body that has stopped contorting itself over a bucket. What Wolf was thinking about his promised land I cannot imagine, as he too gave himself up helplessly to the storm, though not for long. That fragile body is used to sickness and he was soon taking care of the rest of us. Nor can I fathom what he was thinking when he insisted we should celebrate Shabbos just before sunset on the day of our departure from Bremerhaven. Of course it was about 'the exodus from Egypt', but how many years had it been since he and I renounced all religion? He bought some candles from the steward. They were forbidden because of the risk of fire, the man said, looking at my brother with a certain expression, whereupon the little fool gave him as much money again and the candles were delivered wrapped in a towel. Of course Wolf didn't remember how to celebrate Shabbos properly but he lit the candles stuck into puddles of melted wax on our stateroom table and we all covered our heads with the best shawls or headscarves we could find while he wished for a safe voyage to the promised land, with the anxious Danish Frederiksens peeping at us aghast from the adjoining cabin. So we were Jews after all, non-believers – perhaps they feared we would sacrifice and devour their pretty children! But then Wolf hastily extinguished the candles and waved the smoke from them towards the windows with the towel. My dear little brother was like a naughty boy full of glee, but I believe serious as well behind his fun. Of course Catharina enjoyed the charade without understanding it, except inasmuch as Wolf told her he was making the sea calm for her, which she must have found disappointing once we got to the Ärmelkanal where the ship began to heave about and the Danes to wail and pray, and seawater to come down into our cabins. How we endured that week is difficult now to imagine and I for one plan to forget it quickly. How much worse it must have been for those piled up upon each other in the steerage. When it was over we heard that some of the animal pens on the deck above had been swept away and at times it felt as though we all would be lost to the tempest, rich and poor alike.

But after sunset on the day we left there was a beautiful full moon that was reflected on the ocean. See how the moon is trailing her silver sleeve across the waves! exclaimed Josephina to Catharina. How often she finds these kinds of expressions in herself! But what she could not see or say was that her face was also illuminated by a kind of ecstasy that came from within, not from the moon's light. There is surely a poet in that small body that can hardly contain what it perceives and feels. I have seen this effect often with Josephina and it has always shaken me. It is as though the space between the phenomena her body encounters and her perception of them is filled with transformations. How can I not picture the transformations that might shine on her face when what has excited them is love?

The moon was obscured by dark storm clouds about midnight. Josephina was looking out the little window but closed it as the ship began to tip. It's getting dark now, she said in a whisper, but Catharina had been asleep for a long time, and Wolf as well. I could hear the labour of his breathing and some inarticulate night-murmurs from the child. Josephina didn't know I was still awake and watching her in the darkness. Was she talking to herself or to that transforming spirit that lives inside her?

Josephina was very pale and weak after the storm. The ship's matron had been abrupt with her at first, disapproving of the arrangements in our cabin and threatening to ask questions of the ship's captain and also of the doctor. The papers that Wolf arranged for us in Bremen declare that we are all Hansens, husband, sister, wife and daughter. The matron's eyes almost parted company in her face while trying to reconcile our appearances. But she soon became Josephina's ally, so she had good soup and clean towels and before long there were little spots of warm colour on her cheeks.

Now we are allowed on deck again where the sailors are exerting themselves with much bustling and business. They are not allowed to talk to the women on the ship but one of them called out to Josephina in Danish. What did he say, I asked her. The warm spots on her cheeks got warmer. He asked if I was called Siren, she said, and why was I hiding my tail? What is a Siren? She's a mythical sea-woman who lures poor sailors to their doom, I told her. She has a glittering fish-tail. Oh no, said Josephina and put her hand over her mouth, at once shocked and fascinated. A kind of Lorelei, she asked herself. I could see that a transformation was already happening in the secret space of her imagination, though imagination is perhaps not the right word, since her transformations invariably involve external phenomena and not just the closed world of mental fancy.

I have no reason to believe that her transformations are always happy since she has had to endure much unhappiness and turmoil in her life. But when I watch her sewing or embroidering, or encounter her clear gaze, I see that she has a gift. What it is I don't pretend to understand, but perhaps because of it she is able to make her own kind of sense of a fearfully incommensurate world.

My dear brother, on the other hand, came down into our stateroom yesterday pale and shaking. Josephina and Catharina were having a nap in the sleeping compartment, and Wolf looked around for them. His fingers are very thin and white and bony with thick tufts of black hair below their middle knuckles, and he had been gnawing at those knuckles on his right hand so that the hairs were wet and flattened against his fingers, like the hair of a cat that has been cleaning itself. Where were they, he asked in a hoarse voice. Where were Catharina and Josephina? Were they on deck? They were sleeping, I told him, but what was the matter? Why was he so distressed?

Then, with trembling lips, and twisting his hands on the table in front of him, he told me about the mistreatment of a young seaman, just a boy of about sixteen. Those who were on deck saw the boy being beaten with a rope end as he went to climb up into the rigging with a tar pot. The officer who was beating him pursued him and continued to beat him with the rope as he ran further out on the yardarm.

‘We were watching,’ said my brother, whose whole body shook with spasms. ‘We just watched.’ They watched as the boy missed a rope he was trying to grasp in order to slide down to the deck, and fell into the sea. From my quiet place in the stateroom I had heard much shouting and the clattering and snapping of sails as the ship changed course, but of course had no idea of the reason for it. The boy was picked up, Wolf told me, but was at once sent aloft again with the tar bucket. Some of the passengers had now begun to mutter, but no one raised their voice in the boy’s defence. Perhaps because he was shaking with cold, or because of the rolling of the ship, he spilled some of the tar on a sail. He was ordered down and the officer who had been beating him tied him to the rigging and exposed his buttocks and back. The captain then gave him many lashes with a knotted whip with several strands. Then, said Wolf, he was cut down and made to kneel before the captain and beg for mercy. And then he was ordered to lie face down on the deck with his bleeding back and buttocks exposed, while the officer dripped vitriol on his wounds from a small vial.

He screamed just once and then lost consciousness and was carried below, said Wolf. My brother’s hands were still now, and his face, though pale, was composed in a kind of expressionless, waxy mask. I know that he will never reconcile this moment in his mind but will add it, untransformed, to the archive of evidence upon which he builds his view of a world fundamentally unjust and governed by brutal power. I understand Wolf’s world and his hope that it can be changed, and of course I share many of his convictions. But unlike his bitter and hopeful emotions, which he will go on forever grooming like a diligent cat, mine will always exist on either side of a great chasm – on one side in the memory of a world made intelligible by love, and on the other in a world from which love has been removed, like the lacerated, unconscious boy to his quarters, out of sight and out of mind.

Now that is enough. I hear Catharina waking up with a little complaint in her voice. Wolf has been conscripted to a team that is rostered to organise the food rations and I have been requested to contribute to the ship's school for children. Both are improbable to say the least but Wolf will do his best I am sure and I will try to do likewise.

Wolf Bloch

To Signor Pasquale Martignetti
c/o Banca Malzone
88 Mulberry Street
Manhattan
New York
America

Monday, November 17, 1879

My very dear Pasquale and of course also Signora Maria and sweet Alessandra:

Your letter was forwarded to us in Bremen by our kind friend Herr Johannes Paul who may be joining you in the Land of Opportunity where we are told our tired, poor, huddled masses are welcomed! I want with all my heart to believe this is possible but my always-watchful sister suggests we wait and see how things turn out for our comrades who have also taken your path. Like them Herr Paul has found the Chancellor's oppressions intolerable and unsustainable, and writes that he can no longer continue his businesses in Hamburg let alone their progressive ancilla such as the sewing room Kita where Catharina and Alessandra became such devoted playmates! No doubt the Chancellor will be glad to see the last of him and will thank America for welcoming this socialist viper into its bosom!

One day soon you will be able to embrace him and his family on our behalf since we were unable to get timely passage from Hamburg to America, having been given too little time to leave our beloved Bloch House and its ghosts, now, of conversations past. We had to take the soonest option available to us from Bremerhaven and so we are now 'on the high seas' to New Zealand, a name that hints at the low country our family skirted with caution on its zigzag towards Hamburg all those years ago but which I hope will offer us a 'new life'.

In this expression lurks the disturbing dogma of being 'born again' promoted with zeal by our travelling companions, a family of devout Christian Danes whose father and husband speaks fervently of this second birth as involving a combination of 'water and spirit', a wish that seemed about to be granted soon after our departure when we endured a fierce storm. They irritate my watchfully critical and forthright sister simply, I think, because they are both religious and a model bourgeois family, but they seem decent folk to me, and hr Cresten Frederiksen and I have managed to have some perfectly civil (though warm) discussions about his reasons for leaving Denmark, mostly to do with the rise of the Left and 'enemies of the Natural Order of Things'. Perhaps hr Frederiksen expects to re-establish this 'Natural Order' in the country to which he is transporting his agreeable family, but I doubt the majority travelling in the steerage of this ship will leave him much room for his ambitions (and none at all if my sister has a say in the matter), though their (not her!) sullen docility may need to be ignited.

This letter is one of a packet I must finish to send ashore at Funchal on the island of Madeira where our ship has been forced to go off-course, having lost provisions and water in a storm. We expect to be there tomorrow morning. I did not suffer greatly from the storm that began in what the

English prefer to call the 'English Channel' and continued for some days into the Bay of Biscay. Theodora was very sick and so was poor Josephina. Little Catharina was miserable for a day or two but then wanted to go outside to look at the waves, which was forbidden. Our little cabin and the stateroom space we share with the hopeful Danes and two devout Catholic Bavarian families became very foul and wet, a situation not improved by the fervently vomited prayers of our neighbours. I thought sometimes of 'The Wreck of the Hesperus' by your now fellow American Henry Longfellow and the terrifying translation by our German Freiligrath! And especially the part where the captain's daughter ('Blue were her eyes as the fairy-flax') is lashed to the mast and freezes to death before being washed ashore with hair like seaweed! Next door the born-again Danes reminded each other at intervals how their Christ had calmed the waves on the Sea of Galilee and beseeched him to do it again in the Bay of Biscay, but Jesus wasn't listening to them.

Now I can delay my most important news no longer. You will wonder how we can travel and be accommodated together, since passenger regulations should separate me from my sister and from Josephina and her child. We are all of us travelling as Hansens with travel-passes I got made up in Bremen. I am now Herr Wolf Hansen, my wife is Frau Josephina Hansen and our daughter is Catharina Hansen. That my sister is Fräulein Theodora Hansen is a condition she will not tolerate any longer than necessary, but for the purposes of our 'new life' it was prudent to erase the alarming name Bloch from our records. What's more, even my own unique physical condition passed safely below the eyes of the examining medical officers. They gave my hump a squeeze, perhaps in case it contained contraband or good fortune, they looked into my mouth, perhaps in search of seditious language, and waved me on. The youthful and healthy Josephina, on the other hand, got their full attention.

You, Signor, and Signora Maria will be happy to know that although Josephina and I are not husband and wife in the conventional bourgeois sense, we are so as comrades and lovers and will be the parents of a child soon after we get to New Zealand if our voyage goes well. My dear sister was quick to suggest this was an unexpected relationship, and I had to agree with her. However, it is one in which both Josephina and I are glad and in which I am grateful, since from a young age the likelihood of my having such a relationship has been discounted as ridiculous. But now our 'new life' will indeed have a new life in it.

For now I am in one of the gangs responsible for handing out provisions to the passengers from steerage. Their lot is miserable indeed after the storm, since it damaged water casks and spoiled some of their essential foods, as well as sweeping away animal pens on the deck where chickens as well as some pigs and sheep were kept. The passengers must obey rules such as getting out of bed at fixed times, cleaning their quarters for inspection and doing work such as scrubbing the decks. There are some who have rebelled against this, especially one man who has now been locked up for refusing to obey orders until the rations are improved. If fresh provisions are not to be had in Madeira we are told the ship will have to call at the Canary Islands, a journey of several days. If this happens and our journey is slowed down even more, the unrest among the steerage passengers and the sailors will certainly increase.

The discipline on the ship is a mirror of class systems with which we are familiar and where the docility of the oppressed will be proportionate to the power of those who rule. The man who currently yells curses from the stockade is a familiar defiant in this drama, though hardly a heroic one. So too was the young sailor who angered one of the ship's officers by being slow to respond to an order. This man then beat the boy cruelly with a length of knotted rope and sent him aloft with a bucket of pitch to paint some spars, from where he fell into the sea! He was brought back on board the ship very cold and almost unconscious but was sent aloft again at once after changing his shirt. When he spilled tar on a sail the captain tied him to the rigging and flogged him on his naked back and buttocks in full view. He then ordered one of the officers to pour vitriol on the poor boy's wounds as he lay on the deck. The crowd of onlookers was aghast at his screams but none of us thought to intervene. Am I to be ashamed that I wish above all to protect our little 'Hansen' family? We are at the mercy of those who own the secret knowledge that directs our path to the future. What are we to do? Perhaps in America this familiar diagram will be different. My dear Comrade Martignetti, I hope to hear from you that it is so, for all our sakes. The revolutions in 'the old country' seem fated to be extinguished like the bright flame of the Paris Commune, 'that sphinx so tantalising to the bourgeois mind'.

We are between two and three weeks on our voyage. The full moon under which we departed Germany has now given way to dark nights. All being well I may send another letter to you from the Canary Islands if we stop there, and yet another from some port south of them, under a new full moon! But if not, then from the place where the 'Hansens' will make their new home and work to rouse Marx's sphinx from its torpor!

'Fräulein and Frau Hansen' send you their warm good wishes, and Catharina asks if Alex remembers her. You will be able to reassure her once we have an address in New Zealand.

I am as always

Your respectful and devoted comrade

Wolf Bloch

Josephina and Catharina

There was Wolf by the rail of the ship, making a group of men and women laugh of course. She could just see him through the jostling crowd on deck. It was hard to stand still among them but she wanted to watch the Wolf theatre for a minute or two without making him stop, as he surely would if he saw her. She wanted to feel alone with him but without him knowing she was there. He was stretching his neck and face out with his arms at his sides, which made his little hump stand up like the one on the waterspout gargoyle on Nikolaikirche in Hamburg, the long stretched-out gargoyle with the beaky face that turned Catharina's eyes into blue and white saucers the first time she saw it high up there where Wolf was pointing. Mutti was calling Herr Bloch just 'Wolf' and they had already gone for some walks.

Wolf was probably telling one of his stories to the laughing people on the deck. Perhaps he was pretending to be a fish or pretending that he wanted to jump overboard and swim beside the ship like the dolphins they had seen. He was making little paddling movements with his hands – she stood still where she was and watched him, hidden by the people milling around her.

The story he told Catharina on the day they saw the gargoyle was that once upon a time a bad man drank up all the fresh water meant for his children, so a good magician turned him to stone and put him up there under the roof of the building where the nice fresh rainwater would always just run through him and out the other side so that he always had water in his body but could never quench his thirst.

And what was the name of the good magician, Catharina wanted to know – and did he live nearby?

The good magician's name was Friedrich Engels and he lived in a faraway place called Primrose Hill, Herr Bloch told her, leaning down close.

Josephina chided him with a nudge of her elbow.

And could the bad thirsty stone man ever do peepees, asked Catharina.

No, never, replied Wolf – he was quite startled but chuckled to conceal his surprise from her – because, because, because . . . the water always just ran away backwards, no, forwards, and out of his mouth, it never came out as peepees!

And where did this child learn about water going in at the top and coming out as peepees at the bottom, he asked Josephina out of the side of his mouth.

From me, Josephina told him, because I think she should learn about things.

But she was very young, suggested Wolf.

But what was so secret about water going in at the top and coming out at the bottom as peepees, Josephina wanted to know. It was very simple after all and the child should understand how her body works.

Catharina was noticing that her mutti and Herr Bloch were looking at each other for a long time with funny smiles on their faces, so she began to tug at Josephina's skirt to make them keep walking. They were going to Holzbrücke where on some days there was the band of gypsies with the dancing monkey. It was quite near to where they used to live at Herr Andersen's house, and sometimes that reminded Catharina of the Kita where she used to play with Alex. It reminded Josephina of the woman in the pale evening dress with silk flowers on the bosom standing on the stairs of Herr

Andersen's house with Catharina in her arms, but Catharina liked to go to the bridge and so they did, sometimes, even though Josephina felt anxious about meeting Frau Andersen. On that day, out walking with Wolf and Catharina, her worry was almost hidden, like the currents that pushed the surface of the river into ripples.

First they looked over the balustrade at the brown, sluggish flow – Was it true, as written in the *Bürger Zeitung*, that the river water could make people sick?

Wolf was holding Catharina up so she could lean over. It was a matter of public sanitation that mostly affected the poor. This information he provided while pretending to tip Catharina over the edge so that she screamed. And children, he added.

Did Wolf know why they had left Herr Andersen's house? Which was nearby on Deichstrasse?

Yes, he understood why it might have been necessary, he told her.

Then he put Catharina down again. He was nodding at Josephina in a way that said clearly he knew about the situation at the Andersen house. Until then they had never spoken about it.

Catharina was tugging on Josephina's skirt again because Mutti and Herr Bloch were talking to each other with their faces quite close together, but the gypsies and the fuzzy monkey weren't at the bridge so Herr Bloch got a cab with a nice black horse and she was allowed to ride up top with the driver.

Giddy up! she shouted as they clopped away – while inside the cab Josephina leaned towards Wolf and thanked him and then picked up his hand and held it between both of hers for a moment, with a little squeeze. Then she sat back. He was kind and he listened to her, she thanked him for that and for his affectionate way with Catharina. He was looking at her with an absurd expression on his face – it was a mixture of surprise and gratitude, his mouth was open but no words came out, and Wolf was certainly never at a loss for words.

But it wasn't his loss of words, it was his gratitude that touched her the most there in the cab with its rather stale smell of tobacco. He noticed her wrinkling her nose and trying to pull down the window-glass, and so reached across her to help. Excuse me, Josephina? Unlike the cab, Wolf had quite a nice smell – he kept a little bottle of syrup of violets and almond oil by his bed, for his cough; Josephina had taken out the cork and sniffed it when tidying his room, the smell was in his bed as well, and it seemed he dabbed some on his chest before going out – though there was also of course the aroma of himself, and his warmth.

Over by the rail of the ship the group had dispersed and Wolf was leaning back and looking towards her with his head on one side, that was his way. He gave a little 'Come over here' wave.

Of course she knew why she'd picked up his hand in the cab. It wasn't just a thoughtless impulse.

What silly nonsense was he telling those people?

She took his arm.

He was telling them about the only time he'd ever tried to swim. He'd believed all you had to do was dive into the water and make yourself the shape of a fish, he'd almost drowned. That was in Uelzen, in the river Gerdau, which was pure and ran between lovely grasslands and forests, made even purer and lovelier you might think by his young schoolmates who swam in it and had urged him to jump in. He still remembered the ghastly sensation of sinking! But Josephina, she was a Siren now, so Theodora had told him, she'd have to let him ride on her tail and they'd be saved! They could swim together to an island like her favourite one in *The Swiss Family Robinson*, though please without the self-satisfied Schweizer! Who were even worse than the Frederiksens! Or those Bavarians!

But she hoped he hadn't told those people about her being a Siren? And her tail?

'What, the Frederiksens?'

'The people you were telling the fishy story to, silly man. But also the Frederiksens!'

Her tail was their secret, he reassured her – theirs and Theodora's, he added, as his sister came towards them with Catharina.

'This is the Atlantic Ocean,' Catharina told them proudly, extending her arms. 'All of it!'

'Oceans,' explained Theodora, who looked tired. 'We've been learning oceans. Some of us, at least.'

The three Frederiksen children went past in a little herd managed by fru Frederiksen, and the girl called Gudrun poked her tongue out at Catharina. Fru Frederiksen preferred to instruct her children in the Bible away from the common schoolroom. She had a way of parting the crowd on the deck as they hurried towards the stateroom. Could she go with them, Catharina begged with a sweet expression for her mutti. She liked the stories such as the one about the time Jesus made one fish and one loaf of bread increase until it satisfied 'a multitude'.

Theodora said something inaudible.

Yes, of course she could, said Josephina – did she want Mutti to come with her? As far as their cabin?

There was a band with a violin and a flageolet, and some

people had begun to dance. Dancing was encouraged as a way of exercising on board the ship, so they were all told. But it was the nice weather and the sunshine that had lifted the mood of the passengers, as it had Josephina's, so she thought it was quite simple, surely? Unless Catharina would prefer to stay and listen to the music? She could have a little dance with her mutti? But not too fast?

But no, Catharina wanted to go to be with her friend Gudrun, she liked her, they had a secret language.

Wolf allowed his hand to press Josephina's stomach as he took his arm from her waist.

There was that expression on Theodora's face again – was it more sad than annoyed or more annoyed than sad? But what did it mean to think of it as an expression, an out-looking, since what Theodora's face was doing was mostly concealing what she thought or felt? Or in-looking, looking in at what she was thinking, looking at herself? And in any case, Catharina was *her* daughter, not Theodora's, she had raised her to be a friendly child and to be curious about things like reading, which she was learning to do with *The Swiss Family Robinson*, and about oceans, for example – what right did Theodora have to those expressions that were not quite truthful?

Then Catharina was pulling her away towards the Frederiksens. Probably now Wolf and his sister would have their discussion about the Danes, it was usually the same one, with Theodora being annoyed and Wolf being amused, which annoyed her even more, which amused him even more, and so on. She'd leave them to find a way of changing how they discussed the Danes, or going back to the beginning again, or coming to an agreement! – while she went with Catharina to be with her friend Gudrun and the stories from the Bible that she herself remembered well from the days at Pastor Köhler's hot musty schoolroom so long ago now it seemed, when in summer the big dung flies would come droning in from the cow meadow. *Boring boring boring* Elke would mumble under her breath, imitating them and Pastor Köhler, and *thwack* would go the wooden spoon on her back!

And then she continued rather tired through to her own space in the cabin where she'd begun to put nice blue chain-stitch borders on the little garments she was making, starting with a muslin night-shift long enough to cover the baby's feet. She was also going to do a little antlered deer on the front, with its mountain peak and a pine tree, more interesting than an owl, though she didn't have much thread and had begun to unpick some of the embroidery work on her own things to get enough different colours.

The sound of the sea – of the Atlantic Ocean! – never went away from the sides of the ship, nor did the sounds of the ship itself, its creaking and snapping and moaning so terrible at first and the sounds of wind and sails, and especially when their hatch was open the hubbub of people on the deck when they were allowed to be out there, and now the sound of fru Frederiksen next door in the stateroom reading from the Bible in the Danish that Catharina said she understood, she understood perfectly! – though of course she hardly did, since she was only just talking when they left Sønderborg, her funny mixture of Danish and German with Finn's made-up words as well. The sounds were soothing and the sewing was intimate, the way it repeated was both dreamy and careful, and there was just enough wave-flicker light from the porthole window if she sat below it on the bunk bed she sometimes shared with Catharina but not Wolf these days.

Ah, it was so nice to be alone but also nice to feel her body occupied a little by desire – it was the pleasing atmosphere of the cabin that did that but also Wolf's absence, the thought of him saying 'little bird wings, how lovely' in his room with its dim lamp, his hesitant fingers on her shoulder blades, his uncertainty – and as earlier in the cab with the black horse and Catharina shouting with excitement up there with the driver who was also by then shouting giddy up! – that look of astonishment and gratitude when she took his hand, but later in his dim room his fuzzy chest rising and falling with his difficult breaths. The funny, fuzzy chest he'd been too shy for her to uncover, at first.

'You're a fuzzy monkey! So now I know!'

'And you're a little bird.' He could only just manage to say it once.

'A Rohrsänger.'

Gasping, 'A what?'

No, she wouldn't do the little deer on its mountain with the pine tree, or the owl with its solemn round face turned out to stare straight ahead – no, it would be the Rohrsänger on the delicate pale muslin, a pair of them, they would have tiny blushes of redness and dark streaks along their wings and pale breasts of bare muslin, they would have small bright black eyes – where could she get some black beads, perhaps she could dye some grains with Wolf's ink, but how could she attach them? – and they could rest there on the thin muslin, the little Rohrsänger, and sway a little in the breeze that was the baby breathing, and then one day they would arrive at last after their long journey at the place that oranges came from. And that was the story she would tell her baby, not the story of the little deer that would only ever stay behind, and not the story of the owl that could only ever make its first evening hoot from the edge of the woods over beyond the Bauernhaus – there always had to be a first one as the daylight faded, and it would always be where Elke was.

Now she was crying and had to put the muslin aside, which was when Wolf and Theodora came in. Theodora turned at once and went out again into the stateroom, closing the door on Catharina's worried face looking towards her. It had begun to rain outside, it was a 'squall' Wolf told her, and indeed the ship had leaned over – but then he sat down beside her on the bed and carefully put his hand on her back, the bones he liked.

'What's the matter, little bird?'

What was the matter? What was the matter? Nothing was the matter, she couldn't really explain it, she was feeling so happy and even would he believe a little amorous, yes, just a little, it was so nice, she was liking the peace of their cabin and the sewing, she even liked remembering her sister Elke, nothing was the matter, really nothing.

Now she just had to unpick some things because she didn't have enough thread. She'd been remembering.

Remembering what, he wanted to know.

'That first time we . . .'

His pleased ah-hum, the prickle of his whiskers on her jaw.

But no, that wasn't it.

She gently pushed him away.

'I don't understand what the world means. I don't understand where it is.'

His face and whole body were silent.

'Sometimes it overcomes me.'

Catharina's querulous voice on the other side of the door.

'Just give me a little kiss, please, Wolf, and then tell the others they can come in if they want to.'

The very sweet tender little kiss. His hand on the side of her neck.

'Thank you, Monkey.'

Catharina came in first. She knew Mutti's crying from the redness of the eyes.

Would she like to help her mutti with some unpicking, so they could have some more thread for the baby's nightdress?

Then they sat down together to do the work.

Tuesday, the 25th of November, The Atlantic Ocean

My dear sisters Elke and Greta I kiss you both many many times.

Yes of course I've cried sometimes thinking of you! And also thinking about Papa, and of course Finn and Otto who will both be big boys now especially that naughty Finn! And perhaps Elke will have something special to write me about when she has time away from her handsome Franzose!

I promised to write a letter about my life in Hamburg but it has been very different and busy and in any case we all saw each other at Elke's wedding and so you know that I was living with Catharina at the Bloch House of Herr Wolf Bloch and Fräulein Theodora Bloch and liking it, it was a nice house by the lake, and very hospitable.

Since the wedding and the happy memories I have of those days much has happened and some of that is why I haven't written you the letter I promised, it was because I was unsure how to tell you about the things that have happened in my life which is also Catharina's life, I was afraid you would judge me or be angry with me. But I was wrong and foolish to be afraid because I know you love me. No matter how wide the distance is between us we are always close in the world and will be for ever.

Elke you will read this first and so will Papa and perhaps Tante Elizabeth, but please send it to Greta as soon as you can because you all need to know that Wolf and Theodora Bloch and Catharina and I have left Hamburg because of laws against the Socialists, it had become dangerous. We are now all on a ship going to New Zealand many weeks journey away but it will be a safe place where we can have a new life.

You will want to know why I am going to this distant place with strangers since the laws are attacking them but not your little sister or Catharina. The reason is that Wolf Bloch and your little sister are now in a marriage and I am going to have this man's child. Yes Elke I know you will at this moment be screaming what a fool your sister must be and have I allowed myself to be taken advantage of again but I can tell you and you must believe me nothing could be more different. Firstly because I did not allow myself to be taken advantage of in that house on Faulstrasse and of course you know why that was so, but secondly because I am married to Wolf and bearing his child because I chose to and you know I can choose my path, you have seen me do it before. He is a very gentle man and also funny but not strong in his body, it is the strength of his nature that I love and his kindness to me and also to Catharina who calls him Papa Wolf. Yes it is true that we are not married in the usual way with a pastor like you Greta to your Danish man who carried you far away across the Alsund to Sønderborg where your uncles were killed by the Danes, in case you forgot! And you Elke to a penniless Franzose who says things in his beard about the revolutions of forty-eight and so is surely seditious!

But we are all married in the way that matters which is about love, and so Elke and Greta you have to be happy for me and for Catharina and for the sister or brother that she will have in our new life.

And now at last I will tell you something about what has been happening and what it is like to be sailing across the Atlantic Ocean in this ship with hundreds of others also hoping for a new life. We had to run from Hamburg in a hurry because the Chancellor's men closed Wolf's Bürger Zeitung newspaper down and took his property and would have sent him to prison if we hadn't gone to Bremen. He wanted to go to America where some of his comrades were already living but there was no time. The friends of the Bürger Zeitung collected enough money for an intermediate class voyage and so we are travelling in better conditions than most of the passengers. There are four intermediate class cabins on the ship, two on each side of it, and each one has two sleeping compartments with four beds in each, the beds are stacked two high so it is very close. There are about thirty of us altogether in these cabins and a lesser number in the most expensive first class ones, they keep to themselves and stay on the upper deck at the back of the ship, sometimes people on the lower deck gather to look at them and discuss their clothes!

In our class there is a small shared room for each pair of cabins where we can eat our meals and shelter during the day. We are sharing ours with a Danish family with three children whose sleeping space is the closest to us, of course they speak mostly Danish and are Lutherans like Pastor Jepsen who christened Catharina in Sønderborg, you will remember him Elke, you said he was buttoned-up. The others on our side of the ship who also share this stateroom are two families from a place called Starnberg in the south, they are related to each other and all look the same, they speak a funny kind of German and are Catholics and are travelling to be with even more of their family in New Zealand, perhaps one day you will think of doing this! And then there is our family which the others think is Jewish even though Wolf and Theodora are Socialists and don't believe in religion and Catharina and I are not. Wolf tries to have conversations with these different believers but Theodora keeps to herself. We have all been thrown together by circumstances and will have to remain friendly for many weeks but I think this will not be easy. There is a shared washroom with a privy that spills over when the sea is stormy but no bath, some of the men go on deck and have seawater thrown over them in the morning.

There was a big storm soon after we left Bremerhaven, both Theodora and I were very sick but Catharina was not bad and Wolf looked after us all as much as possible dear man. There were animal pens on the deck and most of them were swept away into the waves that came over the ship and also came in to our cabins and flooded them. We had to go in to the Island of Madeira to get supplies since many of those were spoiled or lost in the storm, but there was a dispute about these provisions at the port and so now the ship's captain has told us we are going to the Canary Islands. All that came on board at Madeira was some wine and fresh fruit for the rich passengers, which made the others angry and no wonder!

So now some people are angry about the supplies and the delays in our voyage and the captain and his officers are walking about with weapons. But today was mostly sunny and warm and people were dancing up on the deck where we are allowed to go for certain times every day if the weather is good. When the weather is bad we have to stay shut up with all the doors and windows closed, which is bad for us but much worse for the people in the mass accommodations who have to live crowded together in a single space, and so we are lucky. There is a school for the children that Catharina goes to, and I still have the Swiss Family Robinson that you hid in my bag Greta on that day Catharina and I left you that I will never forget.

But now we all have to put our lights out, the ship has many orders like this, and so I will stop here and promise to write again. This letter will have to go ashore in the Canary Islands where we hope to be before too long so that another ship can carry it back the way we have come, to my dear sisters in those places I will always remember because of you.

Your sister and daughter Josephina
and your niece and granddaughter Catharina who can now write her own name here.

Catharina

Papa Wolf was having a bucket wash with the men. They pulled the bucket up out of the sea on the end of a rope and threw it over each other. Papa Wolf only had his underdrawers on, he was covered all over in hair and was jumping up and down and going hoo hoo too cold! She helped Tante make breakfast in the big kitchen, Tante had to do it for Gudrun and all the others, it was her turn, Tante said, thank you Catharina for helping to stir the pot, you're a good stirrer! Papa Wolf would be getting dressed while she and Tante made the breakfast, of course he had to cover up his hairiness because it was funny. There were people waiting to make their breakfast and some of them began to shout. Then she helped Tante carry the breakfast to their room where the others were waiting, they had to go carefully because the ship was rocking and also go carefully down the steps. Then Gudrun's papa said a Danish prayer and they all waited. She and Gudrun were staring at each other with their secret look. Then one of the Bayern papas said one of their prayers and they all waited again and those ones all made touching movements on their fronts because they were catlickers Papa Wolf said. No one waited for Papa Wolf to say a prayer. Breakfast was oatmeal but there wasn't any milk to drink only coffee so she had water, it tasted funny. There was also some cheese but no more oranges, they were all gone. They had to hold on to their plates to eat. The oranges were from the Canary Islands that Tante said was in the middle of the Atlantic Ocean, they also got some big and little goats, mostly brown and black with big bubbies hanging down, some of them were for milk but there wasn't any yet. The goats lived in pens on the deck and had funny eyes. Then she helped tidy up their beds. Mutti could feel the baby moving, would Catharina like to put her hand on her tummy and feel her little brother or sister? It felt as though the baby was jumping around but not as much as Papa Wolf getting his bucket wash and shouting! Would the baby be hairy like Papa Wolf, she wondered. Or it could be like its big sister, suggested Mutti. With Kornblume eyes? But now it was time for her to go to school, first she must use the privy and wash her face, here was a towel and the piece of lavender soap that was almost all gone now, be careful not to drop it, now give your mutti a sweet kiss please. Mutti's face was nice and soft but she had tired eyes, so Catharina kissed them on their lids. Have a rest, Mutti. Yes she would, but first she'd come with Catharina to the school after she'd had her wash, she'd better hurry because there would be others waiting as well. Then they were up on deck in the bright sunshine. Mutti wished they still had some oranges from the Canary Islands, and didn't Catha also miss them? It was the smell of the oranges that she liked as well as their taste, she'd have liked to see the place where the orange trees grew on the Canary Islands, Mutti told her. Yes, Mutti's eyes were tired, she was blinking them, but maybe that was because it was so sunny outside. The goats didn't blink theirs, they were yellow with black stripes across them. Why were the goats' eyes like that? Mutti thought it might be because they spent so much time looking at the faraway edge of the Atlantic Ocean, what did Catha think? Catharina thought they'd better not let the baby do that, look at the edge of the Atlantic Ocean, but then Gudrun took her hand and they left Mutti behind.

Theodora

Thursday, 4 December, 1879, Atlantic Ocean, south of Canary Islands

Today it is sunny and not cold even for this time of year, and so very pleasant. I was on deck early when Wolf and his newfound friends were hurling buckets of seawater at each other. Of course my brother was conspicuous in this gang as you would expect since all except for him are big loud hearty men who smack their thighs and chests and bellies and bellow like wild animals as they compete to be enjoying their drenching even more than their herd-fellows. This is a small as well as incongruous miracle I must suppose, since before now Wolf has avoided like the plague anything resembling a bucket of cold water for fear of getting a sick chest and has to my knowledge never agreed to appear half naked in public, except for a notorious incident at Uelzen when his school mates conspired to drown him like a sick cat and very nearly succeeded. But now it is as though the ship with its crowded mass of undernourished optimists has become a Sanitarium at least as far as Wolf is concerned, and he clearly fears no malice from his fellow bathers.

Today it was also my turn to prepare breakfast for our mismatched stateroom of sixteen gaping mouths and Catharina was helping me to fill them. We were on our way to the kitchen when we passed Wolf working up his appetite for the spoonsful of oats and the measure of coffee that would be his reward for the morning's exertions. He performed an extravagant caper for Catharina's benefit rather than mine and made a comical hooting sound as the seawater struck him.

Catharina calls him Papa Wolf, and Papa Wolf it was who made her laugh until she hiccupped this morning. Of course I must rejoice at my brother's changed behaviour springing as it does from the newfound joy that emerges in disbelief from his paternal relationship with Catharina and also of course even more from his inconceivable relationship with her mother. He seems at times to be living in a space stretched between bliss and disbelief in which even his miserable little body has been renewed. That Catharina loves her Papa Wolf I don't doubt and I am sure Josephina does too, but in her case I fear that the rewards of this unlikely love have been borrowed against compromised capital, the past that sits in her heart like a loan shark waiting his moment to call in the debt with all its scandalous interest. I see that she knows this and fears the contingency of her happiness. At the same time she is evidently glad in the clear-eyed and clear-sighted critical way of which she is capable. That her eyes are sometimes red from tears can be as much from gladness as dread. That she also grieves for her own family left behind is obvious although she refuses to talk about them, and so I see that the further we go away from the place where her map of the world was first drawn in a small space but with large consequences for her thinking about fate and the future, the more resolute she tells herself she must become. She wept suddenly and was unable to hide it when a basket of sweet oranges was delivered to our cabins in the Canary Islands. It was as though what had been presented to her was at once her hope and her grief, her hope for what might be sweet in the future and her grief at leaving what had been sweet in her childhood now long past and distant behind her.

But now I am speculating about what I cannot truthfully know, although I see that Josephina is watching me watch her and sees that I do so with a blatancy she prefers to turn from rather than stare down, as would be her usual manner. And so we are all locked here in this floating Sanitarium in the middle of the vast Atlantic Ocean in which these dramas of sensibility and affection are being played out as a kind of mummery upon which the confines of the cabin press in stiflingly when the weather is bad and which inflates its absurd dramas in proportion to the bewildering expanse of ocean when the weather is benign.

To this must be added our microcosm of the religious wars that have gone on devastating the human world ever since mankind first erected altars to gods, since we are now subjected to the glares and shrugs of Christian sects who hate not only each other but also the shipmates they believe to be Jews.

And of course there are many degrees of simmering nationalist resentment and suspicion among the passengers, not least those in our small compound. Danes and Germans, Germans from the south and those from the north, and all and sundry looking askance at these Ostjuden whose origins and loyalties owe nothing to the Homeland and who are presumed to be opportunist beggars and pants-sellers. Where once we were parasites on the soil of Germany, now it seems we benefit from the misdirected charity of those who would like to assist our departure from that soil. In addition, of course, our immigrant nation of beggars and intellectuals has been branded unpatriotic and subversive by association with socialists and not least with that arch-communist fiend Karl Marx. What right do we have to be enjoying the privileges of our comfort on board this ship when so many are suffering between decks, and so forth!

Though our Danish cabin neighbours are politely apprehensive rather than hostile, those family members from the Bavarian south make no attempt to conceal their distaste for the proximity into which they have been thrust, though, to be fair, their opprobrium is directed almost as much at their Protestant Danish neighbours as at our small cell of Jewish degenerates. The worst of them are their three glowering sons and head-tossing daughter aged somewhere between fifteen and twenty, who expect to be reunited with their older siblings when they get to New Zealand, where their seniors have been preparing for them. And so the inbred hostilities of the Old Homeland have already been transplanted to the New Homeland and await the arrival of fresh recruits. Wolf, it has to be said, deflects these tiresome glowers with his usual mixture of insouciance and riposte. When asked by one of the braver lads where he came from, Wolf replied that he came from his mother's womb, adding, with a straight face, And you?

Two mornings ago I asked Wolf why he was so happy that morning and said I was waiting to hear why he hadn't told me the reason for it. This is a little dialogue we've reprised most of our lives, but his reply on this occasion gave me a fright. He was planning to publish an on-board newspaper, he told me, to circulate the news of the ship, such as its progress and what had been reported of the world from the most recent port visit, and to include some entertainments such as stories of life on the ship 'and so forth'.

'And so forth', I suggested to my blandly smiling brother, might not include political material, surely, given certain vulnerabilities to which he might expose us? He avoided my question by saying with mischievous convolutions that he hadn't told me why he was happy because he didn't at that stage know what there was to tell me, if anything. But now, I asked. Now, as it turned out, one of his bucket-wash companions was a printer called Oats who had on board the basic means to set a few pages of type, as well as a small broadsheet hand-press, and who was a nice fellow and bored enough to print anything he was given.

Then, anticipating me asking whether 'and so forth' and 'anything he was given' included material many on board including the captain would consider inflammatory and even mutinous, he very carefully presented me with a question that I took to be rhetorical. When are men indiscriminate thugs by nature, and when is their violence politically directed and particular as to its occasion? He then at once answered his own question, as he often likes to. Our Danish companion hr Frederiksen had described to him the mutinous and violent passenger in the stockade as a thoughtless thug who would be a violent presence no matter what the circumstances. On the other hand, the good Dane believed the violence inflicted on the poor young sailor whose back had been lacerated by flogging, while horrible, had been the product not of mindless thuggery and incoherent rage but of a system of punishment enshrined in the disciplinary codes of the ship to which we all as passengers, or if you like as citizens, owed our safety and well-being in the Natural Order of Things.

Wolf knew very well that I believe, as does he, that the man in the stockade, while no hero, appears as a violent thug only in relation to that disciplinary code and the powers it enshrines, when in fact his conditions and his relative powerlessness have made his rage not only comprehensive but also comprehensible. And so, was this the polemic with which Wolf planned to inaugurate his newspaper? Which was to be called, what? The Mutineer? No, replied my brother, whose spirits were very high, the first issue might commence a discussion of recipes for making salt beef with pickled cabbage taste like fresh baby goat stew with a carafe of good Canary Island malvasia.

We are now making passage towards the port of Praia in Cape Verde, about two weeks distant and yet another stop at which only some cabin passengers will be permitted to go ashore, with predictable consequences. Wolf plans to buy a small stock of broadsheet paper there with which to begin his newspaper, in the first edition of which he promises a schedule of entertainments including concerts, dances, puppet shows and floggings.

Ah my dear little brother, your happiness is almost enough to make me happy too, but the reason it falls short is constantly within your reach.

Beth and Frank

No point asking Frank why he turned off the main highway about an hour later – he'd said 'Okay' but not to her as they left Taumarunui and it seemed the turn-off further along was what he'd agreed to with himself. Singing in a growly whisper, 'I'm an ordinary joker growin' old before me time, 'cause me heart's in Taumarunui on the Main Trunk Line', but when Beth joined the chorus of 'In Taumarunui, Taumarunui, Taumarunui on the Main Trunk Line', he turned to her with a startled look and stopped singing. A campervan passed them with a cheerful toot-ti-toot; there were T-shirts and undies flapping from the wound-up windows. Frank drove at a steady eighty and not all passers were as amiable as the camper. Clouds in the sky seemed to be going too slow as well.

They continued to dawdle at Frank's speed for a while. Then the obscure turn-off. They dawdled on across some unremarkable deforested, chopped-up hilly country with miserly grass cover on the slopes. Some sheep. There was a Clydesdale horse stud in a greenish valley-flat. Now that was an option Grandad Wolf hadn't considered.

'Pouakani,' Frank said, after a while. And then, 'Sorry we never visited you that last time.'

'So was I,' she said.

'There was this big tree,' he said. 'Helen wanted to see it.'

'Bit more interesting than an old stump.'

'Nothing of the sort and don't be packing a sad, it's not like you. It was just her thing – she was pretty crook, she wanted to look at some splendid old trees. Then we had to get home.' He reached for her hand. 'You up for a short walk?'

Beth knew the big old tree called Pouakani quite well, and the short bush walk. She and Noel had tramped in the Pureora with the kids a few times. He was photographing for *Nat Geo*. 'Pity I never got to meet your Helen, all the same. And I'm not packing a sad. I'd have liked to.'

'Chuck a sad?'

'Meet her.' She lifted his hand back on the steering wheel, it was a twisty bit of road. 'How come you know this way in? We always came over from the Taupō road.'

'It was in that brochure back at the hotel. I was led to the page by Helen's invisible hand. She ran out of puff when we got to the old tree, threw up at the base of it – we had a nebuliser in the car but she forgot to bring it on the walk.' He gave the steering wheel a whack. 'Fuck,' he said, with venom, and then, 'But meanwhile.' And then, 'I taught her that song.'

Then the silence of the bare landscape invaded the car. Beth considered putting some music in the player. What would that be? She had the 1990 remastered CD of the 1957 Solisti di Zagreb recording of Vivaldi's *Four Seasons* with the appropriate showmanship of the Argentinian Jan Tomasow's violin, Noel's favourite. She'd played it often after he'd forgotten who she was but recognised every note of the music. Sometimes they'd go for drives to his favourite spots.

Of course now if she put the CD on it would inevitably begin with Spring, but the parched hills receding slowly behind them were all about late summer. Oh, for Christ's sake. It was even tedious, the way everything couldn't be simple. Just play the damn thing.

And then Frank said, 'You got the old grave, I get the old tree, we're quits, okay?'

She took the CD out of the glovebox and stuck it in the player. 'Springtime is upon us, the birds celebrate her return with festive song, and murmuring streams are softly caressed by the breezes.' She knew the translations of the *Four Seasons* sonnets by heart: she and Noel would say them in unison over and over, he remembered those as well. She pushed play and Frank began immediately to laugh.

'Genius,' he said. 'Touché!'

Some native forest, briefly, past Benneydale, and squashed possums on the road. She was humming along with the *Seasons* in her head.

It was Autumn by the time they got to the Pouakani track. Frank pulled the car over and turned off the ignition. Autumn had just begun its *Adagio molto.*

'Everyone is made to forget their cares and to sing and dance by the air which is tempered with pleasure,' said Beth into the silence. Frank was looking out his driver's window at the place where the track started. The faded green sign had white graffiti scrawled across it.

'Should have done that,' said Frank.

'Done what?'

'Signed her out. She sat with her back against that tree for quite a while. Did her good, I think. Then we went back to Taupō and stayed in a motel called Chateau Suisse, she pissed herself over that. Where the fuck are we, she said. And how the fuck did we get here?' He opened his car door. 'You don't have to come if you don't want to,' he said, and climbed out with a grunt of discomfort.

'There's no arse left in your dockers,' said Beth as she followed him to the track. 'You're way too skinny. We should have a damn good lunch after this.'

She followed his arse-less strides the short distance to

the place where the trunk of the huge old tōtara called Pouakani rose ahead like a fissured cliff. He tipped his head back to look up at the tree's dishevelled crown. She waited for a bit, thinking Frank needed some time to himself, but then without turning around he held one arm out, making beckoning movements with his fingers, so she stepped into his hug and felt the sobs heaving in his chest.

Then, 'Okay, thanks,' he said. 'We should get that lunch.'

Then, after a long silence in the car, 'What's the difference between recalcitrant and refractory?'

'Recalcitrants have a bad attitude to authority, refractories can't be persuaded. Pretty much the same.'

'Helen said she was like a recalcitrant seed because she wouldn't survive drying or freezing, but she was refractory because she chose not to believe that.'

Beth was taking a turn driving; they were passing the gloomy pine forest that fed the Kinleith paper mill, a dreary expanse of dark trees with here and there clearings filled with the wreckage of felled timber. Then the nasty chemical stink of the mill itself.

'She'd have preferred to be a tree, for sure, but not one of those poor wood-pulp buggers. She was always taking the kids to look at trees – they used to say you like trees better than us. Not true of course, but still.' Frank was squirming around in his seat, checking out the surroundings. 'I worked here in the holidays after my first year at uni, before we went to Aussie. Boy was I green. A foreman had a log dropped on him because he got offside with a certain work gang. On paydays a bus used to pull in to the work camp with a bunch of prostitutes on board. The place was full of fucked-up guys with maintenance orders out on them, lots of keep-your-head-down crims. Lots of PI overstayers lying low and trying to save some money to send their families in town – these days we'd call them refugees. In the pub on Fridays there'd be jugs flying across the room and big brawls in the carpark. I met this old guy called Hick, he wasn't allowed to see his kids because he was a drunk, he had a hermaphrodite pal called Joey, talk about an odd couple. We used to go for Sunday drives to places like Mangakino – they'd get completely pissed on Waikato Draught and I'd drive their clapped-out Ford Popular home to the camp. We'd stop on the way so they could spew or get their strides off to beer-shit by the side of the road. I hitched back to the city when the plant shut down at Christmas and the night I got home with my hard-earned cash Mum told me and Ruth we were going to Australia, she'd scored a subeditor job in Brisbane, time for a fresh start. She'd been a widow for thirteen years, had a couple of see-ya-later boyfriends, never stopped working, stayed in the same house. Ruth and me were nineteen. She was pushing sixty. You can stay here if you like, she said, but what were the chances?'

Beth knew some of this but not the sordid Kinleith part. It was way more than Frank had said all week except for the story of Ruth getting killed in Jordan, as if both were his ways of telling her or himself about something else. The stories were like semi-transparent wrapping. 'I remember Mum threw a goodbye party for you guys at our place,' she said. 'You told me not to cry. Fat chance. You promised to send me stuff.'

'And I did, didn't I? Heaps of it.'

'You sent me jokes and photos of koalas and later on girls in bikinis – your girlfriends you said, but I never believed you.'

'You were what, about ten?'

‘It lasted quite a few years.’ Beth drove through Tokoroa without stopping for their lunch, no way, it was a ghost town.

‘Still got any of that stuff?’

‘What do you think?’

Frank didn’t answer – he thought not was her guess, that was what his silence suggested. But those letters might still be there somewhere in one of the boxes under the house. What did it even mean to say she couldn’t remember? Quite a bit of the junk was Noel’s. Boxes and boxes of full 35mm colour-slide containers. She’d been meaning to have a cleanout ever since he died. There was a warped mast for an old Cherub sailing dinghy. That was what always made her turn around and go back up the stairs. He’d dumped the useless thing in front of her racks of stuff. The hull it belonged to went long before Noel did. She’d have to get around to chucking it.

Wolf Bloch

To Herr Aksel Andersen
Deichstrasse 31
Hamburg

Friday, December 12, 1879

To my respected colleague and friend Herr Aksel Andersen, greetings from the middle of the Atlantic Ocean!

My sister Theodora and I also send our greetings and best wishes to Frau Andersen.

Dear Friend, I am writing to you in the hope that you and Frau Andersen have not yet joined the exodus to America, as you sometimes spoke of doing in the months before the Bloch House was obliged to pack its remaining belongings and leave Hamburg. This letter will be returned from Cape Verde along our journey's path and so will not reach Hamburg for some weeks. If you have not departed and do receive it, may I ask you to circulate its contents to those friends of Bloch House whose names are familiar to you. You were not a member of our circle but your sympathies were appreciated since we, like you, care about the conditions of workers who contribute to Hamburg's prosperity but share little of it.

You will know better than me by this time that those of us identified as seditious face dangerous consequences if the Chancellor's networks of spies, agents provocateurs and interrogators notice our communications and meetings. I am therefore taking the precaution and liberty of sending this letter to you, my respected friend. There is no reason to believe you will have joined the list of those whose communications may be investigated, as was the case with my colleagues Signor Martignetti and Herr Johannes Paul, whom you knew at arm's length so to speak, and who like Fräulein Bloch and myself have had to seek a safe haven elsewhere.

First of all, would you be so kind as to pass on, to one of the friends of Bloch House, Theodora's and my grateful thanks for the generous support we received from that circle. Any one of them will be able to circulate this message, which must reach as many as possible. Without their support we could not have afforded papers with which to travel safely, nor could we have afforded the accommodation we now have on board our ship. Though not luxurious, it is better than the conditions shared by the majority. Therefore, our friends should know if they do not already that we are safely on our way to New Zealand.

They should also know that we are travelling under the name of the young woman who joined our household, whose identity is known to you. You may communicate this identity to the person of your choice, but please ask them not to record it or the use to which it has been put. It may seem melodramatic to say that we wish to disappear 'without trace', as hunters say of their elusive prey. However, until we are able to scrutinise the conditions of immigration at our destination, and the kinds of official record-keeping that pertain in New Zealand, and indeed the political temper of the country, we prefer to be new people coming anew to a new land. As far as the authorities in Hamburg are concerned we will still be in Germany, though like the clever little speckled partridge of my childhood we will be presumed to have merged with the autumn margins of the wheat fields in some obscure place like Uelzen where we can hardly be expected to trouble the status quo, thus thwarting the hunters eager for our blood.

The following information is also important and, like our innocuous grey partridge plumage, must be kept hidden from all except those I am, with emotion, calling the friends of Bloch House. All significant records of our dear Bürger Zeitung are now in the vaults of Behrenberg-Gossler, a place unlikely to come under the gaze of the Chancellor's agents. The bank has an affiliate in America, which may be useful to us in future. The records are deposited under the name of the young woman mentioned earlier, and once we are settled in New Zealand either I or one of our colleagues in America will be able to provide letters of authority to a secure party. In the deposit there are also journals and research diaries made by Theodora and myself which, all being well, we may be able to make use of in future, once we have recovered them.

Finally, my kind friend, a very brief description of our situation here in the middle of the Atlantic Ocean. We are sharing space with thirteen others in four sleeping cabins arranged as pairs, with a common stateroom and washroom. A similar arrangement exists on the other side of the ship. We are lucky to be where we are, and are thought to be so by those who live in crowded conditions. There are accommodations far superior to ours in a closely guarded compound at the back of the ship, where those with the means to afford it are served the food and drink prepared for them from livestock penned on deck and from a store of superior wines and the fresh produce taken on board at ports-of-call. This manifest privilege, while familiar, has caused unrest among those denied access to its fruits. It seems probable that this diagram of class will be transplanted to, or will conform with, conditions in the place we will soon be calling home. Thus, the work with which we have engaged these past years seems likely to continue on new soil in which we may be able to sow some seeds of change.

With this hope in mind, I will close by wishing you and Frau Andersen good fortune on whatever path you choose to take. I have no doubt your generous and progressive instincts will win you friends wherever you decide to settle. You may even decide to join us there in New Zealand. If you do, you can be confident of a warm welcome and all assistance possible.

Finally, please urge the friends of Bloch House to remember us and be prepared to re-open the channels of communication that will be our means to advance our causes in the furthest parts of the world.

I am and will remain

Your grateful and devoted friend and colleague

Wolf Bloch

To Friedrich Engels, in Primrose Hill, London
Friday, December 12, 1879

My dear Engels

Unlikely as it may seem, I am writing to you from the middle of the Atlantic Ocean, somewhere between the Canary Islands and Cape Verde. The distant horizon encircles us like the future we seem fated to approach by imperceptible degrees, though always with hope.

Like your Anti-Dühring that I was lucky to read and admire on the eve of its persecution, we were banned by Bismarck's anti-socialist laws as I intimated we might be in my last letter to you. We have escaped with very little, but thanks to the generosity and bravery of our comrades in Hamburg have been able to get passage on a ship bound for New Zealand. It was our wish to go to America, following not only Germany's own 'Forty-Eighters' but also our contemporaries including, as you know, the Martignetti family, now resident in New York. However, given the need to move as quickly as possible, we have had to commit ourselves in good faith to this interesting alternative.

New Zealand is a place about which I know very little except that the 'New' in its name I read as a promise, whereas my dear sister Theodora, who I admit is wiser than me in most respects, utters the word with a prudent shaping of her lips. However that may be, the purpose of this short letter is to inform you of our status as refugees from the Chancellor's stool pigeons and agents provocateurs.

I also want to express my sincere hope, dear Comrade,

that our exchanges of information will continue in the future about which we know little except that it may contain useful challenges to the old orders against which we have struggled. That both Theodora and I hope to lend our voices to these challenges goes without saying.

For reasons that you will understand well, we have found it necessary to obtain new identities. From henceforth, and until we see how these matters are treated in the New place, we are a family of Hansens. I am Herr Wolf Hansen, my sister is Fräulein Theodora Hansen, and our beloved travelling companion and her daughter are Josephina and Catharina Hansen. It is their name that we have adopted, and it will be to that name that you must address any future communications. As we do not yet have an address in what will become our new home, it will be best to send letters to an appropriate agency in the town called Wellington, until we are able to give you an address. That there may be a Deutscher Verein or consulate in a remote town named after the English duke may speak to the break-up of Old World hegemonies, and I look forward to writing to you if that is so. I am mindful, however, that it was Wellington who organised counter-revolutionary forces in London as protection against the expected uprisings of 1848, and perhaps, some thirty years later, the shadow of his name now lies upon the distant town named after him.

I have learned that the late Duke's courts were for some years sending their unfortunates with the abbreviated stigma of 'convicts' to New Zealand's neighbour, New South Wales, a practice that has only recently ceased. This information was provided by an on-board acquaintance from the ship's mass accommodations, a printer by profession, whose skills may be useful to us in future. He is English with the wholesome name Oats but speaks some German, having been there as a journeyman. The man's brother was deported to a convict settlement some twenty years ago on a charge of forgery but has since moved to New Zealand, and my new friend hopes to be reunited with him. I do not believe our destination has ever been a penal colony. Rather, it is clear that a proportion of those passengers confined 'between decks' are the victims of what you have called social murder. A presumption that boredom is the prerogative of the idle rich is soon overturned by the rebellious expression of this underclass, confined as it is both by its cramped quarters and by the tedium of its daily disciplines. Perhaps this repressed mutiny will find its appropriate outlet once its cadre has been released into a new place of fresh opportunity.

Now I must end my letter with a promise to send bulletins from the front line where our rebellious travelling companions coming ashore in Wellington confront the ghost battalions of the Old Duke.

We must live in hope, my dear Comrade, and so I close with that and with the additional hope that you are well and busy at Primrose Hill and recovering from the loss of your beloved Lizzie.

Ever your admiring disciple and colleague

Wolf Bloch

Catharina

Papa Wolf was sick in the morning, he made a funny noise like a goat and fell out of his bed. There was a bad smell because he'd messed in his bed. He was lying on the floor making the goat noise. Then Tante came back with some men and they carried Papa Wolf away. She and Tante went outside with Mutti. The sun was just coming up over the edge of the hills on the island. Look, said Mutti, the trees are. But she was just looking at them. Her mouth was moving but no more words came out. Then she said that the trees were waving at the sun, could Catha see them? Some people were washing the deck with buckets from the sea – was that because of Papa Wolf, Catharina wanted to know. Silly Papa, said Mutti, he ate some bad fish and shells on the island, also something squishy called papaya and some drink called grog. But they weren't washing the deck because of Papa Wolf, they did that every morning, Catha knew that didn't she? But where was Papa Wolf? He was in the infirmary. And what was the infirmary? It was where you went if you were sick so the doctor could look after you. But why didn't they go there when there was the storm? Because too many people were sick, there wasn't room for everybody. But why was Mutti angry, was it because of Papa Wolf? No, it wasn't because of Papa Wolf, and she wasn't angry, it was just because she was worried about Papa Wolf, wasn't Catha also worried about her poor papa? There were some other men who went to the island, two of them hadn't come back, but her papa did! Then Gudrun and her mutti came out, they were going to make their own morgenmad, Gudrun told her with a special look.

Then Gudrun's papa and her two silly brothers came out, one of the brothers held his nose and made a rude noise and his papa gave him a push. They went and stood on the other side of the ship with a big crowd waiting for breakfast. Don't worry about them, Mutti told her, they are just silly boys. Would Catha please come with her, they could make their breakfast and also for the Bayern while Tante was cleaning up their cabin where Papa Wolf had been sick. But then all the Bayern that Papa Wolf called catlickers came out and stood near Mutti, and one of their papas asked what was the matter with Herr Hansen? It was nothing, Mutti told them, the silly man ate some bad fish stew on the island, and he had some of their strong drink. And was the doctor examining him now? And he was quarantined? Yes, Herr Hansen was in the infirmary. Mutti expected that he would be out again in a day or two, the sickness would pass quickly. She and Catharina could make their breakfast now if they were ready – there were some fresh fruits from the island, they were called papayas, would they like some? Was that what Herr Wolf ate, asked the catlicker papa. Yes he ate some, Mutti told them, but so did she when he brought them back, she didn't like them, they were too soft. Well, serve him right, said one of the big boys, not everyone was lucky enough to go to the island. Then the catlickers were going to make their own breakfast just like Gudrun's family. Would Catha mind waiting until they'd finished, asked Mutti. But when could they see Papa Wolf? Could Catha please stop asking questions? Because she didn't know when, Mutti told her. She didn't know, perhaps tomorrow? Then she'd see, Catha would see her Papa Wolf having the buckets of seawater thrown at him again! He'd be jumping up and down like a fuzzy Papa Monkey! Going hoo hoo!

Josephina and Catharina

Oh my dear little Wolf.

Oh Wolf.

The sailors tipped the plank and Wolf went down into the sea. He was wrapped in sacking with thick jute cord ties, the cords were choking him.

Oh my fuzzy Monkey.

But he couldn't swim. Those boys tried to drown him.

Theodora snatched the bible from the doctor. Don't you dare read that shit to my brother!

Give me the bible please ma'am, it's the way we do it here, I'm sorry. Please don't do that.

She was going to throw the bible into the sea.

Papa Wolf had gone.

Josephina took the bible from Tante and gave it back to the doctor.

Thank you, Frau Hansen. Then he went away to the afterdeck. No one was coming near them.

I wanted to unwrap him, said Josephina.

I wanted to see him.

They went down to their cabin. No one else was there. The cabin smelled of chlorine, not syrup of violets and almond oil.

It was the stink of Wolf gone into the sea.

I wanted to see him.

Come here, Mutti. Lie down.

Catharina lay down close beside her.

At first he wouldn't let me take his clothes off. He was afraid I wouldn't like him, poor little Wolf. He was ashamed that time. But then he let me and I did it.

And you did like him, didn't you, Mutti?

I loved him very much.

Catharina's little bony chest going up and down with the life in it.

Theodora was sitting up straight close by on the other bed.

Yes, and he loved you, Josephina.

Josephina closed her eyes and put her face in Catharina's hair.

She didn't need Theodora to tell her that.

The sound of the sea going away past the side of the ship.

Theodora

Thursday, 8 January, 1880, Equatorial zone

It is now two weeks since my dear brother died from eating fresh food at Praia in the Cape Verde Islands. Fresh food! It took barely four days for this fresh food to empty his body of the stubborn forces that had animated it against all expectations for more than forty years. There was a shore party of boastful young single men freed from their quarters. They announced that they were hopeful of meeting the island's young women. Two of them failed to return to the ship and Wolf made Josephina laugh with a scandalous scenario of their lives as castaways in which they were undressed by the island maidens and made to perform savage rituals undreamed of by the innocents of Swiss Family Robinson. They continued to laugh together for a long time as we watched the island slowly diminish behind us.

It was clear that I should keep a certain distance from their intimacy. The distance wounded me almost as much as the reason for it made me happy on Wolf's behalf. If it was jealousy I felt, then it was also a kind of perverse desire. I wanted to be the invisible breath they shared as they laughed into each other's face. I wanted to be the breath that passed between those sweet lips into my brother's mouth, and to be the breath that returned out of his careless smile to Josephina's shining tongue. Now I should find the memory of that moment abhorrent, and yet it is the last one I have of my brother in which he remains fully alive in his defiant nature.

This was the nature I had adored and battled with since he was the poor little thing whose life had often depended on the vigilance of his older sister. Then, as if an epoch had slid from time, that life depended on the young woman whose gaze had first opened my heart to the paradox of jealousy doubling as joy, and to the pain of redundancy. If this opening is a wound, then I must try to heal it and not allow it to infect the woman and child my brother loved, nor the child he will never see. I do not know how I can accomplish this healing, but the need to do so is where I must start.

None of the young men who returned singing to the ship died from the fresh food they consumed on the island, though all were drunk. Whatever they drank seems to have enlivened them. Some of the first-class passengers, men and women and their children, were also permitted to go ashore, and returned in lighters laden with the fresh food that seems to have done none of them any harm, since they continued to enjoy it in the days that Wolf lay dying in the infirmary. Wolf had been permitted to go ashore past the scowls and mutters of the majority, since with his usual graces he had persuaded the captain that a ship's newspaper would be an entertainment and distraction and would lighten the dissatisfied mood of the passengers, and he undertook to bring back what was required.

Now that I can write again and can think clearly about what it is I am writing, I know there is no intelligent reason to believe Wolf was poisoned by any agency other than the fresh food and liquor he ate and drank apparently with such pleasure. However 'fresh food' is a term I can only write with a grimace of horror, knowing that some of it must have been a poison to Wolf, whether because it was not fresh or because it was something his body could not tolerate. And yet, of course, the fearful thought I have had to wait two weeks to set aside in a kind of mental quarantine remains with me, in my mind and in my dreams.

That Wolf was poisoned by a human agent is improbable in our present circumstances, though he seldom hid the views that might have earned him enemies on the ship. It is the history of our lives together and in particular the stresses of the past months that have made me vulnerable to the suspicion that he was the victim of old venom rather than fresh food. This malign thought persists inside me next to the rational one I have managed to raise against it, and I fear it will never entirely leave me. I, too, have been poisoned first by jealousy and then by irrational suspicion and must now doubly beware of infecting those around me, especially the two whom Wolf loved utterly in his last months and who made him happier than I was ever able to. I must do this in spite of or against the contradictory force of my memory of Wolf and Josephina laughing in each other's face as their erotic island slowly sank beneath the waves but rose over and over again in their expressions.

After Wolf was sent to his final resting place Josephina was unable to look at the sea and would not leave our cabin except to relieve herself. She soon stopped weeping but seemed to retire within herself and to stop looking at the world, even at the narrow span of it that is our cabin. If she saw me there it was as though she did not perceive me with her senses and thoughts but merely with a dull, passive unrecognition. The bright, penetrating gaze that is the unmistakable signature of her nature had been shut down by her grief. The doctor visited her and prescribed brandy, which she quickly drank, but she seldom seemed to sleep. The matron brought her special broths and fresh goat's milk and urged her to eat them for the unborn child's sake, which she did as though through the agency of another Josephina hidden within the one I saw before me. I hoped that this hidden, determined Josephina would emerge soon and once again demonstrate that she was her own agent, but I was powerless to assist her to do so.

Catharina seldom left her, and had stopped going to the school. Sometimes she went out for short times to play with her Danish friend. But mostly she and Josephina lay or sat together, sometimes Catharina sang to her, and the child persuaded her to do some of the sewing work they had begun some weeks earlier. But Josephina's slender fingers, so quick and intelligent, simply stopped moving after a while, whereupon Catharina took the needle and thread from her and carefully folded the cloth away. How can a child so young know that it is she who must take care of this woman she can hardly recognise as her mother? After several days our Danish neighbour fru Frederiksen knocked fearfully at the cabin door and when I admitted her ignored me and asked Josephina in the patient tones of someone addressing an idiot if she would like her to read some comfort from the bible. Josephina's silence might as well have been the screeches of a fork-tongued devil given the haste with which the poor woman then retreated.

The weather has now become very hot and on some days there is scarcely any wind either to drive the ship towards the longed-for end of our journey or to cool the moods of those who swelter on deck. Below in our cabin and in the stateroom it is even warmer and so our neighbours are usually outside in the shade of awnings where space to rest is often contested. The small rations of water we are permitted also become objects of dispute.

Today when Josephina finally came up from the cabin she was soon allowed space to sit in the shade, whether because she still carried the taint of infection or out of sympathy was not clear from the expressions of those who moved to make room for her and Catharina. But the sociable intentions of the man who approached her with a bottle of water were obvious, as was his courteous posture as he also held out to her some papers rolled up and tied with a piece of string. Josephina is now about seven months' pregnant and moves very slowly and heavily, especially after the weeks she spent below barely moving. It was Catharina who stood and took the water and the rolled-up papers, whereupon the man made a little bow and shook her hand. He appeared to be giving a short formal speech and then stepped away respectfully. He saw me where I was sitting with my small class of listless children in shade below the afterdeck, and raised his hat, but then moved off.

While my mutinous children droned 'A B C the cat ran in the snow' I watched Josephina unfurl the roll of paper, and saw from the expression on Catharina's face as she looked in my direction that her mutti had not only emerged at last from the cabin but had also come back out from the self in which she had been confined for so long. Catharina's face shone with delight but also with a kind of challenge. The direct gaze I knew so well was not an invitation to share her joy. Then she was in Josephina's arms. As I was asking my children if they knew why there was never ever any snow where the ship was now almost becalmed, though there was a cat on the ship whose job was to catch mice, I saw that Josephina was reading to Catharina what was on the paper that had been so ceremoniously delivered to her.

There was no snow because we were in the equatorial zone and did anyone know what that was? There was one boy who thought it was the place where the earth was divided in two: white people lived on the top part and knew how to speak but on the bottom part the people were black from being burned in the sun and they didn't know how to speak. And is the bottom part where we are going, I asked the boy. Josephina had stood up and on her face, as on Catharina's, I saw that expression at once enlivened and obdurate. Yes, the boy told me, and his father was going to teach the burned people how to speak.

There once again was that familiar, intractable laminate of effects as I transferred my attention from one situation to another. On the one hand I was offered a chance to educate this misinformed child, and on the other I saw the familiar tableau of Josephina and her daughter confronting me in unison with their unflinching interrogation. Then they walked across to the rail of the ship and inserted themselves among those looking at the placid sea.

Later in the day when we had eaten our supper and were once again on deck, but all together this time, Josephina told me, with a careful smile, that the paper given her by Mister Oats the printer was two pages of what would have become their ship's bulletin. He had printed one copy for her but did not expect there would be any more to come. He had liked Herr Bloch very much and had enjoyed his company, and was sad for her sake and the sake of her daughter that they would now be arriving in their new land without such a fine husband and father. His German was very strange, Josephina said, but he had prepared his address carefully and she could tell that he was a very sincere man. When I asked her what was printed on the sheets she told me that the first contained a list of entertainments planned for the remainder of the voyage, including a series of concerts by a trio of violinists from Vienna which she looked forward to. And then she paused before telling me that the second sheet had a poem by Wolf. She saw that I guessed from her hesitation that the poem was addressed to her, but she held my gaze and, whether out of sympathy or not, said only that I should see this fragment of what my brother had hoped to do with his newspaper, and that she would treasure it.

I have written this without having read the fragment, and may never do so. I have had much of substance from my brother during the years of our work together, and these memories will not be ephemeral. Now Josephina and Catharina are asleep and soon I shall have to extinguish my lamp. It is good to be simply glad to see Josephina recovered and perhaps my dreams will now allow me to sleep peacefully again, though I doubt it.

Wolf Bloch

To my wife
'Little Bird'
Together with me on the Atlantic Ocean

December 14, 1879
'Water, water, every where'

I searched for you along the wild paths of life, the one
Who hand in hand with me would voyage bravely to our
New Home.
I had no wish to go to joyful festivals alone,
To see at last our tired, poor, huddled masses welcome;
And yet, my Little Seagull, look what you and I have done
Because we always dreamed together of what we might
become
And know we can't buy love for gold, no matter what they
say,
Nor futures, with the dragon-hoard of Reichskanzler
Dismay.

From calm blue Alster Lakes to seas of storm and stress;
From summer's trees reflected in the placid water's sheen
That gentle forest creatures ripple with their thirsty kiss
To far horizons undisturbed by flags of forest green –
Carried forward by your knowledge of suffering and
distress
And brave wish to leave behind whatever might have been,
My captain Little Bird steers our ship towards the day

The sun will rise beyond the gaze of Reichskanzler Dismay.

Always your loving and admiring comrade
Wolf Bloch

Beth and Frank

No, he hadn't planned to stop over any longer. He had a crack-of-dawn Virgin Australia flight and a room at the Novotel. He could walk over to the terminal in the morning. Hadn't he told her?

He probably had.

'It's got a bar,' he said. 'With a living wall.'

Beth found the 'living wall' sad, but didn't say so. It was a blocky, two-storey thing with abundant assorted ferns and creepers. Lurking somewhere within the greenery was the native epiphytic orchid *Winika cunninghamii*, or so the informative text on the wine list said. 'This indigenous orchid grows on native Podocarpus totara trees, one of which was used to make the hull of a sacred waka (great ocean-going canoe) belonging to Tainui people.'

'Poor wee Winika,' she said. They were 'sharing' a bottle of pretty good pinot noir which Frank would drink most of because she was driving home later. Then he'd have another, after she'd gone. Then he'd share a joke with Helen, alone in his room.

'Who's Winika?'

Beth waved the informative wine list at the living wall. 'It's an orchid, in there somewhere. It grows on tōtara usually.' She didn't add, You should tell Helen.

'I'll tell Helen,' he said, and raised his glass at the green wall.

Beth could feel his imminent departure opening up the space between them. He was looking past her with an incurious expression at what she guessed was an Asian trade delegation or some such – she could hear them exclaiming enthusiastically about the wall as a woman explained in carefully enunciated English that it had won heaps and heaps of prizes.

'Do you think they get "heaps"?' Now he was looking to have some fun. His grin was an invitation to play. 'Can visualise them, the heaps? The heaps and heaps of them?' He was waiting for her. 'When we first got to Oz I thought the other guys were talking about black people when they said wogs, then I found out it meant immigrants who hid gold chains in their chest hair.' His expression said, Don't want to play? 'Wogs wore tracksuits, called trackies.' He leaned towards her across the table. 'They hung out with their cousins a lot.'

They didn't have much time left.

Frank gave it one last try. 'It was tough, being new to the place. For me and the wogs. Getting the hang of the lingo.'

That was some kind of opening, at least. 'Tell me about your grandmother.'

Frank poured himself a glass and blew a sigh through pursed lips. 'Not letting up, are you, Beth.'

'And your mum. Tell me about Granny Cath and Auntie Greta.'

'I already did.'

'Not much. Not enough. Hardly anything, really.' There'd been these lacunae or held breaths or incommunicative looks during chats and reminiscences back at the reunion. Frank could mostly be found enjoying the company of others disinclined to open what one keen family historian called 'cans of worms'.

'You remember Grandma Cath down at the river when we were kids, though.'

‘I was all of six or something the first time I saw her. Maybe I remember her singing. I remember her sitting in the river splashing herself. I think I was nervous of her, she had a way of looking at you. She was really old.’

Their olives had come with a container of toothpicks. Frank began to make a shape with them.

‘Besides,’ said Beth, ‘after a while you can’t really tell what’s a memory and what’s been planted somehow. There were photos – my mum had some. Your grandma was pretty chic. Even her old-lady togs. But do I really remember them?’

Frank had made a fat two-sided toothpick track with bars across it. It went across the table towards her. He put a black olive at the front. ‘Witchetty grub,’ he said. ‘I remember the first one I saw. But no, like you, not Grandma Cath’s togs.’ Then he swept the toothpicks up and returned them to their container. He put the olive in his mouth and chewed it slowly. ‘What I know and what I remember are vastly different,’ he said. Then he took the olive stone from his mouth and held it, looking at her. Then he put it carefully on the little snack tray. Either he was thinking slowly or he was stalling. ‘The trouble with what I know and what I remember being vastly different is that they don’t add up to a lot, even when I put them together into some kind of story. So you’ll have to cut me some slack here, cuzzie.’

Down the other end of the bar the trade delegation or whatever it was had begun to shout about everything that had been cool. Frank was looking at them.

‘Imagine, for example,’ he said, ‘that one of those people down there went back after their visit to New Zealand and told everyone about the giant tooter tree they’d seen, and the wonderful exotic orchid called Winnie, and the great voyaging canoe called Awaken. Which in truth they only encountered at the living wall in the airport hotel, itself surrounded by many heaps of glittering prizes. And they saw them, too, the heaps and heaps of them. Know what I mean?' He gave her a little slosh of wine. 'So don't expect me to do much better, okay?' He waited again, for a moment. 'So don't try to untangle what you think I know from what you think I remember, including what I remember being told that someone or other knew or remembered, because you'll go crazy.'

'Try me.'

'Grandma Cath was really smart. She distinguished herself at school where she was dux and, after a spell teaching little kids, at university in Wellington. She graduated with honours, one of the first women to get a degree in New Zealand. It was her mother Josephina who encouraged her.' Frank sipped his wine. 'Feel like something to eat?'

'Don't stall, Frank.'

'I'm not stalling, I'm starving. I'm going to order something.'

'Go for it, but I'm okay, thanks.'

Frank continued his account while scanning the bar menu. 'Grandma Cath was also encouraged by a German professor whose name I've either never known or have forgotten – comes down to the same thing. I'm getting some crumbed calamari with aioli and a small bowl of tomatoes with torn basil. You're welcome to help yourself.'

'The encouraging German professor,' said Beth.

'Ah yes, the encouraging German professor.' Frank was getting the barman's attention. 'Grandma Cath was by now in her late twenties, unmarried, a strikingly beautiful woman by all accounts but don't take my word for it. She may have done some encouraging of her own because – The crumbed calamari with the tomato and basil salad please, and chuck in a few extra squiddy bits for my companion.'

'Do you want two servings, sir?' asked the waiter. He was now withholding his charming smile.

'Not really,' said Frank. 'My companion doesn't feel hungry, but she'll probably want some when she sees mine. Pretty sure she will.'

'I'll see what I can do,' said the waiter. 'Let's call it a serving and a half.'

'Why don't we do that,' said Frank, and as the waiter left, 'Charming man.'

'The German professor?'

'You're remorseless. No, the waiter. Where I come from now in the redneck north of Australia he'd be called a wog. My mother Greta's father would have been called a Hun, except he ran away to South America long before the First World War broke out.'

'The German professor.'

'My grandfather, the nameless German professor.'

'I think I knew that.'

'So no surprises there then.' Frank's face was contorting with the pressure of a forced smile.

'I'm sorry, sir,' said the waiter.

'Okay, make it two servings then.'

At the far end of the room, half the corporates were singing something in Chinese, each line followed by the other half singing what Beth guessed was the English translation. They all kept cracking up. *I never knew . . . to forget a person*

. . . it's so difficult . . . I never knew . . . to forget that feeling . . . isn't that easy . . .

'They're singing our song,' she said.

Frank gave her a look that said he was pretending he

couldn't hear it. 'And as for Greta, our mum, she was closing in on forty when she had us. Dad came back from the war early, he was a nervous wreck and minus a leg, there was ongoing pain. We were his last accomplishment. Pretty much drank himself to death by the time we went to primary school. He left us in the car a few times while he went into the pub for a couple of quick ones. He brought us out Cokes, they were the thing. Then we'd go and get the fish and chips he'd been sent out for. There was always a little pack of hot chips for us to have in the back seat while he drove home. He drove with immense, deliberate care. With one real leg, mind you. I can picture the back of his head and the smell of the chips. Ruth and me had burping competitions with the Cokes.' He tried to fill her wine glass, but she put her hand over it. 'Once he fell forward at the table and put his face in his dinner. Greta gave us a look so we just kept on eating while he stayed put. They had big rows. Afterwards he sometimes took his prosthetic off and sat outside and smoked. We knew he wasn't really there any more than his leg was, just the breathing thing that made smoke come out of his nose. Other times he'd pretend to be a three-legged sheep dog and round us up – we loved it when he did that kind of stuff. He could be pretty funny. He did a great Oliver Hardy impersonation with a little stove-black false moustache. We saw Laurel and Hardy in *Busy Bodies* at the RSA, they had a 16-millimetre projector for family nights. Bert would be sneaking drinks with his mates.' Frank's grimacing smile as the calamari arrived. The waiter said you're welcome even though Frank hadn't thanked him.

'Didn't get a mention at the reunion,' said Beth. 'Bert, I mean.'

'Albert Didn't-get-a-mention Parks,' said Frank. He bit

a calamari ring in half. 'Poor bugger. Poor bloody Oliver Hardy impersonator.'

'Just a half, please,' said Beth. Then she raised her glass. 'Albert Parks.'

'Otherwise known as the Parks Department,' said Frank. He waved his glass at her plate. 'You should try them.'

The waiter was back. 'And how is everything?'

'Marvellous,' said Frank. 'Bloody marvellous. Ripper.'

So that was going to be that, then. She sampled a crumbed calamari ring. It was horrible, oily and limp. Time to go. It was clear Frank wasn't going to talk about his mother Greta, or her 'fresh start', not this time.

But then he said, 'I'll send you some things of Greta's when I get home.'

'What kind of things?'

'She was a journo, remember? Guess where Ruth got the bug.' He poked his fork at her calamari. 'Disgusting, eh. Time to get home for some bloody big Dingo Beach tiger prawns. You should come over.'

His body was very thin and bony, and he held her tightly. She sat in the car for a while before taking the exit to the motorway. There were processions of headlights in both directions, coming and going, impossible to tell which was which.

Josephina

It was even a rather silly poem, but Josephina couldn't say that to Catharina, who had asked her to read it again many times in the days after Mister Oats politely handed it to her and gently shook her hand. Catharina's expression was solemn and tragic whenever she heard the poem read again, and it was easy to see that the poem Papa Wolf had written for her mutti had become a magical object. Josephina was now Little Bird! – but Little Bird couldn't tell Catharina that she was not completely happy with Papa Wolf's intention to publish his intimate name for her, especially as it was about the shoulder blades he'd liked to stroke.

And who was Reichskanzler Dismay, Catharina wanted to know, and asked to be told again, and then again. Josephina would explain that he was the Chancellor of Germany and was called Bismarck, he was a very powerful man who had made it dangerous for all of them to stay in Hamburg, and had also made it dangerous for Alex and her mutti and papa to stay there, but Catha already knew that, didn't she?

So was he a monster? Catharina made her fingers into claws and bared her teeth.

Yes, he was a kind of monster. But not like that.

But did the Chancellor eat children, like Krampus?

No, he didn't eat children. But he was very cruel to people he didn't like.

And was Papa Wolf fighting him?

Yes, Papa Wolf was fighting him, but he was fighting with words, not with a sword.

So he was fighting with words like the ones in the poem?

Yes, like the ones in the poem.

So around they went, around and back again. Soon Catharina knew the poem by heart. *The sun will rise beyond the gaze of Reichskanzler Dismay.* She and Josephina would say the words together, looking at each other's lips as they made the shapes of the words, and Catharina would widen her eyes as far as they could go. Sometimes Catharina would put one finger on her mutti's lips as she said the magic words. Then Catharina would say, 'Brave Papa Wolf!' and shake her fist in the air.

Brave Papa Wolf!

What Josephina could not explain to Catharina was that this monster Reichskanzler Dismay was a man Wolf had in his thoughts all the time, but he wasn't someone Catharina's mutti thought about as much, and so the poem was perhaps not so much about her, but even a bit more about what Wolf had in his mind when he wrote it, which was what he usually had there, the things he thought about all the time, including the Chancellor.

And of course he had meant the lines about the Chancellor, and about 'our tired, poor, huddled masses', to be read by others on the ship, not just her. In fact, mostly by others on the ship.

And of course he would have done that.

And what she could not explain to Catharina, nor even very well to herself, was that she didn't mind knowing that Wolf had almost published his intimate name for her and her shoulder blades so that everyone on the ship could read it, and that the poem addressed to Little Bird was as much about what he always had in his mind and often talked about with Theodora, and had talked and talked about with the visitors who came to the Bloch House. Because that was who he was, that was her Wolf, that was who he always would be for ever, and the things that were not quite right about the poem were what allowed her to have him, but also allowed her to let him go a little, little by little. Really it was because the poem had made her laugh at Wolf, at her Wolf, and then the laugh had opened a gap in her grief and the world had begun to come back in, just a little bit at a time.

Now the weather was cooler and there were strong steady winds blowing from behind the ship. In the evening, Josephina liked to stand by the rail and turn her stomach with the heavy child in it towards the wind and the sunsets. Sometimes she did this with Catharina when she wasn't playing with her friends. Then they'd be sailing into the future and towards the next day's dawn – she and Catharina and the baby were going there – but she could see the past sliding slowly away along the hull of the ship and getting left behind. It was always there, like the sea, and always sliding away at the same time. And Wolf was always there, and always sliding away.

And what she could perhaps never say to Catharina, or only when Catharina was much older, and could only now think to herself, was that what had woken her up to being back in the present, on the deck of the ship the day she came up out of the cabin with Catharina, had been the almost-silliness of Wolf's poem – how it was about her and how he loved her but also about what Wolf could never get out of his thoughts – that was what had made her laugh, the Wolfness of it. It was the laughter that had surprised her and woken her up as if from a long dream in which time had just stopped or didn't exist.

Catharina had seen her laugh, the first time for weeks, and had at once looked across at Theodora who was watching from the shade by the afterdeck while some of her pupils made rude gestures behind her back. Yes, Josephina had seen Catharina look across at Tante Theodora and claim her mutti's laugh for herself, and stare down the rude gestures of the children. Then they had hugged each other with the Wolf-poem pressed between them, and Theodora had seen that too.

Now Catharina was going to school again in the mornings and sometimes in the afternoon after their lunch. Sometimes Theodora was at the school, and when it wasn't her turn to do that she would often sit by herself in the stateroom or in a sheltered place on the deck and write in her book. Sometimes they talked about what they would do when they got to New Zealand, and they agreed that they would have to get some work. For example, Josephina could do sewing and Theodora could be a tutor to the children of well-off families – a suggestion that made her say ugh. But this conversation they could really only have once and then repeat. It was the same when Theodora would ask how was Josephina feeling, was the baby moving around a lot? To which Josephina could reply that she was feeling fine, but very heavy and tired now, it was difficult to sleep, she was looking forward to getting the baby out, and it was going to be a running and jumping child, of that she was certain. There was nothing else for them to talk about, and it seemed to Josephina that Theodora was keeping her distance – she made it clear, for instance, that she didn't want to talk about Wolf and their lives together. Josephina would have liked to hear about Theodora's experience of Wolf, but she turned her face away when Josephina asked and said, only, that Josephina had known one Wolf and she another.

Of course, Theodora was always thoughtful and ready to help. But that made no difference to the loneliness Josephina had begun to feel.

And now there was no Wolf to talk to and play with –

none of the funny stories he made up, or the ones he told about what he'd heard was going on in the ship, because he was always talking to people, that was how he behaved. He told her the story of the young men from the single men's quarters who, one night, took a small pig from its pen on the deck and put it down the hatch of the single women's quarters, where it ran around squealing until one of the women took hold of it and threw it out on the deck for the night watch to chase. Another time some women stood outside the captain's cabin and wouldn't let him out until he agreed they could hang their washing in the rigging to dry, including their undergarments – then she'd understood why the sailors were always saluting the washing. And of course she no longer had Wolf's tender touch, on her big stomach or on the shoulder blades he loved.

Josephina was sitting outside with her sewing when fru Frederiksen sat down beside her. She spoke Danish carefully, with some German mixed in, as if she was trying to translate for Josephina's benefit. And what was the meaning of the little birds that Frau Hansen was embroidering on the front of the baby nightgown? And where had she learned to do such fine work? And then, after a pause, before Josephina could reply, she said carefully, as though her words were memorised, that all her family were very sorry about Herr Hansen's death, she hadn't wished to approach Frau Hansen at first to say that, or at least not until she had come out from her mourning, not that there was an end to mourning, of course. And then she stopped, as if she had kept going past the end of her prepared speech.

The little birds were Rohrsänger, perhaps fru Frederiksen knew them? Perhaps they had them where her family came from? They lived in the reeds close to the sea. In the autumn they all flew away to somewhere warm, perhaps the places where oranges came from? Like the Canary Islands? Did fru Frederiksen remember the oranges they got there, in the Canary Islands? She herself had always loved getting some of them when they came in to Kielerhafen, that was where she lived as a child. Her papa used to bring them home.

Then Josephina couldn't talk anymore.

The fat tears just came and would not stop, they were falling on the baby's nightgown and on the back of Josephina's hand there. Fru Frederiksen's hand came over and rested on top of Josephina's – some tears fell on it but she left it there, on top of Josephina's.

Yes, she said after a while, they had those birds where their Frederiksen family came from – it was up at Haderslev, the birds nested around the lake.

Fru Frederiksen's hand was warm and her fingers a little swollen and purplish. A glove was tucked under the wristband of her sleeve. The sleeve had a narrow crochet lace trim, the pattern like one Greta had on her church dress, very plain circles and squares.

Josephina put the forefinger of her free hand on the lace trim. She needed to make her speech work again.

Her sister Greta had that one, a trim like that one, it was a present from her family in Sønderborg.

Ah, so quite close to Haderslev, and was Sønderborg where Frau Hansen's family lived now?

Now Josephina's tears had stopped. She wanted to wipe her eyes but left her hands where they were, with fru Frederiksen's slightly swollen purple one and the baby's nightgown with its unfinished pair of Rohrsänger.

Her sister was married to a Danish man. That was why she was in Sønderborg.

But Frau Hansen spoke some Danish? And her daughter Catharina also?

Yes, she had visited her sister there and stayed for a while.

And would fru Frederiksen now ask if her sister in Sønderborg knew Pastor Jepsen? But she did not. Fru Frederiksen carefully took her hand away from Josephina's and dabbed at the tears on it with the glove she took from her sleeve with its Danish lace trim. Josephina, too, wiped her tears and her nose on an offcut piece of muslin from her sewing bag.

Did Frau Hansen know of women who could help her with the birth of her baby? Because there were midwives on the ship, the matron knew who they were, there was a list. The baby must be quite close now? She herself had three children, as Josephina knew, and . . .

Josephina guessed fru Frederiksen had been about to tell her that she had also lost some of her babies. She heard it in the little silence after her cabin neighbour's unfinished sentence.

And yes, they were neighbours, after all.

'Please,' she said. 'Call me Josephina. We have been neighbours for a while now, after all. And thank you for your kindness.'

'And I am Ada.'

'Thank you, Ada.'

Yes, naturally it had made her weep after being alone, when Ada spoke kindly to her and touched her hand. But now Josephina could picture Pastor and fru Jepsen from the Saincte Marie church in Sønderborg; they were perched up on the spar above her and were looking down at Ada whom they certainly recognised because the Frederiksens were good church people, and of course at Josephina who had arrived in Sønderborg as a young widow pregnant with her first child, whom the Pastor had christened Catharina Elke Lange Hansen – and now here was Josephina again, widowed and pregnant again, but still called Hansen?

And over there was Ada's friendship group. They were three women about the same age, they often sat together.

Would Josephina like to join her friends, Ada wondered. There they were, Josephina probably recognised them, they often sat together? They would certainly be interested in the embroidery work she was doing, so fine and pretty. Sometimes they sewed together, but just mending and so forth.

Josephina put the baby's nightgown in her sewing bag. It was quite difficult to stand up from the hatch cover; she had to press down hard with one arm, and her dress tightened uncomfortably against her stomach. She would have to let the gathers out again.

Ada was looking at her with an encouraging expression. Her friends were also looking in her direction.

Josephina thanked Ada but said she needed to have a rest now, she was going to lie down for a while.

Pastor and fru Jepsen were creaking and flapping up on their spar. But of course they were far away now, all of that was very far away.

But had she made a mistake to babble about Kielerhafen, and Sønderborg, and the Rohrsänger?

No, of course she had not. The ship was going on into the future.

The air in the cabin was a little close and smelly; it was much nicer and fresher outside. She took her dress off and lay down in her shift.

She would join Ada's friendship group but not yet, not today.

And what about her sisters?

It was uncomfortable lying on her side and she wasn't really tired. She would get up and write to her sisters. She didn't know when the letter would be able to go to them, but writing it would be like talking. She could easily imagine what they would say, and the different ways they would do it, when she told them what had happened. The big strong hugging arms of Elke's speech, the clear thought of Greta's eyes slowly blinking her words.

Wednesday, the 21st of January, 1880 near Cape Town

My dear sisters Greta and Elke

I am writing to you first of all because I miss you very much and have no one I can talk to the way I can talk to my dear sisters. I can almost hear your voices when I think of you and I can see you when I shut my eyes, but you are not here, that is the truth I have when I am alone.

It is now two months since I wrote my last letter to you, it went ashore at the Canary Islands and so you will have it now I hope. To me the Canary Islands seem much longer ago than they really are, though long enough ago even so. That is not just because time passes very slowly on this ship but because of the terrible thing that happened a few weeks after the Canary Islands. No, my baby is still growing well and Catharina is as well as can be expected in this situation, and has learned to read a little and even write her name, I know you will have worried about them at first when you read that something terrible had happened. What happened after the ship went in to the place called Cape Verde, where we went after the Canary Islands, is that my dear husband and friend Wolf Bloch died from something he ate and his body was slid down into the sea, that is what they do on these ships.

It is now about a month since I saw my beloved husband and kind companion go into the sea for ever and out of my life for ever. I have only just begun to come back out of the grief that was like a fog or a storm that filled up all the time around me. I had Wolf's sister Theodora and of course Catharina with me but they could not take the place of my dear sisters. Now at last I can again go back out into the fresh day, and so my life will begin to go forward again after a long time in which it had stopped completely. I can hardly even remember that time.

So now you know what has happened and that Catharina and I are travelling on alone to New Zealand and must make our new life there by our own efforts. They speak English there and so we must learn that new language. There is a kind man on the ship called Mister Oats who had become one of the many friends my husband made on board the ship. Mister Oats was a journeyman in years gone by and spent some of his travelling time in Germany, and so can speak some German although with a very strange accent. I am going to ask him to teach Catharina and me some English so that we can be better prepared when we get to New Zealand. Catharina has learned a little bit of English at the school they have on the ship, for example how to say hello my name is Catharina and how much does this bread cost, but we will need more than that.

It is very hard to be writing to you without hearing anything back except in my thoughts, where your voices are as clear as if you were with me in this little cabin, but of course you are not here. Please write to me and to Catharina and to our new baby son or daughter who will now certainly be born before we get to New Zealand as the ship has been delayed more than could have been expected. Write some long letters and tell me everything that has been happening where you are there next to the good old Schwentine and the harbour at Sønderborg, which I can still see when I close my eyes. When I know where you must send the letters I will write to you again, but next time it will be from our new home.

Catharina and I send many kisses to my sisters and her aunts, and to my nephews and her cousins Finn and Otto, and to my dear papa and Catharina's grandpapa, and perhaps also to someone Elke will write about when she sends her letter to us in New Zealand.

Now I am going to help Catharina to write you a letter by herself, she can write her own name at the end!

Your sister Josephina

Dear Tante Greta and Tante Elke and Cousin Finn and Cousin Otto and Grandpapa Hansen

Now I can write my name Catharina. Today we saw a big albertoss. Our lunch was soup with biscuits. Mutti is better her baby will come soon.

Catharina

Catharina's kiss is here

Wolf Bloch

Bloch House, Hamburg, April 20th, 1879

It had never occurred to me, before Josephina (over my protestations) opened the fastening of my shirt and put her face against my wretched chest, that there could be any conceivable connection between carnal desire and philosophical thought. Can there be an erotics of thought? The question could never, before that moment of Josephina's insistence, have entered my mind let alone the life in which carnal desire was an affect I could only locate in the base kingdom of cravings such as gluttonous hunger and avaricious greed, neither of which I welcomed in to my nature. Such carnality as I did experience, therefore, I relegated to a vault deep within the fortress of my sensibility, where it mostly declined and wasted pitifully away, uttering only the most feeble of pleas for liberation from time to time, and with ever decreasing frequency.

I knew that there could be an erotics of action, since the hysterias and excitements of combat are plain for all to see when the angry mob rises up or when an army rushes to penetrate the defences of its opponents; tales of such encounters are always swollen with the hyperbole of erotic enthusiasm. Equally hyperbolic are the high colours and rousing music and rhythmical exertions of military parades, which have always dismayed me as false charades of true feeling; they are, in fact, no more than obscene theatres of engorged power in which the rapes committed in the name of nationalism are costumed in the regalia of patriotism, their end purpose being the adoring submission of the cannon-fodder masses.

The exulting rhetoric of those who urge action, for example upon the hesitant among their conscripts, is yet another sign of the primal forces that bind carnality and action; but since I have never had the capacity for exciting action of any kind whatsoever, my experience of such an erotics has been limited to the vicarious emotion aroused by writing about it, and never more so than in poetry, and never more than in the poem I wrote during an unsleeping day and night occasioned by the tragic defeat of the Paris Commune in the cemetery of Père-Lachaise in May 1871.

But the emotion I experienced while writing this poem does not begin to compare with the gratitude I felt as Josephina very tenderly and gently released my wretched carnal prisoner from his pathetic dungeon, thus allowing me to experience, for the first time in my life, a freedom that rose up through my whole body and person and mind. In the days that followed, this liberation was not always so gentle; but however it was enacted, the freedom it generated was a life force that transformed not only how my body felt but also how my mind thought. Furthermore, the two were united or placed in a kind of ecstatic realm of exchanges, a sharing of powers and sympathies that utterly transformed how this poor, deficient creature called Wolf Bloch could now know his own nature and consciousness.

The great French writer Gustave Flaubert, author of the 'Madame Bovary' through which I struggled like a blind man with the aid of my inadequate French and my even more inadequate understanding of human passion, is said to have thought that physical and intellectual gratifications have nothing in common and that the former merely corrupts the latter and is a sin against the Idea. His stern predecessor, the philosopher René Descartes, came early in his life to the conclusion that the mind and the body are separate, and yet in asserting that 'I am' because 'I think' he seems by implication to have insisted also on a space of mental embodiment. Our own Idealist, Friedrich Hegel, bewildered me, but my dear sad sister less so, with his dialectical diagrams of the interactions and interrelationships of spirit and phenomena. With her help, which she tired of offering, I could have thought more productively about the example of our own dear mentor Engels and his discussions of the unity and conflict of opposites. But before that moment when Josephina quite literally opened me to the possibility of a transforming reconciliation between the mind that seemed to animate me and the miserably inadequate body that transported it like a dutiful porter, I had no conception whatsoever of the possibility of an existence vivified by robust conversations between the porter and his mental or spirit burden.

Now, the question that a new Wolf Bloch wants to ask is not, Can there ever be an erotics of philosophical thought, but rather, How can there be any thought worth having that is not produced in the unity and conflict of mind and body, that is to say, through the erotic power of their intercourse?

This was not a gift I expected, nor one I sought, and I can see that my astonished gratitude for it has affected my sister who, while evidently happy for my happiness, may feel herself denied the gift I was so freely given. I know that the possibility of her receiving a gift like mine was not something she could realistically have expected of Josephina, and that her own meagre experiences of an equivalent if different happiness have been few and often short-lived, with one sad exception. But I see now what I was unable to see during the happy years of our household before Josephina joined it, that my sister Theodora's lively equanimity and energy during those years were the rewards of her relationship with the friend who shared our house; and I see that now her existence in the dreary, barren, disappointed space between body and mind is the consequence of her friend and lover Annushka's death, in the same terrible year that our dear friends Aksel and Rana Andersen's daughter Isolde died.

And so for ten years since Annushka's death I have lived obliviously in the unsympathetic space of my own shameful inability to understand or even notice what truly made my dear sister's life joyful, and what infused with intellectual joy the ways she spoke her mind. Now I see that her thought, for all its fiery conviction, seems distant from her heart; and her poor heart distant from the lively world, except that dreadful aspect of it which contains pestilential diseases like the one that took her lover and that prey with catastrophic prejudice upon the defenceless poor.

Theodora

Sunday, 8 February, 1880, Indian Ocean, somewhere between Mauritius and Fremantle

I have two events to record at this juncture, which I will do in a corner of the crowded deck since our space below has been occupied by one of the events. The occupying event is the second of the two that I shall record here not just because the first precedes it in time but because the first one has cast its shadow of significance across the second.

Once again our meandering, slothful ship was required to stop over at another port, a place called Mauritius this time. Its charms seemed Edenic when viewed from the deck, where a muttering crowd idled away the three days of our sojourn. Some of the fresh food that came on board might likewise have been plucked from the trees of a paradise beyond the wildest dreams of the porridge-bloated and unhealthy crowd whose garments were by now infested with persistent vermin. Rather than add my eyes to those that roamed with helpless longing across the charming vista of the harbour and its backdrop of palms and steep mountains where, no doubt, torrents of sparkling fresh water fell in cascades to cooling pools; and rather than dwell again on the culinary seductions that had brought about the death of my poor little brother, I decided to unpack at last some of his belongings that neither I nor Josephina had wanted to look at up to that point.

my dear sad sister . . . her help, which she tired of offering . . . her own meagre experiences . . . her existence in the dreary, barren, disappointed space between body and mind . . . her poor heart distant from the lively world . . . These were but some of the observations I read in the first entry of my brother's journals, the first one I opened and the first and therefore the most recent of the five that were stacked neatly together and bound with a ribbon in the old English valise where he kept them, together with his few most precious books. The valise was a gift from Engels and had arrived with several books in it, including *The Condition of the Working Class in England* with Engels' inscription to his 'dear Comrade Wolf Bloch'. Wolf had long treated the valise as if it were an outsize teffilin for what had become his sacred texts once he renounced religion. It was of course the first time I had opened this special, private bag, intending only to see what he kept in it and what might be done with its contents. The same question had to be asked of his other frugal possessions, his shoes and clothes, the hat that he always replaced with its exact replica when it got too shabby or when I told him it had become so, the neat kit of his medicines and toiletries, the writing utensils he maintained with obsessive care, and not much else.

But my practical if sad task was stopped by the grief and anger I felt after reading these few pages, before closing the notebook and holding it shut tight against me as if to stop it adding to my confusion. I felt grief, of course, because there in these pages were the unmistakable traces of my dear brother's presence and the tireless energy of his thought and speech. But my grief was confused together with anger at my brother's presumed wisdom and misplaced sympathy, and by the question, Why had he never shared these tender concerns with me?

His announcement of the part Josephina had played in what he saw as his transformation did not surprise me, but it wounded me too against my wish not to be affected in this way. Needless to say, I was also affronted by his unlicensed summoning up of my dear friend whose name I have refrained from saying either aloud or in my thoughts, needing to move past that time in my life and make something fruitful out of my loss. Yes, I may have been changed by that loss, but my brother's patronising summary of its effects made me angry with him at the very time such anger was the last emotion I wanted as I surveyed the few material remnants of his short life.

It was at this moment, as I sat weeping with a mixture of grief and rage, that Josephina came in to the cabin and found me surrounded by Wolf's things. I saw at once that this shocked her, even more perhaps than the sight of my tears. She was standing in the doorway with her hands clasped beneath her stomach and her legs braced apart, and from this strong platform she pierced me with the look I have seen only intermittently these past months. Catharina was just behind her, and she turned and very firmly told the child to go outside and play with Gudrun, which she did at once, as if stung by a rare sharpness in her mother's tone.

What was I doing? she demanded to know, in a tone not so different from the one that had made Catharina turn quickly and leave. She continued to fix me with that stare I had once admired for what it seemed to convey of this young woman's clear purpose but that now seemed unsympathetic and even hostile to me, indeed towards me. Her gaze shifted from my face to the journal I was holding tight, and then back to my face. I knew at once that I seemed to her to be clutching the journal possessively, as if to keep it or its contents from her. I put it on the bed beside me and said that I was preparing to look at Wolf's possessions, to see what should be done with them. But why did I think I had the right to do this, Josephina demanded. Was it not appropriate for her, as Wolf's wife, to have a say in what should be done, and to see what might have special meaning for her?

And what was this? she wanted to know, picking up the journal. Wasn't it where she'd seen Wolf writing down his thoughts? Didn't she have the right to read what he'd written there, before any decision could be made about what to do with it? Of course, I said, and there were four more of the journals in Wolf's special bag, she should read all of them if she wished. She sat down opposite me on her bed and opened the journal to its first pages, the very pages I had just read. After a while she put the notebook down beside her and once again confronted me with that clear look. And so, she said, what about the other things? They could be offered to the other passengers, those who might need them? What did I think? But she made no move to return the journal to its bag or to me. And so we proceeded to sort through Wolf's mundane things together, and made a pitifully small pile of what seemed useful, while the journal we had both read some pages from remained where she had put it, on her bed, together with the only other thing she wanted for herself, which was my brother's apothecary's bottle of syrup of violets and almond oil.

The clothes and other things that had once been Wolf's disappeared into the lives of those who took them, the English valise with its books and four of the five journals remained with me, the writing materials Josephina kept for Catharina who now knows how to write her name, and the fifth journal and the bottle of syrup of violets and almond oil Josephina kept for herself, though neither of us ever spoke of the arrangement in such terms. Nor have we ever talked about what we had read in the journal. What was written there, whatever it meant in different ways to either of us, was hidden in the circumspect relationship we then maintained until the second event about which I will write now, remembering still the shadow of circumspection that was present at this moment and clouded the event like an approaching squall.

The birth of Josephina's baby was completed in the very early hours of Saturday morning, on the seventh of February, 1880, apparently with relative ease though after a long labour. It is now Sunday late in the afternoon, and she and the baby have been back in our çabin since just after midday, together with fru Frederiksen and Catharina. The birth took just under a day altogether, beginning with the moment when Josephina came in to the cabin where I was resting. I saw from her expression that her labour had begun, and that her dress was soaked below with that commencement. She very calmly went to wet a towel in the washroom and came back to our cabin to wipe herself clean and change her clothes. Then she sat on the edge of her bed and seemed to retreat into herself. Her eyes were closed and a little smile was the only sign of any emotion.

She had been with the women who associated with our neighbour fru Frederiksen, and this woman, who had recently ingratiated herself to Josephina, knocked at the cabin door and, when admitted, asked if there was anything she could do to help Josephina at this time. The implication of her kind enquiry was that I was not the person with requisite experience in these matters, and of course she was right to suppose so. Josephina, however, declined the woman's offer and said only that she preferred to walk up and down on the deck for as long as possible, and to rest from time to time, and to be alone, but that when the time came she would ask me to find the matron who could then summon the midwife, if that was necessary.

She then looked at me quite directly but without the challenge of our encounter over the journal a week earlier, in fact still with the little smile that had been the outward sign of her inner contemplative state, and said that she hoped I wouldn't mind if she called the child Wolf, if it was a boy. In fact, she thought she might call him Wolf Bloch Hansen, since the Bloch name had been bartered for our safe passage and deserved to be recovered. And if the child was a girl? I asked. A sour lump had risen into my throat, but then was not the time to spit it out as words, and in any case at that moment I had no idea what the words would be, nor whether they would be uttered as a wounded cry of protest or as a grateful cry of assent.

If the baby was a girl, Josephina told me without waiting for my dissent or approval, then she would also like to remember the name Bloch, but would add to it the name of one of her sisters, not Elke which was the one commemorated in Catharina's name, but that of her eldest sister, Greta, the one who lived in Sønderborg, in Denmark, and who together with her husband Danne had given her shelter and love when

Catharina was born. She would like to be able to thank Greta for that loving kindness in the name of the child who would be her niece in a faraway place, whom she might want to visit there one day, if that might be possible. And how did I feel about that? she asked again, using my name, Theodora.

Ah, how did Theodora feel about that? Viewed in the kindest light, Theodora found Josephina's suggestion to be moving, and the request for permission it entailed to be considerate. Viewed unkindly, I, Theodora, found the suggestion to be impudent and brazen, and the request for permission to be disingenuous and sly. And of course, Theodora found the Theodora who viewed the suggestion for naming the child in the kindest light to be the Theodora she wanted to be, indeed the one who mirrored the loving kindness of Josephina's eldest sister in Sønderborg, the one called Greta who might even undertake as punishing a voyage as the one Theodora was now enduring, for no other reason than to visit the niece named after her. But also of course I, Theodora, knew that the Theodora who found Josephina's proposal to be impudent, brazen, disingenuous and sly was the honest Theodora.

It was the Theodora I wanted to be, and knew I had to be at that moment, who told Josephina that of course she should name her child in this way, it was a very generous and touching idea, and after all, Wolf Bloch was indeed the father of this boy or girl child, and his name should indeed travel on to the new land for which he had such high hopes.

At that moment I shocked myself with the thought of taking the child and raising it myself, and at the same moment saw that Josephina did not entirely trust or believe the response of the Theodora I wanted to be, the Theodora who mirrored the loving kindness of her sister Greta in Sønderborg. The bitter lump of unspoken words in my throat sank back to the pit they had come from, and I said, only, that of course Josephina should let me know the moment she wanted to call for the midwife, that she should rely on me to get her anything she needed in the meantime, that I would stay close. Then she kissed my cheek and said she was going out to walk on the deck for a while, it was good to do that, she was happy to be by herself at this time, there was no need for me to stay too close.

She did not say she wished Wolf could be there with her, though I am sure she was thinking it, and I guessed it was in consideration of her acute hearing of the dissonance between us, and her disinclination to irritate it, that she did not say she longed for Wolf's companionship. And so, in the guise of the Theodora I wished to be, I said that it was sad Wolf could not be with her at this time, could not be the one who walked with her on the deck. But he will be, she said, if you know what I mean.

And now there in our cabin is the child called Wolf Bloch Hansen. He has his father's dark hair and his father's dark eyes, and when I last saw him his father's impatience with the tiresome business of getting food. My heart is very full of his presence, my chest and throat are swollen with his sweet smell, and the fingers with which I have written these words remember the clutch of his little hand, which will not let me go. The dark squall I anticipated after the business with Wolf's journal has passed and the air seems brighter and clearer in its wake.

Catharina

Now Mutti said Baby Wolf was a week old and so was growing up quickly but he still cried a lot and made a mess. Mutti said a week was a long time for a baby. Tante told the schoolchildren that a week was seven days. Mostly there were four weeks in a month. Could any of the children say how many days there were in a month? Gudrun's big brother Bendt said twenty-eight, he was ten years old and could read and write. Yes, Tante told the children, Bendt was right, but sometimes there were more, for example thirty days. Could the children please remember thirty days. Each day lasted for twenty-four hours. But how could Bendt be right when he said twenty-eight but there were thirty, Bendt's brother Harald wanted to know, so Bendt poked him with his elbow and then Harald poked Bendt in the stomach. Then Tante said again could all the children please remember thirty days and that each day lasted twenty-four hours, and could any of the children say how many hours there were in a month, but not Bendt or Harald because they had to keep quiet. But none of the children could do the question, it was too difficult. Bendt and Harald were pretending to keep quiet but they couldn't do the question, Catharina could tell, because they were making silly faces at each other. Seven hundred and twenty hours, Tante told the children. That was how many hours there were in most months, it was a lot of hours, and did any of the children know how many months the ship had been sailing to New Zealand? Two hundred, said one of the girls with red hair, her sister had red hair as well, they were called twins. Their names were Julia and Sophie but sometimes Julia pretended to be Sophie and Sophie pretended to be Julia. Was the girl who said two hundred Sophie or Julia, Tante wanted to know. She was Julia, the girl said but the other one gave her a special look. Then Tante told the children that the two hundred months Julia had answered was more than sixteen years and so now Julia would be twenty-four years old and a proper grown-up woman. Did Julia look like a grown-up woman? Then Julia began to cry and so did Sophie, they always cried together. Then Tante told them not to worry, because today was a special day. Today the ship had been sailing for one hundred days, that was fourteen weeks and two days, which was more than three months and was also two thousand and four hundred hours. Now all the children were not sitting still, they were looking around to see what was happening in other parts of the deck, and some of them were standing up. The people with violins were playing music on the high part of the deck at the back of the ship. Yes yes, said Tante, the children could go and listen to the music. But Catharina went with her to see Baby Wolf. He was sleeping and so was Mutti. He was next to Mutti on her bed. Would Catharina like to give Baby Wolf a little kiss, asked Tante, but just a little one so he wouldn't wake up? So she did, she could smell the oil from the little bottle that Papa Wolf had. Then Tante gave the baby a little kiss as well, and they went out to listen to the music. Was Tante happy because of the hundred days, Catharina wanted to know. Or because of the music? Then Tante told her that the music was called a string tree by a man called Franz Schubert, she liked it very much, but she liked Baby Wolf even more, she liked Baby Wolf the most of everything. So that was why Tante was happy. Was that why Catharina was happy as well? Yes, Catharina liked Baby Wolf, but now he was always sleeping with her mutti and he made a lot of mess.

Josephina

Josephina finished embroidering the baby's nightgown with the two little Rohrsänger on its front just a day before the baby was born. She was doing the last thread of the thin black reed-stalk gripped by the bird's tiny claws. She drew the thread through to the back of the cloth and picked up the last couple of stitches. Then she snipped the thread and turned the nightgown right side out.

How good it always felt, to finish something. Then there would be a new thing to start.

There they were, the little birds, facing each other and tweeting with open beaks.

Shall we go? Are you ready?

The baby was very low, now, and seemed to be squirming.

It was a nice breezy day and the deck was very crowded. There was Mister Oats with three men playing cards – he had lifted his hat to her politely when she first came up on deck. Sometimes after she began to be out there again he had brought her a thoughtful gift, some water, for example, or some dried figs from Mauritius. He was helping her with some English words, and she could then pass them on to Catharina.

Water. Weather. Wind. Ship. Wash. They were quite like the German words. But some were not. Fruit. Sky.

Ada's friendship group, by their expressions, were wondering if Mister Oats wasn't somewhat forward?

But the friendship group admired the finished embroidery on the baby's nightgown very much, and especially how Josephina had left patches of the muslin free to represent the breasts of the little birds. The effect was so nice and simple and fresh!

She had already washed the nightgown three or four times because the smell of the baby's puke was strong in the cabin where it was very hot and close, even with the door open to the stateroom and the hatchway. The Rohrsängers' pure little breasts were stained now, and the coloured threads unpicked from other things and used to embroider the birds were already somewhat frayed here and there, so that the outlines of the birds were becoming blurred. The tiny jet beads that one of Ada's friends had given her for the birds' eyes were still there, though, she had been careful with them when washing, and they looked out brightly from the little frayed faces.

Some of Baby Wolf's napkins were cut-up bed sheets from Ada's friendship group. The napkins also smelled worse than Catharina's had at Greta's house, where Josephina could boil them up in the outside wash copper with some of the verbena by the privy and the good yellow soap that came in Danne's boat from Flensburg. Then, she could put her tired face in the drying napkins sweet with the smell of sunshine or fresh with frost out in the yard at the back of Greta's house, and breathe in her happiness.

There was hardly any soap to buy on the ship, they didn't get any more at Fremantle, and the piece she had was very hard and couldn't work with salt water, only with hot water from their ration. The smell of the nightgown with the two little worn Rohrsänger was her grief and it would not go away, not even after she tied the nightgown and the napkins in the rigging and let them flap about in the wind that was taking Baby Wolf to his home. There was her grief, she scrubbed and scrubbed at it on the washboard with the hard piece of soap and rinsed it out with cold salt water, but it stayed, and in her heart she wanted it to stay. There were her grief's flags like the signalling pennants that were hoisted when they saw another ship at sea or when they were going in to a harbour. There, flapping in the rigging for all to see, were the secret signs of what she hid from Catharina and from Theodora, but who could read them? Only she could read them and understand what they were signalling.

Yes, she understood what her flags were saying, that her dear Wolf had gone, and also that she was the only one who could understand the flags, and that the meaning of the flags was her secret. Catharina could not know the meaning because it would hurt her to see her mutti's grief going on and on after the scrubbing and the wind, and Theodora could not know it because it seemed as though the baby had healed an old wound in her, perhaps the loss of her friend that Wolf wrote about in his diary. Now, Theodora would hold the baby while Josephina attended to her own needs, she would take him out and carry him around on the deck or to sit in the shade of an awning, and she was even unwilling to give him back when Josephina asked for him. Of course she pretended it was a game, holding the baby tight and saying, No, you can't have him, he's mine! – but it was plain to see that she meant it in a way.

Was this a good thing? Some of Ada's friends liked to hold him as well, especially the one called Elizabeth who had given her the jet beads, and two of the smaller children were curious about him and wanted to poke him to see what he would do. But of course Theodora's feelings were stronger and more real than those of Ada's friends. Baby Wolf's father was her brother, after all, and she sometimes cried with a trembling mouth that was holding her words together with difficulty, and said she thought about Wolf and how he would have loved to cuddle his son.

Little Wolf had brought Josephina and Theodora together in almost the opposite way to how the grown-up Wolf had driven them apart – it was surely a good thing that they were united in their love for the baby? – and yet sometimes Josephina's strong instinct was to snatch Baby Wolf from his father's sister, from his aunt, which was not right or fair, but she couldn't help it. The desire to snatch her baby back from Theodora was connected to her grief. She didn't want or need to lose her grief, she just wanted to look after it properly and keep it to herself. And so sometimes when she was approaching Theodora and saw how Wolf's sister was adoring the baby and looking at his face and giving him little rockings, she would have to turn away and walk around for a while on the other side of the deck, or look at the sea slowly purling away behind the ship, unhitching itself from its side and sliding away, being there and then not being there.

Then she would go back to Theodora and say that it was time for her to feed Baby Wolf. Theodora would say of course and hold the baby up to her and they would smile at each other over the baby as he was passed between them.

Sometimes he was asleep and it was clear that it wasn't time for her to feed him, but she would take him away to the cabin and wait for him to wake up.

But of course mostly she was grateful for Theodora's help, with Catharina as well as the baby. Without her help and the kindness of Ada's friends and especially Elizabeth it would have been difficult to manage both the baby and her grief, because her happiness and her grief became confused together at times, and then she needed to find a little space for herself, to feel that she was alone when washing the nightgown, for example, even when there were others at the tubs.

Theodora offered to help with the washing but Josephina liked to do it herself, and there was a better supply of water and firewood after Fremantle.

Some sailors had run away when the ship was in Fremantle and some new ones had come on board. On the first morning after they left the port, one of the new sailors pulled all the washing off the ladders in the rigging and threw it on the deck. He was a tall man with a thick yellowish beard, and when Josephina said what did he think he was doing, because the captain permitted them to put washing in the rigging, he stood looking down at her with his teeth showing in his beard.

There were several teeth missing in his smile, if it was a smile, and he stood there pointing his gappy smile down at her for a while before asking, in a strange accent, was she German?

Yes, she was, but what did that have to do with the washing?

It had nothing to do with the washing, merely with how he should tell her, gnädige Frau, respectfully, in language she could understand, that the captain was no doubt a wise man, but that it was not the captain who had to climb up the rigging, where the washing would be in his way if he did try to, so he would probably break his neck and then who would steer the ship? And what was her name?

Then one of the ship's officers shouted angrily at the sailor, who went at once to the rope ladder and climbed quickly up. But he stopped for a moment and leaned out, holding on with one hand, and made a bow to Josephina with a flourish of his free arm. Or perhaps his bow from the rigging was a mocking one, for the benefit of the angry officer. She could just make out his disrespectful grin up there.

Josephina began to tie the napkins and the nightgown back in the rigging but tried to keep the rope ladder as clear as possible. The sailor was too familiar for her liking, but also friendly in his way, and his mocking bow was funny. And there for a moment was the young sailor with the wonderful whorled shell and the bitten-off earlobe and the missing finger and the ruined smile on the harbourside at Kielerhafen – did he get any money for his shell, and what did he do with it? She could feel that her mouth was making a smile, but she hid it from Elizabeth who had come over to help her tie the washing back in the rigging.

How uncouth and rude that sailor was, standing over Josephina like that! – where did those men come from, they were surely criminals running away from the authorities – was Josephina going to complain to the captain?

No, she wasn't going to complain, Josephina told Ada's friend. It wasn't the sailor's fault, after all he was new to the ship.

But standing over her like that!

Elizabeth's mouth pursed around her disapproval.

What she could not know was that Josephina and Theodora and of course Wolf had also been 'running away from the authorities'. It was clear that Ada's friends were not quite sure about 'Frau Hansen' – they had befriended her when she needed help, they admired her needlework, they discussed Baby Wolf's health at nearly three weeks already! – but Josephina sensed there were many questions about Frau Hansen that they discussed among themselves and that were not asked when Frau Hansen was with them. Their conversation bulged with the pressure of the unasked and unanswered questions, like the sails of the ship bulging and quivering with the pressure of the invisible wind.

Why did Josephina demur when asked if she would like to join their Bible reading group? Was it because she had been married to a Jew? What had been Herr Hansen's profession? Why did his sister keep so much to herself? Was Hansen a Jewish name as well as a German and a Danish one?

Josephina rebuked herself for imagining these questions, but she couldn't help doing it. There they were, the kind friendship group women with their heads together while they talked, and she saw that they sometimes glanced in her direction as she crossed the deck, or when she was talking to Mister Oats who was helping her with English.

It should be Hanson not Hansen, Theodora had objected when Wolf brought the papers from the agent in Bremen. Because Hanson was a Jewish name. She exaggerated the different shapes of the Jewish and the German names with her lips.

Ah, what a tremendous historical difference it made, an 'o' or an 'e', Wolf had teased his sister. But it was his married name now, with an 'e', wasn't that true?

But these were the questions Josephina guessed Ada's friendship group asked among themselves when she wasn't with them, and also, why was she talking to that man from the steerage accommodation?

She had learned to sew from her mother, who had learned from *her* mother, Josephina told Ada's friends, because this was the safe question. And she had her grandmother's sampler with her. It was in their trunk in the ship's hold. It had hundreds of stitches in it, many shown in little pictures and stories. Perhaps it was even older than her great-grandmother.

And the Rohrsänger?

No, the Rohrsänger were her own invention.

So clever!

The question about where she had watched the Rohrsänger coming and going with the seasons pressed in. It was a question about how a young woman from the marshy edge of the sea by Kiel could have met and married an older Jewish man.

(An older Jewish man with an ugly crooked back! Called Hansen!)

(From Sønderborg?)

These questions were not asked when Josephina was with them, but she felt their pressure, and sometimes also the presence of Pastor and fru Jepsen from Saincte Marie in Sønderborg, perched up on one of the spars above the friendship group.

The tall sailor with the strange German accent passed by and touched his brow respectfully to Ada's friendship group. They were not happy with his familiarity, nor with the respectful attention of Mister Oats. Josephina was sitting with them and holding Baby Wolf on her lap. His head was on her knees and she was squeezing his little feet in her hands. It was as though she was steering him towards the future through the squally, unasked questions of Ada's friendship group.

Yes, it was the future his father had dreamed of, but now it was hers.

Of course she could always sew, she replied in answer to their question about how she would be able to look after the baby when they got to Wellington, and of course her sister-in-law was an educated woman, she could teach.

Ah yes . . . of course. An educated woman. (There she was, over there, writing something, as usual.)

(But without a husband or even a brother?) That was the question the pause before 'of course' concealed when Elizabeth and Ada and the others agreed with Josephina and her answer to the question, How would she be able to look after the baby?

But the answer was simple, surely? And so was the question, What choice did she have? And the answer, Her own choice? Was that not also simple?

'What choice do we have?' Josephina asked the companions and friends of Ada's friendship group, looking from one to another and seeing their nods begin. She was gently squeezing Baby Wolf's feet and steering him towards the future. It was a question that answered a question the friendship group had not asked, and that they could not answer except by remaining silent and nodding that they understood! – Of course, they nodded, of course, what choice did she have?

But then it was clear that Baby Wolf was not interested in the future but in his hunger, so Josephina took him towards their cabin past the men playing cards, including Mister Oats who acknowledged her by lifting his cap.

Theodora

Saturday, 28 March, 1880, Port of Wellington, New Zealand

Our ship went back and forth in blustery conditions for the better part of a day, keeping its distance from the land. We were between one and two weeks on from our arrival at Sydney where a number of the ship's passengers had disembarked in lighters, many of them singing and cheering as they left their prison of some four months, and who could blame them for that. The ship remained at anchor out in the harbour, perhaps to discourage crew deserters. It was clear that a close watch was being kept on the crew, some of whom perched themselves high in the bare rigging and gazed at the busy signs of life on the shore. Others, however, ran away while getting the passenger baggage ashore, and so we were delayed while replacements were brought on board. Now, within sight of our destination, the word went around that we were delayed yet again because the winds and the tide were not right and the ship was unable to take the Wellington pilot on board. You see how I have begun to adopt an easy familiarity with language that had only ever seemed metaphorical before.

In the distance from time to time we could barely see an inhospitable rocky coast and beyond it some vague misty hills, everything very windswept and a thin line of white breaking water at the land's edge. Black, grey and dirty green-blue were not the obvious colours of a new paradise, nor were the sullen oppressions of the sky, but their grim palette at least carried no hint of false promises such as those flaunted at us in pestilential Cape Verde. Though the ship was rather unsteady and seemed to be going back and forth between two landmasses separated by a wide choppy maelstrom, none of the passengers who had stayed on deck were any longer prone to sickness. Even so, there were some shouts of dismay when the captain and officers ordered all passengers to their quarters as the ship then prepared to make its final approach to our destination. Were we to be denied the reward of a first sighting after so many long weeks, indeed months? But down we sullenly went as if well schooled in the behaviour appropriate to this New Land. Catharina was following with the other children under the firm Danish hand of fru Frederiksen.

In the hour or so before we went below, Josephina had been with her friends, the women associated with fru Frederiksen, all of whom had been unfailingly kind to her in the time after Wolf's death and the birth of his son. I was grateful for their kindness on her behalf and thought it generous rather than charitable, a judgement I confess to arriving at against my own familiar prejudices. At no time did I have any particular wish to join them but, more to the point, I had for some weeks thought it best to treat this opportunity for sociable warmth as being in Josephina's best interests and the best interests of her baby, and so hers to own. My best interests, after all, have become those associated with solitude on the one hand and the company of a speechless infant on the other. It has comforted me perversely since my poor dear brother's death to know how much he would have enjoyed the apparent absurdity of this space of opportunity and choice in the life of his always critical elder sister! And yet it has become a nearly perfect life for me, in which grief can be encountered and measured rather calmly whenever it returns to my thoughts. It has also been a practical life, combining my regular obligation to prepare unappetising food for appropriately ungrateful travelling companions and my attempts to retain the intellectual attentions of children bored to the point of moroncy. My own intellectual stimulation comes to me second-hand from Josephina, who shares the notes on English she gets from Wolf's friend Mister Oats. These permit me to supplement what I have previously been tutored in by the likes of Engels' Conditions and Paine's Rights in their daunting English editions. And so, in time, as well as startling the baker with an assertion that men are born free and equal, I may be able to ask for a loaf of bread and get one.

And of course, despite the circumspections of our relationship as sister and lover of the little man we had both adored in our different ways, and the close confinement of our living conditions, here I have been now for some strange weeks in the inescapably intimate circumstances, at once blissful and intolerable, of living with the young woman whose claim on my heart I cannot disclose, and the child whose claim I cannot conceal.

Given the habits and expectations into which all of these contingencies had moulded me, it was with a shock as we went below that I heard Josephina mutter under her breath, with a venom in her tone that was unlike anything she had said in my presence before, that she was sick to death of the whispered judgements and suspicions of fru Frederiksen's friendship group, and the sooner we could all go ashore and never see them again the better she would be pleased! There was much noisy clattering, shouting, blowing of whistles and snapping of sails as she said this, and so it was only after the hatch cover had been closed and we were in the stateroom with our neighbours that I found myself having to suppress an angry rebuke. Then, leaving Catharina with her friend Gudrun, we went through into our sleeping cabin, where Josephina sat on her bed and began to feed the baby, something both of them had begun to find difficult. What was the reason for the malice in her tone, I asked her. What had happened to turn her against those well-meaning women whose company she regularly sought and seemed to appreciate?

Little Wolf had learned to tangle one hand in a strand of Josephina's hair as he fed and after some initial outcries his cheek was flushed with the work of suckling. Seeing this tender tableau, which I had witnessed often without appearing to seek it out, was as close as I could ever hope to get to a reconciliation of the erotic claim on my heart that I cannot disclose and baby Wolf's claim that I cannot conceal, and my irritation melted away in a sweet warmth. But then Josephina looked over at me with a piercing expression of frustration. It was none of my business, she said coldly, but since I had asked, her anger was precisely because she had no choice but to sit with those women, as the alternative was to add fuel to their suspicions by appearing to avoid their company much as I, Theodora, had chosen to do, as they noticed. Hadn't I seen how they liked to discuss her and indeed me, Theodora, as well, when we weren't listening?

But what suspicions, I asked her. And how could she know what was in their minds or what they were talking about when she wasn't listening? And then she dictated, in a dull staccato, as if from a remorseless, repetitive, inquisitorial voice that played over and over in her mind, a list of things she believed the women were discussing. Most of these seemed harmless to me – for example, how was it credible that a young woman with a German or Danish name could have married a considerably older Jew who could hardly be considered a compelling prospect for such an attractive young woman? I didn't say that the same question had occurred to me, the Jew's own sister, but then I had seen how that unlikely story had unfolded in ways that overruled my own mental whisperings. They were convinced, hissed Josephina with, now, tears in her eyes, that the kindly Mister Oats and even one of the sailors were making improper advances. What could I say to her? That a man's most kindly and generous attentions might become the advance manoeuvres of seduction, as she herself knew well, and this was not such an unreasonable suspicion for the women to have, since they had made caring for Josephina their responsibility?

But then I saw, as baby Wolf began to complain loudly about the agitated messages in his mother's voice and body, that the space left in Josephina's heart by Wolf's death had become a horrible echoing vacuum that had filled up with these imagined whisperings endlessly repeated. She had been locked up with them on this ship where no escape or relief was possible. The wide horizon on all sides had never ceased to be other than a stifling encirclement towards which the ship's grudging movements were endlessly inconclusive. What was driving her mad was this, but also her stubborn refusal to abandon the resource of her own strong will which was itself like a horizon that confined her.

This could have been the moment when I crossed the short space between us in the little cabin and took her in my arms to say that I loved her and Wolf's baby, that we were nearly in a new place where those whisperings would soon blow away, that they didn't matter, that we would do whatever we had to, this was now our choice to make. This was the recitation with which we had lately often encouraged each other. But I did not cross the cabin because Josephina gave a great sigh that was almost a laugh, and said, Well Wolf, here we are, and I couldn't tell if she was talking to her baby or to her dead lover, nor who were the subjects she meant by saying we.

And then, after an hour during which Josephina knelt in silence by the sleeping baby Wolf and looked out the little spray-smudged window as the daylight was beginning to fade, we were allowed back on deck while the ship went very slowly with almost all its sails furled into the broad expanse of a harbour encircled by hills. In the distance was a meagre scattering of lights, with a few more flickering across the slopes. Though it was forbidden to do so, some of the young men climbed up the ladders of the rigging to get a better look at what these lights revealed. There seemed to be a town, they shouted, there were chimneys and smoke, and a number of other ships at anchor. But not much of anything! An almost full moon had begun to rise above the long, blunt mound of a hill below which a line of lights seemed to indicate a foreshore. The evening sky was clearing and the misshapen moon was swept by dark clouds. The air was fresh but not cold.

Josephina was standing next to me with the baby wrapped in a special warm shawl that she treasured. Catharina was nearby, riding aloft on Mister Oats' shoulders, but complained she still couldn't see anything much but hills. There was a great rattling of chain as an anchor was let go. Then I felt Josephina's hand reach very gently around my waist, and her head leaned against my shoulder for a brief while. There is hardly anything here, she said. Her tone was more of wonder than disappointment. Perhaps she meant that there was still room for something, though of course I cannot know that. I was touched by her gesture, which may have been in part an apology for her earlier outburst about fru Frederiksen and her friends. A fiddle and some other instruments had started up and people were dancing. Josephina persuaded Catharina to come with her and I saw them join a circle. Josephina was holding her baby close with both arms but her feet were skipping quickly below the hem of her skirt. Then I was alone again as usual, in the crowd that remained gazing in perplexity towards the strange chimera of our arrival.

And now it is morning. Everybody else is on deck waiting to be told what will happen next. I do not need to be there to know that our instructions will contain little information of any substance about that. What I do know is that this may be the last time I wait for a few seconds in this small room for my breath to dry the gleam of wet ink and then close my journal.

Beth

Really, Noel had liked the appearance of order more than order itself, though his containers of 35mm colour film were an exception of sorts. The containers he liked were flat grey metal Brumberger cases with six slotted rows for twenty-five mounted slides in each row. Always the same containers, he got them from America. So, one hundred and fifty slides in each container. The containers had quite a nice marbled effect on their surfaces and they were definitely stylish industrial modern, the way Noel liked his world. They had metal handles that folded up so you could carry them like a briefcase or a safe-deposit box perhaps. Each container also had a pre-prepared index sheet under the lid. Noel had always filled these in with place, date and, if published, the initials of the magazine. He was finicky. He used a fine-nib Parker fountain pen, nothing else would do. He also wrote the information on the cardboard slide frame, until they became plastic. He complained bitterly when magazines didn't return his slides, which happened regularly. So out there somewhere, in the vaults of forgotten or anachronistic pre-digital publications, without the benefit of Noel's neat index entry, were a whole lot more of the slides, unnamed, out of time and history, undocumented, unloved. The 'orphans'. This much she knew before breaching Noel's barricade. Then, too, there was the way he'd picked a slide out of its slot with elegantly fussy finger and thumb, and the way he'd bent over it on his light table with a magnifying glass.

Behind what was surely the artfully contrived carelessness of the warped and cast-aside Cherub mast's untidy tangle of wire and wood was a ceiling-high rack of blue metal industrial storage shelves. The Brumberger cases were in there, about forty of them at first sight, stacked quite neatly on top of one another in lots of four. So, ten lots with about six hundred 35mm slides in each. So, something like six thousand 35mm colour slides in all.

There was just so damn much of it, no, just too so damn much of it, viewed from a safe distance, from the outside of Noel's barricade. The other barricade, the one she'd constructed every bit as carefully as Noel's crafty one, was the one in her head that kept at bay the thought and, inevitably, the sad/comical image of Noel over the years scrupulously extracting six thousand colour slides and looking at each one on his light table – his rather dandyish long hair, black and then grey and then mostly white, held off his face and the magnifying glass by the spectacles he pushed up above his forehead. Every so often they'd fall off and land on the light table. Sometimes he'd used a rakish blue-and-white spotted bandanna knotted at the back of his head, and sometimes even a pair of his Skants because they had good elastic. He didn't like the hair clips she offered him any more than the flash digital camera he got about the same time his Cherub mast barricade went up and he stopped using Kodachrome film.

The word 'Kodachrome' and the sexy way he'd said it with his lips pushed forward a bit was also kept behind her barricade, or had been until now. They'd joked that he had an erotic relationship with 'Kodachrome', which he'd confessed, serially. The warmth, the glow, the capacity for soft textures. The relationship hid in the camera until he took the shot and then . . . in full sight as he pored over the results of their affair, his and Kodachrome's. Noel with his Skants on his head to hold back the now somewhat straggly hair: 'Can't you see I'm with K'chrome?' One of the last of his many jokes, endlessly repeated. Was that because he didn't remember telling the jokes, or because they just kept repeating themselves to him? Then there were the lunches. Once he got up to three – it was tomato and cream-cheese sandwiches with glasses of the Astrolabe pinot gris he 'insisted on' – and she and 'Sonnyboy Joe' sat in the garden and ate all three without comment. Then Noel washed up for the third time and came back down with his glass of wine. Joe asked him what he thought of the new digital Hasselblad H he'd just bought, and he gave a detailed technical answer. A beautiful machine but he didn't like the relationship it asked him to have with the world.

There was just too much of both kinds of stuff, what was behind her barricade and what was behind Noel's one. Maybe the national museum would like to have what was behind Noel's. She'd have to give Joe a ring and see if he could help with the slides; he could bring the kids round and they could also take the Cherub mast away and turn it into a flagpole over at their place out at Laingholm. Where to put the stuff that was behind her barricade was another matter.

'So how was the ride back with crazy old Frank?' Joe wanted to know. Somewhere in the background one of the boys was trying to get an E5 power chord. 'Straighten your bloody finger!' Joe shouted, adding, 'Not you, Ma!'

'We should pile everybody in cars and go down the valley one summer.' There was a silence, except for the E5 with a straight finger, a couple of times. 'It was okay. He's a cranky old bugger but we had a great road trip. Went to have a look at Pouakani, remember him?'

'How was he?'

'Frank or Pouakani?'

'Both.'

She needed to cut to the chase.

'Listen, Joe, I need to get Dad's slides out of the way.' There was another silence and then a door slammed and the E5 attempts with straight finger faded to the background.

'Why do you need to do that?'

'It's been going on six years, Joe, I need to start clearing stuff out.'

'You can't just chuck them away. A life's work.'

'Come off it. You know I wouldn't chuck that stuff.'

'Stuff.'

'Life's work of warm, glowing, softly textured Kodachrome colour slides.'

Finally, his lovely cackling laugh.

'We could give them to a museum. Maybe Te Papa would want them.'

'Would they pay?'

'They might, I don't care. Could you take it on for me, Joe? I'll chuck in the old Cherub mast for free. You and the boys can make a flagpole.'

'You all right, Ma?'

'Come over at the weekend, have a glass of wine, bring the boys.'

She expected Joe to understand that she needed a clear space to go forward into. It had to be a space that hadn't been gatecrashed by the past. He'd had to do that himself, took his time over it but got there in the end.

'I'll smoke you a fish.' He made a kissing sound close to his phone.

Then she went back downstairs into the drive-in and looked at the unlit space where the Brumberger cases were. There was just a dark mass. Hidden in it were six thousand little windows to the past.

Josephina and Catharina

Now it made her laugh out loud to imagine that the wooden birthing chair with the hard shiny arms was the hull of her heaving ship and she was its full-to-bursting body – the woman who sat behind her in the hull and gripped her tight below her breasts was the helmsman whispering hoarsely that she had to keep steady, the midwife who knelt between her knees was saying that she was nearly there, now she was nearly there at last, and now all at once she was! There was a wide blue-green expanse of ruffled water with sunshine glinting across it, and the purple shadows of slowly passing clouds. The gulls were making a squawky fuss around the ship, and Wolf was making his own squawks until she turned him around in the wrap of the Danish shawl and showed him the sunshine on the water. She even felt an ache low in her belly as if it too was remembering – it was the sunshine and the purple cloud shadows that made her ache there, and as well as that the horizon was gone, there was a proper border to the place they were in, it couldn't keep on unravelling away anymore, her thoughts had a simple space to be in.

Theodora came up from their cabin wearing her plain straw bonnet with the red ribbon around it. Though Josephina had seen the old bonnet many times she got a little shock of surprise – they kept startling her, the things that were familiar. Theodora held out her arms for Wolf and asked what did he think? Did he like the look of this place? Wolf was saying loudly that he didn't like it very much at all and so Theodora took him away for a walk around the deck through the noisy crowd of people.

It had taken so long and so much pain for him to be born that when he arrived at last there was hardly anything else there – the polished wooden arms of the chair weren't there, the woman's hoarse voice in her ear wasn't there anymore, the other woman wasn't kneeling in front of her saying *nearly there*, the pain wasn't there, her own voice crying out wasn't there, she was in an almost empty place with just the baby in it, and he didn't know where or who he was or where he'd come from, and now there was the almost empty expanse of water with hills all around and a range of blue-grey mountains in the distance. The sunshine was nice. There were wispy plumes of smoke blowing away from some buildings.

That's where they were going now, she and Wolf and Theodora, and nobody there knew who they were or where they'd come from. Nobody there had ever known Wolf Bloch the poet or Hauptmann von Zarovich the shithead. Perhaps no one there knew the words or the melody of 'Wie traulich war das Fleckchen' and they'd certainly never heard of Puck Puck – that could hardly be expected! They didn't know who Greta Andersen and Elke Franzose were and they'd never heard of Meister Hansen or poor thin coughing Agatha Hansen. They'd never heard of Alex who was really called Alessandra who lived on the other side of the world in a big city like Hamburg, not like this little place, even though New York had New in its name as well. Perhaps they'd never heard of Kielerhafen or Sønderborg.

Then Catharina was tugging at the sleeve of her dress and telling her that Gudrun's big brother Bendt had told her that this wasn't Wellington after all and that they'd been kidnapped and taken to a secret place to be slaves in the mines, was that true, Mutti? There were gold mines in the mountains over there and children had to pull little wagons deep into the earth, there were Kobold goblins down there, but here they were called Maries, they were black.

Bendt didn't know what he was talking about, Josephina told Catharina's anxious face and widened eyes, and she ran back across to where the children were to tell Bendt.

But perhaps it was true, said Theodora, laughing somewhat sarcastically when she came back with Wolf who had quietened down. It was as likely as anything else, after all. Who could tell what they would discover when they were finally allowed to set foot on that land? Something like a small fishing town with low buildings had been established on some patches of ground scraped bare; there was a rudimentary port with three or four wharves, there was a single unimpressive church spire – had her dear brother envisaged anything like this? She was even enjoying the joke, if it was a joke, and seemed not at all sad. And after all, said Theodora, whose face was speckled with the sunshine coming through her straw bonnet, Wolf would hardly have been surprised to hear that there were gold-mine goblins exploiting children, they were usually to be found everywhere, though of course being Wolf he'd hoped things might be different in the New Land of his hopes and dreams.

Theodora said 'New Land' in English with a familiar twist of her lips. 'And now, see, look, here they are coming,' she added, also in English. And indeed, a boat had rowed out from the shore and come alongside. Half a dozen men climbed on board and went with the captain to his cabin. 'The Kobold have arrived!' said Theodora with a bark. 'Quickly, we had better hide Wolf!'

But then after an hour the six men came back out from the captain's cabin and climbed back down into their longboat and were rowed away. And then it was time for lunch. It was the same barley soup with the carrots from Sydney, but two of the Sydney sheep had also been butchered that morning and so almost everyone on board the ship could perhaps find a small piece of the meat in their soup, although the best parts had gone to the captain's cabin and first-class passengers at the back of the ship.

'A taste of things to come I hope!' exclaimed fru Frederiksen, who was stirring their big soup pot beside Josephina in the kitchen, because as she often reminded her fellow passengers her two eldest sons were farming sheep somewhere inland, it was very successful, and that was where they were going.

But where were Josephina and the baby going, she wondered, without mentioning Theodora.

They were going wherever their own talents might take them, said Josephina, giving her a direct look that made her blink quickly several times.

Why of course, that went without saying, agreed fru Frederiksen, who had perhaps noticed that Josephina had returned to her theme of 'what choice did she have?' but by turning the theme upside down. Now it was that the choices they had were their own to make to the best of their abilities – she and Theodora had decided together that here they were in this new place where no one knew them or expected anything of them, and was that not after all an opportunity and even like giving birth to new hope?

But she didn't say any of this to fru Frederiksen – to Ada – who was now a little flustered by Josephina's direct look, which was hardly fair, because it was true, she had been a good, kind friend. And so Josephina gave her a gentle kiss on her cheek and said that she hoped Ada's grown sons weren't too far away because it would be a pity to lose touch with her and with her family, after all they had endured a long voyage together, not to mention a great deal of soup with no meat in it only beans.

Now Mutti was smiling sometimes and making the shapes of words with her lips but not saying them. She was walking around all the time with Baby Wolf. Perhaps she was singing? Sometimes she was moving her head as if she was singing but without making any sound. Gudrun and Bendt and the other stupid brother called Harald had fresh clothes on and their papa had cut the boys' hair with a pale bare stripe around the side. They had been saving the clothes for when they arrived, Gudrun told her, was Catharina going to do the same? Did she have some? Look, she even had some special shiny shoes, but they were a bit too tight. And she had a special handkerchief from Haderslev, it wasn't their home anymore, but it had a special picture sewn on it, there was a shield with some water and a bridge, but she didn't know if she could remember the bridge. Would Catharina like to come down to the cabin and get some fresh clothes on, asked Tante, with that Tante look, when Catharina told her about Gudrun. That was a good idea, because soon they would be going ashore. Ashore was an English word. But could she have a special handkerchief with a picture, like Gudrun's? No, said Tante, she didn't have a special handkerchief, but Catharina could have the red ribbon from her straw hat – if they made a plait with her hair she could wear the ribbon around it, would she like that? It would make going ashore special? And also it would be a good idea for Catharina to clean her teeth, she could do it with the washcloth around her finger, with some salt on it, they could get some salt from the kitchen, because the men who had come back on board would want to look into her mouth and at her tongue. So then she took her clothes off in the cabin and Tante wiped her all over with the washcloth dipped in a basin of water and with some of the lavender soap, there was just a narrow slice. Then she put on some clean clothes, and Tante did the same. And then she brushed both their hair – Tante piled hers up but did a plait for Catharina and tied the red ribbon around it. Yes, it felt special. But where was Mutti, was she going to change her clothes as well? And Baby Wolf's, because his would certainly be stinky? Tante thought Catharina's mutti might be too happy walking around up on the deck, perhaps she couldn't be bothered. Or perhaps it was because she was very unquiet, Tante thought, perhaps Catharina had noticed how she was walking about in that unquiet way? But what did unquiet mean? Tante thought it might mean that Catharina's mutti was thinking about everything that had happened, about her Papa Wolf getting sick and dying and about Baby Wolf getting born, and about what they were going to do when they went ashore. She used the English word ashore again. But what was ashore? But then they had to wait in a line with Mutti and Baby Wolf because the men had come back in the long rowboat and they wanted to look in everybody's mouth just as Tante had said they would, and so Tante didn't tell her what English ashore meant, and one of the men listened to her chest with a thing like a trumpet that he put in his ear. Tante showed them some papers and spoke to them in English and then they went to wait with some others in a crowd. Mister Oats was there as well, he told them that soon the ship would be towed to the wharf and they would be able to get off. He also told her very slowly that he hoped to see her again, and her mother and aunt, once they had got ashore. But what did ashore mean? Everybody was saying it. Ashore was where flowers and trees grew, said Mister Oats, it was where grass grew for horses and cows to eat, it was where birds could make nests in the trees and where people could make their homes. And was Mister Oats going to make an ashore home as well? Perhaps he would, Mister Oats told her, but first he had to find his brother who had got lost a long time ago. Perhaps once he'd found his brother he could come and see Catharina's ashore home? And visit her mutti and tante? But now Mutti was walking around and around again and laughing, and then suddenly using her special Papa Wolf Poem voice she said, 'The sun will rise beyond the gaze of Reichskanzler Dismay!' – and then Catharina joined in, she was happy to be saying the Poem again, they hadn't done that for a long time, and they said it together in their special Papa Wolf Poem voices while looking at each other's lips. Tante was watching them with a funny expression and Mister Oats walked away!

The rear balcony of the hotel was above the landing steps and faced across the harbour. Often noisy boatmen would come to the hotel that way, and Josephina began to understand more of what they were saying to each other. How many afternoons had she spent sitting on that balcony in the late sunshine listening to the men boasting about the fish they'd caught – they often caught fish by the landing because the hotel's kitchen scraps were thrown into the harbour there – but now it was time for a damn good glass of beer? Or perhaps a couple? The words for glass and beer were the same in German and English, but couple was not. A couple could also be two people who were married. What would Wolf have thought of this place? The evenings were often a melancholy time; it was when the light began to fade. Sometimes she'd sit out there with Baby Wolf on her lap, if he was peaceful. He was getting stronger and more contented and her milk was better and her breasts not sore. Herring was a German word but the boastful watermen also said snapper and gurnard, those were the names of fish. They quite often had snapper or gurnard for their supper, the fish were very plentiful in the harbour. The word fish was the same in German. Very plentiful fish – Catharina made the shapes of the English words very carefully with her mouth, which was full of the very plentiful fish and the boiled potatoes with white sauce. Please don't talk with your mouth full, said Theodora – and especially not English, she added, with a little bark laugh.

There were warm baths on the first floor of the hotel, and Doctor Lichtscheindl said it would be beneficial for her to take one every evening. Beneficial. There were beneficial mineral salts to put in the water, she should dry herself with a very rough towel, she should also drink the beneficial tonic made with cardamom seeds and spirits, and she should add some drops of it to the fresh milk that came to the hotel every day in a cart. She should drink plenty of fresh milk because like her the dear little baby had also been affected by the long sea voyage and the bad diet, he was too thin. Doctor Lichtscheindl believed in watercress, beetroot, onions, apples, and plenty of fresh fish. There was plenty of watercress in the fresh streams around the town. He said they should stay at the hotel until Josephina was completely better, he was only too glad to be in a position to help some fellow Germans in their time of need, and Theodora said the hotel charges were reasonable. There was still some money from the subscription, and a bank draft had arrived at the

Deutscher Verein – Herr Andersen had arranged it from Hamburg. Then they would move to a rented house. These could be found through the Deutscher Verein, Theodora had investigated how it was done. Then they would see what to do next, such as a school for Catharina.

Josephina heard what Doctor Lichtscheindl was telling her while Theodora listened, and what Theodora was patiently saying to her, but what she mostly noticed was the way the weather wove itself across the surface of the harbour, and the way the mountains in the distance changed their complexions from grey to purple to a dull blue-green.

Had Josephina understood what Theodora had just said to her about getting a house and the school for Catharina?

Yes, she had, thank you. Had Theodora noticed how the harbour changed its surface from one moment to the next?

Yes, Josephina, she had.

The harbour was called Nicholson but neither Theodora nor Doctor Lichtscheindl could explain why. The doctor's first name was Josef – after a few weeks she heard Theodora calling him by that name. The hotel was called Empire, and the reason for that was obvious, Theodora thought, since the English had planted their flag in the soil of New Zealand. Perhaps the name Nicholson was obvious for similar reasons, it was an English name after all, but no one seemed to know, not even Josef – he was very well informed in general, was Doctor Josef Lichtscheindl, said Theodora with a droll intonation, but especially about the beneficial properties of watercress.

Now they had a little baby carriage and she could take Wolf for walks along the street where the hotel was, with Catharina helping by holding on to the handle of the carriage. The street was rough with cart tracks in it, but there was a sealed footpath beside it and they could walk the length of it to where the buildings stopped. Work was being done on the harbour at the end of the street, so they would turn around from the noise there and push Wolf 'back home' to the hotel. The word home was quite like the German one, but because it was a little different it didn't really mean home. Sometimes they would go back and forth several times, and then when she was tired she could lie down in their room 'at home' while Theodora took care of Catharina and Wolf. Theodora was helping Catharina to learn English words and then Catharina was helping her mutti.

Breakfast, Mutti – say it.

Breakfast.

Street, road, path, window, fresh air.

No, not fresh iya, fresh eeeaaar.

Fresh eeeeaaar.

The warm little puffs of Catharina's breath on her cheek as she said the words close to her in the bed. Then Wolf would be awake and hungry, so she would feed him by the bedroom window above the street where bullock wagons and some horse carriages came and went, and then take him to the balcony if the weather was fine. Theodora would bring her a glass of milk to drink, and one of Doctor Lichtscheindl's watercress sandwiches made with very coarse yeasty bread, another of the Doctor's dietary prescriptions.

Their big trunk from the ship was in the bedroom – it was full of several different things, but mostly silence. She watched Theodora open it and take out clothes and also some books and other things. She put the silent household things back, the bedding and the knives and forks and some plates and cups, but no words came out of the trunk. The words for what was in it had been left behind.

It was a nice evening, the fresh eeeaaar was blowing gently across the balcony, below it some men were standing outside by the water drinking their beer, or perhaps a couple of beers, bloody beautiful, and the mountains in the distance beyond the end of the harbour were tinted with the glow of late sunshine. Yes, it was quite a beautiful place, bloody beautiful, it was spacious and somewhat empty, perhaps that made it peaceful. But she was so wrapped up in the peacefulness, it was muffled and dull despite the noise of drinking men and the breeze, she might as well be asleep? Wolf was kicking with strong little jerks on her lap and blowing bubbles, he was certainly much stronger and happier, and Doctor Lichtscheindl thought she was too. The English words Catharina was helping her to learn and the ones she heard the drinking men saying below the balcony kept repeating themselves to her as if they were what mattered most.

Fresh eeeaaar.

Bloody beautiful.

But now here were Catharina and Theodora. Catharina was carrying something and Theodora was encouraging her – they came along the balcony together, and Catharina had a special expression on her face, a little solemn and important but with a smile, it was a careful smile and so was Theodora's.

Mutti was holding the rolled-up cloth thing on her lap, it had changed places with Baby Wolf, who Tante carried away screaming to the end of the balcony where there was a big plant in a pot, it was called a fern. Could Mutti see how Baby Wolf was snatching at the spiky leaves of the fern? At least he'd stopped screaming. But Mutti was looking at the big cloth thing in her lap. Oh yes it is the Oma, she said, oh look, here it is! Did Catha remember how Mutti used to show her the stories in it? There was a little deer on a mountain, and some others, there were yellow ducks on a blue lake, and a little red house with a smoking chimney, and some owls, did Catha remember? Yes, perhaps she did, she wasn't sure – Tante had thought Mutti might like to see the Oma thing and so here it was, Tante remembered it going into the big trunk, did Mutti like it? – but wasn't an Oma a grandmother like the one in the churchyard with all the flowers and Tante Elke? She could remember that, and Tante Elke's cow with the eyelashes. Yes it was, said Mutti, an Oma was a grandmother but she called the cloth thing Oma because her own grandmother had given it to her when she was still a girl, didn't Catha remember that story? Surely Mutti had told her that story! Perhaps one day she would give the Oma to Catha! But imagine a grandmother being locked up in the chest, said Catharina – don't worry Mutti, it was a joke! Or in a ship! said Mutti. But shall we look at it? And then she untied the three pieces of thick brown string around the Oma and unrolled it on the floor of the balcony. It had a funny old smell. Yes, of course, now Catharina did remember the little pictures, the red house with grey smoke coming out of the chimney, the blue lake with the yellow ducks, the white mountain with the deer on top and the little pine trees, the owls with huge staring eyes, the writing in different colours, some stars, and look! – an angel flying across the sky, yellow, red and blue flowers, some brown and black horses going around the edge, the writing going around the edge as if the letters were galloping as well, yes now she was remembering it! Could Mutti tell her one of the stories? Well, well, so here you are, here you are! said Mutti to the Oma. They were both kneeling on the floor next to the

Oma and Mutti was carefully stroking her hands back and forth across it, so Catharina did that too – the Oma mostly felt thick and bumpy. But where was the little deer Mutti had told her about, the one that came down off the mountain and went looking for the place where oranges came from? Oh you clever little deer, said Mutti, so you do remember! Yes, Tante was right, the Oma was making Mutti happy. Yes, here I am, said Catharina, making her fingers into antlers on top of her head, here is the Little Deer, are you happy to see me, Mutti? And now Tante was coming back with Wolf, he had a fern leaf in his hand.

Theodora

Monday, 27 September, 1880, Town of Wellington, New Zealand

Here I transcribe from Josephina's dictation what has recently become the ambiguous anthem of our situation here in Wellington. What it might yet become the anthem for remains to be seen. This morning Josephina departed happily with Wolf gesticulating in his carriage and Catharina proudly walking to her school in the Aro Valley. In the early afternoon I went from our modest neighbourhood to the 'official quarter', Thorndon, to introduce the children of a well-to-do family called Cornish to the salient moments of European history and culture, and to teach them the rudiments of the German language. Sometimes before our afternoon tea at five we sing simple songs: for example, the faintly subversive one by August Mühling that we were taught by the politically tone-deaf Chorleiter back in those days of Wolf's and my childhood in Uelzen – 'Froh zu sein bedarf es wenig und wer froh ist, ist ein König!' It takes very little to be happy, and whoever is happy is a king! This task requires a diplomatic circumvention of that history's class struggles of which I mark out a simple diagram in my daily walks between the neighbourhoods of Te Aro and Thorndon. That my suppressed diagram has been transplanted from Europe to the far side of the world no longer surprises me, if indeed such a surprise was ever likely. The nostalgia evoked by Josephina's lament for a lost childhood, in the maudlin lyrics of the song 'Longing for Home', are perhaps even more dispiriting. My anger is another matter, and I shall come back to that, though I cannot pretend to understand it well.

Josephina and I used the transcript of her song as an exercise in translation. Here is the German with our improvised English appended.

Wie traulich war das Fleckchen,
Wo meine Wiege ging!
Kein Bäumchen war, kein Heckchen,
Das nicht voll Träume hing.
Wo nur ein Blümchen blühte,
Da blühten gleich sie mit,
Und alles sang und glühte
Mir zu bei jedem Schritt.
Ich wäre nicht gegangen,
Nicht für die ganze Welt! –
Mein Sehnen, mein Verlangen,
Hier ruht's in Wald und Feld.

How homely was the little spot where my cradle used to rock! There was no little tree or little hedge that wasn't hung full of dreams. Where only a little flower bloomed, my dreams bloomed there too, and everything sang and glowed for me with each step I took. I would not have gone away, not for the whole world! My yearning, my longing dwell here in forest and field.

On Saturday evening last we were gathered in the Deutscher Verein to celebrate the end of winter, a moment that could not have come soon enough for most of those in the rather austere surroundings of the 'hospitality room', where, however, there was an elaborate Bohemian Kachelofen to keep the guests warm, imported to Wellington at great expense no doubt. This was one of a few objects designed to remind the guests both of the homeland they had come from and that they were no longer there. There were other talismanic presences also warming this spirit of too-cheerful nostalgia. These included some apparently rustic country house-style cooking aprons worn over dresses with puffy sleeves – it was Josephina who noticed these. Her reaction to the aprons, which were adorned with flowery embroidery, was sympathetic and interested in proportion to what I confess was my own sceptical reaction: had we come this far only to perpetuate sentimental condescension to romanticised rustic virtue by the Old World bourgeoisie? And what about the hard-working women whose broad aprons would have been filthy with the stains of their toil rather than festooned with elaborate bouquets of bright silk thread? Oh what a sour old doubter and naysayer I am becoming!

And of course there were also the refreshments, some very good coffee, and also beer and some nice cakes. Wolf is now almost eight months old and already has a steady pair of legs that can transport him some distance in a straight line if he has a destination in view. It was Catharina who stopped him before he could pull down the cloth with the cakes on it, which might have signalled the beginnings of a subversive life, Wolf's that is. One can only hope.

The entertainments were also well tuned to the cheerfully nostalgic mood of the evening. A boy and a girl aged about twelve or thirteen sang a comic version of Goethe's 'Erlkönig' in the setting by Schubert, into which they inserted inappropriate English names and expressions, to loud appreciative laughter, since the nervous comedy of inadvertent language mishaps was no doubt a daily happening for many at the Verein. There was a halting but determined piano recital by the same girl, I think of the Allegro section of a Brahms piano sonata.

And then came the evening's special Brahms moment, his setting of the dreadful sentimental poem by the Holsteine poet Klaus Groth, a native of Josephina's birthplace Kiel where, she tells me, he is much revered, not least for his association with Brahms. In this poem, in which is moaned a maudlin desire to return once again to the infantile cosiness of the childhood crib, the guests at the Deutscher Verein heard the perfect expression of their conflicted knowledge that they were now adults in a strange new place and their longing to be once again in the homely spot where their cradle used to rock, to paraphrase Groth's tearful text. Josephina has a very sweet voice and a well-pitched intonation, and she allowed the twelve-year-old piano accompanist plenty of room for small mistakes. At the end of the song, as she smiled shyly and gave the girl a thankful kiss on the cheek, there was I swear not a dry eye in the room. The applause for Josephina's performance was substantial and sincere but I detected a hint of restraint in it, as if too much enthusiasm would reveal the hidden narrative of the song's conflicted affect.

This was perhaps the next stage in the lengthy process of Josephina's recovery from the dreadful melancholy despondency to which the portal had been her strangely restless gaiety in the last days on board ship. The melancholia's most obvious symptom had been her preoccupation with imagined mutterings by her friends and fellow passengers. It now seems clear to me that she had locked herself in this miserable place by her own strength of nature. That clear-eyed determination I had so often admired in this young woman had been the resource with which she sustained a barricade between herself and those with whom she might have shared her suffering. Of course I must ask myself why this should seem familiar, and reply to the obvious question with the obvious answer: that in Josephina's predicament I saw the now faded ghost of my own. The barricade of her proud strong will became thicker as we approached our destination, and when it began to crack at the sight of a place 'with hardly anything there' she was not able to defend herself.

I saw how, some weeks earlier, dear Wolf's poem began to return her from grief only for her to lock herself away from expressing it. I saw how the sight of a place 'with hardly anything there' made her feet skip and dance with gaiety that was the perverse sign of her surrender to the inertia of melancholy. And then I saw how the old sewing sampler revivified those dull senses. And now, six months after our arrival in this place 'with hardly anything there', I saw that singing the Brahms song to sentimental words by her admired poet Groth was another and, I thought at first, perhaps even the last stage of Josephina's arrival with all her senses and capacities in the new place to which her love for my brother had sent her – away from everything she had held dear, her sisters and their children, her childhood home, indeed from the 'homely spot' yearned for by Groth's narrator.

But she was not, I believed, given what I knew of this young woman's strong character and the way in which she had brought herself back out of a deep despondency, responding to the song in the lachrymose manner of many at the Deutscher Verein. Indeed, I have for many weeks been rejoicing in and admiring her vivacity and energy since we took up residence in our strange narrow little cottage in Bute Street, with its muddy road outside and determined beds of parsley but not much else in the yard at the back – so different, I am sure, from the idyll sketched by Herr Groth's 'Where only a little flower bloomed, my dreams bloomed there too'!

Then, at the conclusion of the entertainments and when all the refreshments had been cleared from the long tables, some of those present put out items for sale such as jars of preserves, cakes and biscuits, knitted or embroidered things such as children's garments, some male handicrafts such as wood-turned toys including little wagons and painted soldiers, and also a few curios and exotic objects perhaps obtained during visits to foreign ports on the voyage here. Josephina had some of her own work on one of the tables and was hoping not only for a little money but also to increase the number of people who would know about and might use her skills, which were already in modest demand.

Earlier, she had whispered to me that one of the sailors from our ship was at the Verein, did I recognise him? He was the one who had thrown some of the washing from the rigging to the deck, but who had always made a point of courteously greeting her after she had remonstrated with him. He was the tall man with the yellowish beard and hair, very much trimmed since the time of the voyage, she noted, and wearing a good plain woollen suit.

I did not recognise the man, and had never had any reason to single him out from the crew that came and went around the deck of the ship. But then I saw that he had put some objects on a table not far from where Josephina was showing her work. They seemed to be oriental in nature, and included some painted fans which he had spread partially open on the table, a pair of small portly statuettes, a brocade strip of some sort with tassels, and a paper or cloth scroll that he partially unfurled. He stood behind his modest display with a patient closed-lips smile, greeting people and explaining his objects – he fully spread one of the fans and made a little show of fanning himself before handing it to the young woman who had admired it. The older man who was with her, her father perhaps, bought the thing and they stood talking with the sailor for a while before moving away, the young woman happily fanning herself. I saw that the sailor had a certain charm and I also saw that he had noticed Josephina and touched his fingers to his brow in a respectful salute. Josephina, meanwhile, was being kept busy with people interested in her needlework, and with Wolf who wanted to throw all of it on the floor.

Then was the time for me to intervene and offer to take the two children home, but I allowed myself to be detained by Josef Lichtscheindl who had recently been shown the bones of a giant bird of some kind, which, with his passion for diet, he believed had been eaten to extinction by the Maori inhabitants of this place. I listened with half my attention to this outlandish tale, while the more alert part of me kept watch as Josephina, having sold her little stock of things, left Catharina to play with Wolf and approached the man she had described as 'the sailor'.

They greeted each other very properly, but all at once I was alarmed by an absurd premonition that this man would enter the life Josephina and I had organised in the face of such adversity and which was harmonious in spite of its challenges both practical and emotional. Josephina and the sailor had sat down on opposite sides of the table while she looked at the thing in front of her. The good doctor's tone became somewhat insistent, but I was unable to take my attention away from Josephina as she bent over the scroll that the sailor was unrolling to its full extent. And then I saw that the thing had affected her strongly and that the sailor was looking away from her as if to spare her feelings. I was sorry, I told the good doctor Josef Lichtscheindl, of course I would be interested to see the giant bones, but would he kindly excuse me as I needed to help Josephina to get the children home.

I saw when I confronted her that she had indeed been affected by the scroll, a miserable black-and-grey panorama of little scenes. We should take the children home, I suggested. This is Herr Heinrich Wenczel, Josephina informed me, he has travelled to many parts of the world, he has been showing me this wonderful Chinese scroll. Herr Wenczel and I shook hands as Josephina explained why she had found the scroll so interesting, and then he quickly rolled it up, tied it with a length of yellowed cotton tape, and handed it to Josephina. Please keep it, Frau Hansen, he said, with a carefully restrained glimpse of his few remaining teeth.

I am sure this was a kind and sincere gesture on the part of world traveller Herr Wenczel, but now, still, two days later, there is a painful twist in my heart, the scroll remains tied with its length of old cotton tape on the dresser in our little cottage, and I fear it may be the instrument of another stage in Josephina's journey from Groth's 'homely spot'. 'Ich wäre nicht gegangen, Nicht für die ganze Welt!' – I would never have gone away, not for all the world! cries the poet, but my darling Josephina did, and had to, and perhaps one of us may have to do so again.

And so now late at night with Josephina and the children sleeping peacefully in their little room, I close my entry for this day, unable to dispel the unreasonable and anxious premonition that invaded my thoughts as we celebrated the turn of the seasons. I fear unreasonably and humiliatingly that the departure bemoaned by Josephina's poet of homeliness may in the end have to be mine, that Groth's homely little spot is now none other than this chilly, rattling wooden cottage at the edge of the world where a frugal kind of love has been able to bind our bereft family. I am angry and fearful to the point of trembling, and would like to seize Herr Wenczel by his throat and choke the plausible courtesy from his disagreeable smile. But even worse, I resent the no doubt innocent impulse that made him give Josephina the Chinese scroll, since the very innocence and kindness of his gesture mark my repugnance as unworthy of the enlightened woman I pretend to be. I have no reason to believe that this man will infect our 'homely spot', and yet I do. I would say that I fear this fear.

Now it is late and I will extinguish my lamp and attempt to sleep, though I doubt my rest will be peaceful or free of the jeering thoughts that continue to circulate in my body and mind.

To Friedrich Engels, in Primrose Hill, London
Friday, 8 October, 1880

Respected Comrade Engels

Today I am sitting with your letter that has come to my brother Wolf Bloch here in Wellington care of the Deutscher Verein. It is clear from a number of letters forwarded in the same way that friends and colleagues have become anxious at the absence of news from Wolf, usually the most reliable and sociable of correspondents.

It is therefore my sad task first of all to inform you that my dear brother Wolf died of food poisoning on the twenty-third of December last year, shortly after our ship left Cape Verde. He was buried at sea the following day. You have yourself experienced the anguish of losing a dearly loved companion and so I do not need to describe the grief that I felt as his sister, nor the suffering of the young woman who was shortly afterwards to be the mother of his child, his beloved Josephina.

Now, almost ten months since Wolf was 'consigned to the deep', we are established in a small worker's cottage in this town of Wellington, an unusual little family of mother, daughter, infant son and sister-in-law. At Josephina's insistence, the infant son has been named Wolf Bloch, and so my remarkable brother may live on in this new life and in this new place. We are able to support ourselves, Josephina by her seamstress skills and I by tutoring the children of more well-to-do households, but our life is frugal to say the least and I for one miss the fervour of conversations at our dear Bloch House in Hamburg, itself a distant memory.

It will not surprise you to know that the familiar class

template of workers and landowners has been faithfully imprinted on this town, though there are signs that the enterprise of artisans and small businesses may yet establish a bloc capable of challenging the hegemony of landed privilege and capital. Even so I chafe, as I know Wolf would have, at the disproportions and exploitations that govern how the majority must live. I am therefore grateful, dear Comrade Engels, for the information you sent Wolf and that I may presume to benefit from. I am referring to the establishment in Brisbane in Australia of the Social-Democratic Vanguard Party by Hugo Kunze, our fellow German exile. With your blessing I am sure, I will contact Herr Kunze and see what we might do in concert.

Now I will close this short letter in the hope that my contact with you and Wolf Bloch's many valued comrades will be sustained, as I am determined to continue in the work my brother and I were committed to for many years together.

With respect and in loving memory of our comrade Wolf Bloch

Theodora Bloch

Please continue to use the address of the Deutscher Verein in Wellington as I cannot be sure of our continued place of residence.

To Herr Aksel Andersen
Deichstrasse 31
Hamburg

Friday, 8 October, 1880

Dear Herr Andersen

I am writing first of all to thank you for so kindly organising the remittance that came to us at the Deutscher Verein here in far-off Wellington, New Zealand, not long after our arrival here.

Secondly, since your recent anxious letter was addressed to my brother Wolf Bloch and was responding to one of his sent back to Hamburg from Cape Verde some ten months ago, I have to explain why it is I and not my brother who is now replying to you. Sadly, my dear brother died from food poisoning on the voyage, not quite two weeks after writing to you, and was buried at sea not far on from Cape Verde where his letter to you went ashore.

You and I am sure also Frau Andersen will be glad to hear that the young woman Josephina Hansen who, together with her daughter Catharina, was in your care for some months in Hamburg, and who had joined our family on its voyage, has recovered from a long period of miserable grief and is now the mother of a robust baby boy, my brother Wolf Bloch's son, born towards the end of our journey.

I am aware that Wolf had requested you to act as our discreet agent in Hamburg, and had provided details of our arrangements with Behrenberg-Gossler there. Would you now be so kind as to send the materials stored at the bank to the Deutscher Verein address you have used already. You should continue to use the name Hansen as that is how we are known here in Wellington. Please address the materials to Miss Theodora Hansen. I will inform you as soon as possible should this address change. At present the four of us, myself, Josephina, her daughter Catharina and infant son Wolf, are quite simply and safely accommodated here.

I thank you again for your kindness and in advance for acting on our behalf at Behrenberg-Gossler.

With respectful greetings also to Frau Andersen

Theodora Bloch

To Signor Pasquale Martignetti
c/o Banca Malzone
88 Mulberry Street
Manhattan
New York
America

Friday, 8 October, 1880

Dear Signor and Signora Martignetti

Or, I would rather say, dear Pasquale and Maria

It is now many weeks since your letter to my brother Wolf, with its kind greetings also to myself and to Alessandra's special friend Catharina, was delivered to the Deutscher Verein here in Wellington, New Zealand. You will be wondering why that enthusiastic letter writer Wolf Bloch has been so slow to reply, and so I must be the one who responds with the sad news that our dear friend and brother died as a consequence of food he ate at Cape Verde. He was buried at sea on 24th December last year and it will not be long before we mark the anniversary of the tragedy from which I and Josephina are still recovering.

You will, however, be happy to know that Josephina gave birth to Wolf's son, named Wolf Bloch after him, and this child has without doubt been the chief agent of our recovery from grief.

We are living frugally but securely in a small cottage in the working part of the town, which is divided along lines familiar to us but perhaps no longer to you in 'the land of the free', as Wolf liked to describe America. I hope his optimism has not been disappointed. For my part, though I am grateful to have arrived safely after a long and tedious voyage and after the tragedy that seemed to prolong it, I long for the conversations we had at our dear Bloch House in Hamburg, and for the company of others committed, like us, to the causes of equality and public good.

You should tell Catharina's friend Alex that Catharina can now speak English quite well and is going to a school where she has some new friends, but that she always speaks of Alex as the special one she will never forget.

For reasons that I believe Wolf explained to you, we are living under the name Hansen, and so letters should continue to be addressed to me as Frau Theodora Hansen, or perhaps more appropriately now, as Miss Theodora Hansen, at the poste restante of Deutscher Verein. It is possible that my address will change, and I will inform you as soon as possible if that happens.

One evening soon I will sit Catharina down with paper and pen and have her write a letter to her special friend Alex in New York, America. We will see if we can find a picture of where we are to send you. There is a photographer named Bragge who lives here, I will see if we can purchase one of his prints. What you will see in it will be very different from the surroundings of a metropolis such as Manhattan. The town we live in has barely begun to establish itself, and it may be that I, or Josephina, will one day decide we must move on. Perhaps New York will return as a preferred destination.

For now I will end my short and unfortunately sad letter with affectionate greetings to the three of you, Pasquale, Maria and Alessandra. I will always have fond memories of our time together.

Theodora Bloch

Josephina

A single large tear fell on the scroll and Josephina quickly pushed the old thing away before another tear could wet it, and then covered her face with her shawl, why? – it was not so much to mop the tears and stop them falling on the scroll, nor so the sailor called Wenczel with the broken smile wouldn't be able to see her tears, but because she didn't want to see in his expression the reflection of herself crying.

Because why was she crying? What was in the old scroll with its yellowed paper and the strange writing beside the pictures – what was in there that had suddenly made her eyes flood with huge heavy tears, though no sobs came with them?

When after a short while she took the shawl from her face, she saw that the sailor sitting opposite her at the table was looking with cautious courtesy past her at nothing in particular – there was nothing else for him to look at besides her, and the chattering crowd of guests, and it was as though he'd seen her wish not to be reflected in his expression.

But perhaps he was just shy and awkward, a man unused to the company of women?

To reassure him, and perhaps to explain to herself why the sailor's old yellowed and greyish pictures and foreign writing had affected her so strangely, she was telling him that it was because of the tiny people and animals in the pictures, and the little horses and tilled fields among trees, all seeming to be so far away, like her family, tiny, as if about to disappear . . .

(. . . but no, it was because of the clear, calm empty spaces where a kind of silence was in the picture . . .)

(. . . and also that the writing, though she couldn't read it, was uttering with bold strokes what she was unable to express as words . . .)

(. . . there was a thin, low, dim peninsula reaching out across a pale, slightly soiled emptiness towards some columns of intricate black lettering. A tiny bridge reaching across another hazy void. The piled-up hills were crowned with weathered miniature trees – above them was the soiled silence of the sky. The bold marks of the writing were like pictures or the score of some kind of music. She saw a peaked shape like a roof above black bars that seemed to thump down upon each other. There were tiny people in industrious groups, and a solitary person sitting motionless under a tree – the person, an old woman perhaps, seemed to be gazing into an emptiness beyond which some delicate writing fell like veils of rain from the pale sky. There was a tiny house with animals – horses, perhaps? – and the doors of the house were open wide and its interior was empty. People in narrow boats floating on emptiness. A pale ribbon of road with laden donkeys making their way towards a cluster of farm buildings – a large one and some small structures like animal stalls. Many of the low, fading peninsulas seemed to be pointing away from the land, the farmhouse, the laden donkeys, the solitary person looking across a space that was like silence . . .)

(. . . the old person in the scroll could be her oma sitting under the pear tree above the Schwentine. The old lady had often seemed to be looking further away than Kieler Förde and the ships or the mill where the river ran out past the marshy reeds with the little twittering Rohrsänger – looking away into a space that made her face go silent even when Josephina reached up and touched its soft dry crinkled surface carefully with the tips of her fingers. Was she looking at ghosts, at her husband and foolish sons in the ground over there in a place she'd never seen, at Dybbøl, near Sønderborg? Was she trying to go there in her mind? . . .)

Yes, the simple answer was that the little rustic pictures in the sailor Wenczel's old scroll reminded her of the childhood home she'd left, and both Herr Wenczel and Theodora were nodding sympathetically – but what she couldn't say to them was that it had mostly been the smudged spaces of silence and emptiness in the scroll that had made her eyes flood unexpectedly with big tears. But why was that? What did she want or miss that was in those empty spaces? And how could she want emptiness?

The scroll made her think of her grandmother, she told them. That was at least partly true.

Then she must take it, please, she could not refuse. The sailor Wenczel bent politely over his cautious smile. Please. He held the scroll out to her.

Then they were trundling Wolf home. Catharina was tired and her feet hurt.

'We are nearly there,' said Theodora encouragingly, in very careful English, but her displeasure at the sailor and the scroll entered the cottage with them. Her goodnight kisses were abrupt – she was tired, she said, Josef Lichtscheindl was so exhausting – and she went to her own room without offering to read Catharina some stories. Last night she read 'The Story of the Wild Huntsman' and 'The Story of Johnny Look-in-the-Air' from a book called *Der Struwwelpeter* – it was one of Papa Wolf's favourites when he was at school in Uelzen, but Josephina could see that Catharina was already starting to forget about Papa Wolf.

*

There he was again, the thoughtful scroll sailor, smoking and laughing with some other men outside the Empire Hotel where she had spent those strange weeks she now thought of as being about her study of the harbour and Doctor Lichtscheindl's many ways of making her eat watercress until she almost turned green. That had been hers and Theodora's joke, for a while. She had noticed the sailor there two or three times on her way to the draper's in the weeks after the Verein, and once he had saluted her rather cheerfully and made a bow like the one from the ship's rigging. But why was he no longer on a ship? What was he doing?

Now she was on the other side of Lambton Quay with her new sewing friends Arabella and Victoria. The small, quick one called Victoria reminded her of the little quail that used to bob their heads while running along the margins of the path that led to the pastor's school by the Schwentine, and she was named after the living Queen of England, 'an old pudding'. The big one, Arabella, was named after her late father's favourite thoroughbred breeding mare in Ireland, and it was their joke that Josephina was without doubt named after the son her father had hoped for, with -ina added at the last minute when he saw what he had accomplished.

Arabella's father had been a rich landowner's stable master in a place called Kildare. He was trampled by a horse startled in its stall by the sound of a shotgun fired at starlings.

Josephina withheld her thought about von Zarovich being crushed by his horse.

That was very sad, but what were starlings?

They were nuisance birds. They liked to come after the spilled feed grains, and they raided the grain fields.

That was another new word, starling, but not very new, in German almost the same, Star.

So now Arabella and her brother were in Wellington to see what kind of life there might be here. Her brother was good with horses, he was a skilled groom.

Groom?

Arabella made some broad combing gestures and did a comical neighing sound – she was a strong young woman with large white hands, and her miming reached up and drew the shape of a horse's flank.

Ah yes – Josephina herself had a favourite horse once that she liked to grooom, he was called Gunnar. He aufstöhnte his liking of her groooming deep in his – neck?

She made a groaning noise.

Ah, yes! They were laughing at her impersonation of old Gunnar's pleasure.

And Arabella's mother?

She would not leave, she had remained behind, the wealthy horse breeder was providing for her.

Providing?

Yes, she had somewhere to live, and enough to eat.

And so the talking moved along in a jerky way, with new words, it was enjoyable.

And Victoria's story? Victoria's story was cholera, she too had come with her brother, they were the only ones left from their family. Her brother was a blacksmith, did Josephina understand, horses' shoes? There was plenty of work here, they would do well, better than in Liverpool. People got sick there.

Yes, Josephina knew about cholera, it had happened in Hamburg where she lived before coming to New Zealand.

But no, not while she was there, fortunately.

It was good to laugh at misfortune, Arabella thought, and after all what was wrong with being named after a thoroughbred breeding mare, where she came from it was considered a great honour. All that was missing was a fine stallion of equal merit.

Arabella's laughter suggested that she would rather look forward to the future than dwell on the past.

Yes, of course, they were both on the lookout for good husbands who would provide for them and their children, and their brothers would be casting around for their future wives, though they pretended they weren't interested – and Josephina? Victoria asked in a sympathetic tone.

Josephina began to pay attention to Wolf's bonnet, which had slipped over one eye.

They were walking on the other side of the road from the hotel because they preferred to avoid the men smoking their pipes in the sun there. She was trundling Wolf towards the junction at Customhouse Quay where, around the corner from the bank, was the sailmaker and draper's that had some bolts of heavy blue cotton. It was good for making the plain men's shirts that sold well ready-made from the sailmaker's shop, and Catharina could already sew on the buttons. The sailmaker added his sale commission to the cost of the cloth. Wolf would have to share his cramped pram with the bolt.

It was at the sailmaker's that she had met Arabella and Victoria. They were laughing as she opened the door that time. It had made her smile to hear them. Oh, good morning, ma'am, please excuse us, said Arabella with her hand over her mouth.

They drove a hard bargain, those two, said the sailmaker. His name was Flitch and she could see he liked to joke with them. They were quite comfortable and familiar in their manner and she wished she could be on the inside of their humour – it could be lonely sometimes on the outside of jokes.

But little by little she began to be there.

After all, a flitch was a piece of wood, said Victoria, and she thought Mister Flitch might catch fire one day.

Arabella gave a burnt-finger shake of her hand.

They had come out on the same ship, in the single women's quarters. There were some rough sorts there who bribed the matron for brandy. One girl about fifteen, from a place called Dundee in Scotland, had the most beautiful voice – she could make the brandy drinkers weep even though they couldn't understand what she was singing about. Arabella and Victoria had many stories to tell, and sometimes Josephina told them about her life in the Bauernhaus, and a little bit about the Bloch House in Hamburg.

The sailor Heinrich Wenczel didn't notice her, and she hurried to get around the corner by the bank. Arabella and Victoria took turns distracting Wolf, who was getting too big for his pram, and he was squawking happily at the top of his voice and pulling his bonnet crooked again. Why should she worry that he might attract the sailor's attention? In any case, she hurried. Did she worry what her new friends would think if they saw that one of the smoking men by the hotel knew her and thought it proper to greet her across the street? Yes, a little, perhaps, but really, what did she care?

It was Theodora's bad mood about the scroll and the sailor called Wenczel that made her anxious, but why should she care about that either? The scroll remained where she had put it after the Deutscher Verein because she'd hoped Theodora's mood would lighten, but then their argument about the letters to Wolf that Theodora had opened and read and answered without talking to her continued to spoil the mood of the house.

Why had Theodora not shown her the letters?

Because they were addressed to Wolf Bloch and concerned the work that he and she had been engaged in.

But who were they from?

Friedrich Engels in London. Josephina didn't know about him, did she?

But what about letters from people she did know?

There were letters from Herr Aksel Andersen about the arrangement with Behrenberg-Gossler, which had to do with the affairs of the *Bürger Zeitung*.

But she knew Herr Andersen, he was the uncle of her brother-in-law in Sønderborg! And who else?

Theodora's nostrils were white. There was a letter from Signor Pasquale Martignetti. From New York. And yes, of course he had asked to be remembered to Josephina, and Alessandra was well. But the letter was mostly a discussion of politics in America.

Mostly?

Well, perhaps Josephina would like to write to the Martignettis herself, Theodora was sure they'd be interested in her work sewing things.

Her tone was sarcastic.

But now she was going to prepare the sweet potatoes she'd been given by Mrs Cornish's cook, they were good with some butter and parsley, there was parsley at the back still?

But could she please read the letters from Herr Andersen and Signor Martignetti?

Yes, Theodora would get them for her, after the sweet potatoes. Would she mind waiting?

There was no fun to be had there, in Bute Street.

The street where she and her friends were walking hadn't been cleaned for a while, and she had to wave droning dung flies from Wolf's face. That was what her life with Theodora was like now – she was always waving away an annoying argument.

But soon they were back at the cottage in Bute Street and had begun to work. They worked at Josephina's house because of Catharina coming home from school. They were pinning shirt patterns to the cotton lengths, cutting them out and putting them in tidy piles according to size. There were tall, medium and small sizes, and of course some jokes about which dimension each of them might prefer to cut out. The weather was warm enough to open the door to the little yard at the back and Wolf was having his nap there with a piece of shady muslin above his crib. Theodora was away at the house where she taught the children of a wealthy family – she usually returned in a satirical mood and Josephina hoped her friends would be gone before then. They worked at cutting out the shirt pieces and then put them aside in piles to sew the next day. Then there was time for some tea and a piece of Victoria's cake. It was an apple cake, there was a good young cooking apple tree where she lived in the Aro Valley, and some young peach trees as well. Sometimes the Maoris came to get some, she didn't talk to them.

Catharina came back from school and had a slice. Wolf was awake and sitting on the floor with Catharina and she was feeding him small pieces of her cake. It was true, they hardly looked like sister and brother, but Josephina skirted around the hint in Victoria's observation.

But what was that rolled-up thing on the dresser? Victoria thought it looked old. Was it a picture? May we see it?

They moved the cut-out shirt sections to make room for the scroll, and she unrolled it across the table.

But how curious! Look at the little houses and animals! And the man with the fishing rod in the narrow little boat!

But where had Josephina got it from?

A sailor from the ship she came on from Germany had given it to her, he'd told her he was from somewhere in Silesia, they'd met at the Deutscher Verein where some German people in Wellington gathered to celebrate the end of winter. He had travelled to those parts of the world where the scroll came from.

Victoria and Arabella had waiting expressions on their faces. The scroll was spread out in front of them and they were looking at her across it.

But now she was going to get some paper and pencils so Catharina could draw a picture of Wellington for her friend Alex in New York. Her aunt Theodora had recently bought the pencils, some of them were coloured. Perhaps the scroll would give Catha some ideas.

She could see that the scroll had given Josephina's friends some ideas, but they helped her to move it and make room for Catharina and her pencils. The angry argument she and Theodora had had over Theodora's letter to the Martignettis in New York, with its suggestion that Catharina might make a picture for Alex, had been somewhat soothed by the pencils, which were a kind thought.

Catharina was sitting on a cushion to make her higher and had begun to draw. From time to time the tip of her tongue crept out to help with the management of the pencil. Arabella was holding Wolf on her lap and avoiding the clutches of his hand at her hair, which was somewhat unpinned.

But now it was time for her friends to go. Victoria would be walking up Aro Valley past her brother's forge, and Arabella in the opposite direction to the boarding house where she cooked in the evenings. The establishment was called the Willow Bank Boarding House – but there were no willows and no bank, how silly!

Josephina was struggling to understand willow, a new word, and bank, the same as in German, and why were the words making Arabella laugh heartily with her head on one side while Wolf tugged at her hair? – when the door opened with an angry rattle and Theodora came hurrying in. Arabella's confident laugh stopped in mid yelp and Victoria looked up anxiously from Catharina's drawing, which already had a ship with three masts, a girl's smiling face with pigtails on either side, and a star.

These were her friends Arabella and Victoria, they were just starting their shirt-making plan, and this was her sister-in-law Theodora.

Theodora Bloch, said Theodora. She put her hat down on the scroll.

Then small Victoria and large Arabella were leaving perhaps somewhat hastily – they gave Wolf and Catharina quick kisses – of course they would all three be meeting again the next day, would they not, they could begin sewing the pieces together, was that not so?

Yes of course that was so, Josephina was looking forward to it.

But at present she was looking at Theodora's hat on the scroll, and then also at the expression on her face.

That stupid Cornish woman had told her to leave, Theodora said with a huff of breath. I was influencing the children!

She lifted her hat away from Josephina's look.

And she was sick of using the Hansen name.

Josephina rolled up the scroll and tied the old yellowed length of tape around it.

If Theodora was sick of the name Hansen then she should

stop using it. It was not proper for her to keep using the name if she could not respect it.

'Oh, my dear sweet Josephina,' said Theodora in a voice that was rough and unsteady, as though something was caught in her throat. 'Ich wäre nicht gegangen, nicht für die ganze Welt!' There were tears on her cheeks that she didn't bother to wipe. 'But I am dying here for the loss of Bloch House. What can I do? Who can I talk to? I am Theodora Bloch!'

Catharina was looking at her with big owl eyes.

This was her drawing for Alex, she told her. What did Tante think of it? Of course, it wasn't finished yet, it would take a while, there were a lot of things to put in it, of course it already had her friend Anna whose pigtails hung down over her shoulders.

Yes, Tante agreed, it would take time, there was no need to hurry. Then she went quickly to sit outside while there was still sunshine in the yard.

Wednesday, 17th November, 1880
Our home at 4 Bute Street Wellington (Catharina has made a picture)

To all My Dear Family
But first Elke and Papa, please send this letter to Greta when you have read it

The road outside our little house is narrow and muddy but when I opened the door this morning to see what the sun was doing I saw its dawn glowing in the muddy ruts. There are birds here with little white napkins under their throats and their songs in the late spring are melodious and like playful laughter. A pair of them chortle to each other in a tree across the road. In early spring it was covered in golden pendant flowers and these birds came and went all day to sip at the blossoms. When the breeze blows from the nearby harbour it is very fresh and clean. The harbour is enclosed by hills and at its far end are mountains that change their colours all the time. It can be stormy here with strong gales and then the harbour turns white with spray. This is a rough unfinished place and the town has only begun to exist on land from which the forest has been scraped but that is what I like about it. It is just starting and there is still an emptiness like a deep breath. There is room to breathe. Now you will say that Josephina is talking nonsense again, so here is some simple news. But first I will tell you that tonight there will be a full moon, the sky is very clear and before bed Catharina and I will walk up the hill to look at the moon's path on the harbour. From this you may be able to believe that I am still your sister Josephina, the one you used to say was moony.

Our house is very small and narrow with only one floor and made of wood, but there is a room for me and the two children, and another for Theodora, and there is space for a table and chairs in the room where we cook our food. There are other narrow houses in the row, they are close together and all open on to the street, with a small yard at the back with some parsley, but we are lucky to have it thanks to the Deutscher Verein.

It is now many months since I sent a letter to my old home and my sisters and Papa and the children, I am very sorry to have taken so long. I wrote that one some weeks before we arrived here at Wellington after those events that have changed me so much from the sister you knew that now you might not recognise your little sister, and I can no longer recognise that person either, even though I am still the moony one. As you will know from my letter I lost my dear husband Wolf whose body was dropped into the sea, and for a long time after that I think lost myself as well as though I was drowned. Then came a blessing, it was the son that should have been Wolf's and mine together. His name is Wolf Bloch Hansen and he is now eleven months old. He is a strong and wilful child after having a hard start to his life, perhaps that is why he is obstinate. His hair is very thick and dark, he has dark eyes and is a sturdy walker for his age. Catharina is a good big sister to him, I am proud of her. Her English is much better than mine!

I began to write letters after he was born but did not finish them as I was in an unhappy state for some time and did not want to worry you. Now as I told you the children and I are living with Wolf's sister Theodora in our small cottage in this strange town. We have been helped by Wolf's friends in Hamburg but are now living mostly by our own work. Catharina goes to the school nearby and so I have some time to make shirts and other things with two other sewers. Both speak English and so as well as earning my living I am learning that language more every day. I can earn more than in Hamburg when I lived at Herr Andersen's house but my sewing companions fear this will not last and so they are hoping to find good husbands.

I do not know if Theodora will stay here much longer, she loves little Wolf with all her heart and is his kind Tante but she doesn't care for the town or the tree with yellow flowers or the rough bareness, and I think she will decide to go somewhere else one day. Perhaps she will go to Australia, or to America where some of her friends are now and where Catharina's friend Alessandra is living in New York. If that happens my life with the children will become more difficult but until it does I will go on cultivating my opportunities and enjoying my new life.

With this letter I will send you a photograph of two streets here in Wellington. It was taken last year by a man called Bragge, Theodora found his print shop in the town and bought one for me to send you. In the picture you can see two rough streets, they are called Lambton Quay and Customhouse Quay, they are near the harbour. The small two-floor building on the corner is the chief bank of this town, so you can see that nothing very grand has been built here. To the right of this bank is a small shop that is where I get cloth for my work and also where it is sold. As you can see there are not many people, I can see ten, and one horse-drawn cart! Catharina thinks she can see some ghosts in the picture, one of them is standing between the two policemen, she thinks it looks like her Papa Wolf, but she hardly remembers him, which I find sad. Are the policemen arresting him she asks! The hills all around are mostly quite bare, so you can see that the town has space to grow, as it is doing quickly since most buildings are made of wood of which there is a large supply from nearby forests. Can you picture your sister and her new friends walking in these streets? It is along the one on the left that I go with Wolf in his pram to get cloth from the draper and sailmaker's shop in the street on the right.

Now I will finish, but not before begging you for long letters with news about what is happening by Kieler Förde and Sønderborg, and how is our papa, and of course after a year how is my sister Elke with the handsome Franzose!

Now after my kisses Catharina will write something as well.

Your loving sister and daughter

Josephina

Dear Tante Greta and Tante Elke
and Opa and Finn and Otto

Our house is small but bigger than the ship which was smelly. Wolf is a noisy baby. My friend at school is Anna she has long pigtails. You can see them in my picture. Last night we saw the big moon it has a face. Mutti said it's the man in the moon and he has a little dog but I couldn't see it. There were many stars. When are you coming to see us? Please come soon I can teach Finn English.

Here are my kisses there are many of them like stars
Catharina

Part 3

'the fresh airs of time to come'

Beth and Frank

The otherwise tidy little FedEx box from Australia had a picture of a gaudy galah with upraised crest pasted flauntingly on it and was sealed with a sheet of plastic affixed with slapdash silver masking tape. Inside, on top of some things in cardboard folders, was an envelope containing a letter and a postcard featuring the aquamarine waters of Nudey Beach on Fitzroy Island, Queensland. The hasty writing on the postcard read, What are you waiting for? Frank.

Beth poured herself a glass of the 'cheap but good' Chilean cab sav that Joe had left and took the letter to a chair with strong light – Frank's handwriting was forceful but erratic with occasional lurches of altitude as if he'd needed to adjust how his arm and hand were aligned. He'd made the capital 'F' of his signature into a galah with the top horizontal as a crest and the one below as a beak.

Snapper Court
Cungulla
QLD 4816
Australia

8 April 2017

My Dear 'Comes Second' Cuzzie

What do you call a farting Aussie? Ned Smelly. No, didn't think you'd appreciate that and I will do better.

I can't begin to tell you how lovely it was to see you again 'after all these years' and to venture into the past I thought I'd left behind me. It's not that I want to reopen that old Pandora's Box, but being with you at least allowed me to come along for the ride and on the way to recover something I'd forgotten about or had wilfully sealed off. I've no idea why we do that sealing-off since what harm (or good) can the past do and I for one don't believe we learn much from it except easy stuff like don't play with fire. But then 'play with fire' probably works as a metaphor for all kinds of deep shit, so don't listen to your cousin who is ageing into ill-tempered prejudice and idées fixes. And I have to admit I was looking for a way to get some space between where I am and wherever Helen's gone and so the reunion was a good enough opportunity, though perhaps a misnomer now I think about it.

So what had I forgotten? I got off the plane in Rockhampton which is not the place I love but close to it, and I had the taste of that river in my mouth. I couldn't tell if it was the water we tasted the day we went for a swim a month ago or the water we drank copiously about sixty years ago. You said something clever like, time doesn't flow it just waits for the present to make room, and I think you may be on to something, not quite sure what.

Anyway, thanks to that watery taste I went looking for the stuff Ruth had stashed before she took off to Amman. That was a long time ago and I'd forgotten or chosen to forget about her stuff until the watery thing happened. The stuff is in a beaten-up cabin trunk with brass trims and locks that was connected to the ancestral voyage. Thank Christ the trunk is impregnable, as my house is not, being at the lower end of the market and prone to all kinds of boring bugs as well as what we locals call the swelter. Ever since I moved here after Helen died the trunk has been what I put things on top of and then throw away once I've forgotten why I needed them.

Having now opened my very own Pandora's Box I find that the trunk and most of what's in it came from Ruth's and my mum Greta, and some of it must have come originally from Greta's mother Catharina, the one you thought you remembered as being scary and chic, though I have to point out that's unlikely given you were about three when she died, and yes I am working it all out, never too late. I suspect Ruth planned to write something about our mob one day and was collecting or at least looking after things. I never wanted to open the trunk after she was killed but now I do, thanks to that river. The stuff in the trunk is quite orderly, as was dear Ruth, and includes some of her work folders and copies of some books including Hannah Arendt of course. But mostly it's old stuff.

So now against my better judgement I've embarked on a project and will be sending you items of interest once I've had a look at them. You can send them back if you like, or give them to your kids if they're interested, I don't care who has them. My granddaughter Lizzie and her bloke John and their bub who live here with me while they get sorted had a look but I could see they were being polite. That doesn't matter, so over to you cobber.

That said, Lizzie is a smart kid with what get called 'organisational skills'. She's doing some study of her own and is helping to put the old stuff including me in order. So here's a sample of what she's getting sorted. If you want the bit with me in it you'll have to come over.

The sample is an old pamphlet thing I think was written

by a woman connected to the Wolf Bloch you flushed out of the woodwork or should I say gravestone, otherwise why would it be among these family relics. I'm not sure I get the bit where 'our Van will call around in the morning with the milk, and fire at short range', maybe you can unpack it for me, feels as though something's lost in translation. I quite like 'groping human brain' and 'moulding the plastic minds'. Also in the trunk are some, ahem, rather interesting diaries written by one Frederick Wenczel, Great-grandmother Josephina's son if I remember the reunion account, also a pretty far-out cosmological text by the same Fred, a complex chap it would seem. I'll send this on once I've had a proper look at it. There's quite a lot more where this came from, tell me to stop if you don't want it. If so it can stay in the trunk where it's been all these years and no doubt go to the tip about the time I do.

With love from your happy to be Second Cousin

Frank

Vanguard Tract No. 13 1901

An Appeal to Women
FOR THE VAN
By Comrade Theodora Bloch
Published by Social-Democratic Vanguard,
80A Queen St., Brisbane

WHEN READ, PASS ON

> Every great cause has had its devoted women workers, so to women this appeal for the Ark of the Vanguard – our Van – is written. The text of the appeal is the brief chronicle of the Vanguard.
>
> The Vanguard exists to firmly point out that if we, the workers, grafted sheepskins on our backs, the rich would shear us twice a year, and to teach that we can, by banding together and becoming stronger and wiser, use the shears on the rich instead, until all alike share the earth and its fruits.
>
> This lesson of Co-operation the Vanguard has scattered over the State in 60,000 leaflets, and if one of these messengers has brought light to some groping human brain, we have not lived in vain.

Some practical stuff followed, about the travelling 'Van' of socialist texts and its fundraising efforts, as well as the bit Frank had enjoyed, promising that 'our Van will call around in the morning with the milk, and fire at short range'. This alarming metaphor followed closely a rather contradictory one promising that the Van 'will travel over the State, leaving a blessed stream of Fraternalism in its wake'. Though not wanting to overcook her instinctive pedantry, Beth wondered if the effortful strains of metaphor were the product of an English-as-a-second-language over-exertion? The ghost-voice of her remote German several-times-removed Bloch great-aunt?

> Socialism is for women a living, inspiring religion. Women in the past have done much for creeds that taught sex-slavery, and 'contentment in that state of life to which we are

> called.' Our religion, Socialism, teaches that EQUALITY IS THE ONLY MORAL RELATION BETWEEN MEN AND WOMEN, that wrong must be attacked at the roots, and that by working for the progress of all, each woman will best be helped.
>
> The doctrine of slavery and contentment, judged by its result, is its own condemnation. The great majority of us are at present household drudges and factory and shop wage-slaves, deeply grateful, in the fierce light of competition, to be allowed to toil for bare shelter, food, and clothing, until we marry, when we sink deeper into the economic pit, and become straws in the gale.

She put the old document aside for a moment. How easy it was to scoff about 'straws in the gale' in 'the economic pit' when what she was reading in the layer of text just beneath the surface of the printed page was the voice and presence of a determined woman who had probably been a political refugee, who had grappled with a new language and with an unfamiliar country and culture.

> A bride, in our station of life, ought always to be congratulated with reservations. A single woman in a factory or at service can at least ascend one rung of the industrial ladder by co-operating with her fellow workers to form a Union to fix wages and prices, but a woman who marries under present conditions, when the dependence of a wife does not inspire a man with courage at a trade crisis but impels to submission, sets a period to her own emancipation and rivets her own fetters upon the daughters she brings into the world.

> These grinding conditions are artificial, and CAN BE ALTERED if women will cease accentuating them by burying their talents under a cloud of domestic duties, and in a tangle of commonplace conversation. To be a good housewife is not the ideal status of womanhood, for domesticity means subjection, and the contented household drudge is only queen of the kitchen.

Now it was the rungs, fetters, clouds and tangles that moved her, as if she was with the woman whose voice so insistently lifted itself to the surface of the page and even from it, so that she could hear this Theodora Bloch, this ghost who was probably the sister of that other ghost called Wolf, author of the thumping poem about the Paris Commune, who had flickered into spectral life on the screen of her laptop that night back in National Park when she'd overheard Frank in the next room talking to his dead wife Helen before going out to sit with the yelping dog and look at the moon!

> The brain has no sex, and there is no need for us to remain silent during an intelligent discussion, or make a foolish contribution to it, if we will but read and think a little. Co-operative kitchens and laundries are coming fast, and with few domestic duties to attend to, and better still, few to talk about, women in the homes will simply have to get out of the body to think, and then they will radiate like the tail of a comet.

Or perhaps Frank and his pooch were looking at the tails of comets!

And then in the next paragraph she encountered the Germanish 'stress and storm of life' and knew who she was listening to, and wished she could have been talking to, and was perhaps almost talking to, across the collapsed space of more than a century. And then:

> Charlotte Stetson points out that physically woman belongs to a tall, vigorous, beautiful animal species capable of great and varied exertion, but that, through artificial delicacy, we have so far degenerated that we are now the only animal species in which the female depends on the male for food. Happily this reproach does not apply so much to our own class, but to the idle rich women, for women wage-earners comprise over one-fifth of the adult population of this continent.

It would be interesting to ask Theodora to expand a bit on what she meant by 'our own class' and how the Queensland inflection of that differed from its German counterpart in, what, Bismarck's Germany?

> Women are slow to realise that it is a fine thing to be a woman. Woman is the emotional sex, and humanity's highest expression is emotion. To us, as if in acknowledgement of this truth, Nature has given the exalted task of moulding the plastic minds of the future workers of the world. A socialist motherhood, teaching the children to fear no man, to resist tyrants, to despise riches, and to respect only men and women of moral worth, WOULD SOLVE THE INDUSTRIAL PROBLEM! But, 'unwitting that we bear the ark of human hopes', poor mothers cultivate servility in their children towards the children of the rich, and rich mothers teach their children to expect and demand servility from the children of the poor, and out of Servility and Arrogance come un-ending generations of capitalists

> and captured workers. A thousand luminous sermons could be preached from the text that from an enlightened motherhood will come social salvation. Yet preachers ignore this wondrous theme!
>
> Socialism, then, is the Light in the Darkness leading women out of a maze of confusion, and Vanguard leaflets teach women the gospel of co-operation and sex-equality, and that power degrades both subject and master, and that each is helped by helping all.

There followed an exhortation from the Vanguard asking women 'to receive this light, and help us to spread it to others through our Van' which will be 'a perambulating Vanguard on wheels, a power for good to all struggling, unhappy souls, and a rallying point for all Socialists, slowly, but surely fulfilling its destiny of building up and regenerating human souls.'

> We value a good word for the Van from women as much as a small contribution, but we are confident that women will help to grease its wheels when they know that it will carry tidings of hope to brighten the lives of suffering men, women, and children. The seed sown by our Van may fall in stony places at times, but somewhere, sometime, it will take root and flourish.
>
> Van donations received by Van trustees, Comrades 'Theodora' and 'Eznuk' at 80A Queen Street, Brisbane.
>
> ---
>
> Printed at the ALERT Office, Maryborough, Q.

There was a deep, hollow space where Noel's old Brumberger film cases used to be, and though the naked bulb hanging from the beam above the storage racks lit the empty rows their emptiness seemed very dark. The shadow patterns from the shelving made a calligraphy of blocky chevrons and bars. It was crazy to think of this calligraphy as silent, but it was. The old Cherub junk was also conspicuous not by its absence but by its silence.

But of course it was just the silence of the house in which she was alone.

She sat on a crate and poured another glass of Joe's perfectly adequate Chilean – why was he still defensive about stuff, did he think she was assessing his performance of life? The boys had dismantled the old Cherub rigging with glee while she and Joe peeped into the Brumbergers. No, she hadn't wanted to look at any of it, what would be the point of that?

Maybe keep just a few special ones?

But what would have made any of them special? Most of the time she wouldn't even have known where the slides were taken – forests, mountains, beaches, toetoe plumes at sunset, the glitter of moonlight on a lagoon somewhere, a bleak plain strewn with dark basalt slabs of rock, 'exotic' locations overseas. She remembered them as objects that had progressively faded into anonymity, though each slide had been fussily indexed.

Noel's vestiges were in the indexes, not the pictures.

Away they went, the Auckland Museum was taking them, but as a gift with copyright fees attached in case anyone ever wanted to use the things.

You never know, was Joe's judgement on that. There might be the odd windfall.

They sat outside on the deck while the boys worked out how to secure the mast along the tray of the ute and on to its roof. It was sticking up at the roof end, and overshot the ute's tray.

They'd figure it out, Joe reckoned. Paulie was pretty handy and Tim would do what Paulie told him to.

They were shouting Fuck! Shit!

'Sorry, Ma,' said Joe.

And the music?

He was a bloody natural, Tim. That was half the trouble. He learned without trying, and so didn't learn to try. 'Bit like his dad, eh Ma!'

But now it was silent and she'd managed to get herself a bit sloshed.

The slightly wrong language of the pamphlet Frank had sent her with the distant, stilted phantom of German in it – '. . . through all the stress and storm of life . . .'! Sturm und Drang and the issue of Goethe's morbid investment in his Doppelgänger the miserable young Werther had been exultant grist to the mill of sexy radical Professor Schreiber back in the day.

Showing has to be shown! Show that you are showing!

'Das Zeigen muss gezeigt werden!'

But now she was talking to herself. Or to the ghosts of language, or the ghosty author of the pamphlet whose voice had so unexpectedly moved her, or the ghosty photographs that haunted the storage rack's empty space with its ghosty calligraphy, or the ghost of Professor Schreiber whose grinning relish of exact English pro-nun-ci-ation had been funny and sexy, and wouldn't he have loved Vanguard Tract No. 13 1901! That laugh, at once gleeful and a bit vindictive and scornful.

The box labelled 'Treasures' containing some of her favourite Frank letters from the distant past was in the dark space behind where the Brumbergers had been. The Brumberger barricades! The top of the box was covered in dust and cobwebs – leave it to daytime, she'd come back down with the vacuum cleaner.

The boys when they were younger used to play Ghostbusters down here with torches and the vacuum cleaner hose. Noel would come down and do his mouahhhahah routine – it didn't scare the kids after the first time but he kept on doing it anyway, dear old ghost, and the kids quite liked pretending to get spooked if it made him happy. He had a three-hole ski-mask balaclava, you could see his grin in it, and the way his eyes crinkled.

Catharina

Papa Hein was being a pirate with his pencil between his teeth like a dagger. Oh yes, the Moors in their boat with a fierce painted devil's head on the front were approaching! The devil's head was biting at the waves! There were tigers walking up and down on the deck waiting to eat the captives! Could Catharina write 'tiger' or 'pirate'? Here was the pencil. Oh yes of course he should wipe it first. He could do that on his beard, was that good enough? And now perhaps she could draw pictures of them? In English?

Pictures in English, Catharina wanted to know, teasing Papa Hein.

But what was the use of learning words like 'tiger' and 'pirate', Mutti asked as she walked past.

Ah, but there would always be pirates and tigers in the world, Papa Hein said as he snatched Wolf away from Mutti's skirt, and wolves, mad wolves!

Grrr, went Wolf, trying to bite Papa Hein's arm. He already had a mouthful of big sharp teeth.

But now Papa Hein had to go to work, he had to protect the city from pirates coming in to the harbour!

Take care of your mother, he told Catharina in very careful English. And this wild animal. This. Wild. Animal.

(Dieses wilde Tier!)

He whispered the German but went Shhh!

He handed the mad Wolf to Catharina and went out, quickly closing the kitchen door to keep the room warm. Then the front door banged, that was his way. There was a storm outside, a cold draught came in under the kitchen door and made the stove puff smoke.

He hadn't filled the coal scuttle, Mutti complained. Could Catharina go out the back and get some? The bread was only just in the oven, but she had to go to work at Mrs Sanderson's, it was 'her Saturday'.

There was 'mending' to do, she said in a sarcastic tone.

And take the loaves out in thirty minutes, tip them out of the tins. And keep the fireguard in front of the stove!

But of course Catharina knew how to do that, and also that the big black spiders in the coal bin were harmless, but she wouldn't tell Wolf they were, she'd say she hit one with the ash shovel, see? – she'd squashed one of those stinky yellow autumn berries by the back door – see the poison?

And speak English. With Wolf. Because.

But of course, Mutti, she knew to do that as well. He was already able to say that he didn't like his soup because it was dis-gus-ting.

A word Papa Hein had taught him.

Today they were having split pea soup with a ham bone in it, and some of the fresh bread once it had cooled (Wolf wasn't allowed to break a piece off early).

The-butter-in-Wellington-is-nice. Say it.

Not boo-tter – auf diese Weise, bah-ter.

Bah-ter.

Then Mutti would come home.

After supper they were reading *The Swiss Family Robinson* in English. Wolf would try to turn the pages to look at the pictures of the boys with their several guns. Mutti got it from the library on Wakefield Steet that Papa Hein said was too expensive.

And so was the language.

The language too expensive?

Nobody talks like that around here. 'After a moment of reflection, I perceived that I had better come at once to the determination of carrying him across my shoulders . . .'!

Verschone mich!

Sometimes Papa Hein smelled a little of brandy when he came back from the harbour. Arfra momintif refleckshin. Then he would go to sleep in a chair. But then sometimes he would put Wolf to bed. He had a 'nice singing voice'. He was allowed to sing to Wolf in German. 'Guten Abend, gut' Nacht, von Englein bewacht.'

Sometimes he and Mutti sang together. *Wie traulich war das Fleckchen, Wo meine Wiege ging.*

That was how they met, said Papa Hein. When he heard your mutti, sorry! – mother, your mother, singing. Like. An. Angel. At the Deutscher Verein. The. German. Asso-ciation!

He didn't really have to speak English to her so carefully. She already knew lots of words.

She and Wolf were meant to say 'Mum' not 'Mutti' but she almost couldn't because it sounded silly. Wolf sometimes said Mumti.

Papa Hein said Feinsliebchen, Geliebte, also Gnädige Frau Wenczel.

Sometimes he said Mumti.

Come here Mumti my darling.

Mumti Szelwen!

Such memories were 'cheap at the price' she sometimes thought but without regret or bitterness, and partly because the English phrase now came naturally to her, the kind of naturalness she would sometimes still notice with a little surprise even after quite a few years 'if the truth be told'.

What she chiefly noticed somewhat wryly at this moment, however, was that she was choosing to mention Goethe's *Faust* rather than the luridly illustrated *Swiss Family Robinson* that her stepfather had read to her in an effort to improve her English.

'Sometimes when I was little he'd read Goethe's *Faust* aloud at the top of his voice in bed, when he was perhaps inebriated.'

Should she add 'which was seldom'? But that wasn't really true.

Catharina wasn't sure what Professor von Welden would make of this intimate family snippet about her childhood and her stepfather. She meant to convey that even a harbour pilot (she almost thought 'pirate') – but the 'even' in her thought irritated her, so she stopped the story at that point.

She and Professor von Welden were walking in the Botanic Garden that he said reminded him of Austria, but she thought he was almost certainly being polite.

Was he reminded because of the conifers?

Indeed, the fresh smell of the air where there are pines and so forth. So refreshing and stimulating.

But he'd 'walked past' her comment about Papa Hein. She sensed that he liked to stride – he was wearing 'salt and pepper' knickerbockers and had his Spazierstock with a steel tip. But now he was walking slowly, as if needing to pace his thoughts. And besides, it would be impolite for him to stride. He was certainly always polite. He'd invited her to discuss her studies 'in the fresh air'.

In der frischen Luft! (They were meant to be speaking English.)

But his thoughts seemed to be elsewhere.

But now they returned, but not to her studies.

So, your father, Mister Wenczel. A well-read man?

But of course he knew her name was Hansen. This was a familiar manoeuvre, she was used to it by now.

Catharina stopped where there was a small decorative pond enclosed by a rustic wooden fence of crooked sticks. Yes, Professor Hugo von Welden was trying to walk around the side of her story about Papa Hein to see what was behind it.

Her *step-father* was a sailor, she told him, breaking the word into distinct parts while looking at the exotic floating water lilies in the pond. Then he'd been a pilot on the harbour, he'd brought in the sailing ships, but after a time there were fewer of those. He'd been to many places in the world. The Orient, for example. He'd collected a number of exotic things. He spoke German of course but also quite good French and good English.

Professor von Welden was mimicking with his slender, tanned hands the gentle floating movements of the lotus leaves.

And her stepfather had also spoken Polish because that was where his origins were, over there in that much-dissected part of Europe. It was possible he'd had to make himself scarce at some stage, like so many who now find their homes here in New Zealand, wouldn't you agree, Professor?

The professor's hands had ceased to be lotus leaves.

And her stepfather had a damaged leg, Catharina informed the smiling professor, her tutor in Romance Languages and Literature. When she and her brother Wolf were little Papa Hein used to tell them he'd been bitten by a crocodile. The teeth marks, see? He'd obliged by pulling up his trouser leg. There were the blue indentations. But her mother told them it was because of a gunshot. She said Papa Hein blamed 'the

Austrians'. Neither Catharina nor Wolf had known what or who 'the Austrians' were. Were they pirates?

But even now she, Catharina, wasn't entirely familiar with that history, and after all here they were, Professor, on the other side of the world, where the old world animosities could be forgotten, wasn't that so? Along with a great many outmoded social conventions, she suggested.

Professor von Welden made a little bow and smiled.

Catharina's face was returning the professor's smile, but her thoughts were lying in wait behind her own smile. No, she wouldn't yet suggest that the smiling professor could by all means call her Catharina if he felt comfortable being on 'first-name terms' since they had much in common, for example being German, and could be friends as well as teacher and student. That would be quite proper, now, under the circumstances? And perhaps he would like to meet her mother, Mrs Josephina Wenczel, who had 'encouraged' her to attend university? If the professor were to meet her mother he'd understand what was meant by 'encouraged'.

But of course not if he felt uncomfortable with her suggestion.

She didn't wish to seem familiar.

The professor appeared to be parsing her smiling silence. He was calm. People passed them, walking and talking. Some of them had dogs – one of them, a small bristling creature, took a ferocious interest in the ducks that were negotiating the lily pads.

The professor shook his head disapprovingly but continued to smile at the surroundings, the young pines, the new borders of flowers and low shrubs. He wasn't in a hurry.

Not long ago, Mutti had told her the story of Papa Wolf asking if she, Josephina, would mind calling him 'just Wolf'?

That was when Mutti considered her old enough to know about 'certain things'.

And look what that led to, she'd said, laughing, and with tears that were both sad and happy.

Which she'd quickly wiped away. Her dear little mutti who preferred not to dwell on the past, so she said with that piercing Mutti look.

But even so, 'He was a very special little man,' she'd said. 'Ein besonderes Männlein. And so funny! He believed in the future!'

Mutti's tone had been at once mocking and affectionate.

But now Catharina could barely remember the 'special little man' except for an image of him in his sad baggy under-drawers on the deck of the ship, and having a bucket of seawater thrown over him. He was hairy all over, with a funny sticking-out chest. That, and his head tipped on one side as if his smile pulled it that way. And of course he was Wolf's father, not hers. Even though Wolf had been given Papa Hein's Wenczel name 'for convenience'.

For a time she'd struggled with the idea that being 'on first-name terms' could result in Wolf.

He was a very kind, sweet man, was the most Mutti would say. And he believed there was a new world and that they were all going to it.

But alas.

'Ah yes,' said Professor von Welden, finally, with approving nods of his head. 'Outmoded social conventions indeed, Catharina.'

So, 'Catharina' now, not Miss Hansen.

He had a pleasant smile and was very clean-shaven, even somewhat shiny – there were little humour-creases at the otherwise smooth corners of his mouth.

'Please, Catharina, do call me Hugo if you like!'

They'd agreed to speak English. His was somewhat fastidious.

He had rather pale blue eyes and kept them fixed on her in a manner that was either frank or a little too persistent.

'But perhaps not in our classes.'

No, perhaps not.

'And *your* father, Catharina?'

The annoying bristly dog was being dragged away by its collar. Its portly owner attempted to give it a kick but missed. It fled towards a rustic archway that a gang of young men were putting up – its owner walked belligerently towards their jeers.

'He was a soldier,' said Catharina. 'He was killed.'

There was yelling and derisive laughter down by the rustic archway.

'Before I was born,' Catharina added.

It wasn't clear whether the professor's rueful expression was because of the soldier's death or the confrontation along the path.

At the university in Professor von Welden's German literature seminar they were studying Goethe's *Die Leiden des jungen Werthers*, which the professor considered was inadequately translated as 'The sorrows of young Werther' since he believed it missed the connotations of sickness and morbidity – 'sorrows', after all, were the effects of outside events, whereas the young Werther's miserable condition was in large part the result of his own vulnerable and even sickly nature.

Or so the professor had suggested, inviting his students to offer their opinions.

Few had any.

The young men cutting up manuka sticks for the rustic archway were too polite to pay obvious attention to her, but she sensed the professor's firm posture was 'en garde'.

Catharina wasn't ready for 'Hugo' just yet. Nor for 'Catharina'.

But what about the purported reason for their walk?

With respect to the subject of the professor's seminar, she wondered, wasn't 'suffering' a better than plausible translation, given that tragic love could hurt even those who weren't morbid by nature?

She kept the thought *such as my own mother* to herself.

The professor inclined his head as if to acknowledge her deflection of their intimate conversation up to that point.

'That's quite an interesting thought,' he said, with a pause that he seemed hesitant to fill with either 'Miss Hansen' or 'Catharina'. 'And of course Goethe went on to substantially revise and republish the book, in a sense revising and republishing himself in the process.'

Quite an interesting thought.

Perhaps the professor's tendency to drain the impetus from conversation was merely the consequence of his slightly pedantic English.

Catharina's mutti had had three children with three fathers. Two of the fathers she'd mourned (one in particular) and the other she'd said she no longer needed to hate. Her son Wolf (by the father 'in particular') had been apprenticed to a blacksmith, having left school as soon as he could, against his mother's wishes. Now he was already a married man, and his wife was expecting their first child. The youngest, Freddy, the son of the kindly Polish deserter-sailor who'd drowned while drunk, had been bullied at school and had no memory of his father. Their mother had insisted they speak English at home whenever possible. She had worked to support them, with a little help from the widow's fund at the Deutscher Verein. She'd been on the electoral roll for two years. She spoke frankly with her daughter about these things, though without dwelling on them.

Their mother had needed to 'revise herself' frequently, if not exactly 'republish'. She was now in her forties. One day it was possible she might meet the professor and then she'd be able to tell him about her 'revisions', if she chose to.

Catharina and Professor von Welden walked back down the hill in silence, having made rather little progress with their discussion of her 'studies'. Nonetheless, he suggested as they said goodbye, he looked forward to hearing more of 'Catharina's' views on the works they were studying. She was clearly a perceptive reader and had 'a mind of her own'.

Yes, and her hands were 'my own' as well, thought Catharina, noticing that 'Hugo's' was lean and warm as she shook it goodbye – she could feel the bones in his fingers, they were elegant without much fleshy padding, and the slightly prominent wristbone that emerged from his sleeve was covered in fine golden hair.

At the moment his warm hand released hers after a perceptible pause, it was as though the past of her childhood with Mutti and the kindly pirate-sailor, and the future into which Professor Hugo von Welden seemed to be advancing, began to look sideways at each other, like individuals at a social gathering unsure of the appropriate protocols of engagement.

Yes, well, we shall see, she thought as the professor strode firmly away.

*

'No more, Hein,' said Mutti.

Papa Hein was looking with his funny smile at her and the baby in the armchair. He'd knocked into the side of the kitchen door when he came in – that meant he'd been drinking brandy.

'No more, Hein,' Mutti said again. Her face was quite pale with red blotches. The women who had helped with the baby were cleaning the bedroom. The one called Arabella said something that made the other laugh, then Arabella went Shhh. Then they came out with the towels and sheets and went out the back. One of them said, 'Congratulations Mister Wenczel' with a tone.

'No more.' Papa Hein repeated what Mutti had said like an echo and as if there was something in his mouth. Then he pretended to tip a drink into his Papa Hein smile. 'But a father is permitted to celebrate the birth of his first child, Mumti, surely?' His eyes were wet and red.

'No more babies,' said Mutti as Papa Hein was leaning down to look at the baby. He was holding himself there with one hand on the arm of Mutti's chair. It looked as though he was going to fall over on top of Mutti and the baby. 'No more babies, Hein,' Mutti said again, and put one hand against his chest, was it to stop Papa Hein from falling? 'No more babies. Keine Babys mehr. Verstehst du?'

Then the women came back with fresh things for the bed and beckoned at her almost impatiently, so she went to help them. The big one Mutti called Bella who knew a lot about having babies closed the bedroom door, but Catharina could still hear the sounds of Mutti's and Papa Hein's voices, they went on and on. Then she had to go over at once quickly right now to get Wolf from Miss Vicky's house by the forge.

Soon it would be dark but she stopped for a piece of

Vicky's apple cake, which was more like a batter with apples, she knew that already. The door to the back yard was open because it was so warm and the chickens were making a fuss, it was probably Vicky's big blacksmith brother doing something, perhaps he was chopping one of their heads off. Sometimes she was allowed to give them the food scraps from the kitchen and some green weeds and they made a big fuss about it throwing the stalks in the air. Wolf was banging an old horseshoe against the kindling box in the kitchen, so she picked him up.

It was a boy, she told Victoria, another one, he was quite small.

Yes, Mutti was all right.

She was very tired, Catharina thought.

Yes, Mister Wenczel was there now.

Then they were leaving.

Yes, Wolf could bring the horseshoe but he'd have to carry it himself otherwise she'd throw it into the bushes where he'd never find it.

On the way, Wolf carefully hid the horseshoe in the bushes. Oh yes, he was a clever one. Then he walked all the way home without holding her hand.

At home Mutti was back in her fresh bed with the baby, and Papa Hein was asleep in the armchair with one boot off and one on. Mutti was asleep too and Catharina wouldn't let Wolf wake her up. The baby was all rolled up, so they couldn't see him. She got Wolf a piece of bread and dripping and a cup of milk. He was poking holes in the bread and poking his tongue through, but she didn't care, it didn't matter. Then she took him to have a pee outside. It was dark with only a little light from the kitchen door. No, the spiders in the coal bin were asleep, they wouldn't jump out on to his little willy.

Inside, the armchair was empty but Papa Hein was on Wolf's bed. He still had one boot on and he was snoring but not loudly, it just sounded like a draught rattling the blind. She let Wolf wet his fingers and pinch out the candle and pretend that he was hurt and then she and Wolf climbed into her bed and she told him the story that Papa Hein did sometimes, about the huge octopus that wrapped itself around the ship he was sailing on, and how he and the other sailors had to chop the octopus's arms off and how after it had let the ship go they sliced one of the arms up and cooked it for their dinner.

But what did it taste like, Wolf asked, but really he was already asleep and anyway he always asked that question. It tasted stupid what do you think she said to the back of his head even though Papa Hein always said it tasted delicious like chicken only better, one day he would bring some octopus arms home for their dinner. They had a roasted chicken at her sixth birthday, that was already two years ago, it was at the Verein, and that was where Mutti and Papa Hein met again and he gave her a fan for her birthday present, but now it was broken, Wolf did that. The next time they had chicken was when Mutti and Papa Hein got married, they sang Mutti's favourite song 'Wie traulich war das Fleckchen' together at the Verein afterwards. Papa Hein had a nice voice for singing and everyone threw rice at them out in the street. The wedding chickens were from Vicky but now that Papa Hein was there they could buy chops twice a week and often rabbits to make into pies and sometimes there were special treats like sweet cable twist that Papa Hein hid in his pockets, and sometimes little oranges from a place called up the coast, they were what Mutti liked the most, especially while she was growing the new baby.

Perhaps she could creep into the bed with Mutti and the baby later. Some angry men were shouting at the end of their street, they'd better not wake the baby up. Perhaps tomorrow she could stay home from school, but perhaps it would be better to go there, she could tell everyone about the new baby at her house.

Ah yes, Hugo's slender fingers had been so careful, and there her corset had lain where she had put it on the little chaise longue where his trousers were also. It was those empty objects comically together that had made her laugh at the same time as Hugo's caressing fingers were finding out what was enjoyable, or mostly so.

But why was she laughing, he wanted to know in a rather gruff tone, as if he was even somewhat offended, though the offence didn't obstruct his attentions, which were quite industrious.

Because of their silly garments over there on the chaise longue, she told him, but, oh! – oh, never mind, now it didn't matter.

There was a fuzzy line of hair from the end of his spine down to his pale bottom and she kept her hand there once he had stopped hurting her, it was a simple tactile sensation that was almost pleasant, the feel of the fuzz against her fingers.

It was when he withdrew quickly from her and then groaned with his own satisfaction that she felt something sympathetic but not very much. She didn't really want his breath around her face at that point, a cool breeze through the curtains would have been more welcome.

There was some blood that she knew was to be expected,

but not so expected was Hugo's rather triumphant tone when he said, 'Wenn alle untreu werden, so bleib' ich dir noch treu,' adding the name Novalis.

But then after a while and a glass of the riesling – 'all the way from the Rhinegau!' – they did it again and this time was better and the pleasure of his fingers in her after he had taken his willy out was irresistible. She liked his willy, too, though that was the word she had used when Wolf was little and she had helped him to pee with his tiny worm of a thing, and not appropriate for Hugo's sturdy shaft with the rosy-coloured collar around its sleek emerging head.

That was where his animal sensitivity was, he told her somewhat breathlessly, helping her hand to the correct position.

Stop trying to teach me, she told the professor, about Novalis for the love of god, Hugo, but also about this. What we might know together may not have to be taught or even known before.

Hugo was at that point somewhat crestfallen.

There were their comical cast-off garments on the other side of the room on the chaise longue, and there was their bottle of wine 'all the way from the Rhinegau', and there was a pleasant tingling lassitude, but there was also at that somewhat dreamy moment the unsteady memory of her lovely little mutti after Papa Hein's funeral on that spring day, saying to her when she was no longer a child but still more ignorant than she thought herself to be, 'He was a very good kind man but he was also notfalls, do you know what that means, Catha, my dear foolish Hein, he was ne-ces-sary, we both understood that, and I was notfalls as well, we could help each other, it was better to be married, the world is not kind.'

And yes, she had understood in a way, and perhaps she had been old enough to understand, their lives had not been simple or easy, and her mutti's least of all.

Papa Hein's comrades from the harbour, where the watersiders' strike had happened that winter, carried his coffin from the little church on the corner of Ghuznee Street to the hearse with its two black-plumed horses that Wolf admired with a quiet whistle. The comrades, with Mutti, Wolf and herself in front, walked in a procession behind the hearse, together with the Maoris who were his crew in the pilot boat, and there was a small brass band from the wharf because Mister Wenczel had been very well liked, the man said, taking his hat off and shaking Mutti's hand, her husband had been strong during the strike, and had taken a beating, and would she please accept this subscription as a mark of their respect for a brother worker? He gave her an envelope with a black border around it. One of the Maoris gave Mutti a greenstone pendant like a little hatchet to hang around her neck, and he shook hands with Wolf and Freddy. And then there he was, a small grey stone with his name on it in the Bolton Street cemetery, the comrades had paid for it.

He had always liked the spring narcissi that made their own way into the spring air, and so every year on a Sunday near the anniversary she and Wolf and Freddy would go with Mutti to take some narcissi to the funny pirate's grave. Mutti told her she sometimes went there by herself, it was a good quiet place for her to think, and it was better to think in a place of thankfulness than in one ruled by disappointment or anger.

They were on opposite sides of the kitchen table, folding some ironed tablecloths that Mutti had edged with simple green loops and with a few fern-leaf shapes in the body.

More and more she was preferring to do plain designs with much clear space – not all her customers liked the simplicity she said, but why should she go on making those stuffy overcrowded arrangements of many-coloured flowers just because they ordered them?

Mutti had also stopped wearing puffed shoulders so that now she looked at once younger and yet older than she was.

Her mutti's rather piercing look at that moment, those clear blue eyes asking firmly that Catha not turn away. They had just agreed that she should continue with her schooling, that they could manage, there was a small pension from the Verein, there were still customers who liked her plain needlework and for the garments, there was often fish from Hein's Maori friends at the harbour, and vegetables and eggs from Vicky, and soon Wolf would be apprenticed, it was what he wanted, he could contribute.

Did Catha understand the difference between gratitude and thankfulness? Because it was important. She used a German word, Schirmherrschaft, it meant something like patronage. One should not be grateful for favours. It had been the hope of favours that had made her own poor mutti sick to death back by Kielerhafen.

But now, how was Catharina to leave Hugo's lodgings? She had requested some privacy as she washed and then dressed herself. There was the issue of the professor's reputation and, of course, of hers.

Professor von Welden was smoking his pipe with resourceful puffs in the drawing room and he withdrew it to bestow an enthusiastic smile on her. Her satchel with the books she had brought to his private lodgings were on the table. Her hat was on a chair nearby. She gave the professor a long kiss while he held his pipe at arm's length with one hand and pressed her waist with the other. Then she pinned her hat on and picked up her satchel.

Would Hugo mind walking her to the tram?

Yes, there had been a hesitation like a little flinch in his smile before his mock-formal bow.

Why yes, of course, it would be his pleasure to do so!

There were some patches of rosy-coloured light on the floor below the stained glass of the professor's rather splendid front door with its polished brass doorknob. He twisted the knob with a muscular flourish, and out she went into the nice sunshine with his hand against her shoulder as he followed. Then she paused by the arched wrought-iron gate while he locked his door. The wrought-iron arch had a 'pineapple' on top, like the ones Wolf had learned to make at the forge. The iron was pleasantly cool under her hand as she waited for Hugo and traced the 'pineapple' patterns with her fingers.

Wolf

Papa Hein was reading in his book-growly voice. The dog called Turk killed the mother monkey and ate it. Her baby hid in the grass. Then the baby jumped on to Fritz's shoulders.

'. . . he has lost his mother, and he adopts you for his father; perhaps he discovered in you something of the air of a father of a family.' Papa Hein stopped reading and made his hrrrmm hrrrmm noise.

In the coloured picture the little monkey was clinging to Fritz's hair. Fritz had a long musket across his back and a pistol in his belt. His father had a musket too.

Wolf made his arm into a musket and shot little monkey Freddy who was trying to climb up Papa Hein's leg.

No, of course Freddy couldn't understand the story, Papa Hein agreed. What he understood was in-fan-tile. But he could sit with them. That would make him peaceful.

'. . . I will give him all my share of the cocoa-nuts till we get our cows and goats; and who knows? His monkey instinct may one day assist us in discovering some wholesome fruits.'

'Whole-some fruits,' Papa Hein said again, making a funny shape with his mouth and wiggling his beard.

Freddy liked the wiggling beard and took hold of it.

Did Wolf know what a cocoa-nut was? Oh yes, he, Heinrich Wenczel, had drunk of the milk of the cocoa-nut, very delicious and sweet the milk was, it was at a tropical island where hungry tigers prowled along the beach waiting for thirsty sailors to jump out of their boats and run to the cocoa-nut trees and climb up to the juicy nuts. And perhaps

Freddy would rather play with Papa's watch?

But how did they get back to their boat with the nuts?

Ah, the trick was to drop a nut on the tiger's head and then run to the boat while the tiger was un-con-scious.

Un-con-scious.

Yes, un-con-scious. Wolf would be un-con-scious if someone dropped a cocoa-nut on his head.

But was that true? About the beach with the tigers?

It was true if Wolf could see the beach and the tigers when he closed his eyes. That was the best way to find out.

Wolf could almost see Days Bay where there were poisonous spiders. They went there twice with cold-meat sandwiches that got sand in them. Catha was trying to swim.

Papa Hein was turning the pages of *The Swiss Family Robinson* and humming in his chest. Wolf kept his eyes closed waiting for a different beach with tigers to appear. Meanwhile he could almost see Papa Hein in the sea. He could swim and he made a waterspout with his mouth. He was being a whale. He'd seen whales as long as a ship.

But then Papa Hein found another picture. The Swiss family father with the red shirt was firing his pistol with a flame coming out of it. The mother buffalo was crashing its face into the ground. Its tongue was hanging out the side of its mouth. Jack was running away from the buffalo with his musket in his hand. But where was Fritz?

'This one, a female, was no doubt the mother of the young buffalo which the dogs had seized . . .' hrrrmmm hrrrmmm '. . . was advancing in her rage, and would have torn them to pieces, if I had not prevented her by firing upon her with my double-barrelled gun, and thus putting an end to her existence.'

'Verschone mich!' Papa Hein held his head with one hand and Freddy with the other.

But that was enough bloodshed for one night, did Wolf agree?

Papa Hein put Freddy down on the floor but put his watch back in his pocket.

And yes, it was a pity about the mama monkey and the mama buffalo. Yes, it was indeed sad. Yes, it was! But now, could Wolf tell Papa what he'd done today that didn't involve shooting mamas, Papa Hein hoped.

He went to the forge with Catha.

But school? Papa Hein made a frown that was also a wink.

It was after school. Catha was walking home with him but he could do that by himself.

'But she is your big sister and you have to obey her.'

Wolf wasn't sure if Papa Hein's frown was real.

'Continue, please, go on,' Papa Hein said, turning his frown into a smile and making a wheel movement with his free hand. The other one was keeping Freddy's hand out of his watch pocket.

'Catha went to see Miss Vicky . . .'

'. . . and got a nice piece of cake!' Papa Hein was shaking his head. 'Poor hungry little Wolf!'

But he hadn't wanted any of Miss Vicky's cake. It was always hard. He'd wanted to . . .

'So you went to the forge!'

Was Papa Hein angry? It was hard to tell what it meant when he shook his head like that.

Miss Vicky called the man at the forge Bob but his proper name was Mister Kelly. Could Wolf help him with the bellows? That way Doyle could go for his cup of tea. Doyle's ears stuck out and they went red when Mister Kelly told him to go for his tea.

But first Doyle had to put another shovel of coke on the fire.

Doyle did it and dropped the shovel beside the forge.

'And stand that shovel up!' Mister Kelly shouted. Doyle came back and stood the shovel up. He gave Wolf a mean look as he went out.

'What are you waiting for!' Mister Kelly shouted, but he was smiling so Wolf began to bellows as hard as he could. Soon his arms ached but he kept going. The coke turned from red to white. His face was red hot but maybe it was white. Mister Kelly was making spear shapes for a fence, or they were pointy leaves. Then Catha came in and said they had to go, so he didn't see Mister Kelly hammering the red rod. Another time he'd seen him pouring melted iron into an iron box to make round things called pine apples.

Now Catha was reading a book by herself. She wasn't listening to anyone.

But what did Wolf like so much about Mister Kelly, Papa Hein wanted to know.

He liked the way he made something hard into something soft and then into something hard again but different. It was magic.

Papa Hein had the happy look on his face. He liked to hold his top lip inside the bottom one and make his eyes crinkle at the edges.

'Ah, yes,' he said, 'magic!' But that was all he said.

But magic was real. That was what he wanted to say to Papa Hein. The hard iron could be soft or melted and then be something else. That was different from Papa Hein's stories about the cocoa-nuts and tigers because he couldn't see them when he closed his eyes. But he could see what Mister Kelly did to the red iron and what happened when he poured some of the melted iron into the special iron box. And he'd seen that special magic look on Papa Hein's face when he was reading out loud from one of the German books in his old chest. Papa Hein was seeing what the words did. Sometimes Catha made the shapes of Papa Hein's words behind his back and goggled her eyes. O Erd O Sonne O Glück O Lust O Lieb O Liebe.

But now Papa Hein had to go down to the wharf. It was his turn to guard the harbour during the night.

Guard against pirates?

But of course. And also against the giant octopus that lived under the wharf. Sometimes it reached up with its arms and tried to steal Papa's supper. But Papa had his cutlass and he could cut the arm off.

But the arm could grow again.

Yes it could. Had Papa told Wolf that already?

Papa Hein was putting his boots on and then his big coat.

But where was his cutlass?

It was down at the wharf, and so was his pistol.

Papa Hein was in a hurry. He might have to go out in the pilot boat and guard the ship that was trying to come in past the octopus.

But now Catha would have to take her nose out of her book and get the supper ready before Mama came home from Mrs Sanderson's. And would she please make sure Freddy had a pee before supper because otherwise. And make sure the kettle was hot for Mama's tea.

Catha was looking at Papa Hein over the top of her book but she was hiding the rest of her face.

Then he went out making the door bang.

They were having the cold rabbit pie from the meat safe

with some bread and also apples. She hoped the flies hadn't found it. Maybe Mama would bring something else. What would Wolf like?

He liked cherries. But once Freddy got one stuck in his throat. Papa Hein had to squeeze him and he was sick on the table.

Catha hoped Mama would bring some fresh peas. Then they could pop the pods.

Pop the pods!

Freddy tried to say it too. He already had some words.

Plop the plods!

Catha stopped laughing first when Mama came in, because of the expression on her face. She put her bag down and sat in the chair where Papa Hein had been. Then she began to cry.

'My papa has died. My papa in Germany.' She held her arms out. 'Come here, my babies.'

When he thought about the moment Mama told them about her papa being dead he didn't see her as very small. But of course she was always small, and now that was how she appeared day by day, very straight but small and neat. Her fair hair pulled back, and that blue-and-white brooch at her throat some days, and on other days the greenstone axe shape. But when he remembered the day she told them about her papa there was another outline of her, the size of the one that had held out her arms. Her spread-out arms had been wide enough to fit them all in then, though Freddy got her lap and took up most of the space. Her neck had smelled of the lavender water she shook on cloths before ironing them. That smell he would never forget.

Now she could barely put her arms around him and her head rested quite low on his chest.

How did this giant come about when his dear little papa had been such a lustiger kleiner Gnom?

Catharina was certain she remembered the 'little gnome' and told their mama off for making fun of him. She was also certain she remembered her grandfather from the farm near Kiel, but he didn't believe that. There were lots of bees, she said. It was summer. They sat outside at night singing under a tree. There was an auntie who sang the loudest. She was big and soft, but her grandfather had been a tall thin man with very bright blue eyes looking at her all the time. She played with a big cousin called Tilda.

But how could she remember all that! She'd have been, what, three or something?

But she insisted, that insistent sister of his. There was no point going on about it.

Now – Papa Hein when he drowned and the Maori men brought him to the house on a cart dripping water! That he could remember as if it were yesterday.

Well, compared to her remembering her grandfather with the blue eyes, Papa Hein's death might as well have been yesterday, wouldn't he agree?

Of course, he had to agree with that. There was nothing to argue about with that one. But what about his Wolf father? What did she remember about him?

The 'little gnome'?

She shouldn't call him that. He'd have liked to know him. The wolf whose name he had.

He was a funny little man, very quick like a bird, not anything like a wolf, with very shiny black eyes and a slight mound on his back. He talked a lot. He hopped around and stood with his head on one side. She could tell that their mama had loved him very much. She remembered him having a cold seawater bucket wash on the deck of the ship. He was very hairy!

What was it about people's eyes, with her? Why did she always notice them?

The windows to the soul.

But her tone was a little mocking. He didn't really know what to make of her remark, as usual.

They didn't talk about *her* father. He was a silence in which their mama's eyes, also very blue, seemed not to blink for a while. But once Catha had told him what Mama had told her about it. That wasn't going to happen to her, Catha said. And you behave yourself!

But didn't she want to marry a good man and have children?

But what was the hurry? And where were the good men?

What about Miss Vicky's brother Mister Kelly?

Catha tipped her head on one side and gave him a look.

She'd end up being the last apple on the tree, the one with wrinkles and cracks.

Rather that than fall into the grinning mouth of the first fool that came along!

But now she was teaching. Didn't she like the little children? Didn't she want to have some? And what was all this talk about going to the university college? What was the use of that?

It was when she laughed in her Catha way that he knew she had him by the neck and would soon shake the truth out of him.

Ah! So that was it!

Yes. And why not? Of course he would like to have some

kiddies one day. What was the matter with that?

But then he went out quickly to split the kindling. That was Freddy's job, but he hadn't done it. If he stayed inside any longer Catha would find the lever to open what he saw when he closed his eyes. The magic of Ettie and the way her smile trembled because she tried too hard to control it. And now he was a man, after all. He was earning money and had learned his skills. One day he would be a father. He knew what was real and what was not. The jarring in his forearm when he struck the anvil. How it became the shape of the thought of it. How the thought became the thing. How the thing that was real in the world had begun as magic.

There was an owl somewhere up the hill a little way. Some big soft moths arrived and flew at the lantern. There was the small tree whose white trumpets had a strong sweet smell at night. As usual there were some noisy drunks down the end of the street. What would it be like to be in a quiet place in the country? Their house was too small now that Mama and Catha were sharing a room, while he was in with Freddy. He could picture himself in a place cleared of trees except for an orchard. There was smoke coming from the chimney of his house. He was holding one child in the crook of his arm, and another by her hand. Yes, that one was a daughter, she had her doll, and their big old dog was lying at her feet. The little one was a boy, he was holding an apple. Was there already a tree with apples? How long had he been there?

Catha and Mama were sitting by the fire when he came back in with kindling for the box.

So Freddy wasn't home yet? It was time he learned to do his share. They both mollycoddled him! What was he up to, out at night? He gave the fire a poke to stir it up and put a shovel of coal on it. Were they waiting for Freddy fly-by-night to have their supper?

Mama was laughing. Well now, just listen to him! My big man!

But Catha was waving a letter. She'd been waiting for Mama to come home from Mrs Sanderson's – and by the way, how much longer was she going to go on running to and fro to that place? Because, look!

It was a letter from the university college. Because she'd done excellently in her matriculation she'd been offered a scholarship. Next year or perhaps the year after she could go there. She could go to the university.

Catha got up and did a little dance, waving her letter.

Mama's lips were making the shape of the word excellently. But she was looking at his expression.

Why the fish-face, she wanted to know.

Of course he couldn't answer that it was she who had urged Catha to do it, the matriculation, and it had been she who tried to dissuade him from going to the smithy so soon.

But he had to say it. Had he not also done excellently at the smithy?

Oh, he should not look so jealous like that, she scolded him. He should be proud of his sister. She herself had met his father Wolf in a house that made her feel ignorant at first. No one should feel like that! And his father had believed so. But it was not just about book-learning!

She reached up to pull his face down for a kiss. And then she fetched out the bottle of brandy from the cupboard where she kept her sewing things.

'Prost!'

The blue-and-white brooch at her throat made a skip as she swallowed her brandy. It was an oval shape with a fine chain rim. On a blue base was a white picture of two little naked people under a tree. A dog had its front feet up against the trunk of the tree as if it was chasing something. When he was little she used to take it off and give it to him to look at.

What was the dog chasing, he'd ask?

That was for him to find out.

And were they in a forest with wild animals? And perhaps one had climbed up the tree?

One day perhaps he'd be able to tell her.

But didn't Mama know?

It was better for him to find out for himself. Perhaps he would have a dream about it. Or perhaps one day he would go to the place in the picture. What did he think?

Now he could still picture the place in the brooch when he closed his eyes. But of course it was still just in the brooch. Though perhaps one of the little people was Ettie and the other one was him. Perhaps they had taken their clothes off. And that was their dog, and their orchard tree.

He gave Catha a kiss and said he was proud of his sister. He could feel her own pride in the warmth of her cheek against his lips.

Then Freddy came in. The drunks at the end of the street had annoyed him. His sullen expression said that he expected to be scolded, but no one did that.

Then they had fish soup from the pot on the stove. Mama had made it with some big fish heads from the snapper Papa Hein's old Maori friends had brought round.

They hadn't forgotten him after all these years. The carrots and potatoes in the soup came from Vicky. It was good to live in a place where people cared about each other. What did Freddy think? And what did he think of his big sister's news about the university college?

Freddy looked across the table at her. His little smile had

some parsley in it. He licked it off his teeth.

Perhaps the university college would make Catha want to leave the place where people cared about each other. Didn't Mama do that once herself, when she was about the same age as Catha?

He had that little smile, did Freddy. Now Mama had one too.

'Oh, Freddy,' she said. 'Don't be too clever too soon.'

Then, to make up for not chopping the kindling, he took the dishes away to wash. When they went to bed he turned his back and went to sleep. So they didn't talk about what was happening.

Beth and Frank

Brought out of the ghosty shadows of the downstairs storage shelves, the carton labelled 'Treasures' had a forlorn appearance – yellowed, cobwebby, dusty – and the cardboard gave off a vaguely thymey smell, as if haunted by an aromatic former life – as what? All these neglected years barricaded behind Noel's Brumberger film cases. She'd vacuumed off the dust and cobwebs downstairs, and now up in the daylight she gave the thing a good wipe and then pulled the brittle masking tape from the folded-over seal on the top. There were various large manila envelopes much as she remembered them, each one identified by her girly-swottish labels. Qualifications, Birth Certificates, Dad's Letters (written after he left Elke for the woman she described as 'the flutterer' because of her way with her eyelashes), and a set of beautiful hand-coloured Italian postcards from Dad's time there during the war, labelled noncommittally as Italian Postcards.

Frank's postcards, not in an envelope, were just held together in batches by thick perished rubber bands that had pretty much decomposed and stuck to the cards. She picked the remains of the bands off (why 'perished'?) and there they were, about ten years' worth, maybe four or five a year? – and just as she'd remembered them, the girls in modest 1960s bikinis on a beach (she'd have been about twelve?), the one with the joke about premature ejaculation (fifteen?), a surfer cutting back off a monstrous curling wave with Frank's arrow and the word 'Me!' added (sixteen?), then the one of a strange vaguely reptilian armoured creature with a snout and Frank's handwritten scrawl across it, 'Joh Bjelke-Petersen'.

That one was to do with the 1971 Springbok tour to Australia and the anti-apartheid demonstrations, and Frank's note on the back wasn't a joke. Instead it described in short sharp sentences what the police had done to demonstrators in Brisbane. He'd been there and got bashed by the cops. The curt intelligence of his note pushed his joker self aside. It read like a message to her: 'Get this.' She'd have been eighteen and Frank twenty-eight. He already had a pack of kids. He'd signed off, 'Party's over', and that was the last card she got. Had he meant their party, the game he'd gone on playing with his little Kiwi cousin, or the fun of his life in Queensland? Or just the illusion that life could hop forward from joke to joke? Or had there been a crisis in his life that cut him off? His marriage before Helen?

It was a nice sunny day, so she took her unwilling tears out to the deck and sat there having a mop-up and a glass of water. Had she written to him after the Bjelke-Petersen postcard? What was almost sadder than his 'Party's over' was her inability to remember the shape or substance of the time after that postcard, as if the childhood thing with Frank had simply done its dash and she hadn't really even noticed when the postcards stopped.

The thing was, though, she'd kept them. They were in the 'Treasures' box along with her mother Elke's favourite bits of dreadful old yellowed lace that had come from Great-great-grandmother Josephina, a blue-and-white Wedgwood-type brooch ditto, a strange grey Astrakhan hat that her dad had brought back from one of his overseas jobs, and a pair of brass doorknobs, provenance unknown. Among other things. She'd have taped the box shut and labelled it when she and Noel came to the house twenty years ago. Joe was just turning twenty and had canned out of uni and gone to Japan with his girlfriend Sakura. He sent photos of them making joined-up snow angels at a resort out of Tokyo where they were instructing kids, or so he'd said. They ended up running a bar in Roppongi, then Sakura dumped him and took off to Copenhagen with a banker. It was about then that he went off the rails.

There was nothing from Joe in the 'Treasures' box, obviously, it was sealed before he took off, and she didn't have the photos of snow angels or the Roppongi bar, only what remained in her head. What wasn't in her head was what if anything happened in the time and space between her and Frank from 1971 until his email via the reunion mailing list some forty years later. But what was there, like the pressure of a headache coming on, was an insistence that something should have been, and was, but got lost.

'Dear Beth, remember me?' his email had read. 'I used to chuck you in the river down the Kaitieke. Are you coming to this reunion thing? If you are, then I will too. Your long lost Second-ed Cousin Frank.'

And then there he'd been, tall, stringy, with a weather-leathered face and a mop of dishevelled white hair. He was just a bit stooped. He had a glass of wine in his hand that he was waving precariously as he talked to a younger man whose shoulders seemed to have been drawn up a bit defensively. She saw him recognise her over the defensive man's shoulder at the same time as she recognised him. Then he'd just walked straight towards her from the abandoned conversation as the bloke half-turned to see where he'd gone.

'Jesus fucking Christ. It's Beth.'

But of course their up-to-date photo-thumbnails had been included in the reunion attachment. Otherwise, who knows?

But of course she knew she'd have recognised him without the photo.

But of course she also recognised him from the photo.

So what had happened in the space between those two? What was in that space between the Frank she'd have recognised and the Frank she did recognise? What was it that had been in that space that had gone, if it had gone? And if it hadn't gone, the memory, or whatever it was called – and if it had gone then of course you couldn't call it a memory anymore! – then where was it in this person she was, this Beth? And if there never had been a memory in the first place, then why did it seem to matter so much it had made her cry?

Her loud arrgh of annoyance frightened the lovely yellow-beaked blackbird that was often her companion in the tree by the deck or down on the lawn probing with alert intelligence for worms. The bird flew off decisively.

'Sorry, mate,' she said. Perhaps she meant that for bloody old Frank as well, though it had been he who'd picked up the loose end of the maze-thread and found his way back to the time when he'd sent her those silly postcards, and then the last one that wasn't.

When Joe came over for a meal with the boys a couple of days later, she tried to explain the uncomfortable sense of a gap between what she remembered and what she thought she should have remembered, and the sad feeling that she'd lost not just some part of an old friend but also some part of herself in the gap.

They'd finished off the pineapple he'd brought for dessert and the boys were squabbling over who should do what over at the dishwasher.

Joe wasn't drinking but he didn't care if she did. She

poured herself another glass of the Aussie shiraz that was on special at New World. He was looking at her with a Joe grin, almost but not quite mocking.

'Probably Alzheimer's,' he said. 'Or booze.' He paused for effect. 'Or both.'

But of course it was neither.

Then he made an announcement. Next time they came around he'd bring his new friend. Her name was Frankie, but his ma shouldn't allow that to confuse her in her mind any more than she already was with the weird old Frank thing.

And what did Frankie do, she asked, feeling a tiny pang at Joe's lippy tone.

He leaned forward with a conspiratorial expression. 'She gets on top,' he said.

In the morning she was up early and went for a good brisk walk down along the Cox's Bay creek. Out in the bay the sailing boats were all lying on their sides on the low-tide mud. There was a sluggish flow of murky water from the creek, with a cargo of green mangrove pods and plastic junk. The breeze was nice, a mixture of low-tide pong and fresh breeze off the Gulf.

The youthful and wannabe-youthful women in matching black tights and caps ran past her towards unknowable goals. She had a strong black coffee and a poppy seed roll with jam at the German bakery. She made a point of always speaking German with the Bavarian proprietor and his wife, or the young women who seemed to change regularly – they were probably exchange students – and she almost believed that this amounted to a certain kind of appropriate intimacy or at least courtesy, but of course all it did was confirm her as cosmopolitan or pretentious or both. However, it was nice to feel the different shape of the language in her mouth, and to encounter the friendly correctness of the staff. They all got dressed up Bavarian-style for Oktoberfest, the young women in fetching Dirndls and the plump owner in Lederhosen. Then she took her fresh sourdough loaf homewards past the stream of commuter cars and checked her postbox on the way.

There was a yellow card in it that said she had a parcel to collect that was too big for the box.

It was from Frank, with extravagant and unnecessary stamps. They had John Gerrard Keulemans' lovely paintings of Christmas Island birds on them, and she knew straight away that they were telling her to come over and visit. She put the parcel with its enticing stamps on top of the rubbish bin in the postbox annex, and leaned there for a moment with her eyes shut, because the pictures of birds had tumbled simply into the space that had made her sad a few days ago, and that had made Joe get a bit satirical last night.

Then she carried the parcel past the guy who camped out by the bank ATM with his placard that read, 'Got nowhere to go. Spare a coin.' She dropped her change from the bakery into his plastic cup and said, 'Good luck mate.' The thought that she'd contributed to his fund for going nowhere cheered or amused her briefly as usual, and then she was home.

There was a very brief note from Frank on top of the bundled notebooks in the package. It read: 'This is all very sad and a bit shocking but also wonderful. I think we'd both have liked to know Frederick. Your great-granduncle and my granduncle or great-uncle if I've got the wiring diagram right. Father must have been the Wenczel immortalised on Josephina's headstone in the charming rustic Raurimu cemetery we visited on the memorable never-to-be-forgotten day when we unwisely took the lid off our Pandora's Box. Now I can't help thinking what Ruth was going to do with all this, and of course I'll die wondering. Book your ticket, we'll go and look at some beautiful birds.'

The first little notebook was a Whitcombe and Tombs 'New Zealand Pocket Diary for 1898'. It was covered in scuffed black leather with a fold-over tongue that would once have slotted into a loop, since torn off. There was a little sheath for a miniature pencil inside the front flap. There were advertisements for a Handbook of New Zealand Gardening and for Edison's Mimeograph on the front two pages, and after the title page there were six pages covering the phases of the moon, with rates of postage and stamp duties along the bottom of the pages, and then several pages showing telegraphic rates, N.Z. Railways passenger fares, a page listing members of the Royal Family, an N.Z. Government Directory, and a national population count (census April 1891) showing Wellington at 97,876, and total including the Chatham Islands and the Kermadec Islands, and including 'Chinese and Half-Castes, of 626,830'.

The page with the Edison's Mimeograph advertisement had Frederick's signature on it. The signature had bold, experimental flourishes, and was followed by the line 'Age 15 and "Growing in Wisdom and Stature"' – a biblical quote? – and a date: 15/1/98. How much use would fifteen-year-old Frederick have had for the informative matter at the front of his diary? The first entry on Saturday 15th of January 1898 read, 'Went to Baths. Birth of my diary. Bought it for 3/-. No more events in the life of this famous man "what's goin' to be" will be lost to posterity. Cricket match B. Barr & self agst J Barr W. Wedde & A Scoular. Defeated. Average match Two top scores 19 & 16.' The entry for the following Sunday read, 'Baths. Stayed home all day. Read Persival, Kearne, Marrayat.'

She could imagine fifteen-year-old Frederick immersed in Captain Marrayat's ripping yarn *Mister Midshipman Easy*, though not perhaps in its seesawing libertarian politics, but who was Persival – the Knight of the Round Table? And Kearne?

The entries for the following Monday, Tuesday and Thursday all included visits to the Baths. At the back of the diary there were pages for Cash Accounts. Pedantically responsible and un-teen-like entries for the 15th, 16th, 17th and 19th all included the costs of going to the Baths, along with 'Peaches', 'Paper', 'Gullivers Travels', 'Tattooed Man', 'Shout' (6 pence) and others. But the most persistent cash entry was Baths, and usually specified 'Self and Will', a combined cost of 6 pence a time. Frederick was also shouting a Fritz to the Baths, and there were other entries for Shouts ('Alex & self', 'Pies').

Turning pages. On Bank Holiday, Friday 18th March, which Frederick noted was after Saint Patrick's Day, he went for a walk up to Wadestown in the morning with Will, and then for a 'stroll up stream'. Then this: 'Liked the smell of his cock but he was too rough and in a hurry.'

The closed diary was on the table beside her while she looked out at the garden and managed the sense of shame and intrusion. But what was so surprising about two teenage boys sharing a wank in the bush? Or at the Baths, for that matter? What was more surprising was that he'd risked writing about it in his diary. But she put the diary back in the box with the others. She'd have another look at them later – or not. There were a lot of them, the little pocket-sized ones but also large journals. Then she had a shower, trying not to think about washing away prurience, and got dressed for lunch.

Her fortnightly at the Staff Club was fun and she looked forward to it, especially since Noel's death, though she had to stop the conversation bogging down in university politics. Taking early retirement to look after Noel had been one of the best decisions in her life. Her postgrad courses in postwar German prose, German literature and film, and German culture and the Pacific were in need of makeovers she couldn't be bothered doing – even the course titles wearied her with their airs of resigned anachronism – and so she was becoming what she despised, a bored teacher on repeat. Instead, she could sit with Noel while his mind reinvented entire tranches of their lives together, or go for lovely walks while his presence and consciousness meandered through unconnected timescapes and weirdly off-target locations. They'd be walking through Cornwall Park in the week the spring daffodils came out along the oak boulevard, and he'd be in the flower markets of Kashmir as the civil war tore the place apart – his look of dismay switching back and forth with one of ecstasy. Then after a while she was his sister, or Joe's ex-wife, or nobody he knew, and then he was no longer able to walk safely. Then, as she'd liked to repeat for a while, he was gone before he went.

The same could be said of her lunch friends' sympathy, but today she caught them looking at her, quick glances that became a collective, unspoken interrogation: Was something wrong?

They were sitting outside under a large sun umbrella, with a nice view across the freshly mowed lawn and the well-kept shrubs and flowerbeds, very tidy and organised and responsibility-free. It all smelled warm and summery and was where she wanted to be, unlike the dim, musty interior of the Common Room. Of course there were birds hopping about or flitting among the trees – she was noticing them since getting Frank's parcel.

Sorry to be a bit distracted. She'd begun to be haunted.

A beat. Then variations on awkward condolences.

No, not Noel, it was her great-granduncle Frederick Wenczel.

Ah, so a secret project! But why hadn't she told them?

Because there'd been nothing to tell. Some material had just come to light.

What she couldn't, or just didn't, say to her former colleagues, whose manner was at once solicitous and envious, was that the 'material' had begun to light up – wake up? – the part of her that her German ancestors might have called Geist, her soul-mind or spirit-mind or something like that, the capacity that had become dull or lazy or perhaps self-protective once Noel had gone. Nothing as grandiose as Hegel's version, something more like the bright, alert attention of her blackbird which, on most days, would hardly be noticing the human sitting motionless on the deck with a cup of coffee and a book or finding useful enough things to do in the garden.

Yes, the road trip with Frank had been the start of it, his asymmetrical provocations and kindnesses, and the blurred memories he'd revived. But it was the little diary that had now begun to insert itself into the uncanny gap where her memory seemed to have lost its purchase on how she knew what. The little fragment of a fifteen-year-old's secret life back in 1898, a kid at once overconfident and vulnerable – weren't they all? – who could easily have been one of her own kids or grandkids, and who was, in any case, connected to her through some thin filament that her sensible mind told her was too ephemeral to matter but that had wrapped itself around her heart in spite of that.

'Growing in Wisdom and Stature' at the front of the diary, and at the back the earnestly diligent and try-hard adult Cash Account entries – May 9 1895: Treasure Island 2/-, June 3: Lollies 6d, July 29: Shout Ma to Play 2/-. They made her smile, or laugh sometimes, and they were breaking her heart.

Catharina

'Mutti?' she said. She heard the faint hint of a plea in her tone before she'd even said what she was going to. She saw her mutti hear the tone but also saw that she'd been expecting it. Or had expected something other than their usual coffee-time chat – Catharina's reports on what she was doing at the university college that Mutti listened to as if with those attentive blue eyes rather than with her ears, and Mutti's reports, increasingly sarcastic, on the 'appearances' of her 'Thorndons'. One of them had described her newly commissioned table linens as 'impoverished'. The word had caused Mutti to show her teeth in a smile across the coffee table – there were some gaps in the smile now and she seldom revealed them unless the joke was especially 'schlau', which meant smart.

'Schlau, nicht wahr?'

Her mutti had been on the electoral roll for almost nine years. Her English was good if sometimes oddly imprecise and she often chose, now, to use it at home. She interpolated German words where she deemed them 'better'. She liked schlau, and also 'echt' for truthful because it sounded 'more sincere'. Her accounts of the 'impoverished linens' and other such topics were delivered with mocking relish, and with the interpolation of certain indispensable German expressions. 'Bitte, verschone mich! Please spare me *impoverished*!'

Papa Hein had also liked to say 'Verschone mich!'

Mutti reached up and took off the scarf she'd knotted over her head. She gave her hair a shake, as if to free her thoughts. There were now white threads in her fair hair, which she requested Catharina cut shorter than before.

'Oh Catha, have you been unwise?'

Of course it was no secret that she and Professor Hugo von Welden had become friends during her final year. There was gossip. And she had graduated with top honours by her own capacities despite what the gossips thought. She'd seen that her mutti was both proud and envious, but that her envy was also a kind of pride.

But even though Wolf's bulky occupancy of their cottage had been transferred to the house on Mount Cook that he now filled up proudly and manfully along with Ettie and their infant Agatha, the place she still shared with Mutti and Freddy remained an intimate one in which to sustain or conceal a bodily secret, especially as she shared a bedroom with her little Mutti whose sleep-whisperings and mutterings were the same as they had always been, though now Catharina heard more of them through the wakeful nights that had become longer since Hugo.

There was a pressure and a pain in her chest. It was where two answers to Mutti's question as to whether she had been 'unwise' were contesting. Yes, she had been unwise to permit her affair with Professor Hugo von Welden to come to this; no, she had not been unwise – what had happened was a natural consequence of a decision she had made – to have the relationship.

She was ten years older than her mutti had been when her unequal and unchosen encounter with the Prussian had made her a young mother – the same age as Ettie! – whose future had to be hidden not only from those close by but also from herself, until she was able at last, after much difficulty, by the economical account she had given Catharina but also by what Catharina had witnessed, to take large control of her own fate and the decisions both of the heart and also of the mind that had put her where she was now, across the table with its coffee pot and cups and the slices of a plum cake, the rich aroma of which had made Catharina nauseous.

Mutti's fingernail tapped the edge of the plate with the slices of cake on it.

Ah yes, those eyes. That had seen it.

It depended what one meant by 'unwise', she began in answer to Mutti's question, but felt herself almost slip ridiculously back into girlhood and her fear of appearing foolish to her mutti, who would always wait for her to find a way to finish saying what she had begun, even if it was likely to make her sound stupid to herself as well as to Mutti.

So she began again, with the intention of finishing.

'Unwise, perhaps, unlucky perhaps, but then perhaps neither.'

The woman who was now as much her friend as her mother maintained her steady gaze, though she had begun to blink more often as if in preparation for clenching her eyes against her anger, or perhaps because she might be about to weep, though the latter was unlikely.

'I am twenty-seven years old, Mutti, you began early to teach me to make my own decisions.'

Across the table, the woman who was both her mother and her friend tilted her head from side to side three or four times, as if to ask, Which is it, then: that you are almost what they call eine alte Jungfer, a spinster, or that I am to blame for your predicament because of my example?

'To be clear,' said her mutti in that 'to be clear' way of hers, 'you are pregnant to that professor?'

'Yes, Mutti, I am.' The relief of saying it so simply.

The professor and Mutti had met twice, both times at the

kiosk in the Botanic Garden. His charm had failed to get past her sceptical scrutiny, though she had given him credit for having it.

'Reizvoll, the Herr Professor, and he has very good manners. And also a very fine watch.'

The Herr Professor had consulted his 'very fine watch' at a certain point, and had excused himself on account of some urgent matter.

'Reiz' of course mostly signified something like 'appeal', and so the professor had been deemed to be 'full of appeal', indeed perhaps 'appealing', but appealing for what, exactly? Her mutti's approval?

As usual, then, her mutti had enjoyed wrapping her approving comments in these hints. But now she gave a deep sigh with 'Ah Catha!' in it, and at last allowed her eyes to fill with tears that spilled briefly until she stopped them with her handkerchief. It was one of those she had edged with the swan motif in her favourite blue silk thread. Half a dozen dabs, and the swans swam back inside her sleeve.

So now the blunt question. Did the Herr Professor know? And another – had the Herr Professor indicated that his intentions were serious 'in the longer term'? She uttered the formally respectful term 'Herr Professor' with a little smile that was more like a sceptical grimace.

'Ah.' That was all the small straight-backed woman with unbound hair had to say at that point, when Catharina shook her head, not trusting herself to speak words.

But then Mutti stood up in that quick way she had and walked around the table and stood behind Catharina and took her cheeks between her small, dry palms, and put her mouth in Catharina's hair so that she felt her warm breath on the top of her head, and her kiss there.

'Well, then,' said Mutti into her daughter's hair, 'it's time surely that the Professor heard the good news.' Was that a huff of laughter like a quick cough, or of anger, or of determination that she then felt in her hair? And then, '*Notfalls*, Catha, don't you think?'

Of course the word was even somewhat historical.

And then Mutti returned to her side of the table and stood behind her chair with her hands resting on its back. Her fingers were long and had always looked too delicate for work, but now the knuckles and joints had become somewhat thickened. She tapped the fingers two or three times against the chair. Wolf had burned fern-leaf patterns in the back with a red-hot poker.

'Wolf can do it,' she said. And yes, it was a little Mutti smile that briefly straightened her lips as she made an encircling gesture to indicate the persuasive height and bulk of him.

Of course Catharina could 'do it' herself, and it would not be her muscular dimensions that mattered when she confronted Hugo with the news that he would be the fortunate father of her child! But what mattered more at this moment was that she was glad to be having a baby – indeed 'glad' could not begin to describe something that had not been spoken of so far, her happiness. The happiness filled every part of her from head to toe, her mind no less than her body. She had never experienced anything like this happiness or known it might be possible. The happiness had first overcome dismay at what had perhaps been a moment of recklessness, then fear of its immediate consequence, the painful birth of a child, then dread of the longer consequence, which would be her certain disgrace and perhaps the uncertain future of her child; lastly the happiness had overcome her apprehension about another uncertain future, which she had not fully imagined with Hugo installed in it. But the happiness had nonetheless recovered and fastened in her the memory of utter undefended pleasure when, feeling his cock seeming to thicken inside her, she had closed her legs more tightly across his back and heard him exclaim, or curse – 'Gott!' – before he pulled away.

'I'm very happy, Mutti,' she said.

Her mother's hand reaching across the table.

'Then so am I, my darling.'

It wasn't at all clear whether her mutti's happiness was because she believed Catha had agreed to Wolf being the official bearer of glad tidings to the 'Herr Professor', or because she'd heard finally that Catha was happy to be pregnant with the professor's child. The latter was unlikely to be uncomplicated by anger, fear and disappointment on her mutti's part. One day, without doubt, they would have a conversation about that – but not now, or not yet. In the meantime, as was not unusual – indeed, as was only to be expected – her mutti's brevity and straightforwardness disguised clever knots that would need to be unpicked in due course.

Nor was it yet time for her and Mutti to talk about what it might mean for them to live apart, should that happen, despite it being unimaginable.

But no more or less unimaginable than when Wolf married Ettie and left the little house in Bute Street that he had crowded with his quiet bulk and his presence within which Mutti had stood even a little incongruously.

*

Yes – oh yes it was a beautiful day, Mutti had agreed.

But she was looking in the opposite direction from the early-morning sunlight that fell grudgingly between the neighbouring buildings and across the narrow back yard of their house in Bute Street. She was looking at the back door of the house that the sunlight had not yet reached – pausing as if impeded by an invisible obstacle in her brisk movements around the washing line. Then she put out a hand to open the door though she was still two or three steps from its handle.

'Perhaps we should move,' she said, without turning around. Then she took the necessary two steps to the back door and went inside. She had Wolf's best white shirt and was going to iron it while it was still damp.

What had Catharina just witnessed? She herself had begun to reach out towards Mutti, fearing there was something wrong, but was left holding her absence.

It was like a little jolt in the passage of time. Her mutti's motion stopped momentarily as she approached this juncture in her future.

Catharina stood there looking at the door as it closed, and caught a brief glimpse of Wolf's tall shadowy bulk within the room. He moved out of sight a moment before Mutti pulled the door shut.

Wolf's former master at the smithy, Mister Kelly, had agreed to be his best man and witness. Ettie's uncle, City Councillor Hastings (known as Councillor 'Hasty'), the well-known master carpenter and now house builder who was 'throwing up' wooden dwellings and getting rich quickly, led her to the altar, since Ettie's father had recently died of pneumonia – the family had come to New Zealand because of his 'weak chest' but had not anticipated the southerly winds in a land they'd been led to believe was tropical with fruits and land aplenty.

Now, however, they were 'making the most of it', which was the theme of the councillor's droll wedding-breakfast speech as he wagged his finger in the direction of Wolf. Wolf stood with his hands clasped in front of him – his expression suggested he was paying attention, but whether to the councillor or to an interior voice was not clear. He seemed to be restraining his hands from reaching towards Ettie who stood beside him with a polite smile for her enthusiastic uncle.

The wedding had taken place in the same little church on the corner of Ghuznee Street where Papa Hein's funeral had been conducted when Wolf was ten years old. Now he was barely twenty, and Ettie in her hat with its descending veil was not yet quite eighteen and looked as though she was 'dressing up'. They ran a gauntlet of rice-throwing guests and were driven off to the wedding breakfast in a buggy. They were to live in a house that had been built by Councillor Hasty on the slope of Mount Cook. He had 'helped them into it' but Wolf was expected to work off the debt, not least, it was clear, by discounting his own expertise with the hammer and anvil and the moulding of wrought iron.

She, the older sister of the groom, on the other hand, would still be living with their mother and her young brother, and was twenty-six years of age. In just under a year's time she would graduate with a university degree, the utility of which 'interested' the councillor. Their Bute Street house was small and in an unfavoured part of the town and so the wedding breakfast, which could not be held in the Deutscher Verein because Ettie, in the opinion of the councillor, 'was not from there', was celebrated in the spacious garden at the councillor's house.

Catharina could visualise Professor Hugo von Welden, with whom she had recently strolled in the nearby Botanic Garden, in the extensive and richly planted garden at the councillor's house, but of course he was not there. A tennis court was there, however, and she could visualise him on it, in his whites.

Her mutti's elegance was noticed and complimented, as was the fact that it owed much to its 'simplicity'.

The councillor was a self-made man and professed to have no time for the toffs in his neighbourhood, but the weighty furnishings and ornate plantings of his home and garden were more than adequate announcements of the status his success deserved to win for his family, now enlarged by the fortunate addition of strong new blood captured by the charms of his niece.

Thus, in as many approximate words, ended the councillor's toast on the freshly mowed lawn of his house, upon which the severed shapes of daisy plants stood out like small blots. Catharina found herself with downcast eyes counting the blots as he approached the end of his peroration.

There were at least fifteen kinds of sandwich, each with a little flag identifying what was in it – cream cheese and lemon curd, egg and olive, and others even more dainty. After the champagne for the toast there was a bowl of fruit punch and also cups of tea. A string trio was being ignored in a corner of the tennis court.

She watched Freddy reading the little sandwich flags and sampling a number of the delicacies – he caught her eye and winked. He was sun-dark from his time as a survey field cadet and his grin was a bright flash of wickedness as he popped his sandwich past it.

The extended families were there, and some friends of the bride and groom – But no one from the university college, Miss Hansen?

Councillor Hasty was paying her the compliment of an appraisal.

She noticed the appraisal but was looking past his looming broadcloth shoulder at her lanky, newly wed brother, and was distracted for a moment by the way he bent attentively towards and sometimes over the people he spoke to – at that moment it was Ettie's mother, the widow Francis, who still wore a black mourning rosette at her bosom. Mrs Francis had taken both of his hands between hers and was speaking earnestly up into his face. His dark hair fell forward across his forehead and he politely released one hand from hers and swept the hair back, holding it from his eyes while he answered her question. The dark hair, of course, he had from the little man who was the father he never met. He got his father's hair but not his small stature, nor the tidy stature of his little mother. How did that come about? And how thoughtful he appeared without trying to seem so. His slow, careful speech, likewise, seemed always to be fastened to thought, and the thought to what he saw in his mind as he composed the words in his mouth, which he then spoke with care, as if each one mattered as much as the next. They were often surprising because what he had perceived in his mind had been so. He could have been a poet, she thought, and perhaps he was – a poet of the forge!

Would Mister Hastings please excuse her inattention, she'd been distracted by the sight of her brother and his evident happiness! – and how fortunate he was to have found Miss Francis, a sweet young woman! – and what was the councillor's question again?

Councillor Hastings' appraising gaze had hardened a little. He'd wondered about her friends and colleagues at the university college, for example the distinguished German professor who'd become quite well known in the town, but never mind, Miss Hansen would understand if his duties as host called him away at that point.

He inclined his head and then moved off quickly to greet a recent arrival, a tall man with a luxuriant moustache above a rather pouty bottom lip. It was the mayor, Mister Johnston, the one who had organised the famous Jubilee Parade. Was he also a 'friend of the family'?

But of course it was the councillor's escutcheons that were on display here, his selection of sandwiches and his imported champagne, his house and lawns and tennis court and the beds of roses that surely required the attention of gardeners – this was the situation into which her thoughtful, courteous brother had indentured himself.

And then, as the last of the sun warmed the drab flanks of Mount Victoria in the east and the string trio struck up jauntily from the western shadows of the tennis court, the bride emerged from her uncle's house in a plum-coloured going-away dress and was driven off in a trap by her husband who remained stooped over the reins and didn't look back as she turned to wave with one hand while the other held her hat with two long crimson ribbons at the back – the breeze caught them as the trap rounded the gatepost at the end of the driveway, and their flutter was the last thing Catharina saw before she felt Mutti's hand slide under her arm and grip it tightly.

'Ah, so, there he goes,' said Mutti. 'My big Wolf.' Then, after a while and a long intake of breath, she was looking around. 'We had better find Freddy,' she said. 'He's eating all the little *schnacks.*' She relished her odd pronunciation of the word, making it sound like their old Kieler Plattdeutsch word for gossip.

And indeed, there he was, sharing a joke with Ettie's brother Will. He performed a mime of weeping, rubbing his eyes with his knuckles, before giving his mother a kiss on the cheek.

'It's all right, Ma,' he said. 'You still have me.'

Wolf

So what exactly had been in his mind, if there was one in that great block of a head? That was what the councillor had wanted to know about his niece's husband's thinking when he was told about Wolf's encounter with *Fon* Welden, a member of the town's educated class and an aristocrat and wealthy so far as could be seen. And connected to the class of person building mansions out at Karori. Was the councillor and mayoral candidate to be associated with the blockhead's giving-herself-airs slut sister? Whose brazen character would be seen by all?

Wolf stood there and let the man run out of breath before taking him by the shoulder and sitting him back down in his chair.

The professor had agreed to marry his sister after listening to what he had to say to him on her behalf, and on behalf of her mother and family. If the councillor called his sister a slut again he would break his neck and take the consequences.

The councillor had come up hard from hard times and was not a man who surrendered easily. As if to mark the fact that he had come up hard and now commanded a good view of what went on about the town, his offices were on the top floor of a grand building on Featherston Street. The building was entered past a uniformed porter with a high opinion of his own importance as well as that of the councillor. He sent a boy up to Mister Hastings with a message. To Wolf's way of thinking the offices were intended by their fittings and furniture to make him feel small in the presence of the councillor but failed to do so.

Wolf spoke with care because the councillor was a hard man as well as a generous one. He had for two going on three years regularly paid his mortgage into the councillor's account. He had undertaken work at a discount on the councillor's properties. The councillor's niece had given birth to a fine little girl called Agatha, named after her dadda's German grandmother, in the house on Mount Cook. He had improved the house by the skill and hard work of his own hands, as well as building a sound hen house and tool shed at the back and installing well-forged palings at the front, the envy of their neighbours. He had taken good care of the councillor's fatherless niece as was expected of a husband and father, even one as young as he. The councillor had no right to speak to him like that.

The councillor remained seated and appeared to be listening to Wolf who had not yet stepped back from the man's chair, though he had seen the effect on him of the mention of Agatha's German great-grandmother and of course of the indignity of being made to sit. But then when the councillor stood up against Wolf's chest he did step back and give the man room enough to feel respected, though his words about Catharina had not earned him respect. One of the room's sash windows was open to its full extent and a cool breeze came by fits and starts into the room with its strong smell of the councillor's tobacco. How often he had thought that the harbour's breezes might be blowing over the blue ranges from country far in the interior where a man might be free to raise his family away from the reek of command that came from rooms such as this one.

Yes he was a good provider, the councillor was acknowledging as Wolf looked away from him in the direction of the window, but that was not the issue. The issue was why by all accounts, including Wolf's own, the Wenczel family from a squalid part of the town had dispatched their eldest son to *stand over* the distinguished professor? And further, why that eldest son had now thought it necessary to *stand over* the benefactor of himself and his family, and what did he expect would come of that? Did Wolf expect that the councillor would become the patron of Miss Catharina Hansen's marriage to the distinguished professor, as he had been of Wolf's marriage to the councillor's niece, the daughter of his sadly deceased brother?

Wolf redirected his attention from the window to the councillor, who was looking into a silence where there should have been respect. He was sorry, he told the man who kept the keys of his and Ettie's house, and also of their future, in his locked bureau, he had not meant to stand over him, nor had he stood over the professor despite what gossip may have got around the town. He had merely told the professor the fact of his sister's condition and requested he have the decency to consider his responsibility. And as for his visit to the councillor's office, he had simply wished, on behalf of his mother and sister, and in the interests of courtesy towards a family to which they were glad to be connected, to clear the air of hurtful gossip by telling the councillor the facts of the situation, including the happy fact of his sister's forthcoming marriage, which would take place in the Deutscher Verein, and to which the councillor and his family would be invited as was only appropriate, given their connection to his, and now his niece's, family.

What both he and the councillor knew these thoughtful remarks concealed was the fact that the so-called gossip had got loose from the councillor's own nephew, Ettie's brother Will, who was Freddy's best pal, the same Freddy who had been the source of it, but of course the councillor was well aware of that, though not of the way Freddy's mother had expressed her anger at her thoughtless son and, by extension, at the councillor's nephew Will who had also shared his story with his sister Ettie.

Oh yes, he could play the councillor's game. It was clear from the man's refusal to budge from the space provided by Wolf's stepping-back that it was he, Councillor Hastings, who was accustomed to doing the inviting and he who chose when and with whom to associate his family. Well then, let him accept the wedding invitation or not, and let him associate with the bride's family or not, what did it matter.

The councillor was measuring him with his eye but would not strike him, that was sure. But the man's ill will was also clear, and no doubt its consequence would itself be clear soon enough.

Wolf thanked the councillor for hearing him out, and hoped to see him again in the not distant future. And then he went down slowly into the bustling street that seemed to have blowing through it the fresh airs of time to come. The fresh breeze was at his back as he went towards the forge in the Aro Valley. All he had to do was turn and go towards the time and place the fresh breeze came from.

It was at once something simple and something that could barely be understood inside the moment of its happening. It was as though time was a flap that opened and shut on where you were, but like the lid on the forge's casting box. There would be the empty shape of the thing and then the liquid metal and then the hard thing that would always also be the molten thing and the empty shape of the thing. It was where he had been in the empty shape of the moment and it was where he was now.

Now there was Agatha's little bony hand holding the last two fingers of his right one, and there was the stink of Adam's shit in the napkin he'd filled while grunting comfortably across his daddy's forearm. There was the curly-haired black bitch setter that Ettie had named Curly who was panting in the heat and had taken care to lie across Agatha's feet as if minding her pup. Because of the heat there was also the stink of the trench dunny a little way off at the bush line. Everything was dusty, including Curly. The mud heaped up around the slab-timber base of the tent wall had baked into shapes that showed where the roots of trees had been and in many places the roots and stumps were still there and men had used them as anchors for the tent walls. Behind the tents, that were almost becoming cottages made from the material spaces where the trees had been, great trees still rose into the hazy sky. The hot sunny bush behind was ticking like kindling in a new campfire, and far away across the range in the next valley, the one they were going to, smoke haze from the burn-offs turned the air blue. The vaporous sky above the dry ranges was at once the sign of what had been there before the fire, what was there now, and what would be there after the smoke had blown away and with it the last branchy rubbish of the trees. All of that stuff would be ash. Then, by that time, his fancy told him, he would have built their house in the next valley out of what could be made of what otherwise made smoke. And the ash would become grass and the grass would become wool. The trees were already wool, once you lifted the time lid.

There was Yorky with his pants rolled up below the knee showing his scrawny white shanks and with a wire-handled kerosene tin in his right hand. Back at the forge in Wellington they'd used top-cut-off kerosene tins to hold water for the fix trough. In his other hand Yorky had an empty wicker basket. He was looking at Agatha and it was already clear why he was doing that, even though that moment hadn't happened. Even though it hadn't it might as well have.

The others were all waiting but none of them had kids. Ambrose had his axe and was striking a ready-for-work pose, and old Bill had his camp oven for making bread and his patient expression. The other two were smoking. The Italian had his hat on at an angle above one eye as was his way.

Would Miss Aggie like to take the basket up to the bush just over there and get some dry twigs to light the fire for old Bill? Then they could all have some bread with their tea when that time came.

Yorky's teeth were all gone, and the way he said bread made his lips stick out past his moustache before they got sucked in again. Agatha put her doll over her mouth to stop her giggle.

And since the brrreahdth would be all the tastier without the stink of shit, would Wolf mind taking his bhoohy to the dunny and filling its water tin on his way there? If he went by way of the creek to fill the tin, well then Miss Aggie could go with him?

Yorky held out the basket and the kerosene tin. He smiled at Agatha who looked at his gums and then up at her papa with an anxious expression, but the look Wolf saw next directed at him by Yorky was a lesser kind of smile and a less kind one. It said that if his work was to be minding his own children then the sooner he was on his way down the valley the better.

By all means, Yorky, that will be my pleasure, were the

words he thought but did not say.

No he would not rise to the taunt that all he was good for was running errands for the Yorkshireman.

Off they went with Curly trotting along.

Oh yes the sooner the better, and just as soon as Ettie was better, and the sooner she was better the better. Off they would go down the valley. He was already in that moment.

After scraping the shit off Adam's napkin into the scrub he left the kiddies getting twigs for old Bill's cooking fire while he washed the napkin in the creek, giving it a good sound bashing on a rock, and then filled the kerosene tin. Then he knotted the damp napkin back on Adam who struggled and screamed against it and they went back down towards the camp. One of Yorky's boys was squatting across the dunny pole when he put the full kerosene tin of water there. He had the skitters and looked at Wolf with a horrible smile while the shit squirted out of him into the trench.

'Thanks for the water, Wolf,' he said. 'Oh Lord I wish this would stop.'

Oh yes they had to get out of there the sooner the better and over the hill and far away from the camp sickness and into the smoke that would soon enough be blowing clear away from their house.

But now could he kindly go across to the smithy, said Yorky when he got back, they needed a couple of boxes of three-inch square-head nails, rough as guts would be fine, the fools were nailing slab timber down in the valley and couldn't get enough of them nails.

Wolf was meant to be away from that forge work because it was unsafe with the kiddies. Yorky knew that. They'd agreed upon it. And he could hardly go to the railway cuttings with the navvy gangs and take the kiddies with him.

Yorky sucked his toothless cheeks in and made a popping sound with his mouth while he waited for an answer.

'You know I won't do that work while Ettie's sick.'

'Well, then you can fuck off and wipe all their arses somewhere else.'

So that was it, the thing that had already happened in his mind's time was going to happen where he was, with Agatha holding on to his hand and Adam escaping the crook of his arm and Curly pressing herself wearily against his leg. It was the wise dog that then led the way back to where Ettie was lying on her cot, with the bucket next to it and the big flies droning to and fro in the stink of her sick.

'Hello Wolf my darling man,' she said with an expression that was both a brave smile and a sign that she knew what was happening in that moment and had perhaps expected it. 'So we're off now is it?'

Adam was trying to climb up on her cot and get her bottle of cordial but Agatha was standing by the door flap and holding her nose. There was a streak of sunlight from the open flap, it extended across the hard dirt and at its limit wavered on the edge of Ettie's sheet. She dipped her hand in it and moved her fingers as if dabbling in the bright creek where he'd been with the children not long before. It was as though that feeble dabble was all she had the strength for. How could he now put her on the pack-horse with their kit like a roll of camp canvas or a sack of flour? She could not be expected to walk from Raurimu the long day or more it would take to get to their block – he had done it himself to see the place and to measure what they would need at first, and got back two nights later bone weary as he would not have been even after a day working with Yorky's gang in the railway cuttings or at the smithy forging the tie bolts and plates for sleepers.

Ettie's wedding ring glinting in the streak of sunlight on her sheet was a generous gift from her uncle, and also his signal by day and night and for as long as it had taken to raise two kiddies and improve the soundness and value of the house that was never theirs on the bare slope of Mount Cook above the town, that they but especially Wolf and his family were beholden to Councillor Hastings, the man people called 'Hasty' behind his back and for good reason. It had always until now been a reminder of that generosity and what it entailed. But now it glinted in the watery sunlight as if the weak stirring of Ettie's hand was signalling to him, but also to her angered uncle back in Wellington, that the ring no longer guaranteed their debt.

'Fix not thy heart on that which is transitory; for the Dijlah, or Tigris, will continue to flow through Baghdad after the race of caliphs is extinct,' said Ettie in her special pretend-solemn voice and with that wicked little smile, weak and trembling now but still Ettie's, the smile that had some time ago unlocked her secret nature to him and for him to share, and so he joined in the rest, making his voice solemn as he imagined Thoreau's might have been, 'if thy hand has plenty, be liberal as the date tree; but if it affords nothing to give away, be an azad, or free man, like the cypress.'

It was memorised out of her favourite book that she had got from her father who had dreamed of a better life where there was land and fresh water aplenty but had not found it.

How much did they still need for a second pack-horse? Because he couldn't leave her while he went over with a load.

Ten shillings a day at the smithy, and seven for bushwhacking and roading and other jobbing. He was owed a week from before Ettie got sick and three part-days at seven shillings less time lost, doing what he could manage with the kiddies. That was three pounds near enough, he calculated, after his share of the bread and tea was taken off. He owed seven shillings at the shop. That was two pound thirteen near enough to add to the kitty.

Off they went again with Curly trailing along. Adam could just walk but was not very steady on his feet that kept tripping in the hard ruts. Agatha was being a big girl and trying to hold his hand but he shook it off. Soon enough he had to be carried again.

Yorky was at the depot where the Italian and the boy with the skitters were unloading. He could have been doing that too and earning while keeping an eye on the kiddies.

Yes he'd be taking his smithy kit, the whole lot, he'd be needing it down the valley. He didn't say too bad Yorky hadn't thought of that. He was a head above the Yorkshireman but was still holding Adam. He could see the fresh sweat break out across Yorky's forehead, so he stood still and waited until the man stepped away. He would come back to the smithy for his kit later, it had better still all be there.

Well then he could get his wages later too, and had better or what? said Yorky, turning back to the job of unloading.

Adam began to wail when he was handed to the Italian but stopped when he got the man's floppy hat to play with. Agatha stood with her doll in her mouth. A hot gust of breeze made little dust devils in the road and blew her hair across her eyes but she just stood there and let it. The Italian was showing his teeth in a smile that left his moustache where it was. The Yorkshireman's muscles were thin and hard like tool handles where he gripped the man's arm and steered him to the depot doorway.

Just what was in the ledger as owing, not a penny more or

less, that was all he was asking. Then he'd be gone for good. And good luck to you with finding another smith within the day.

Then they were heading back to Ettie. Even though Adam was staggering slow and tumbled over several times into the dust, the present was moving quickly towards what Wolf could already see, which was the scrubby place on the bank above the river down there where the flood gravels stopped below a good dry flat easily cleared for a tent. It was light sandy soil that would drain. They could get there downhill across the slope through big trees from where the pack-horse track ended at the Kaitieke Block settlement. There was a creek in a gully they'd have to cross on foot while he led the horse. He would have to take the horse with Ettie and the kiddies on it down first and go back for the other one once they were down there by the river. They would be where it was shallow near where the bend joined another arm and ran on past some of the other ballots. No doubt they would be meeting those other ones before very long. They were already burning off. He could see it all clearly, and Ettie holding on tight as he led the uncertain horse slowly down the slope. Perhaps Aggie could walk the last bit. That would be one of his first jobs, to cut a good track down there and bridge the creek. And then she could sit there in the quiet with the kiddies while he went back for the other horse and brought it down. They would be hearing the birds, unless the kiddies made a racket and frightened them. He would get them all a drink of water, it was very clear and cool over there in the valley. He had tried it when he went on his recce and the taste stayed with you – it was the taste of stones and leaves. Here in the camp it got filthy.

There was enough in the kitty now to pay the store off and

for provisions to get them started. He could lease another horse with the ring as collateral and the anvil from his kit thrown in as well because it would be too heavy to take over there at first.

But Ettie had already slid the ring halfway off her finger before he had finished. Her face was very warm to his touch but she had that smile. So he took the tired children to the cookhouse and when they had finished Agatha proudly carried the billy of soup back for Ma. Some of the navvy ragamuffins were running up and down kicking a ball in their bare feet. The ruts in the road were baked hard and she had to be careful not to trip and spill the soup. The ruts were like the gullies they would be crossing in a day or two, he told her, only now they could pretend they were giants, walking across the rough steep land and the mountains and tall thick trees to their home.

Then he left them to play peacefully outside the tent where Ma could see or hear them and not disturb her for just as long as it took to go with the barrow to the smithy and get his kit, not long, because time seemed to be striding quickly away like a giant towards their green cool place by the river. In the morning he would arrange the second horse. The other one was already theirs. He had lifted Agatha up to meet its gaze and the horse had snuffed at her dress and blown a big hrruff breath out into it.

Always the sound of birds had woken him back at the railhead camp at the edge of the tall bush in the dim light just before dawn. The first few calls in darkness soon multiplied until the air was full of them, calls and songs of many kinds, a joyous sound and dense as though the songs had substance in the air. You could not even talk over that sound. He expected that when he stepped out through the tent's flap he would feel the bird songs brushing his face and arms. Sometimes the birds came close to touching him, especially the cheeky little ones with flirting tails that came to greet him at the edge of the bush. Their call was a wittering, clever and alert. But they didn't follow him back from the creek once he'd left the bush with his bucket of water, and as the camp's noise increased and the morning brightened the birds were quieter. The bush was their home and its border was the mess of branches and stumps that marked the camp's extent and the hard labour of the men who lived in it.

And now it was his and Ettie's labour alone that had begun to clear a space in the forest where he and Ettie and the children could live on the dry above the river. Their needs would clear the bush border back as far as was required for their hill pasture and the flat ground where they could have gardens and crops. But he would leave the steep gullies because they were difficult to fell and the birds could have their homes there. There was good rimu timber and more than enough of it on the ridges and broader slopes. There was a place nearby called Pukerimu, it meant rimu hill. Back in town Councillor Hastings was throwing up his mansions built out of it on the Karori hills. But in the valley the smoke of burn-offs from neighbouring ballots was already filling the air the birds had owned with their songs and their flitting so quick and sure. In time the smoke would clear, and there they would be in their own mansions, and he and Ettie and the children in their one.

He lugged Freddy's theodolite and tripod along the riverbank where he had cleared a path through the scrub. The western limit of his ballot was close to where the two streams met, so his map said. A shallow just upstream of the junction allowed him to cross if it had not rained. There were no clear sightlines from the ridge where the tall timber was, so he would have to measure his land from the valley bottom up towards the top. Now he would see if he could remember what Freddy had taught him. He had the big weighty compass as well, a thing he found beautiful, as was the theodolite, and he had the map of ballots with theirs on it, and his axe. Once he had found the right place by the river and with Freddy's theodolite the right angle of sightline up to the ridge, well then he could get his compass bearing right and begin to blaze a track up the slope from the river where the two arms joined up just by the shallow. That would be his west border and he would cut timber along it and mill the best of it that could be brought down in sections. The ridge was his northern border as near enough as mattered for now. What lay beyond he could get to later. The eastern one would run down to the river a couple of miles upstream of the junction. For now he would deal with what he could see and with what he could imagine.

He could bridge the river and run rails across it to get timber to the flat where it could be milled. He would have to get some train wheels for the sledge and borrow a team of horses. He began to make a plan that was also already vivid, with him sitting astride a log on the sledge while the bridge creaked under its weight. Ettie was leaving in the light one-horse buggy with the kiddies but they reined in to watch the log being towed across the bridge towards them. The team of five horses harnessed in line were snorting hard with the weight of the timber and the kiddies were shouting Giddy up! at them from over the other side. Then Ettie and the kiddies would go on up the road he had cut across the hillside to the settlement. The road was well formed with gravel from the river-junction shallows.

But of course that was a while away! Meanwhile he had to sight up the hill and establish his border. The theodolite found the ridgeline across the river and up the hill and the line along which he would climb with his axe to mark his border, just as Freddy had showed him it could. Then he could write the distance and the bearing on the ballot map and go from there with the compass.

But the clever instrument's eye could not measure the distance to Freddy or what direction he was in. And in what quarter of the world would Freddy's fine compass find its true owner?

He sat for a while on the riverbank next to a little creek choked with watercress to let the grief and dismay settle back down in his chest. He was even quite used to it. The birds started up again while he was still, but quietened when he jumped down to the shingle with the loudest shout he could summon and sank his face in the river's cool running water and then climbed back up and put his wet dripping face to the instrument. It was good to imagine Freddy here helping with the work and scoffing with that laugh of his at his big brother's mad ideas, but the pity of Freddy's disgrace would not go away and neither the cool river water nor working to the point of falling down flat to sleep at night could take it away.

His brother was a filthy little bugger and his sister a whore and his mother gave herself airs because she could sing songs in German though she lived in the same slum as always and who was his sister's father anyway, was what the councillor shouted in his face with froth at the corners of his mouth, but they had got the result of their ballot which was what he had come to tell the councillor about and had done so and so they were leaving anyway. So he left the councillor's office for the last time without another word because why waste them, and they packed up their cosy Mount Cook house and were gone. And so now she would only have their chickens for company was Ma's joke, but she could come up to the valley soon enough when all was ready for her.

There was a tall rimu that viewed from below stood a hand's width above the rest on the top of the ridge near enough to the point Freddy's theodolite had found for him up there. He might leave that one – that one could be Freddy's tree. The clouds moved on along the ridge but he could still find the tree – it had a couple of long outstretched branches near its crown, he could line it up by sight as well as with Freddy's compass, and that tree with its arms would be his end marker as he crossed the river at the shallows in fast water up to his knees and began to cut blazes every twenty yards or so on the way up. At each fresh cut of his axe he shouted his brother's name aloud and felt the name thump in his chest as the thick chip flew to the ground. This was where he would be, this was his mark. Fred-dy, Fred-dy, Fred-dy – it already felt better to have Freddy ghosting there along the trees with perhaps his laughter, and perhaps one day he would see the place and his tree. But of course he would not.

He had marked out the western line, he told Ettie when he got back wet and dog tired as darkness fell. He hung his pants to dry by the fire and sat bare-legged to eat his supper. His legs were like tree trunks, said Ettie with a mock grimace, weren't there already enough here? There was bread with some watercress and the last of the cold mutton from Dick. His chewing jaws were tired as if from the cold water of the river even though it was warm in the hut. He was talking around his mouthful of supper because he could feel his thoughts tiring. Soon they would have enough timber to wall the hut properly and tin for the roof. He would get some lads from the settlement where the mill was, and Dick would come over from his place downstream to help with felling the trees along the line. They knew how to drive down a whole lot of trees at one go. They could have a share of the timber, not that there was any lack of the stuff. He could hardly get his mouth around the word timber and when warm Adam climbed on to his lap he took him to the bed and fell asleep with him lying across his chest. He woke when the birds started up. Ettie and Aggie were in the bed too and he had not even noticed.

That ground mist was there when he went out to piss, and of course the birds. He went barefoot to the river and stripped off to wash. The light was just coming up over the treeline to the east. Oh lord yes, one of these days very soon he would have to go out that way again and get Ettie's ring back and not before time. The pale-gold light along the ridge reminded him of that.

Catharina

Yes my dear Hugo, Mutti was still insisting she preferred to be by herself in the 'miserable' Bute Street house, aside that is from Wolf's 'dirty' chickens in the little yard at the back. She did not find her house 'miserable' and she was fond of the 'dirty' chickens. It might reassure him to know that she had named some of the chickens after characters in the books she claimed she had time to read 'at last'. There was an Emma, Bovary of course, and also of course the Charlotte who bewitched poor unfortunate Werther – it was her copy of the book that Mutti had now, very well thumbed and with her daughter's student scribbles in the margins throughout. And others, even a chicken Isolde! – a dirty Isolde! There was a Mutti story associated with the Isolde chicken, one day she would tell Hugo about it because she herself was in the story. But alas no filthy old Chanticleer. He had met the ruthless edge of Mutti's kindling axe because his enthusiasm was unbearable in the early morning when, these days, she had the chance to lie in bed for a while longer 'at last'.

Hugo was looking at her with an affronted expression, but then, thankfully, laughed, a little too heartily perhaps – Ha! A dirty Emma Bovary! And a filthy old Chanticleer! Bravo!

Mutti's tone as she told her daughter about these celebrated chickens had been between sarcastic and affectionate, as it was when she wondered aloud whether the chickens missed her bravely pioneering son Wolf.

The other one, Freddy, she had banished from their conversation less by decree than by her own silence. It was a silence that occupied her face as much as her speech. No, she would not speak about him nor about the reasons for her silence. And what could she, Catharina, say to this silence – that it was not fair for Mutti to embrace her daughter's no doubt scandalous marriage while cursing Freddy with her renunciation; that the renunciation was unreasonable for a woman who had lived beyond the rape that had made her, Catharina; that the renunciation of Freddy and the obdurate silence that conveyed it were unjust when read in the story that also contained Mutti's marriage-of-some-kind to the poet Wolf Bloch and marriage-of-convenience to the absconded sailor with a murky past, the kindly father of the silenced Freddy! – but no, she could not even begin to compose a way to say these thoughts in her mutti's presence, and in any case could not help but keep flickeringly alight the little thought that her mutti's silence was her way of protecting if not Freddy in person then her own implacable embodiment of him. Those Kornblume eyes and the glint, now, of the spectacles she wore to read and sew, and the line of her mouth that would not smile again until Freddy's presence had been fumigated by her unsmiling mouth and her glint, and by her refusal to admit him to the present she now occupied with discussion about other things, for example her granddaughter Greta's uncertain health which, at age two, was still a worry to her – could those unblinking eyes, and the glint, and the implacable set of her lips, and her deflection of conversation into mundanity, not also be her way of protecting Freddy?

But of course her granddaughter Greta's uncertain health at age two was also a worry to Hugo, her daughter insisted, continuing to commit herself to her husband's defence while leaving Freddy outside the perimeter of their mother's silence.

Mutti's tone was droll. Of course, and how was the

Professor these days?

Or for that matter, they could deflect the absence of Freddy by complaining in chorus about the despicable Councillor Hasty whose recent elevation to the position of mayor enraged the professor and his mother-in-law in equal measure, because the pompöser Dummkopf had grossly insulted his wife and her daughter – and unfortunately 'the pioneer' Wolf had not felt it necessary to make the full extent of the man's gross discourtesy clear to him in a traditional way.

But then neither had the professor.

Ah, but the pioneer was a very different kind of man, they all agreed about that, though without agreeing entirely on what constituted his difference.

But wouldn't Catharina's mother Josephina – Hugo had only recently gone so far as to call her Josephina – like to come and live with them, he asked rather dutifully, but also, his wife suspected, because in the twenty-five years her mutti had lived in the little cottage in Bute Street its environs had become more and more run down and disreputable, to the point where having chickens to keep in the small back yard might even be construed as a mark of affluence in that neighbourhood though perhaps quaint elsewhere in the town, for example in Karori. And perhaps unsanitary, from that lofty quarter's point of view?

But no, she would not prefer to move to her daughter's and the *Professor's* house, much as she was grateful for the thoughtfulness of the invitation. And so there she remained, with her Chinese scroll that Wolf had mounted for her in a long frame with glass to protect it from fly spots, and her dirty bookish chickens. But she would come over to the house with its fine wrought-iron palings to look after Greta whenever they needed, and sometimes Greta could be left with her in disreputable Bute Street, where she liked the chickens very much and could sometimes even hold Emma, the quiet one, in her lap and let it peck at grains in a tin or even in the palm of her hand, although that made her shriek.

Her grandmother had had a favourite chicken when she was little, Josephina told Greta, it was called Puck Puck, she had loved Puck Puck passionately and had carried it everywhere, it was an especially brave chicken and if Greta liked she could tell her some of Puck Puck's adventures. The adventures had happened a long way from where the chicken called Emma now scratched and pecked around in a little back yard in Bute Street in this town on the other side of the world.

But why the *Professor* as well as the chicken called Emma Bovary lived in this town on the other side of the world was a question that also preoccupied Mutti with that sharp look for Catharina from behind her spectacles. They had gone back and forth with this topic many a time. Mutti had not had a simple life when it came to the stories of her men and her children, but that did not mean she was of right her daughter's confidante in all intimate matters. Catharina would not be telling her mutti about the time some years ago when Hugo had wept copiously upon the smooth, stretched pale dome of her swollen belly with its protuberant button and said that yes, it was true what she had, not suspected, no, what she had *intuited*, it was her *intuition* that he had seen and admired, that this was indeed not the first time he had expected the birth of a child *aus seinen Lenden* – which had sounded so comically like something to do with loins of pork or other meat that she had burst out laughing, which had transformed his tears into a huff.

But that was the truth of the matter – he had then taken

the opportunity to enlarge upon his peccadillo as he liked to call it – Hugo von Welden had indeed impregnated a young woman in a rash moment of youthful indiscretion, not his first it was true but his most foolish, and had been banished along with his modest degree and equally modest entitlements to a place as far away from the young woman's respectable family and the town of Giessen as his family could find by consulting maps and the accounts of the town's somewhat famous explorer Ernst Dieffenbach, who had been to New Zealand in the earlier years of its development as a civilised country where a youngish man (such as himself!) might make something of himself (as had Dieffenbach!) – and had she by any chance read Dieffenbach, because if not he could give her the *Travels in New Zealand*? He had made a famous ascent of a mountain, for example? And had been enchanted by the songs of the birds of the forest?

Ah well, Hugo, she had said quite gently, lifting his heavy moist face from her stomach, now you have the opportunity to show yourself to be the better man your family hoped you might become. And no, she had not had the opportunity to read Professor Dieffenbach's account of his mountainous conquest, perhaps she could do so while she was laid up with this gigantic mountain of her stomach that Hugo rather liked to occupy the summit of.

But the issue of Greta's health. Despite the mountainous dimensions of her mother's stomach, which was after all usually rather small, the little girl had been born somewhat prematurely and was a weak, fractious baby whose despairing yowls had driven her papa into a frenzy of vacillation between anxiety and impatience, for which the remedy was mostly found in his study with the door shut. Mutti's response to this information was that the *Professor* was probably more use there. They would take Greta for walks in the Botanic Garden where a cavalcade of prams circulated around the ornamental lotus pond on fine days, or paraded through the rose garden, and then sometimes Mutti would wheel the child back to Bute Street for an hour or two. But Greta was thin and often vomited her milk because of the colic, and once she was grown enough to crawl around began to sneeze and wheeze and have a runny nose.

Now, it was the chicken called Emma that made her sneeze – but what was the point, Mutti said, of keeping her away from all the things in the world that might affect her? She was almost four years old and look what her mother had come through by that age, and 'the pioneer' also, including a long journey by sea!

Of course the issue of Greta's health, to Hugo's way of thinking, had something to do with the miserable conditions at Bute Street. Of course, to Catharina's way of thinking, he had no right to imply that her mother's house was unhealthy.

But there was a silent emptiness at the centre of this little politics as it revolved around the child who was prone to sneezing, and of course the silence and emptiness were where Freddy existed but existed through the incontrovertible fact of his absence. Yes, of course his Ma would keep the house from which he had been absent going on two years, the house that was filled with his absence, and of course she would seek to occupy that empty space with the sound of Greta's sneezes and the need to discuss what the sneezes meant. And of course the discussion of the sneezes animated what would otherwise have been the resolute glinting unsmiling impassivity of her expression when the absence of Freddy was either apparent or perhaps about to be discussed.

*

What Professor Hugo von Welden had preferred to call their nuptials had been celebrated modestly, first of all in the same little church as Wolf's and Ettie's and then, also modestly, at the Deutscher Verein. Her brother Wolf, whom Hugo referred to admiringly as the giant Rübezahl who walks with such a heavy tread that the earth shakes, walked her with restrained strides to the altar but was distracted by the mews of his new-born Agatha and kept glancing over his shoulder. The modesty of both the nuptial ceremony and the Hochzeitsessen at the Verein owed something to the unmentioned non-attendance of Councillor Hastings and his immediate family – the councillor's generous patronage of his niece's marriage to the giant Rübezahl had included the dainty sandwiches with little flags that Freddy had so relished along with his pal Will.

But the councillor's niece Ettie was there with her babe in arms, along with her brother Will, and their mother the widow Francis, and their uncle who was Wolf's former forge master Mister Kelly, and half a dozen of Hugo's colleagues from the university college, and a dozen of Catharina's friends, and Mutti's best friends Victoria and Arabella – and so the councillor's non-attendance passed without comment except by Freddy who lamented the lack of those special little sandwiches they'd had at Wolf's and Ettie's wedding. He pulled a sad face and turned his hands palm-up and asked where were the sandwiches with flags? And especially the ones with egg and olive, so delicious?

Of course he was just being naughty – she saw Will give him a sharp rebuking poke with his elbow, and then saw Freddy squeeze the elbow against himself before he moved it away, and saw that Mutti was watching them from the corner of her eye. Perhaps she feared that Freddy would embarrass the family with one of his ill-judged pranks. But then there was dancing to a violin and an accordion, and Hugo swept Frau Wenczel away. Her mutti was still very light on her feet and daintily graceful in the way she moved, and Hugo complimented her with a bow and took her to the refreshments table for a glass of his favourite Rhinegau – the wine was a contribution from his department at the university college.

They drank some more of the wine at his house that was already somewhat familiar to her after leaving the Verein through a ribald guard of honour from 'his department' – at the last minute she saw Mutti turn and take Freddy by the arm, because of course now it would just be the two of them in the house in Bute Street, she and her youngest, her baby Freddy – but, after the wine, Hugo was not able to accomplish much in the way of love-making and fell sound asleep, while she lay awake for a time with that dissatisfaction mingling with the image of her mutti taking Freddy's arm, and his head tousled from dancing bending down so he could kiss his mother's cheek, and then kiss her again so sweetly when she turned to smile up at him.

But now three years later Freddy was gone, his abrupt departure a horrible counterpoise to the happily anticipated arrival of the second child Adam in their giant brother's house on Mount Cook. The counterpoise had a grotesque quality, like a mechanical device that jerked one character out of sight behind a slammed door, pursued by the jeers of the mob, while another was thrust forward to welcoming applause, the apparatus managed by some kind of malignant puppeteer.

That was how it seemed to her, she told Hugo, disliking how her voice trembled – it was like a horrible mechanical nightmare that repeated itself over and over, she could not get them out of her mind, the jeers and the cheers, over and over, and what was it that had given these events such a horrible persistence, and was it this persistence or something like it that had sealed her mother off within a fortress of not-talking about what had happened to Freddy or what Freddy had done? While at the same time not wasting any opportunity to talk about Adam? As if talking about Adam, who had as yet done nothing more than be born and shit in his napkins and puke, was more important than talking about what had befallen Freddy, or for that matter about Greta's health and her sneezes, or her cousin Agatha's health and her complete sneezelessness! – the infant Adam who, after all, had been named after her mother's father Adam Hansen, the same Adam Hansen who had banished his pregnant daughter to her sister's place in Sønderborg, where she, Catharina, had been born and spent the first years of her life? Something her mother had not wished to dwell on but had nonetheless talked about frankly when she considered her daughter to be old enough to understand the concept of necessity?

Her mother had borne the brunt of cruel family judgement; she herself had lived alongside her mother as she made her way into a life of her own despite that judgement or even because of it – she could hardly be seen as a model of respectability in the eyes of the classes that were even now erecting pretentious mansions in the outer suburbs of this wretched town where respectability was bought at any cost. Why could her mother's compassion learned at great cost not decant her own experience of banishment into the plight of her own child Freddy? Whom of course she loved despite all the obdurate signs of her rejection. And chiefly her silence?

Ah, but of course she could tell by Hugo's silence that he knew she, like her mother, had worked hard for a quota of respectability, so who was she to judge?

Oh, but she was sorry, so sorry, she told Hugo, who was holding her rather carefully against his side in the lounge where they liked to sit together peacefully for a while after Greta was asleep, and would usually read and even sometimes read to each other – really and truly she had not meant to talk in such a confused way, nor to burden him with her confusion not to mention her memory of the time Mutti threw poor Freddy's things into the street outside the little house they had shared for those few years, but what could she do?

Ah, necessity! Hugo was breathing slowly and calmly as he drew the word out into its four parts, and she liked the quiet vibration of his voice against her, even though for a moment it seemed he was about to commence one of his philosophical disquisitions, in this case on the subject of necessity, and she began to prepare to move free of his comforting embrace because really she would not be able to bear the tone of a lecture at this moment, his condescension that was all the more irritating for being unintentional and even well-meaning.

But no, he just suggested rather simply that the time for necessity had perhaps passed and what was needed – again, only perhaps – was for Catharina to find a way to free her mother from the anguish of her denial, since the poor woman was clearly suffering from a grief that had turned in upon her and was wounding her from within, all the more painful because there was no doubt that, in spite of everything, she still loved her son!

And then, reverting somewhat to his usual enjoyment of 'following a train of thought', he added, with a little chuckle, that as for ne-ces-si-ty, had that not been a factor in the way their lives, his and hers and Greta's, had been shaped, as well as by contingency and chance? And had they not embraced the necessity with open arms – so to speak! – having already welcomed the embraces of contingency?

No, of course he could not help himself, but there was some truth in what he had said.

Well, of course he was perfectly right, she said, but what was she to do?

'You must insist on talking to Josephina about Freddy.' He gave her a squeeze and pressed his lips against the side of her head. 'You must talk to Josephina,' he said into her hair, and then kept his mouth there with its warm breath.

And that was the first time he had easily spoken her mother's given name, her mutti's name, Mutti's name. It was as though at that moment, with his warm breath in her hair and his nose breathing in its scent that he always said he loved – at that moment he stepped inside the misshapen perimeter of her family's story and was there in it.

And after all, he added, while the sound of his voice speaking her mother's name was still a kind of shock or gasp in her thoughts, was it not also true that Wolf had just days ago won a farm ballot somewhere in the wilderness and had begun to make plans to leave the city, and then would not Josephina be even more bereft?

And besides, he added after a short pause that seemed to be making a space for her to speak, but she could not do so at that moment – was it not true that the sexual behaviour that some regarded as beastly and indeed against the law was only natural for Freddy? And could the acts of which he had been accused be treated as a category in themselves, when they were in all likelihood inseparable from the nature of the man himself? And therefore natural in their way, however beastly a man like himself might find them? Moreover, Freddy was not the only man he knew whose nature was that way inclined. Even Goethe, whom of course he knew only by his works! – even Wolfgang von Goethe had clearly been indifferent to the kinds of laws that had driven Freddy into exile god knows where.

'Even Wolfgang von Goethe,' she said, and was able to laugh before kissing him. 'We shall see how Mutti responds to that.'

But of course Hugo was right, if not about Goethe then about the necessity of talking to Mutti, because only she could do so. And it was true that within the year or thereabouts Wolf would be gone somewhere into the wilderness, along with Ettie and Agatha and, now, Adam – and then Mutti would indeed be more alone than ever with the grief that Hugo imagined devouring her from within, and then might be the moment when Mutti could be helped to find the way to speak Freddy's name again and bring him back by at least that much.

It was Ettie who had run in breathlessly to say that Mrs Wenczel had thrown all of Freddy's things into the street outside the house. Wolf had tried to collect them up and speak to her, but she wouldn't listen, and could Catharina please come quickly and try to talk to her mother? Wolf had gone back again to Mrs Wenczel's house and was staying there with her, but could Catharina please come? It was to do with Freddy and the police and Wolf said it was the last straw.

The housekeeper was there preparing dinner and so they left Greta with her, and could she please tell the professor they were at Mrs Wenczel's, and hurried to the tram. On the way Ettie said Freddy had been reported to the police because he had been discovered by Will's landlady performing an indecent act with Will in that boarding house on Cuba Street where Will lived.

She said 'performing an indecent act' as though copying an official account, and that the policeman had called at their house where Wolf was having his tea and asked Wolf to accompany him to 'the miscreant's place of residence', since Wolf was 'the senior male relative'. Nobody knew where Freddy and Will were now.

Then it wasn't far from the tram stop to the house in Bute Street where a small muttering crowd had gathered in the gloom a few houses down from Mutti's. A dog ran yapping at them as they went through the gathering and a man kicked the animal against a fence. Its yelps followed them into the room where Mutti and Wolf were sitting on opposite sides of the kitchen table. Mutti was gripping a cup of tea and looking at it as if mesmerised.

'I took his stuff to the forge,' said Wolf without taking his eyes off his mother, 'but if he wants any of it he'd better be quick, because if he's not away from here by morning Mister Hastings will see to it that he's charged on account of Will.' Then he turned his head slowly to look at her. 'You stay here, Catha, because Ettie and me are going home. We left Ma Francis there with the kiddies.'

Then they left without another word, with Ettie going first and Wolf's hand on her shoulder steering from behind, and Catharina sat down in the chair Wolf had vacated and reached for Mutti's hand across the table. But Mutti would not relinquish the teacup. It was as if the world was whirling around her grip and she was holding on tight to time and its chaos of comings and goings.

Did Mutti know that even Wolfgang von Goethe was given to buggery or at least was not particular in his pleasures? – and no, just in case Mutti wondered, she had not included this information in her lessons at the High School!

She meant the reference to her lessons as a little joke but did not risk an encouraging chuckle.

Mutti's birthday party was over and they were walking off their lunch.

The day was overcast with clouds that seemed to sag with the weight of rain needing to fall. They were pushed ponderously along by the wind. That chilly wind was gusting over from the south-west, it had the tang of the sea in it, and from time to time Mutti had been sniffing it with a look of enjoyment on her face, wrinkling up her nose and top lip and closing her eyes. She was well wrapped in her old Danish shawl. The Botanic Garden in winter was somewhat dreary and the salty breeze was an enhancement, given the comfort of the shawl. She was in the middle of a sniff when Catharina said what she did about 'even' Wolfgang von Goethe, whereupon her mutti's eyes sprang open. The rims of her nostrils, somewhat reddened by the chill, turned white. Greta had run on to meet her school friends by the rotunda, and so Mutti was able to pause and stand face to face with her daughter.

Which of them would speak first? Mutti filled her meagre chest with a great intake of the cold air and then let it out again in a sigh through lips that almost smiled. The sigh was not words but it was eloquent. 'Oh, Catha, why do you try me?' was what it seemed to say clearly enough, but the hint of a smile was more difficult – was it just how the sigh had shaped her lips? Then her thin hand gripped Catharina's quite hard and she led her briskly to a park bench within sight of the rotunda and the girls who were running around it being squawking seagulls with outstretched arms in the gusts of wind. They sat down with Mutti still gripping her hand.

'They believe they are really flying,' said Mutti. 'That is the wonder of being a child.'

What was the hint almost but not quite concealed in that remark – that then perhaps sadly we know we must have our feet firmly on the ground? Must know what is meant by ne-ces-si-ty? By what is ne-ces-sary? What is *notfalls*? Or was Mutti just avoiding the issue of Freddy, as usual?

'Mutti, it's been nearly three years since Freddy went. Why can we not talk about him?'

The girls ran squawking to the ornamental pond with water lilies and then back to the rotunda. Greta had been promised cake at the kiosk and she was allowed to invite a friend. She and Catharina had discussed how she would choose the one friend, a problem so complex the child had wept with the agony of it and the fear of discounting even one of her classmates. She and Mutti had laughed about it on the way to the Gardens.

For once, Mutti was talking without looking at her, without immobilising her with that *direkt in die Augen schauen* – she was looking at the seagull-girls and smiling about their game, or at least it was likely that was what was making her smile, rather than her daughter's insistence.

'It was the fear of shame and disgrace and gossip that

killed my mother,' she said, making each word clear. 'I did not allow that to happen when you became pregnant to the professor. I did not allow it to happen to me at that time, but nor did I allow it to happen to you. That boy had his fun with the gossip about you and the professor and Wolf, and so did his friend, they were foolish and thoughtless and thought they were clever. You saw that I was angry then, but that passed in due course. I saw how they were together those two and that no good would come of it, but what could I do? Now after three years he is just as gone as he was on that morning. Do you expect that to change, Catha? If I talk about it? He cannot come back and talking will not make him. Now we should go and have some cake, and there is a way to help Greta choose her special friend, it's called Ene mene miste, es rappelt in der Kiste, ene mene Meck, und du bist weg! Do you remember that one?' Now Mutti was looking straight at her and the smile was for her – a little closed-lips smile, not exactly humorous. 'Und du bist weg, and you are gone! Friedrich is gone.' A glint of teeth in the smile now. 'And so is Wolfgang von Goethe, for the love of God, Catha, what do you or more likely the *Professor* take me for? Now come!'

Friedrich. She had never called him that, only Freddy. So she had not really called him by name and so had not really brought him back into their world. But a phantom of Freddy had been acknowledged, an insubstantial and abstract kind of being that did not quite merit attention, but perhaps he was present in a way sufficient for Mutti, at least for now, he was present in her secret or private heart where after all much else was hidden and kept safe.

Beth and Frank

The attempt to Skype with Frank hadn't gone all that well. His uneasiness with the process made him turn this way and that away from the camera, as if avoiding its and her gaze, or as if looking around for her in the room where he was sitting awkwardly at a table with the laptop on it. The room was large and bare, with strong light coming in through wide folding doors from what looked like a veranda behind him, so that his backlit face was darkened. At one point he bent to pat a dog but kept talking more or less inaudibly as he did so – the pooch, an ageing kelpie, wandered out of sight on to the veranda. A young woman with a small child on her hip, perhaps his granddaughter Lizzie and 'Frank Junior', appeared briefly in the doorway the dog had gone out through. She seemed to be checking that the call was going okay, and waved, but didn't come into the room.

He'd begun to feel a bit queasy reading bits and pieces of the stuff he'd fished out of the trunk, was what he'd been saying as he bent to pat the dog, and so Beth missed the part that came before he said the names Ruth and Greta as he reappeared.

'Missed a bit there, Frank, while you were smooching your pup.'

His face, already in shadow and hard to read, was still for a while, as if he was trying to remember what he'd just said. His uncertain manner was un-Frank-like – vague and anxious.

'I was saying that they've begun to get on my nerves, those bloody ghosts, Granny Cath and my mum Greta, and my sis

Ruth. Not to mention that Frederick chappie's stuff I sent you last time. Seems it was Granny Cath who kept everything, then Greta inherited it and was planning a book after she came over here with us but never got round to it, and then poor Ruth got the ghosty bug and started organising the relics but of course she never finished the job either.' Then, at last, a loud Frank laugh or bark – the kelpie appeared briefly in the doorway, ears pricked. 'Oh fuck,' Frank said, 'bloody King Tut's curse or something Germanic!' Another Frank bark, but this time the dog couldn't be bothered responding. 'And don't forget the Krauts got poor old Albert Parks' bloody leg as well!'

He'd had enough of it, too many dead people, was all he was trying to say, so would she mind if he just sent the rest over? Better still, she could come and collect it. He'd send one more lot, the last batch he'd had a peek at, but that was it for him. He needed to go and listen to some birds for a while.

'Get those voices out of my head, know what I mean, Beth?'

She guessed he also meant they were drowning out Helen.

And then, some weeks later, the email with an attachment. It was an image of Frank with the head of a galah photoshopped over his. It had its crest up and was looking at her from a sideways tilt of its head. Of Frank's head. His feathers were pinkish-red up as far as his beak, and the rest of his head was grey-white. His single visible black iris regarded her intently.

Dearest Kiwi bird cuzzie, Greetings from the Happy Country. Lizzie is writing this down for me because I've had a wee stroke and can't work my claws. In addition my beak is a bit numb so we can't really chat very well at least for now because I mumble. The vet says I'll get better but it may take a while. Meanwhile I have to take it easy and rest the crest as we galahs say which means not too much excitement. Lizzie has sent you another batch of the haunted Germanics so I hope you don't get struck down by the Curse when you open it. Do come over, would love to crack a few nuts with you. With love from Frank.

Then there was an added note from Lizzie.

Dear Beth, grandad's not too bad but can't do much, he probably wouldn't want me to say this, but he's such a special old guy and I know it would do him the world of good to see you. It would be nice to meet you, he talks about you a lot. Best wishes from Lizzie, John and Frank (junior).

Yes, there was the time on their road trip when she'd done a kind of faint on the way to pay respects to Helen and Pouakani, and had come to lying on her back between Frank's skinny shanks with her head propped up on his tummy, but nothing fainty like that had happened to her since, and it was true she'd been agitated at the time, as much about Frank's bad manners as anything else, so nothing to worry about there, not that she was going to take Frank seriously re the 'Curse'! She remembered his lozenged argyle socks quite vividly, but perhaps that was just because they were pretty much the first things she'd seen when she unfainted.

I'm being haunted by Frank's socks, she told herself, but it didn't work, because of course reading those ghosty fragments did your head in after a while, and that was what had happened to Frank – he'd had his head done in by the ancestors in that trunk.

Would Joe please come over on Saturday, she needed to have a chat. And by all means bring Frankie and the boys, maybe they could bring some stuff for a barbie?

'You'll love this,' she said, trying to keep her tone light. 'Frank's granddaughter who lives with him has a wee boy called Frank. Frank Junior. Invasion of the Franks and Frankies.'

Frankie and the boys were goofing about while setting up the barbie at the other end of the deck, and Joe was watching them with a sooky look of blind love. Compared to squarish, baldish Joe, Frankie was a tall skinny thing with messy black curls on top. She was vegan; they were going to grill aubergines and courgettes and 'stuff like that'. The boys weren't all that keen, said moist-eyed Joe, but they were pretty crazy about Frankie.

How humans went on making such unlikely choices was one of the great mysteries. What would Joe and Frankie's kids look like, if they had any? Where would the veering progress of their genes land them? The budding guitarist Tim hurled an aubergine down the garden quarterback-style and Frankie gave a piercing farm-girl whistle – her long arm shot out and the other boy ran to fetch.

'See what I mean? Best of mates.'

'And you two?'

'I got lucky, Ma.' Then he was looking at her with a so-what's-up expression. 'You've been in touch with old Frank again?' He pushed a forefinger against his temple and twisted it around. 'You two been messing around with that old stuff again?'

'Frank's had a stroke. He wants me to come over. I don't think it's all that bad, but you never know.' The image of

Frank with the pink-and-greyish galah head stuck on top was all at once so vividly present she knew she'd been hiding it away somewhere in the back of her mind – she caught her sob with one hand while grabbing Joe's arm with the other. 'I'm afraid, Joe.'

'Well then, you should bloody well go, what are you waiting for, for the old guy to conk out before you get there?'

His big hand landed emphatically on top of hers.

The veges were on the grill and Frankie and the boys were dancing about fencing with tongs and spatulas. There was a world just down the other end of the deck that was also hers, that was hers if she wanted it, of course it was hers and of course she wanted it, but now she'd inserted herself into another world as well and the two of them couldn't quite fit together.

'Of course,' she said. 'I just wanted to hear you say that. What else have we got cooking?'

'The aubergines are going to be something called baba ganoush, and there's hot pita bread and salady stuff.' Joe patted his stomach. 'Lost a few kilos, too.' He took his hand off hers and made a whip-cracking gesture. 'Real tough task-master, that one.' His grin. 'Task-mistress. Oh, the pain.'

She kept Joe company by not having a glass or two of wine with the baba ganoush – which was truly delicious – but after they'd gone she poured herself one and prepared to open the large box from Lizzie in Cungulla somewhere near a place called Dingo Beach where there were tiger prawns. Frank had promised to take her to Dingo Beach for the prawns.

Wolf

The lads had cleared out to higher ground on a little ridge to the east of the drive while he and Dick did the honours and finished the final two-man cross-cut. Then Dick scampered away up the slope with the saw while he bashed the wedges in the way he had learned to and followed Dick with the sledgehammer over his shoulder as the cut began to split with a twang. Behind him the first of the big trees let out a long loud creaking groan, and he turned to watch. It was as though he was watching the loudest noise he had heard since coming down the valley. The tree, twice his arm span wide, began to fall slowly at first, and then fast. And then an almighty crash as it landed against the two below and down they went, and two more big fellows below them – that was all of them except two of the seven they had got ready over the two days leading up. There was a great outcry of birds that had flown up from the falling trees and from all around, as well as whooping and shouting from the lads. The cold overcast air was full of sawdust and windblown rubbish and the smell of smashed branches, but there was also now broad grey daylight where before there had been dim shapes of light and shadow. The drive swathe was a mess of broken and splintered stuff, with the five big trunks lying this way and that down the slope, and a great many smaller ones snapped and broken.

Then it was quiet except for the lads calling out after Tom as they came jumping down the slope. Who had seen him? Their faces wore that look he had seen back at the railhead when one of the navvies got his legs run over on the track by a buggy. Tom must have gone back across the river. But why would the fool do that and miss all the fun?

It was Curly who found the boy and began to bark and bark down the bottom of the drive slope just as it was getting dark. He ran back to the hut for a spade and a lamp and dug under the boy's body enough to get him out. He was not even a hundred yards from the river – perhaps he had planned to cross it and watch the drive from the other side. It was a big elbowy branch on the last tree that had knocked him down and fallen across him. His chest and jaw and shoulders were crushed, God only knows if he had seen the branch coming or what had happened, God only knows why he had decided to go down there in the path of the drive and not up the hill with the rest of them.

God only knows was all he could find to say to Ettie after he got back from the settlement where they had taken Tom's body to his house. Four of them carried him there in a canvas sling. The good canvas that had been their roof at first was all bloody, so he left it, he told Dick to burn it. God only knows, the poor boy was boarding at the settlement and getting piecework, he was a good worker, he had done plenty of cutting, he knew what to do, he had helped to cut the scarfs on some of the trees that went down, he knew the trade, he would be owed a share of the timber, he would have been owed a share.

'God only knows, it was me, Ettie, it was me that drove the wedges on the first one that went down. I should have looked out for the poor lad.' He was trembling in the bed, and she put her arms around him and held him from behind, saying it could not have been foreseen, but the trembling would not stop. He could feel the beginning roundness of her belly against him and that would usually have been a joy and a comfort after losing the last one but now it was not. It was wrong to have the thought that Tom had been the price to pay for their new child, but that was the thought he had at the moment he fell steeply into sleep, hearing what sounded like the tree's loud groan as it began to go.

In the morning it was the birds that woke him as usual, it was as though nothing had happened to them, that was how noisy and songful they were. He walked along beside the river in a chilly shower of rain to where the drive's swathe was filling up with weak early light. Oh lord the place did look cursed now.

But later when he rode over to Dick's place to have a talk about what had to be done, Dick said that poor young Tom was not the first and would not be the last to lose his life down here or over at the railway, the graveyard already had a few killed in the timber, as well there had been a leg off at the knee that he knew of from a cut foot that went rotten and a hand with no fingers from the sawmill, not to mention an arm gone from the elbow, that was a bloke called Horne, and the fires had done some harm, one man's life taken at the end of the summer just passed when the wind shifted and another he knew of who had lost the sight in one eye from a spark. A few kiddies that got sick and died from the chill. There was a girl that drowned, most people thought she had meant to do it. The rest of them were lucky, Dick thought, and were only getting luckier as the country opened up. Wolf would get plenty of good timber out of that drive, enough to build a decent house, he should get on with the job of clearing some more and start burning off.

Dick meant well enough going on like that, but the list of misfortunes was no help and nor was the word he used, 'few'. What was the real meaning of that word when what it said was not many when what it meant was many while what it denied was too many? He and Ettie both already knew about most of the few and more of the same, not to mention their baby that was never more than a lumpy mess of blood, and as for getting on with the job, he knew about that too and intended to do so. But before he could do it and keep his mind on the view of his clean cleared hillsides well sown with fresh green grass and stocked with sheep, he crossed the stream where they had bridged it at the narrow and walked down on the other side to where the lad had been crushed. There was no need for Freddy's sextant to help him find the place, the sextant and compass were in his mind now and he found where he had dug out under the great elbow of the branch to free the lad's body. It was already like a grave and should remain so. He would fence it when the tree was gone because that was decent and the least he could do.

He felt the bee hit his cheek before the pang of its sting, and then another and another on his neck and face. Then he saw that they were everywhere around the fallen tree and the droning sound of them all around him, and suddenly louder and shriller as they stung. His hat was covered with them when he tore it off to wave the bees away, and they chased him as he ran to the riverbank and jumped in. The water was freezing and when his feet found the shingle at the river junction he was shaking with cold but also with the shock of the stings. There were stings on his face and neck and also on his hands and some of the bees had got inside his shirt and stung him on the chest. He got his coat and shirt off and brushed the bees away into the stream. His face and eyes were swelling up and the pain of the stings was very sharp. When he got home, Ettie pulled his boots and his wet gear off and nipped the stings out with tweezers – she knew not to squeeze the poison. Then she put bluebag on them. There were maybe two score of them, she said. He could hardly see her face through the swelling. Then he lay down on the bed and she covered him with a couple of blankets to warm him up.

He thought he had not slept at all but had only been seeing the dark stained crack in the fallen tree trunk around which the bees had been flying. There was a strangely shaped collar of broken brown honeycomb around the crack. The image was very clear and sharp as if he was paying it special attention. But then next there above him were the faces of Aggie and Adam and he could hardly see them clearly at all.

It was bees from their nest in the tree that got knocked down, he told them through lips that were numb and thick.

The meaning of it was clear but he could hardly speak what he thought that was.

By next afternoon the swelling was somewhat gone but his face was still red and tender and the bites had become itchy. The rain came down steadily, cool and with its dripping rustling sound in the trees, as he rode over to the settlement to see about some help with trimming branches from the fallen trunks. He lifted his face up to let the rain in under his hat brim and down his neck to his chest. In his mind still the image of the bees' nest and along with it the image of the shallow scooped-out place where young Tom's crushed body had lain. And the kiddies' faces, blurred and worried.

Were the bees angry, Adam asked?

That he did not know, he told them. At any rate the bees had been disturbed when the tree with their nest in it was pushed over.

But did they know who had pushed the tree over, and would they remember? Aggie's brow was wrinkled with worry and with the effort of looking into the future where her daddy would always be hunted by the angry bees.

That he did not know either, but he doubted it.

'My God!' said Dick when he saw his face. 'They had you in their sights! But never troubled us when we were cutting the scarfs and whatnot the other day.'

But at that time of course the nest had been high up?

But perhaps it was the bees that had chased young Tom down the hill when he should have been going up? Wolf kept this thought to himself because he doubted it but also because the two images, that of the dark honeycombed nest and that of the shallow scoop under the great branch elbow, could not be joined up in his thoughts. Both were there but each one was itself. They made a meaning not by being joined up but by being next to each other.

Dick thought the bees were a swarm that had got away from the Badem place a bit further down the river. They had hives there with honey bees they'd brought in, they'd begun planting orchards a few years back. Wolf should chuck some kerosene into the nest and burn the buggers out before anyone went back to work there.

A story began to be laid out after Wolf decided there and then to ride on a bit further from Dick's to the Badem place and talk to the beekeeper. He did not hurry and nor did the story. In a way it was as though the story was telling him, not the other way around. Now the part with the almost sore stretched sensation in his arms and shoulders as he drove the last wedge into the drive's uppermost back-cut was followed by the long loud creaking groan of the tree as it began to fall, and that groan by the clamour of birds flying up into the sky, and that racket by the silence that filled the shallow scoop where poor Tom's body had been, and that scooped-out silence amid the sounds of the early-morning forest was followed by the all-around whine of the bees, and that sound and the pangs of the stings that came with it by the image of the dark opening to the bees' nest and the crooked collar of brown honeycomb around it – and now that succession of story-parts, laid out along the path of the horse Blackie's careful treads through the rainy scrub and the piles of half-burned rubbish along the valley floor, was joined by the sound of Ettie laughing and laughing as she looked at their finished handiwork, the dwelling on the cleared flat delta above the river that was half tent and half hut back then in that summer past, and her saying she thought old Thoreau would have run away for all he was worth.

And each time he got to that part with the sound of Ettie's laughter and the sight of her face still thin from being sick and then from losing the baby, another part got added, such as the picture he had in his mind now of the bees' nest flaming up from a lit dousing of kerosene. And then, plod plod, Blackie's hooves on the wet track. She huffed and gave her head a shake from time to time as if to say that the story would tell itself again and something more would always be added to it, but meanwhile she would just keep going.

But when he saw the beehives on the far side of the cleared bush, the story halted and he reined the horse in and sat there looking at them. The rain had stopped and it was quiet in the clearing without the sound of it. The hives were simple wooden boxes stacked up three or four high, each stack with a flat plank on top and a large river stone on top of that. There were about a dozen of them in groups of two or three along the untidy edge of the clearing. The scrub had grown back behind them, the scruffy manuka stuff that Yorky cut his tea leaf with back at the railhead. The story had stopped at the bees' nest burning with the stink of kerosene, or rather it had stopped with his decision not to do that, and now he wanted to turn around and go home but instead he hopped off Blackie and led her cautiously toward the hives. There was no sign of any bees around them but he kept his distance in any case. Then he heard a whistle and a shout and saw a man coming from the other side of the clearing.

He was Wolf Wenczel from just up the river a bit, he had only wanted to have a closer look at the beehives, he told the man, he was sorry if he had trespassed, and was he Badem? Had they not met once back at the settlement when he was setting up his forge?

The man was looking at Wolf's face. 'Well, well,' he said. 'It's the blackasmith. So you've madeah their acquaintanceah.' He was thin and dark with some streaks of grey in his beard and in his speech added an 'ah' to some words as if the thought they contained was not quite finished, though his manner was very quick and sure. Why didn't Wolf walk back to the house with him and have a glass of tea? Then he could tell him 'whereaboutah he got stungah'. He said blackasmith and glass not cup, whereaboutah not whereabouts and stungah not stung as if English was not his usual speech. So they walked along to the house with Wolf leading Blackie. And so the story started up again, with Denis's sharp look and the glint of a gold tooth in his mouth.

When he got home that night he told Ettie about the Turk Badem who was from Levant near a town called Is-ken-der-un and whose name meant almond. They drank tea black out of glasses, with a spoon of honey to stir in. He was a widower but had his son and daughter-in-law with him. Where he came from was beautiful near the sea and mostly warm but there had been trouble and so they left. His joke was that no one could grow almonds down here in the valley where it was too cold in winter, but that his son was doing a good job of it – there were three little almonds already.

And there they had been, running around. They were the same ages as Aggie and Adam but of course there was one more, the third, who had just begun to stagger, a little boy who flung his arms out to keep his balance, 'like a dancer', said Badem, kissing him.

And why were the almonds here in the middle of nowhere, Ettie wanted to know. What was the matter with Levant wherever that was?

Well, what had been the matter with Hamburg in Germany, was his reply. She should ask Ma when she came up here. And he bet she didn't know that when it was cold in winter the bees all cuddled up together around their queen to keep her warm and hardly ever went outside. Just like this. He was holding her from behind in bed and telling his story in her ear.

That was a fib he was just making up, Ettie reckoned – but she was almost falling asleep, and so he left out the part where Badem whose familiar name was Denis told him that the nest of bees that had stung him must have come from his place a while ago because the ones from around here were not like honey bees and could not sting. They must have come out after the tree was felled and their hive was broken. That would have made them angry because they would have been keeping their queen warm in there. He had bared his teeth with that glint of gold on one side and made a bzzz noise.

'Bzzz,' Wolf went in Ettie's ear but she was asleep.

What he would not be telling Ettie about was that the little Badem almonds were very beautiful, with dark serious eyes, and he had imagined picking the smallest of them up as they stood in a polite line to say goodbye to their grandpapa's guest with the funny red face and bringing the little almond back to his and Ettie's place, because she was missing one and was thin and unhappy. He had ridden back as it began to be dark in the bush, and the picture of borrowing the smallest almond had ridden along with him for a while but had left when he saw the lights of their place on the cleared flat above the river.

The story that had begun to tell him earlier in the day was peaceful now next to Ettie's slow breaths. The story was resting as if waiting for him to start telling it himself.

The train came grinding slowly into the station as if exhausted, and stopped with a long screech in a cloud of steam. The screech and the steam frightened Henry who began to cry in Ettie's arms but Aggie and Adam were standing up straight because they had their best clean clothes on including their new shoes, which were too hot said Aggie. Aggie had the fresh flowers that Henry wanted to snatch and so she was standing with Adam between her and Ettie to keep the flowers out of Henry's reach. They were a mixture including pink and blue sweet peas that would soon droop in the heat, and red and yellow zinnias that grew well in the hot summer down the valley.

The best idea, Ettie reckoned, was as soon as possible to show his Ma something different from all the bloomin' dark forest that she would have seen for those hours on the train. And perhaps they would lighten her mood before she saw the house that was still mostly just walls and a roof and some of the windows with greased paper in them.

Ah, but she had her own room with its glass window on to the veranda and a view to the river. And her comfortable new bed with a proper mattress, not a straw one. What more could she expect?

Ah well, they would soon be seeing how wide the gap was between what his Ma was getting and what she might have been expecting. And the view of the river was usually much the same from one day to the next – she might well get over the great loveliness of it before too long, didn't he think?

Ah, but perhaps she did not know his Ma as well as he did? And after all he was her son and he had not yet got over the great loveliness of the river as she put it.

Yes, well, that was certainly true, Ettie agreed, he could often be seen looking at the river or the hill for periods of time with no other sign of life in him, but after all now she would be getting the chance to match him in knowing his Ma since they would be together much of the time and not least while he was away at the forge or with his trees and bees, if not looking at the river or the hill.

She made treeees and beeees sound like a long extent of time by drawing the length of the words out.

But of course she was just teasing him, that was her way, and he even mostly liked it – it was as much Ettie as the rusty colour of her hair or the bend of her neck as she sat to read by the lamp at night or the way she screwed her eyes shut when she hurt herself and then always said arse!

But now here Ma came with steam hissing across the platform and around her ankles, that small upright woman in a plain straw bonnet with a blue band around it that he recognised at once, carrying a single old carpetbag that he also recognised, as he did the fact that she was not wearing gloves. She kissed Ettie first and admired Henry whom she called Heinrich and who she said would get used to her after a while, and then Aggie and Adam whom she thanked for the flowers, and then finally he had her attention.

He bent down towards her face and she lifted it up towards him, and there they remained for a moment while he kept his eyes shut. Then he felt her warm damp palms against his cheeks, and her quick kiss on his lips.

'Oh my big Wolf.'

There was no need for him to be blubbing, she suggested, surely she had not changed so much for the worse? And my God, they had certainly come to the back end of the world had they not? And the train had crossed an unmöglich high narrow bridge on stilts that was surely the last defence against the outside world?

But she was laughing and laughing with happiness, or was it relief? – and then so was Ettie who was not very respectfully repeating 'back end of the world' and 'welcome to the arse end of the world!' while the two big kiddies looked on with wide eyes and Henry began to howl with dismay.

For weeks before she arrived he had repeated to the river mostly but also to the ground he was clearing and to the place he had fenced where Tom had lain that night, and to the rhythm of hammering as he laid the veranda planks, and to the plod of Blackie's hooves up the hill to the forge, and to the wheezing of the bellows there, that he was sorry, Ma, for the lost grandchild that might have been saved if their conditions had not been so hard here – at the back end of the world as she called it now even though she was almost joking and had yet to see their house by the river with its fine garden of vegetables but also of sweet peas and zinnias – but now she was here and the words he had tried out over and over lost their will to be said and stopped just like the motionless train.

There they stood for a moment next to the train while it seemed to be catching its breath with huffs and puffs.

But now they should get the rest of her luggage?

There was one old leather trunk with wooden straps and brass rivets that had belonged to the man he knew was his father but whom he had never met. For all the years of his childhood it had been in Ma's room at Bute Street and she had kept her best linens and an ancient sewing sampler in it. Sometimes she had taken the sampler out and shown him the pictures in coloured threads. The pictures had stories. There were owls that he had liked for their large eyes. Catha had liked the picture of a little house with a smoking chimney, and another of a little deer on a mountain. Well, now here they all were where there were owls in the bush at night and a house with a chimney from which smoke often blew away across the river. In the sampler there had been a pond with yellow ducks but no river. He lifted the chest to his shoulder and carried it towards the cart. There did not seem to be much in the carpetbag he had in his spare hand. Blackie was stood there with her nose in a feedbag, and gave him a backwards look when he lifted the chest and the bag into the cart.

But was that all?

She had sold off the old furniture and everything in the house. Catha had kept some books and things, she no longer knew what nor cared.

His Ma gave him a steady look. 'I did not need to bring all that with me. And I did not need to leave it where it might think it could call me back.' A little pause while she kept her look on him. 'Also, weg! Off we go!'

Perhaps Ma had been prepared to say that. Her preparedness and her interest in getting going suggested it. He helped her up to the step and into the cart where he had fastened a couple of benches along the sides. Then Ettie hopped up and he gave her Henry. Then Aggie and Adam in their shoes that it was clear were making their feet feel as if they were no longer feet. They sat looking at their feet, and sometimes at their grandma. She was holding the flowers and then gave a red zinnia to Henry. Of course Heinrich was the name requested by Ma in honour of Papa Hein, even though he had not been Henry's grandpa, but they would have to work their way around that.

Then off they went down the bumpy valley road that was a packhorse track the first time back then. Ma had persuaded Heinrich to sit on her lap waving his zinnia.

'Hoppe hoppe Reiter,' she was saying to him as they bounced along. 'Wenn er fällt, dann schreit er, fällt er in den Sumpf, dann macht der Reiter' – she opened her legs and let him drop with a shriek of joy into her spread-out skirt – 'Plumps!'

Of course he remembered that plumps game from Bute Street – Papa Hein had played it with Freddy and had dropped him on the floor between his legs by accident once or twice at the plumps moment. When that happened Catha always said he had been drinking brandy. Ma might think she had left almost everything behind, but most of what she had brought would not be in the old trunk or the carpetbag for that matter.

How many birds there were! she remarked later when they were sitting together on the veranda and looking across the river at the trees and at the part of the hillside he had cleared and sown. Was it always like this in the evenings? And what about the part without trees?

Yes it was, he told her, and after rain even more so. After rain at dawn and just before sunset, that was the time. He especially loved that time. He often sat here to listen to them, there were many kinds. And he would not be cutting more trees. The grass that grew afterwards did not last well. One day there would not be enough for the sheep. Ettie would say that he had spent a lot of time looking, and it was true, but there was a reason. He was also watching to see what was happening. He saw that it was the same as with her. When she got sick the baby could not survive.

He had told her this, but not the other part of the story, which was that when the bees' nest was destroyed they could not keep their queen warm.

And then after a while she had told him about Catha and the man she always called the Professor, how Catha was now teaching at the girls' college and how that annoyed the Professor almost as much as the fact that Catha seemed not to be able to have another baby after Greta – which of course was her fault and not the Professor's, she added with that quick bark of a laugh.

They were going around but not arriving.

And then there was a silence that the birds filled up.

'And Freddy?' asked Wolf. 'Has there been any word from that boy?'

'No,' said his Ma, and took hold of his hand. 'He has taken himself away. And now so have I, from that house.'

Her meaning was clear.

'So west is that way,' she said, looking westwards and lifting his hand to point at the red tinge in the sky above the range with its dark spikes of treetops. It was an unnecessary thing to say but necessity was not why she had said it, which was obvious.

Yes it is, he told her.

As if she did not know already in what quarter the sun would set tomorrow and the days after that.

Catharina

'Alles zu seiner Zeit,' had been Mutti's answer to Hugo's polite question about when she was planning to leave her house 'over there'. 'All-in-good-time!' she added unnecessarily but in order, perhaps, to give herself the chance to emphasise the simple meanings of the words in case the Professor found them difficult to grasp.

The polite scorn of Mutti's smile was familiar to those, including Hugo after several years of observation, who knew well her habit of leaving unsaid what she considered obvious.

He had not found the words difficult to grasp, clearly, and had soon busied himself with preparing for the birthday toast, now that 'the ice has been broken'. Would Catharina like to help him?

She had directed a frown at Hugo to indicate that his ice-breaking choice of phrase was perhaps inappropriate under the circumstances of her mutti's birthday, as had been his question about when she would be leaving the house 'over there', and he had rewarded the frown with a nice smile. He had recently cultivated a beard and enjoyed smiling through it.

Then they had saluted Mutti's fifty-first birthday with glasses of champagne all round. Arabella and Victoria, and herself and Hugo, and Greta, and of course Mutti who had stepped down from the hired trap wrapped against the chill in her favourite Danish shawl.

For some months now Mutti's moods had often been thoughtful and withdrawn, but the toast and the glass of champagne had brightened her.

The room had been full of beautiful winter camellias in vases, some of them borrowed for the occasion. The secret purpose of the profusion of camellias had been to emphasise that Mutti could not hope to grow flowers 'over there' in Bute Street. Greta had tried a chaplet of bright cornflowers but was sure they increased her sneezes – the chaplet had been used instead as an additional ornament for the birthday Kirschtorte.

After lunch and slices of the Kirschtorte, and some coffee and chatter – Hugo was especially charming – she and Mutti had taken Greta to the Botanic Garden to meet her school friends and have even more cake at the kiosk. There the now famous 'Goethe was a bugger' moment had taken place – famous in her and Hugo's discourse but needless to say not further afield.

'You don't have to believe everything the Professor tells you,' had been Mutti's crisp parting advice as she stepped up to the tram on her way back to the house 'over there'. But of course she had never believed everything Hugo told her; they often had quite long discussions over his 'trains of thought', enjoyable discussions for the most part that sometimes became flirtatious and only occasionally turned into arguments, and the sting of Mutti's remark had lingered for a long time after her fifty-first birthday and long after the camellias in vases had been thrown away, having failed to lure her from the house 'over there' in Bute Street.

But now here they were again a year later, planning the occasion of Mutti's fifty-second birthday, which would be without the useless camellias and also, at Mutti's request, without her best friends Victoria and Arabella.

But why no Arabella or Victoria?

She and Mutti were drinking verbena tea at the table in

the house in Bute Street. There was also one of Vicky's nice custard tarts. The interior of the little house was especially neat and tidy, and she had remarked on that when she first came in – had Mutti been getting rid of some old things in anticipation of spring cleaning?

There was something she wanted to show her family, was Mutti's response to the question about Arabella and Victoria. It was a private family matter. And Catha would just have to wait like a good girl until her mutti's birthday next week, because that would be the appropriate moment, it was decided, no argument.

Mutti had a certain wicked pleased look about her that she had not seen for a long time.

And then it was the nearest Saturday after Mutti's birthday, as it had been the previous year, when both she and Hugo were free from teaching and when Greta was not at school, exactly as had been agreed the year before; and in a strangely disconcerting reprise of that event Mutti stepped down nimbly from the hired trap with the Danish shawl around her shoulders and with the help of the coachman – but this time the coachman reached back into the trap and brought out a parcel that he carried in through the wrought-iron gate with its 'pineapples' and up the path to where Greta was waiting with a bunch of flowers for her grandma. She was in her best dress with cuffs and a collar embroidered by Grandma, standing quite straight on a step two down from the top, with her mama on the one above her and her papa above her on the threshold.

How nice they all looked! was Mutti's opening remark, to which she added that they were arranged rather like the little puppets that came in and out of the clock on the Rathaus in Kiel, which of course was a reminder – as if she needed one! – of how many years had passed since she last saw that funny old clock!

It was a little odd that Mutti should at that moment have remembered the old Rathaus clock.

Then Hugo gave the coachman his fare and carried the parcel inside. The others but especially Greta were looking at it – where should he put 'this mysterious object'?

The table was already set for lunch and there was a bottle of champagne in a bucket. It was a cold lunch this time, with some pastries and sandwiches and of course the requisite Kirschtorte. She had already seen what was in the parcel, Mutti said, but she had wrapped it up again so it could be a surprise. So would Hugo mind putting it out of the way somewhere while they had their lunch and then she would unwrap it for them?

So Hugo put the parcel on the little occasional table at the end of the room by the bay windows where it was lit by pleasant winter sunshine coming in there – it was a sunny day with no wind, unlike the previous year's. And there the well-lit parcel sat tantalisingly while the conversation around the table tried to ignore it.

But then perhaps it was the distracting presence of the parcel that caused the conversation to take an unwelcome swerve towards her work at the Girls' High School, something she and Mutti talked about sometimes at the house in Bute Street.

Yes, thank you Mutti, she was still enjoying teaching very much indeed. It was a pleasure to be engaging with young minds, not to mention engaging with her own.

It was her remark, intended lightly, about engaging with her own mind that caused Hugo's frown to persist for as long as it took him to eat two of the sandwiches with a good swallow of his wine and a brusque napkinning of his moustache – she saw the frown there and saw that her mother had noticed it as well.

Ah yes, said Mutti, who as usual was eating very little and taking only small sips of her wine, perhaps she could be forgiven on her birthday for reminiscing a little, something she usually did not like to do, about how – she paused, searching for a word, and looked at Catharina as if for help – how *befreiend*, was that the right word? How freeing it had been when she was still young to meet Wolf's father Wolf Bloch and his sister Theodora, whom Catha of course would remember from Hamburg and sadly also from their voyage, who had encouraged her to engage with her mind and had insisted that it was hers, that 'she had a mind of her own'.

This, again, was a topic usually confined to Bute Street.

Hugo was looking down at his right forefinger and its nicely trimmed nail that was scratching quickly at the tablecloth in front of him as if trying to erase a spilled dot of mayonnaise.

And she had learned a lot from the talk at Bloch House, as Wolf and Theodora's house in Hamburg was called, not just from what was talked about by the many visitors there, though that had been full of interest and she had learned much by listening to it, but also from the way in which the talking took place, which involved as much if not more listening than talking, and so involved both passion and patience.

'Oho!' exclaimed Hugo. 'Passion and patience! And was that the motto of Herr Bloch's socialist politics?'

He enlisted his beard's help to send a quick, roguish look at his wife. He had views on the subject of Bloch's politics, which he had learned about while enquiring after the 'circumstances' of her interesting family.

'No, Hugo,' said the woman he now called Josephina. 'That was just what it was like in that Bloch house where I, although very young, was also invited to sit and talk and where I was listened to.'

There was a silence in which Greta was lifting the top slice of a sandwich and peeping to see what was inside.

'Please, Greta,' cooed Hugo with a smile and a little shake of the busy forefinger, 'you know it's bad manners to look inside your sandwich like that, what do you expect to find, a socialist?'

'But I'm just trying to see what's in it,' said Greta, and added quickly, 'in case it doesn't agree with me.' Then she sank down in her chair and waited.

'And besides,' said Catharina as Hugo's mouth began to open again, 'I enjoy getting out of the house and I like the company of the other teachers and especially of the principal, Mary McLean, a very interesting woman.'

'And without children to take care of,' said Hugo. 'A bluestocking.'

The term 'bluestocking' had recently become a favourite of Hugo's.

'It's cucumber,' said Catharina, ignoring him. 'You like it.'

Then she stood up from the table. There were topics she could sense approaching that she would not allow to spoil the birthday lunch, however much Mutti's special little smile suggested she had enjoyed the passion and patience of their conversation up to that point, and would willingly have continued it a while longer. But after all it was not entirely Hugo's fault that he felt his standing as the household's breadwinner and as a salaried professor at the university college were challenged or even discredited by his wife earning money as a teacher at Wellington Girls' High School; nor entirely his fault that he believed her freedom to do so was the consequence of their not having more children, which was also noticed and not just by Mutti.

But was it fair that the reason for this sad reproductive state of affairs should be implied in her direction rather than in his? This had been the theme of Mutti's contributions to conversations they had been repeating for some months at the house in Bute Street.

Now perhaps was a good time for Mutti to open her surprise parcel, and then they could have the cake? What did they think?

That was when Mutti, as she stood up quickly and agreed about the parcel, and perhaps also with her daughter's adroit management of the passion and patience, nonetheless remarked in an offhand way that it was no doubt helpful that Catha could contribute to the family's income, especially as she and Hugo no longer had a small child to take care of, which gave her more time.

And then she went straight to the parcel in its appealing patch of sunlight and brought it back to the table.

'So,' she said. 'Let's have a little space.'

Hugo had abruptly excused himself for a moment.

By the time he came back the parcel had been unwrapped and its contents laid out on the table. Greta was gazing at them in dismay, but her mama and grandma were still laughing with their arms around each other's waist. Was it tears of laughter that were running down their cheeks, or were they sad in some way that the laughter could not explain?

The objects were an apple, a hank of fresh shorn wool, a jar of honey and a slender black iron nail. They were laid out on a long rectangle of bleached canvas. There was also a letter written in a careful, upright script with strong downward strokes and delicate upward ones. It was on two sheets of plain white foolscap paper torn from a pad like those used by surveyors for sketching maps. The sketching pad had been Freddy's and belonged with his theodolite and compass.

Would Greta like to read him the letter, asked Hugo. It seemed to have come from a fairy-tale place with some magic objects included, so she would no doubt understand it better than her papa!

He was looking at his wife and mother-in-law as he spoke, as if he rather suspected their strange laughter was at his expense.

'Dear Ma,' Greta began, and then looked up anxiously because was she allowed to call her grandma 'dear Ma'? But then after a little cough she continued in the special voice that was needed for standing-up recitations at school.

> Now after almost four years it is time for you to come to your home in this beautiful valley. There is no longer any reason for you to delay. You must come once winter is over and can do so on the train that will stop for you at Raurimu station.

Greta had some difficulty with 'Raurimu' but, having got no help, went on a little more quickly.

> The canvas that I have sent a piece of was once stretched down the wall of our first home that was more a tent than a house. Ettie bleached the canvas with lye and washed it in the river below our house . . .

'They have a river?' Greta was astonished and had begun to enter the marvellous valley near the place called Raw-ri-moo – but then,

'Continue, darling!' said Hugo a little curtly.

> . . . and then spread it over bushes in the sunshine so you could see that this place is fresh and clean and also that the tent walls have now been replaced with good tight timber milled from our hillside.

'They have a hill?' But by now Greta in her wonderment had entered the secret beautiful valley with the river and the hill, and the 'go on' nods of the grown-ups made no impression – she continued to read in a tone of entrancement rather than with her special recitation voice.

> The apple is from a neighbour's tree but those I have planted will bear fruit in five more years. Though many in this valley are clearing land for sheep we will have fewer than them as I do not think the soil will last well. But there will be more than enough good thick wool for yarn.

The thick hank of wool had a sheepy smell but seemed not to affect Greta's tendency to sneeze – she picked the wool up and gave it a sniff.

> The honey we will have from our own hives soon now that they are established. One of our neighbours is a beekeeper from the Levant and this jar is a gift from him. His name is Denis Badem which means almond in his language, and he looks forward to meeting my Anne, that is their word for mother, as do others in our community, you will be welcomed.

At 'Levant' Hugo's lips became pursed within the neat frame of his whiskers.

> The nail is from my own forge and others like it have fastened our house together. It is warm and will be a secure home for many years. In the morning and at evening the sound of the birds in the forest is enough to make us believe we are in paradise though the journey to get here has been a hard one. There is a room ready for you, please come. Ettie and the children will be glad to see you. Your loving son, Wolf.

'Oh please, can we go? Please, please?' pleaded Greta, gazing in wonderment at the mundane objects on the plain piece of bleached canvas.

'You can come and visit me after a while,' said her grandma, 'because I am going, yes, I am going there as soon as the weather warms up, and now you all know.'

Of course 'after a while' and the kiss Mutti bestowed on her sneezy granddaughter's head of clean, brushed, shiny hair suggested that the house with the wrought-iron palings with pineapples on top and the housekeeper who was even then clearing the lunch things from the table on which they had been pushed aside to make way for Uncle Wolf's magic objects – the kiss and the 'after a while' implied with Mutti's familiar wry humour that Greta might find the actual situation in the magic valley with its river and hillside, its honey and strange language and intriguing thick wool and its apple which must certainly have special properties, and the nail from a forge on the same page as Vulcan in her schoolbook of famous stories! – that she might find the magic valley to be more like the place her grandma had come from a long time ago, where the cows and horse had pissed and shat inside the Bauernhaus in winter, than the house in which she lived with her papa the professor and her mama who taught at the Girls' High School not far from the Botanic Garden and the kiosk where there was always cake.

Did Catha remember the time they went to the Bauernhaus above the Schwentine when her Tante Elke was to be married to that handsome Franzose? Did she remember going with her cousin Mathilde to take the Franzose his supper and a bottle of beer where he was being kept apart in one of the animal stalls inside? While the rest of them sat outside under the tree with the lamp hung up in it, and sang? While waiting for Tante Greta and the others to come up Kieler Förde in Danne's boat?

Oh yes, almost – or not really? – perhaps she remembered something to do with a chicken. And her opa's bony shoulders when he carried her on them. And there were lots of flowers, and bees.

But really, did she remember? Or was it the memory of being told about it? What she was seeing was that her mutti did remember, she remembered all of it and more after having tidied it away for many years; and seeing also that Mutti's memory seemed now to have reached out ahead into the summer when she would catch the train to the place called Raurimu and go down into the valley where Wolf had prepared for a return rather than an arrival.

'A chicken?' exclaimed Greta in excitement.

'Yes,' said her grandma who was going to the magic valley. 'It was like that one I told you about called Puck Puck. Perhaps there will be a Puck Puck at Uncle Wolf's place? Then you can hold it the way you did with Emma.'

Then, without noticing the moment she had decided to

do so, but with a strange sensation of having shifted this person called Catharina out of the time and place of the birthday party, she was standing by herself in the last of the pale sunshine at the window end of the room and watching the vivacious woman who was now as much her friend as her mutti – Mutti who had not been vivacious and happy in this way for a long time, but who it seemed now had been re-animated by the potent apple or the nail with Vulcan's warming powers or the sweetness of the gifted honey.

More and more over the years this woman had withdrawn herself into her own tidiness, as though she needed to reduce the amount and complication of what was in her life and perhaps also in her memory. This friend-Mutti had been her closest companion for fifteen years or so, even after Hugo, but she had long ago stopped referring to her life back in 'the old country' or telling stories about it, except when there was important news, such as her sister Elke's babies; but after a while she seldom any longer spoke of even that kind of news. And certainly she had long ago stopped describing what her life had been like as a child and a young woman, with the animals and so forth, though she had done so when Catharina was young.

So why now, feeling even a little faint, and watching her mutti lean in close to the aura of wonder with which her granddaughter had surrounded herself, did she all at once have in her mind Mutti's description from long ago of the animals in the Bauernhaus, and her own memory, if indeed it was her own and not the one Mutti had given her, of her opa's bony shoulders, and the flowers, and the bees?

It was almost as though the special package from Wolf and the magic objects in it had unlocked Mutti's tidied-away memories, and they had found their way into her, Catha's, mind, not because she was a child like Greta with her shining eyes, but because she was her mother's closest friend and she would need to be the one who understood what was happening to her.

Then she was sitting down in the hard armchair with the whorled mahogany arms pressing up against her, and Hugo was offering her a cup of tea with lemon – it had some of the special honey in it, and was she feeling all right? She had gone very quiet and looked rather pale.

Oh he could be so kind, her dear Hugo, but how could she possibly explain to him what had happened just now when she had barely begun to understand it herself?

Do you remember the time we went to the Bauernhaus above the Schwentine when your Tante Elke was to be married to that handsome Franzose? Do you remember going with your cousin Mathilde to take the Franzose his supper and a bottle of beer where he was being kept apart in one of the animal stalls inside? While the rest of us sat outside under the tree with the lamp hung up in it, and sang? While waiting for Tante Greta and the others to come up Kieler Förde in Danne's boat?

Did she? It was impossible to know, but now the story was back in her mind where perhaps it had been once before when she was a child, and before that perhaps the memory itself had been there for a little while.

But why had Mutti asked the question? After all these years? Surely it was because Wolf's magic had unlocked it and she was really asking herself, not Catha?

And then, after some tea, Mutti was preparing to leave. She and Catha and Greta would not go for a walk in the Botanic Garden today because Catha looked tired, perhaps from her work at the High School?

Mutti had her little smile suggesting that by 'work' she

might mean engaging with 'her own mind' as well as those of her pupils.

She had a box with some of the leftover sandwiches kindly wrapped in greaseproof paper by Mrs Tilley the housekeeper – they would keep her going for days! – and would Greta like to keep one of the special things from her uncle and auntie's place? Because her grandmother would like to keep some herself, to remind her of what was going to happen in the summer!

Then Greta was looking at the apple, wool, honey and nail on their piece of pale canvas. Her eyes filled with tears that then poured down past her mouth that had begun to tremble, because how could she decide which of the magic objects she would like the most?

'Choose the honey, my darling,' advised her grandma, 'because that is the most special. And you can have a little every morning with your breakfast. It will remind you that one day you will visit me at uncle and auntie's place.'

And then she was quickly wrapping up the other things and tying the parcel's string with a deft knot. Hugo had himself hurried down to the end of the street to re-call the trap – she offered her cheek for his gallant kiss before stepping up into it. The cool afternoon sunshine was casting the intermittent shadows of houses across the road, and Mutti flickered away through them and round the corner.

Agatha

Dear cusin greta I miss you very much. Granny josie says you will come to see us plese come soon now its summer again we can swim in the river. Granny has been here for a whole year since last summer I think you must miss her she helps with a lot of things mostly henry and she is helping me to write this letta. She ses I must tell you the news mummy will have another baby soon. Now I am almost nine adam is five and henry is two so granny says there will soon be four little wolfs. I hope the new one will be a girl because Henry is a bad wolf who treys to bite me but granny says he is just treying his teeth. Our dog curly dide we are all very sad. Daddy says he will get a new one but it wont be as good as curly. Curly is buried near the gooseberies we made a cross with a sheep bone in it one of the sheep fell in the river and some eels ate it. Now we have one cow two horses some chickens also some sheep they live on the other side of the river unles they fall in that is a joke. Also now we have bees and daddy and mister badem are bilding a honey house near the river how would you like to live in a honey house I would. In the morning I go to school with daddy on the horse its name is blackie of course you will love it. Our teacher is missis fletcher she mostly likes singing. Now we know how to sing a lot of songs my favorite is the fields of athenry, low lie the fields of athenry where once we watched the small free birds fly our love was on the wing we had dreams and songs to sing its so lonely round the fields of athenry. Now granny is teaching me a song in german here are some of the words she helped with, vie traulich var das flekchen vo mine viga ging. When

I know all the words I can sing it for missis fletcher at school. Asian badem is at the school he sang a song in turk his name asian means lion so now there is a wolf and a lion in the school is what daddy says. There are sixteen children at the school some of the big ones help missis fletcher how is your school in wellington? Soon this letta will go to wellington on the trane and then you can send one back so we can have your news or better still send your self. The address is Wenczel kaitieke which means eat a bird called tieke. There are a lot of birds here besides our chickens they live in the forest no not the chickens that is another joke. Soon mister badem will come to have a cup of tea he and granny josie like to talk so I have to finish my letter. Granny josie sends you love and kisses and here are mine xx.

Greta

Dear Cousin Aggie

Thank you for the letter it was very nice to get it and read about your news and animals. Mama was very happy to hear about the new Baby that you will have in the Valley soon, the news made her cry with joy. She says thankyou for the Gooseberries and the eggs that came on the train with your letter. Mrs Tilley made a Gooseberry Tart and we enjoyed it very much with Cream.

Mama and Papa say I can go on the train to visit you in the Valley in the Summer Holidays after Christmas. Mama says she will come on the train to get me at the end of the Holiday and then she will see for herself what the Valley is like. I know it will be magic with all the Birds and the Honey Bees.

Are there Eels in the river where we will swim? I have been learning to swim at the Te Aro Baths. I go there once a week with the girls from my School. Also I go on the Ferry with Papa to Days Bay where there is icecream at the Pavilion.

At School we are learning Reading, Writing and Arithmetic as well as Physical Education, we do that outside with Stretches and Skipping ropes. We also have Cooking and Sewing and Papa is teaching me German in the evening, he knows that song you are learning, he says it is Wie traulich war das Fleckchen wo meine Wiege ging and the song's title is Heimweh by Johannes Brahms. Also we are starting to do some French. Comment allez vous is how you say How Are You in French.

Grandma Josephina told me she had a special Chicken

called Puck Puck when she was little. Do you have a special Chicken in the Valley that you are allowed to carry around? I hope so because then I can have a turn when I come to visit. I was allowed to hold the chicken called Emma at Grandma's house before she went to stay with you in the Valley.

Now I will close this Letter and get it ready to send to you on the Train at Wenczel Kaitieke, but next time I hope I will send myself.

With love from your faraway Cousin

Greta

Beth and Frank

It was unnaturally quiet in the garden with Joe's mob gone, normal nice quiet but minus an extra amount of quietness with their happy racket subtracted from the norm. Both her head and the garden itself seemed muffled, as if their spaces were conjoined and invaded by a dull vacuum that was really the absence of Joe's lanky Frankie and his boisterous boys. Her visiting blackbird came and went without a sound, not even the deft flit of its wings as it departed.

She refilled her glass with the uninteresting pinot gris snatched off a shelf at New World after the galah-head Frank email and the phone call to Joe. At the supermarket it had been the noisy opposite of too-quiet deafness that had made her hasty with the wine and lazy with her selection of fruits and cheese for the lunch with Joe's mob the next day, and at the self-checkout she'd cancelled her transaction and begun to take her basket back to the shelves to start again but had then said 'Fuck it' out loud and returned to the checkout queue where the assistant gave her a fishy look and who could blame her. The place was filled with a tinny racket of bad music tracks on the shop sound-system and in front of her a man talking too loudly into a cellphone mike dangling under his chin – he kept shouting 'No I don't get it, I do not get it, Francis!' while gesticulating with his full basket of stuff. She'd almost pushed him towards the next vacated checkout station, where he continued to expostulate while doing his efficiently angry transaction. On the way home in the car she'd first of all turned the radio on to banish the 'I do not get it, Francis!' from her head, but had then turned it off and opened all the windows to let the muggy air blow Francis away.

Bit of a Noel moment back there. Some way along in his fading he couldn't handle supermarkets, it was the profusion of choices and his inability to know how to make any that led to tragi-comic events, not least the time he set about rearranging the canned tuna shelves. That time he was escorted from the premises by a big Samoan security guard who recommended a nice walk along the row of plane trees over the road in Victoria Park – 'Nice and quiet over there, sir, lovely trees,' was what Noel reported the man had said when she caught up with him after the security guy told her he'd directed the elderly man in khaki dockers and a Panama hat to the park. The organising principle of the tuna display had been 'anomalous', but the plane trees were just right!

Of course it hadn't just been the effect of the emailed image of Frank with the photoshopped galah head that had rattled her and summoned the memory of Noel waving his Panama in gracious sweeps to demonstrate the symmetrical enfilade of the plane trees, but also the sturdy brown cardboard box about fifty-something centimetres square and thirty-something deep plastered on the front with Aussie bird stamps à la Frank and with a crudely drawn Edvard Munch *The Scream* on the back. Now at last she set her glass of wine to one side and ripped the masking tape from the box seals.

The stuff inside was neatly and tightly packed within fresh new white foolscap archive file-boxes surrounded by supporting bubblewrap and with a scattering of what she took to be anti-bug capsules – someone's careful loving handiwork, not Frank's and certainly not anyone historical. There were three archive boxes, each one with a neat handwritten entry on its lid. One entry read 'SDP + KUNZE', another had

'CATHARINA/GRETA?', and the third one the name 'FREDERICK' with a quickly sketched smiley-face emoji. Though the saggy-face Munch-scream sketch on the back of the box could plausibly have been Frank's before the 'can't work my claws' moment, the archive box labels were not – they were done in careful but decisive capital letters, using a skinny-tip black magic marker. Probably granddaughter Lizzie while holding Frank Junior at bay with her free hand. Was she the one with anti-bug knowledge, and where did she get it?

And now poor old Noel again pleading to be noticed and included, his scrupulously organised Brumberger cases of 35mm colour slides, his too-neat handwritten labels. All carted off now, to the Auckland Museum.

A sip of the wine, the second glass better than the first.

There was also a postcard in the box, as was only to be expected, this time of a winking emu, one eye shut next to its crazed amber counterpart, its dishevelled head feathers in a punkish mohawk crest, a straw clenched in its derisive, grinning beak. It was stuck to the FREDERICK package by a little piece of clear tape. No written message.

Yes of course she should be thrilled to be encountering another batch of the Catharina/Greta/Ruth things, and she was even a bit trembly as she opened the CATHARINA/GRETA? box, but also apprehensive because of what Joe had meant a bit earlier with his finger screwing into his temple.

But okay, why not go all the way and invite Noel to the party?

She found the vinyl Jan Tomasow with Solisti di Zagreb *Four Seasons*, Noel's favourite, and put it on the turntable that had been one of the last devices he could manage.

'Give us a hand, Noel dear, please.'

Giunt' è la Primavera e festosetti, he said into the place where the garden and her brain overlapped, and the foggy confused space filled up with the happy, purposeful cheer of the Allegro. While it played briskly he would often have been poring very, very slowly over the details of the slide on his light table, his magnifying eyepiece creeping about with minute care within the headlong movement of the music.

In the fresh new CATHARINA/GRETA? box were a number of much older envelopes. The first of them was A4, brown and not very full to the touch, with a faded mauve handwritten note on the top – ink mauve from age? – the small, cursive letters elegant and precise and somehow old-fashioned. Too old to be Frank's twin Ruth, killed at twenty-three in 1970? Could be her and Frank's mother Greta? On their road trip, somewhere around the stinky stretch of highway near the Kinleith paper mill, Frank had said Greta took the Granny Cath stuff to Queensland with them for her 'fresh start' when she herself was in her fifties – so early sixties? Still didn't feel right, the mauveness, the old-fashionedness, the precise elegance.

For dear particular Noel, the examination of detail had never been slapdash or boring. He called it 'forensic looking' and advocated stubbornly for 'the truth of the detail' when his picture editors argued for 'story' and 'big picture'. He almost always lost the arguments, but never changed his mind.

Forensic looking.

So that left Greta's mother Catharina as the likely author of the faded mauve handwritten note, Catharina the daughter of Josephina Wenczel, the latter now at rest beneath the sheepy hillside of the Raurimu cemetery – the Catharina who, according to the reunion's querulous tree, had taken back her maiden name Hansen when her husband and Greta's father, one Hugo von Welden, was incarcerated on Somes Island at the outbreak of war in 1914. The daughter Greta who, when she married the Oliver Hardy impersonator Albert Parks, awarded herself the hyphen in Hansen-Parks, most likely because her mother Catharina had also prudently stripped her daughter of the von Welden moniker at the same time as she rebranded herself as non-alien.

Beth raised her glass in a salute to Great-aunt Catharina Hansen, because of course it had to be she who wrote the words 'Film Reviews, Evening Post, October 1920' on the outside of the brown envelope. The wine was warm from late sunshine on the deck, so she took it to the kitchen and tipped it down the sink. A fresh, crisp, cool glass seemed no more than Catharina Hansen's crisp, just-so handwriting deserved.

The envelope flap had long ago lost its stickiness and the yellowed and somewhat foxed newspaper clippings slid out on to the table.

PRINCESS THEATRE.

> There commenced at the Princess Theatre to-day the screening of a gripping story of Paris, entitled 'L'Apache', in which Dorothy Dalton does some of the best work of her career.

Had Great-aunt Catharina been a film buff? There were a number of clippings. The next one stated that, '"Salome," William Fox's greatest achievement, commenced a season at the Queen's Theatre to-day. It reflects the glory of Judea forty years before the time of Christ – and the shame of it – and scenes of Old Jerusalem are remarkably reproduced.' Like the first clip, this one went on for a good quarter-page column, ending, 'The celebrated episode which climaxed her career, the Dance of the Seven Veils, is an opportunity which, histrionically as well as scenically, it is naturally assumed is made the most of by the producer, J. Gordon Edwards.'

Madge Kennedy was at Everybody's Theatre in a Goldwyn Production, 'Leave it to Susan'. Here, the reviewer's careful restraint revealed a prissy flash of character: 'This bright photo-play is replete with moments of refreshing fun, wholesome and clean. In this satire of a Western thriller, the dainty star has a thoroughly delightful subject, in that she is given unbounded opportunities to display her talents as a comedienne.'

'Leave it to Susan' was also shown at Our Theatre, Newtown, where the critic's response was even a bit droll: 'Madge Kennedy will be seen surrounded by cow-punchers and bandits, in addition to four-footed denizens of the desert, on which she is stranded.'

Stranded on the four-footed denizens?

But the real question was, who in a family keeps clippings of so little interest to a real film buff? Either the person who wrote them, or the person who was proud of the person who wrote them.

If the writing on the envelope with the clippings in it was Great-aunt Catharina's, then the reviewer who wrote the awkward film notes for the *Evening Post* in Wellington had to be her daughter Greta Hansen/Greta von Welden of whom her mother was proud and who, in 1920, would have been about seventeen? A budding cadet journalist just out of high school sent out to sharpen her quill on film notes for the trivia pages?

Her wine-glass hand was a bit shaky and there was a

lump in her throat because thanks in part to Noel's phantom forensic looking, not to mention his stubborn maddening patience, not to mention her irritation with Joe's dismissive finger-screwing gesture, without which she might well have just fossicked on impatiently and set the stuff aside as being of minor interest – because she'd channelled Noel and resisted Joe and made demands of her own perfectly adequate attention to 'the truth of the detail' and her powers of observation, she'd found this precious thing, wrapped in its layers of protections and lost secrets, this little brittle hoard of a mother's dreams for her daughter, her love, hope and pride.

Enough for now.

The light was fading outside on the deck, so she carefully packed everything back in the box.

And bloody old Frank hadn't even bothered to look?

Evening sounds had returned to the garden, the whisperings of leaves, birds calling to each other, laughter and kid-noise from neighbouring houses, cars on the main road at the end of the street. Nice, ordinary stuff. The police helicopter battered past overhead. Somewhere in the mid-distance someone had the music turned up in their back yard – it was the Phoenix Foundation's 'Give Up Your Dreams', Joe's favourite album last year, 'Give up your dreams, can anyone help me, it's starting to fall apart at the seams', a genius song, he reckoned, about not buying the hype, about finding transcendence in what was real. He and the boys put their own version together in the basement at their place, then he said Frankie came along and subverted the lyrics with stuff like 'Give me your creams, can anyone help me, my face is falling apart at the seams'.

Kind of the point.

Nice to just sit outside for a while longer, with a bit of leftover baba ganoush and a fresh glass of wine, in the company of her gentle ghosts and her gentle heartache.

Catharina

10 December 1915

Dear dearest Mutti

It's been many weeks since I wrote to you and the family far away in what I think of as Wolf's Haven Valley. It's been hard for me to find a cheerful tone let alone cheerful things to tell you. Now it's no longer enough for me to thank you all in the valley for the provisions you have been able to send from time to time, though they have been very welcome and even sometimes essential under the circumstances. Nor can I any longer put on a happy tone in response to your stories about the children and Wolf's marvellous ingenuities. Now I have to be truthful and write simply that every day is very very hard here, every day I think about you and Wolf, Ettie and the children, and I worry day and night that last year's declaration will by now have extended its effects into your distant valley. Please write and tell me that all is well.

I ask for that reassurance because here in the town all has not been well for some months. Indeed this last year has been very hard for us on account of hostility towards those whose names unambiguously declare them to be enemy aliens. The name von Welden has been among the least ambiguous it would seem on account of the 'von'. 'Where are you von?' is the cruel taunt to which Greta has been subjected at school. Wohnsiedler the butcher's son had to board up his shop, his dear old father was so kind to us when times were hard. I remember the pork bones and trotters he would add to our parcel. Papa Hein's old friend from the wharf, Heinrich Reepen, was pushed into the Hutt River where he was fishing, for God's sake a harmless man in his seventies who you will remember was fond of singing German songs after a drink or two at the Verein. He died of pneumonia from the cold water.

My most important news is that Hugo was removed from his position at the university college last month because of an expedient law banning what it called Alien Enemy Teachers. This happened despite interventions on his behalf by the university council, and this week he was taken away and sent to that prison island in the harbour. It is possible he was unwise in conversation or overconfident in his views on matters of interest, as you Mutti know very well the dear silly man can be, though what danger could be expected to result from his ill-considered or too hasty opinions I cannot imagine, as my poor Hugo is not by any stretch of the imagination a sabre-rattling militarist or a sabre-slashing duellist, let alone a spy of some sort, what a comical idea!

I too am no longer permitted to teach at the High School though the principal Mary McLean argued on my behalf as having been brought up here since childhood. However, my married name and the fact that I can speak German are enough to put me beyond the pale. Worst of all, Greta continues to be bullied with the 'von' since the declaration and so I am hoping to send her to you at Wolf's place so long as you can reassure me that the loyal patriotic enthusiasm of the town is not directed at children in your remote place of safety. Please let me know as soon as possible that this will be all right and if Wolf and Ettie are willing to take yet another child into their expanding fold.

It is for Greta's sake that I ask this as I fear for her state of mind here in the town. She quite often wakes in the night in terror of being murdered, and comes into my bed trembling and startling at sounds outside the house, even a dog barking. I would love very much to come up to the Valley myself, as I have such blissful memories of our visits these past summers and especially of lying in the cool river and letting the current wash my cares away. However I must remain here for Hugo's sake and to take care of the house in anticipation of his return. Dear Mrs Tilley left some time ago, she said it was not because of us but because of what her friends thought of her working in a German house. That was just as well, as there is no longer money to pay her. The university college gave Hugo a severance payment when he was dismissed but his other funds have been frozen by the government.

And so I am commissioning you, Mutti, to approach Wolf and Ettie about Greta on my behalf, as I know very well that they would just say yes if I were to ask them directly. If it will be too much of a burden then you must tell me honestly and of course if that is the case then Greta will stay here and we will work together with those who are not thoughtlessly vindictive towards any person deemed to be an enemy and especially a child.

Fortunately such thoughtful people do exist, for example the admirable Miss McLean who has arranged for me to take private lessons at home. The payments for these will not come through the High School as that is now forbidden, but through the goodwill of those who would like to help us and their own children, though not in learning the German language needless to say, nor the best ways in which to get an understanding of the sufferings of Young Werther!

If Greta is able to come to the Valley for a time, please take care always to use the surname Hansen as I'm sure that will relieve her anxiety and will not attract the bigoted attention of those who God forbid may have been infected with anti-Hun sentiment. I too will take steps to return to my maiden name if that can be done under the present circumstances, and will begin to use it as a matter of course in any case.

My dear Mutti, it must be hard for you to imagine what may be the fates of your nephews there in the north at Kiel by the naval base or wherever Tante Elke's five boys have ended up, even though you have never met them and now will not have the possibility of writing to anyone there. Of course those who live on the Danish side of the water in Sønderborg will be all right, including that cousin Finn whom I cannot remember except through the stories you told me, for example one about a giant fish that frightened him with its huge mouth and bulging eyes. I wish all memories of terror could be as innocent as that one. I think sometimes these days of the stories you told me about your grandfather and uncles who lost their lives up at the Danish borders near where Tante Greta lives, and how your grandmother said they had been bewitched by the shiny new Prussian guns. God help us if such terrible enchantments should reach into the minds of boys in your peaceful valley.

I will send this letter directly on the train in Wolf's returned provisions crate with his details on it well known to his good friends at Raurimu station, together with some things you may find useful such as some bedding that I saw the house was lacking last time I visited, for example the good winter quilt that I no longer need here. Alas I am unable to send any substantial amount of paper for the children to write and draw on as it is rationed, but I will send such odds and ends of fabric that I have and some garments that can be unpicked, as well as such things as buttons and other fasteners if they too can be found. I will also send some English books. Here they sit on their shelves wondering what is wrong with them and why no one will ask them to dance.

I am not sending this letter by post as it would surely be read before it reached you and includes what I have chosen not to write about until now. So it may be some time before you hear from me again, unless that is you return the provisions crate as our faithful courier, perhaps with some more of Wolf's honey and some eggs and those huge cabbages! Then my letter to you could once again be a passenger on the return trip to the Valley, with whatever useful things I can put together.

Dear Mutti, you know there's no need for me to say I miss you, but even so I will say it, and add what I have not said often enough to your dear face with that special little smile on it, that the chief reason I miss you is that you are my best friend in the world and that I hope to be reunited with you before long.

It often seems to me that the stories we are both living and talking about are like that cross-stich you taught me when I was quite little and still clumsy with my needle, and that as you told me your oma taught you and so on back across our forgetfulness of so much else. The stitch is at once what and how we remember. We go forward and back and across and back and up and back down in the patterns of our lives, and the little patterns go forward and then back again and then forward again around the border of some large event or else they fill in the space of something larger than they can become by themselves. This is something you showed me and of course you know it much better than I do, but it is only now as I watch the hesitant movements of my own dear frightened daughter towards a sensible pattern in her life that I see how well you understood that stitch.

And now of course I can see your little smile that says 'Oh Catha what nonsense!' though you have never said the words themselves, that is the way of the mutti I love.

Please fondly kiss Wolf and Ettie and the children for me.

Your loving daughter
Catharina Hansen

Wolf

The small, elegant woman who stepped quickly down from the train into the chilly wind whisking leaves along the platform was no longer as young as she had persisted in his memory of her, though she held herself very upright and tipped her head on one side just as he remembered she always had, and gave a gay little wave with the hat that she had taken off to stop it blowing away, the wave that he also remembered always being her wave, Catha's wave, with a twirl at the end, and the girl who ran fast with a shrill cry along the platform towards her was no longer a child as she had been when she herself had stepped uncertainly down from the train back then with that frightened look and one thin pale hand up to her mouth, yet the elderly woman who meanwhile held his arm a bit too firmly was not at all old, it seemed to him, with her straight back and sure step and neatly dressed hair, even though he had watched her every day down there in the valley getting carefully older going on almost ten years now.

At that moment his heart began to thud as if from effort. It was as though he was in a space like the empty ones in Ma's Chinese scroll on the wall of her room down the valley. Time had been emptied from those pale smudged spaces, or rather whatever it was that time measured such as change had been emptied from them, and he peered into the empty spaces on the wall of Ma's room sometimes knowing what their effect on him would likely be, that thudding in his chest as if air and blood were being drained out of him, as if the air and blood of his body were what time consisted of when it was inside him. Sometimes something like the thudding happened, or a shortness of breath, when he had a chance to sit by himself on the riverbank up beyond the honey house and to look back down the valley the way the water was flowing until the movement of the river's surface stopped being a movement and became a still pattern, and the windy shaking of scrub leaves along the bank also stopped being a shaking and became a kind of writing or picturing across the shapes of branches and twigs and the shadowy spaces between them. Sometimes if he waited long enough in that space there would also be a kind of hum in his hearing and the sounds of water and leaves and even of the birds would be taken over by the hum. And then when he took some deep breaths and blinked his eyes the sounds and the movements would return. It was both something that just happened to him and something he invited. He was a bloody hopeless dreamer, Ettie thought, but it wasn't dreaming because he was wide awake, even more wide awake than usual, and if she got annoyed sometimes when he'd stopped paying attention and she asked where did you go, Wolf, what, were you dreaming or what? the answer was that he hadn't gone anywhere, but he couldn't say it was time that had gone somewhere else, it was time that had drained out of him and taken away his attention to the present moment, because she would say that was daft and rightly so, it was daft.

But then there was Catha's head against his chest and her faint scent of lavender that was the same as he remembered, not as it had always been but for as long as he had thought of her as no longer his big sister but as the lightly stepping woman who had held his arm to walk down the aisle on the day of her wedding to Professor Hugo von Welden while behind him in the pews wee Aggie had been mewling like a lost hungry kitten.

But where were all the others, where was the wolf pack, she wanted to know. The pack of little brats? Still within the reach of his arms was Catha with her quick cheeky questions, and Greta was there as well, nearly the same height as her mother now, and Ma was there still with her grip on his arm as if it was him she wanted to hold steady rather than herself.

Why, what she called the little brats were mostly at school where all good children belonged of course, including her ma's little namesake Josie who'd just started! Except Greta who as she could see was no longer a little brat and just for the day because! And wee Grace, she was with Ettie back at the house, along with Peter. Adam was working over at Denis Badem's, he was doing early pruning. No more school for that boy.

Of course there were empty places in his roll call that were like the pale smudged emptinesses in Ma's scroll, three spaces from which time had been emptied out rather than stopped, or they were like chimney smoke that even as it was blowing away was always there, but they were for him to keep in his mind, and Ettie of course, not for Catha to find a place in hers.

And Agatha? That sweet girl?

Aggie was housekeeping down at Smithy's place.

Perhaps Catha heard his tone, which he hadn't meant to be obvious. He saw how his clever sister's eyebrows went deliberately up and down in a moment's silence, but then she lifted Ma's old shawl to her face – she had missed 'dieses alte Dänische Ding', she said into it, and was both laughing and crying and then peeping up at him with that wicked Catha look, because although the war was over going on six months it was stupid to speak German and she knew it, but who was going to notice here on the little windy platform with only two other people walking away towards the transports and young Smith from the far end of the valley unloading his seed sacks and whistling? Smithy made a grand sweeping wave as if sowing and gave a thumbs-up but the only enemy aliens he had to deal with down there aside from Aggie Wenczel were the blasted ragworts he wasted his time grubbing out of the ailing pasture.

Although it shamed him to admit it to himself, he'd expected that Catha would admire the good wooden body he'd built for the Model-T chassis and motor and the fold-down seats on the truck's tray, but she climbed up without saying anything, and she and Greta sat there in the chilly autumn breeze with their arms around each other as if the truck was just an everyday thing, and perhaps it was, back in the town. But then she leaned around the cab as he was cranking at the front of the truck and shouted Giddy up! with just a little taunt in her voice, and so they still knew each other just the same.

Then there was work to be done preparing the hives for winter. In a week or two there could be snow on the hilltops, the year before there were heavy spring falls in the valley just before the war ended, earlier in September someone had thrown a lit can of kerosene into 'the Turk' Badem's woodpile – what had they wanted to accomplish by that, freezing the little almonds? So he'd driven over with Adam and a truckload of dry wood – no one had had the guts to say a single word to him about that either then or later. But even so, they were not as far from that kind of thing as Catha might imagine where she was now sitting in the warm parlour drinking tea with Ma and nibbling on a piece of

Ettie's honey cake while feeding little bits to Grace on her lap – it was a scene he had often pictured and held in his thoughts and now there it was – and then Adam came in out of the chilly evening, and when his Aunt Catharina stood up to kiss him with Grace squashed between them he was head and shoulders above her!

But what news of the Professor?

Ettie gave him a look from behind Catha, but his sister just said 'Gone,' with no particular expression, adding 'South America' after a pause that indicated she was unwilling to add even that much.

It was Smithy who'd galloped over from his place at first light – they'd better watch out because some bad buggers had set fire to the Badems' woodpile shed and Smithy reckoned Wolf's lot might be next in line. The Badem woodpile was still smouldering under its collapsed roof when he and Adam arrived with the truckload of firewood. Denis said he and Omer had doused the fire with water from their tank and then with buckets passed up from the river by the two older kids and Omer's wife Nehir. Did he know her name meant river, asked Omer through teeth whitened by the sooty darkness of his face – and just as fucking well they had a river on their side, but she was pregnant again and if anything had happened to her while she was being a pregnant fucking river in the freezing cold he'd have got along to the settlement with his gun for the bastards that did this, he could guess who the fucking bastards were, the same ones who'd knocked over half a dozen hives the week before.

Shush Omer, said Denis, what good would that do? And thank God the woodpile wasn't the house-ah one in the lean-to because then the house-ah would be gone. He and Omer were raking out the logs that could still be used from under the remains of the shed roof and dousing the smoulder. Thank you Wolf, thank you Adam, he said. That is what matters now, to say thank you for the good, not to run offah with your gun like a angry boy.

His voice was so hoarse it could hardly make words at all. Omer said something angry in Turk and bashed sparks out of one of the unsplit rounds with the back of his rake. Adam took the rake from Denis and began to drag the big rounds out. You go and get a cup of tea with Dad, Mister Badem, he said. I can do this. Omer and me can do this, can't we Omer.

He saw Adam's quick look and the jerk of his head that meant bugger off, Dad. The lad was already as tall as Omer who was small and quick like a bird, and when he put his arm around the angry little man's shoulders and turned him towards the work and away from his father, his brawny boy outline obscured Omer's for a while as they began to reach with their rakes into the woodpile.

He stood and watched the smoke that still rose in breezy wisps from the pile as Adam and Omer carefully raked, because it was the three littlies Ettie had lost that were rising and blowing like wispy smoke, the two that were never formed properly and the one that died, the one before Henry that might have been called Henry that Ettie bled out as just a mess that hard first year after she was sick back at the camp, and the one before Josephina that might have been called Josephina that also bled out but you could see the little curled bean-sprout beginning shape of her, and the one that died before Peter that they called Grace who only lived for two weeks because she could never breathe properly and was the sweet colour of a plum, but then there was the last one after Peter that was born strong and noisy that they also called Grace so they could always have the little plum with them.

Winter ade, scheiden tut weh, Goodbye winter, departing hurts, sang the first wisp that could have been Henry as it blew away towards the river where mist was rising while the morning warmed, that was the song Mutti said she sang over and over to Adam at her little house in Bute Street when he was the baby who could never sleep and Ettie had to look after Aggie when she was sick that time with the sore swollen cheeks. Also she sometimes sang *Wie traulich war das Fleckchen wo meine Wiege ging,* it was a song about the cosy spot where a child's cradle had rocked, that one he remembered in the part of his mind that was like the world just before night fell when certain sounds like the morepork's hoot were not exactly anywhere. Across the river was the slope of cleared land that Badem leased to Smithy where the ragwort was doing well. Some of Smithy's sheep were bleating hoarsely over there but it was the second wisp he could hear, *Winter ade, scheiden tut weh,* how could such a guttural sound come from such a tiny little curled thing? – and then the Grace that only lived for two weeks was singing as she blew away into the river mist.

Winter ade, scheiden tut weh.

What are you singing, Dad? Go and get your cup of tea.

Adam's big boy hand on his shoulder steering him towards the kitchen door where Denis Badem was waiting.

Are you all right, Dad?

Smoke and mist and the hoarse cries of spirits across the river.

Then Adam was sitting him down at the Badems' kitchen table.

Nehir who was a river, the glasses of tea, some of the honey.

Adam should drive you home, said Denis, you don't lookah so good. Can you drive, Adam? Thank you for the firewood. We are all right now. You go home. Adam, take your father home. He don't lookah so good.

But he was all right.

Winter ade, scheiden tut weh, under his breath.

'Isn't that the song you used to sing?' said Ettie to Ma in the kitchen as he and Adam came in. 'For the love of God, what made you think of that song, you mad bugger? Go and have a lie-down for goodness sake, Wolf, I'll keep the littlies out of your hair for a bit.'

He lay down in his longjohns without washing off the smell of smoke and Ettie threw the covers over him. The next thing he knew sunlight was coming in the window on the west side of the room, it was already early afternoon at least.

Voices on the other side of the house, Ettie and Ma, and Peter who already had some words, one of them was 'more'.

'More, more!' Banging with his spoon on the table.

He walked through the kitchen past the questions on Ma's and Ettie's faces and took off the longjohns and washed himself all over in freezing water at the tank with the bit of yellow soap there. No, he couldn't tell them that he hadn't wanted to wash off the smell of smoke at first because, because what?

No, he couldn't tell them that.

He put on a good shirt and the fresh suit of clothes he'd taken out of the wardrobe and stood on the porch in the afternoon sunshine polishing his good boots. Bandy little Peter swaggered out so he gave him a boot and a brush to have a go with.

Ettie came out too and frowned at him but he shook his head at her – either she'd guessed what he was up to or she hadn't, either way it made no difference. The kids were going over to Smithy's place for a bit after school, Ettie said, so why was he getting dressed up like that? Of course she probably guessed why.

It was that nice time of day in winter when the air was fresh and clear and the long late-afternoon tree shadows were making stretched-out patterns across the cleared ground down to the river, especially when the house-smoke was blowing away. It was still blowing steadily in the direction of the river and across it, as it had been earlier at Badems', when that old song had come into his head.

Adam hadn't gone to school after driving the truck back from the Badems'. There was little point anyway – in a year or two he'd be working. He'd been keeping an eye out for those buggers, he said, meaning the ones who'd lit the fire. He'd done a bit of clearing-out work over in the veges. Where was Dad going? Could he come?

No, he could not and he needed to saddle Blackie up and be ready to come over quick if anything happened back here at the house. And it was a bit slushy from the frost-melt around the shady back of the house, could Adam get a couple of buckets of gravel from the river?

Come over where?

He'd be at the pub.

Then he cranked the truck and drove slowly up the hill through the rows of poplars he'd planted for their good straight grain. He could start felling some in another four or five years. He could measure how long he and Ettie had already been there by the length of the poplar shadows.

*

They were eating Ma's rabbit stew with the last of the winter carrots. Oh, they had no idea how delicious it was after the food back in town, said Catha with her head thrown back. There they all were around the table, except for Peter who was asleep. Adam had already pushed his empty plate to one side but was waiting for his second helping. Henry had his head down and was shovelling up the stew. Josie was picking at hers. Greta had made an organisation of the carrot pieces and the pieces of rabbit and was rearranging them each time she got one of them on her spoon. Aggie had ridden over from Smithy's and was sneaking looks at her Auntie Cath. Grace was on her auntie's lap, and that Catha sister of his was interrogating him with those sharp blue eyes of hers over the child's head.

Really? Nothing had happened after the woodpile? No one ever bothered the noble house of Wenczel? What was her brother hiding under those wolf eyebrows?

'Das ist aber Wolfscheisse,' she said so the children wouldn't hear the bad word.

He wasn't going to talk about it.

Yes, they were lucky, he said, putting some rabbit in his mouth. Adam was a good shot.

What? He had Adam keeping guard like a trooper?

Of course she was teasing him.

'Rabbits,' he said.

'What, the ones that burned the woodpile?'

He took a swallow of tea and looked No at his sister across the table. No he did not wish to talk about it. She had that smile.

'He went up to the pub,' said Ma. 'It's a story they tell around here now. But what do we know, we weren't there.'

'Ma,' he said.

'He ordered drinks for everybody, so the story goes,' said Ettie. 'There were either a dozen of them, or fifty, depending on who's telling the story. And he was about nine foot tall at the time.'

He pushed his chair back and went out through the kitchen door into the cold night. It was clear and windless and the stars were very bright in the sky. There was one of those owls they called morepork on the other side of the river. It was nearly always there.

More pork, More pork.

My shout, he'd said. Line them up. He'd already spotted the pair he guessed had lit Badems' woodpile. I want to thank you all for your kindness, so come on boys, drink up. Three of my children have died in this valley, this is where we belong. Thank you for your brotherhood.

Then he'd drunk his glass and left. He hadn't waited to see whether the two who'd lit the woodpile drank theirs. It didn't matter. They'd be known, anyway. When he got home Adam was sitting on the porch next to his 303 and who could blame him, still just a boy despite his size, and scared as well, and scared of showing he was scared. He'd thanked Adam and then picked up the gun and ejected the five rounds from its chamber. That was five lives, he told Adam, without anger but holding the boy's still smooth face close to his own with a hand under his chin – five lives that times five is twenty-five and that is already a war, did Adam understand? Now could he go and unsaddle poor old Blackie and give him a good feed, because he wouldn't be needed until school time in the morning, and after he'd done that he could come in and have a cup of tea and some of his ma's honey cake, he was a good boy, his mother and father were proud of him, as well as a bit scared, because he was big as well as brave and might be too brave for his own good sometimes.

A couple of days later Denis Badem rode over with a parcel. This is for you and for your family, for thanksah. Some others had come down to the Badem place with more wood, and with some provisions. Perhaps Missis Josephina would like to open it because she interesting such thingsah?

The thank-you gift was rolled up in sacking like a big sausage and tied with baling twine. Ma frugally undid the knot in the twine, twisted it into a bunch around her hand and tied it off, and then, as if she had been delaying the moment, unrolled the thing on the veranda in the chilly late-afternoon light and then sat back in her chair and looked at it. She and Denis Badem had quite often sat out on the veranda with cups of tea and talked – Ettie had teased her about it at first but had stopped doing that for quite a while now. The gift was a small carpet about six foot long and four-and-a-bit wide. Its colours were old ghosts of red, blue and green. There was a faded blue chain pattern around the border, within that a narrow green border of entwined vines, and within that rows of rectangular frames filled with different kinds of flowers and leaves.

'Is from Iskenderun, old one, silk and a little bit wool.'

Ma was leaning down from her chair and moving her hand across the weave. He couldn't see the expression on her face but could tell what it was like from the way she was moving her hand. Then she sat back and took her handkerchief from the sleeve of her coat and wiped the tears from her cheeks.

'So schön wie ein Traum,' she said.

And yes Denis Badem's carpet was as beautiful as a dream in which things entwined of their own accord – it was surely because the weavers of Iskenderun knew how to show the order that was already in the world, the order they dreamed perhaps even when they were awake and working at their looms. Perhaps they had songs they sang while weaving, songs that had the rhythms of the entwining. He could imagine them sitting and singing at their looms in the patterns of light and shade cast by leaves and branches on the swept tiles of a courtyard, or in the flickers of light that came in to a cool room with old carpets already on the floor, like the ones at the Badem house.

Sometimes Ma sang to herself when she sat sewing on the veranda with the view across the trembling river to the trees on the far side that went on shaking the light from their leaves. *Wie traulich war das Fleckchen.* And now a year later there the carpet was rolled out on the floor away from the table where they had just eaten their tea, where Catha could see it because this was a special occasion with all the family joined up in their own pattern, and she was looking at it and then at him with a question in her brow.

It was a gift of thanks from Denis Badem and his family after the woodpile burning, he told her. He would not take no for an answer, that Denis, such a firm man. And so now a year later it was a reminder that the Badem family and the Wenczel family were connected.

Catha's eyebrow went up.

'And those Hansens, of course,' he added, because now there was Catha in the pattern, and Greta who had always believed the carpet was a magic one from the moment she had watched her grandmother unwrap it under Denis Badem's smiling inspection, and was now looking at the magic carpet as if she expected it to fly off into the night sky at last.

Though it was certainly not the best time to do so and

Ettie's expression said as much, it was then that he asked his thoughtfully gazing sister about Professor Hugo von Welden – perhaps it was because the professor's thread was not included in the pattern of the little carpet spread out for all of them to look at on the kitchen floor of the house he and Ettie had built, starting with slab timber and canvas and ending with verandas on two sides, a honey house just a bit further up the river, good sheds and gardens and hives and some pasture and all the rest of it! And the children who were well fed and schooled and cared for – he didn't say, What kind of man would just bugger off and leave his wife and child and the family that had minded his child for him? – he didn't say it but he guessed from Catha's expression that she had read his thoughts. She tapped with one fingertip on the table and shook her head.

But then she beckoned to Greta who came around the table and stood with her arm around her mother's shoulders. Catha had that look as though she was going to say something – she closed her eyes and made the grimace face he knew happened whenever she was trying to do something she didn't want to – but then it was Greta who piped up clearly and her mother's head turned towards her as if astonished that her quiet daughter would do this.

It was all very well for them all to be all friendly and sympathetic towards the Badems, who were nice enough people, but her father had been a nice kind man as well and had loved her, except the difference was that he had been put in prison and that was different. So who was going to be kind to him when he came out? Probably no one. So now he was in Buenos Aires in Argentina which was in South America next to Chile and Uruguay, and she hoped he would be happy there and that one day she would go and visit him.

Greta stood up straight there next to her mother and blinked, but no tears came; it was as though she wouldn't let them.

'Oh God, I'm sure you will, my darling girl, if anyone can it will be you,' Catha said and then pressed her face into her daughter's narrow chest, certainly that was to hug her but also perhaps to conceal her own tears that she couldn't stop.

Ettie got up with a loud grind of her chair legs against the floor and fetched the bottle of brandy from the cupboard. The last time they'd had a nip in company was when Denis Badem came round with the carpet.

They could all do with one of these, she reckoned, and they should raise a glass to the poor old bloody professor over there all by himself in Buenos Aires or wherever he was while they were at it, and wish him all the best.

Ma's loud sigh was between a laugh and something else less amused. She lifted her glass two-thirds of the way to her lips and paused it there while giving him that direct look her daughter Catharina had inherited, *direkt in die Augen schauen!* as Ma had told him her grandmother instructed her many years ago back in Germany when she was a little girl.

'Wolf Bloch whose first name you have was planning New York when we left Hamburg,' she said, looking him in the eye. 'Or Argentina, perhaps, God knows. Not Wellington in New Zealand that we had never heard anything about as though it didn't even exist. But even so here we are. Wir sind alle Reisende, also, prost! I hope the Professor will be happy somewhere or other near Chile or Uruguay or wherever he ends up, who can tell what will happen.'

Then they all began to raise their glasses, but Ma stopped them with one finger lifted off the side of hers and a sharp tut of her tongue. Catha was looking at her with a grin instead of the almost-tears as if she had guessed what was coming next, which was that they should also be remembering those such as her own mutti and papa who had only ever travelled as far as the old graveyard down by the Schwentine, and her sister Elke who had only ever gone as far as the town of Kiel that could be reached by train in less than an hour, and her sister Greta who had gone as far as Sønderborg just across the border in Denmark but whose name at least had travelled all this way to become this lovely one here in Wolf and Ettie's valley, and then there were her grandfather and two uncles who had gone as far as the burial grounds at Dybbøl just across the water from Sønderborg – there were many ways of travelling aside from crossing oceans in ships, she said, and so once again now: Prost!

And so finally as directed by Ma with that glint in her eye they all raised their glasses and said Prost! and drank off their brandies while the young ones watched in bewilderment and then Catha let out a loud impolite guffaw that startled her polite daughter, but for the life of him he couldn't understand exactly why his sister was so entertained if that was even what described her mood, nor could he fathom what exactly had happened at that moment when the patterns in Denis Badem's carpet seemed to have been rearranged on their loom.

Agatha

Dear town cusin Greta
Now it is getting reely cold here in the valley and I wish I cood be in town were you are with some lights and peeple like the time I visited wen we went on the boat to Day Bay and had an icecreem I ofen think of that day even tho we were just little girls then. Well not any more becos of my news which is that I had a baby a little wile ago here at Smiths place were I have been living, the baby is a girl and becos our granny Josie told me to I have called her Elke wich is the name of one of grannys sisters back in Germany, I dont even now her but thats alright I dont care, and anyway you got the name of another granny sister and you didnt turn in to a strange german girl unless you just did. Mum and granny came to help with the baby beeng born, one day you will have to do that and so I wont tell you about it becos it wood scare you off having a baby that is certin. Dad came a few days later he held the baby and then he and Smithy had a talk outside you can probly guess wat that was all about. Well then here I am in this valley at the End of the World and perhaps I can come and visit you agen in town with baby Elke wen she is a bit more growd. I do like her but perhaps I will like her even more after a wile. Anyway that is my news wot else cood there be to tell you about down here and so goodbye until we meet agane

your cusin Aggie

Greta

Dear Cousin Aggie

Well my goodness, first of all congratulations on having baby Elke, I hope you and the baby's father will be very happy and that baby Elke will be healthy and happy as well. Mama told me that you were going to have a baby but of course the news that you have given birth is very special, especially as it comes directly from you the actual mother! I can clearly imagine you and the baby in a cosy chair looking across the dear old river from the porch at the back of your house and I think it must be a kind of heaven. I can tell from your letter that you are not so happy with life in the Valley, but I am sure that you will love it again when you have recovered from the pains of the birth which I understand to be severe. I would love to see you and baby Elke here in town one day and I am sure Mama will be glad too. I will certainly ask her if you can come to visit us. We are moving house soon because this one is too big and so I will write to you when we are in our new one.

My news is not very exciting compared to yours. Mama made me stay in school until the last year which was mostly very boring but now I have begun to be trained as a journalist at the Evening Post Newspaper which is not boring at all, in fact it is exciting and sometimes frightening as well. I am a cadet and mostly am required to write news stories for the Women's Pages, but what I like most is writing reviews of the films that are showing here in town. Some weeks I even go to two or three of them and then have very quickly to write reviews or I get told off by the editor! I think my favourite so far is 'Salome' by William Fox starring Theda Bara as the beautiful and seductive Salome. It was at the Queen's Theatre last week and showed the glory of Judea forty years before the time of Christ, although there were some representatives of the churches in Wellington who protested that the story was untrue and blasphemous and forbade their congregations to see it! I am sure that many of them went anyway because the season was extended by a week. One of the sensations in the film is the Dance of the Seven Veils. Some of the people in the audience when I was there got up and left when Theda Bara was doing her dance, but I thought it was wonderful even if quite revealing sometimes! There is a moment where Salome even shows a part of her naked bosom, and at that moment the sound of the audience gasping (before they left!) could even be heard above the sound of the pianist trying her best to imitate the choreography of the Seven Veils!

Anyway that is enough about me. I can add that Mama is well and very busy with her teaching, but I hope she will be able to rest a bit more soon because I can see that she has begun to be tired more often than she used to. She has begun to play the piano more often too, mostly in the evenings, I think it's because she is finding it harder to read as much as she likes.

I will write to tell you when we have moved to our new house, and meanwhile please send us news of baby Elke and yourself, and of course also of Granny Josie and everybody at Uncle Wolf's and Aunty Ettie's place.

With love from your cousin Greta, and a kiss for baby Elke

Beth

Rangamati Hill District, Chittagong Hill Tracts, Bengal, April 26th, 1937

This is my Cool the Snake Entry as I shall explain in due course though not before prolonging the mystery for a few more sentences, my apologies Dear Reader!

The end of Basanta is nigh, so says Dulal who is writing this for me. I will explain this too, in a while. It should be cool but this morning the sun rose above the river in a thick cloud of its own dry heat. The heat cloud was smouldering dully as if reflecting the ghastly cremation ghats smoking on the riverbank. Now that the spring dysentery season is in full plague cry my entire picking workforce has fled to the Upper Hill Tracts where they believe the air is clean, though it is not the air that infects them as we now know. Well I can only wish them a safe return when the dry season has passed and hope that the fresh tea tips wait patiently for my people to come back and pick them. Meanwhile I must live in peace and boil my water since that is where the good doctor at Chandraghona believes the plague resides and God knows he has evidence enough befouling his compound!

Beth was following the clear and even fastidious handwriting on the page with one hesitant finger, as if the writing itself was hard to grasp and not what it was telling her. So then with a sense of having been caught out struggling to understand what was writ plain, she tucked her anxious finger under the cover of the notebook and read on.

> When Dulal brought our tea to the veranda this morning he said he had found a large snake in the dry monsoon drain behind the kitchen. It was cool in the drain he said, and so he left the snake there, what harm could it do. It was a striking image at this time of peril. If this peaceful snake is an omen I wonder what we should call it: Cool, the snake, perhaps. Yes, let us all Cool The Snake I suggested. Dear Dulal was perhaps somewhat alarmed by my suggestion as I think he took it as a reference to my wretched leg.

The diary was the last one of a dozen or so cheap A5 notebooks in plain brown cardboard covers packed by someone, she thought Frank's granddaughter Lizzie, in their own dedicated foolscap box and labelled FREDERICK with a hand-drawn smiley-face emoji. The sense of order in the box seemed to come from the uniform notebooks themselves as much as from the way they'd been packed. She'd picked the last notebook by date out of those neatly organised in double rows with a couple of envelopes, one large and one small, on top, and opened it about two-thirds through. A bad habit of wanting to just get a glimpse of how the story might end before starting at the beginning – she'd always done it even as a kid. She still remembered the ending of *The Tale of Peter Rabbit* by Beatrix Potter: 'I am sorry to say that Peter was not very well during the evening. His mother put him to bed, and made some chamomile tea; and she gave a dose of it to Peter! "One table-spoonful to be taken at bed-time." But Flopsy, Mopsy, and Cotton-tail had bread and milk and blackberries for supper.'

Saying the words aloud reminded her that she had always insisted Elke read that bit first because it made whatever had caused Peter Rabbit to need the chamomile (whatever that was!) tea into a secret she already gloatingly knew the meaning of.

But of course as yet she had no idea what Freddy meant by 'my wretched leg', nor what being the last diary in the box meant, although that meaning was perhaps bleeding obvious if 'bleeding' was the appropriately sympathetic expression at the juncture of the 'wretched leg', which could have been bleeding uncontrollably for all she knew or just a bit overheated like the poor snake, and she would have to restrain herself for the time being.

But why did or should she even care? She had so far read with curiosity and bewilderment but little interest in Freddy, whom she had encountered previously only in one brief schoolboy diary note that it had even shamed her to have intruded on. She had no special sense of duty to either Frank's mother Greta who had first taken responsibility for the materials in her mother Catharina's care, nor to Frank's sister Ruth who had got them from their mother Greta. Even thinking about the 'tree' of these relationships was a bit of a chore, let alone visualising where her own mother Elke fitted in, if she even did, or if she had ever known or cared about Freddy, and certainly not about his Cool Snake!

But all right, fine! – she could at the very least be doing this for bloody old Frank who might be spooked by his sister Ruth's presence in the stuff.

She could at a stretch think of the two-thirdish 'Cool the Snake' diary entry in April 1937 as a kind of prologue to the tragic finale that she would encounter in due course after she had dutifully begun again at the beginning – but then, as if prompted, the phrase 'a stitch in time' popped up in her head. It was a phrase that her dear disorganised Elke-mum used to utter from time to time with a bewildered expression, as if the segue to 'saves nine' was beyond her, as it probably was, but it aptly enough described the reading methodology that she, Beth, had preferred for most of her life. And save nine what? Other stitches? Sutures? Lives?

Her own grandma the legendary Aggie Wenczel had taken in quite a few stitches-in-time by popping Elke-mum out at barely eighteen, and then wasting no time or stitches by leaving her in the care of the kindly Smiths in the Kaitīeke valley and vanishing without trace via the main trunk line. And then there was the summer visit down the valley 'that time forgot' when Elke had appeared intermittently between the trees on the other side of the Retaruke River, barking like a dog, but why? It had something to do with the fact that 'the bastard', whom she, Beth, as a child barely remembered except as a thick moustache that always seemed to be raised a fraction on one side above a thin show of teeth, had buggered off with the woman known as 'the flutterer' on account of her eyelashes. Of course 'He was all a-flutter' etc, which at age six or was it seven meant she'd pictured her father fluttering away somewhere like a big moustachioed semi-smile, a kind of Edward Lear illustration that she had nurtured into adulthood and understood there, though not with the mercilessly surreal truth of a child.

Frederick – Freddy, rather – continued his 'Cool the Snake' entry for 'April 26th, 1937, Rangamati Hill District, Chittagong Hill Tracts, Bengal' by describing in quite elegant prose the 'rhythmical creaking and plashing' – plashing! – of the long twin dripping oars of a riverboat going downstream 'with an overload of argumentative passengers destined perhaps for the filthy entrepôt of Chittagong and away from the relative sanitariness of the Rangamati' – adding 'poor devils' in a tone that seemed at once sweetly sympathetic and patronising, rather like the 'my people' earlier in his account.

There was a yellowed envelope on top of the diaries that, since it was in fact on top, was perhaps the true beginning of the 'Cool the Snake' narrative, so perhaps she should begin there, having quickly put it aside at first.

It was impossible to tell if the yellowed envelope had been opened before because the gum had lost its stickiness and the envelope flap was unsealed. The neat, faded writing on the front of the envelope addressed it oddly to Mrs Catharina Hansen, Please Care Of Marlborough College, In Stephenson Street, In Blenheim, In New Zealand – the town in which her great-aunt and Frank's grandmother Catharina had ended her days about 1956, if she remembered the reunion's tree correctly, but not before taking certain erratic girls under her firm but kindly educator's wing for summer holidays – for example, her brother Wolf's granddaughter Elke, who had in due course occasionally reminisced about 'Aunty Catha's' kindly orderliness and how she liked to play the piano after supper, which had not increased Elke's own orderliness nor curtailed her propensity to do weird stuff like run along the bank of the Retaruke barking like a dog.

Perhaps the true-to-self honest hand-on-heart reason she'd quickly put the letter aside at first and also ignored the second, larger official-looking one and fled to the last diary in the box was because she guessed the personal-looking letter would open a portal to a whole lot more stuff than she wanted to deal with just now under the knowing, one-eyed squint of Frank's galah head, not to mention the bit-too-patient tone of Joe's voice when he asked how was it going with the tomb-raider stuff, meaning what about the present with him and her grandkids in it?

What indeed. Good question.

However.

The thin double-sided lined paper inside the first, 'Please Care Of Marlborough College' envelope was folded very carefully in three, with writing only on the hidden, folded-over side, and did indeed look as though it had never been unfolded – at any rate, the envelope had not been slit open in the conventional way. Either that, or the letter inside the already unsealed envelope had been refolded with care and put back.

She was dithering. Read the damn thing.

The paper looked like the kind in cheap school exercise books and had a carefully torn-out margin. Its appearance was already another little story-mystery – whose exercise book had it been torn out of? And come to think of it, the letter might well have been written last, after the diaries had been organised as a consignment. So the letter could be the end, not the beginning, of this story in which a snake lay cooling itself in a dry storm drain while people's corpses went up in smoke on the cremation ghats and while her great-granduncle Freddy Wenczel lay nursing his 'wretched leg' in a tea plantation somewhere on the banks of a river upstream from 'the filthy entrepôt of Chittagong' and somewhat below the 'upper hill tracts' deemed healthy by the locals – 'my people' – in somewhere called Rangamati.

The ending that was in fact located at the beginning was in the same well-schooled, old-fashioned handwriting as the notebook entry she'd read first. It too was in what would once have been dark-blue ink, now a bit purplish, and faithfully followed the lines on the paper, with the tails of such letters as 'y' curled precisely below the line and the tops of such upreaching letters as 'l' stopping just a tiny bit below the line above. She was struck by the responsible pattern of the written sheet, without yet considering what was written there. It was like the careful handwriting of a well-schooled, diligent student, not of a grown or even ageing man used to writing quickly and unceremoniously with his thoughts trying to outpace his pen.

But then.

Below a traditionally formal letter-heading that identified the writer as Mister Frederick Wenczel and his place of residence as Waggachara Tea Estate, Rangamati, Bengal, appeared the date of the letter's composition, July 5, 1937.

A kind of hiccup or gasp of grief surprised her at that moment – the Freddy who had remarked so beautifully if also terrifyingly on the thick cloud of the sun's own dry heat and the peaceful snake in its cool drain had perhaps consigned his diaries to the person the letter was addressed to, Mrs Catharina Hansen, not long before his death?

My Dear Sister Catharina

I have obtained your current address through the kind offices of your old school in Wellington which of course shamefully dates my attempt to find you again after all these years. And so first of all I must ask you to forgive me for disappearing so completely from the world in which we began to grow up happily together even allowing for the fact that from early on I inhabited a different world from yours as if I had shaken the poisoned dust of that place off my shoes and set out to find another different place beyond its ken and the gaze of those who had to all intents and purposes banished me.

Of course to all intents and purposes shake the dust off my shoes is what I did but my banishment was never something I felt you were party to Catha, may I call you that again after all these years my dear sister, and so it is you that I wished to find again and to make the consignee and guardian in whatever degree you think appropriate of these few records of my life which has been one lived without regret except for the absence of you my big sister and indeed also of that enigmatic brother of mine, Wolf. I long ago forgave our mother for turning her back on me and I hope her life has been a happy and fulfilling one as I hope have those of my sister and brother.

This letter is being dictated to my dear friend and companion of many years, his name is Dulal Tarafdar. The reason for the dictation is that I am sick with an infection in my leg that together with its remedies including the poppy that is abundant in these hills have rendered me more or less paralysed or prone to ghastly tremors, and so with many a break for refreshing cups of the tea that is also rather abundant hereabouts Dulal and I are progressing slowly and carefully through this letter in which I want first and foremost to send you all my benighted love, and secondly to give a brief account of what I have been doing for thirty or so years God help us, and thirdly to make some provisions if not exactly in the form of a will then in an expression of wishes and hopes.

Let us not dwell on the events that led to my friend Will and myself making ourselves scarce to Sydney before Will's cruel uncle Mayor Hastings could press charges, what a quaint expression. We occupied the ship's rail for most of our squally five bob deckside passage. Will went to seek his fortune in the goldfields of a place called Coolgardie, the name I have never forgotten nor have I ever forgotten my dear pal, though I never heard from him again.

Dulal and I are going very slowly as I have to spell out some of the words he does not know, our progress resembles that of the turgid river below our hill as it meanders imperceptibly towards the ancient effluent city of Chittagong and into the Bay of Bengal where its filthy corona extends in an arc for many miles out to sea. It was this discoloured embrace that welcomed me to the place where I have now resided for close on a decade and where I expect to end my life's journey – but let me retrace my steps.

In Sydney I worked in an excise office where my adequate knowledge of German was appreciated and where I bored myself into departing as soon as I had the means to do so. Had I gone to Coolgardie with Will I might have picked up a nugget of gold the size of my foolish brain and retired in luxury as I hope he did, but I doubt it.

My next port was Bremerhaven, the one from which our mother fled, whence out of curiosity I made my way via Hamburg to the town of her birth, Kiel, from which I too fled in haste without attempting to find remnants of her family anywhere in the environs of what the boring boastful townsfolk called the Kriegshafen, its streets filled with strutting marines and its harbour with boastful flags and bunting fluttering above the grey befunnelled hulls of warships. It was the Flaggengala I was told proudly, we would call it the flag dressing I think. To me it had the simple brutal meaning of a hostile animal enlarging itself and baring its teeth in order to appear terrifying.

I fled from this display back to Hamburg where there was much talk of the injustice of the defeat of the majority social democrats in the elections due to the over-representation of the landed gentry, which reminded me of our mother's scanty accounts of the reasons she and the man she called Wolf Bloch left in the first place on what has now begun to resemble an uncharted dynastic exodus.

Thence to San Francisco thanks to the patronage of the businessman I shall call Uncle Joe, and here I resided quite happily for some years and learned the 'Uncle Joe' ways of money and how not to push too much of it ahead of oneself where it might become prey, but on the other hand how to push enough of it ahead into places where it might become bait and thereby catch some more of itself. Not to mention how to stuff some of it into cave vaults and the grinning pockets of lawyers.

Time for my pipe, that can be written and I shall explain.

Thence in haste to London after the war where Uncle Joe's war gains found profitable opportunities aplenty, whence quite soon at my own whim into the fragrant embrace of the budding Good Will Tea Company, the name of which reawakened my affectionate memories. In addition, Good Will Tea being new to the game of attracting the interest of investors in the capital city of its war weary colonial administration, found my by now well practised 'Uncle Joe' skills useful.

Now I think we should speed up Dulal, please write that down in case my poor sister is about to throw my letter out the window.

My nearly seven years of dutiful Good Will passed within walking distance of the British Museum where I fed my boredom to the arcane fires of cosmological scholarship and got a succession of telescopes none of which could often see through the vile smog that was named after London itself.

I cannot in honesty pretend that London was without pleasures of a less cerebral kind but I shall move past them to the next stage of my life so ho ho. And then my telescopes and I were invited to manage the Good Will estates in Bengal from a base here on this river and under these gorgeous skies that are as clear as any in the universe except when the rains come or the cut and burn tribespeople further up set their fires, and consequently I have spent much of my time in this remote place where the plague seasons come and go with the placid fatalism of centuries, with one eye at my telescope and the other making a show of observing the seasons of plants, people, trade and capital investments.

I came here towards the end of nineteen twenty eight and have never wished to be anywhere else since, and so will now begin to finish my letter to you my dear sister though I am unwilling to do so as this has been as close as I have come to talking to you for the better part of thirty-two years, can either of us believe that! None of what I have written may be of any interest to you of course but I hope the small cosmological document I have included with this letter may tell you something about the strange little brother you lost that will be more enduring and perhaps also endearing, what a marvellous word, than these brief notes.

Now to explain about the pipe. It is the product of the poppy that I inhale from it as that is the only relief I can have from my leg up which the infection rot climbs no matter what I or the good doctor at Chandraghona do, and so it must part company from the rest of me or I from it, who knows which of us will win the race, and in any case the pipe has been my other dearly loved companion for many years here in this place that resembles paradise in many ways not least of which is the snake that from time to time these past months can be seen cooling itself or perhaps lying in wait patiently in a drain not far from where I lie, a man possessed of more knowledge than was ever good for me perhaps but with no regrets.

And so farewell my dear sister Catharina! I always loved you very dearly and believed your life would be a rich one in the best sense of that word if not the sense beloved of Uncle Joe.

And now here are my few wishes. I hope they will not trouble your time. Please believe that I trust you to respect them.

Frederick Wenczel's signature here.

And there the signature was, but only just, F Wencz, with a shaky entwining of the 'c' and 'z' and an ink blot at the end.

Oh lord. She went to the loo and blew her nose into a good handful of toilet paper and then flushed it away with an immature sense of performing a meaningful ritual. How could it be that the dictated message from her great-granduncle could have put the sound of his voice so clearly in her mind?

But there he was, and so was this unexpected grief that seemed to reach out to her own mother Elke, who hadn't even known Freddy, and even to Ruth, whom she had never known except in the life-fragment Frank had told her about.

The next part of the letter, the one with the 'few wishes', was written in a different hand, fluid and unfussy and she presumed Freddy's own from an earlier time in his decline, on a plain unlined sheet of good-quality cream paper. This sheet had enfolded the lined ones that had first captured her interest with their oddness. The plain cream one now seemed bland by comparison and without the presence of Freddy's voice, perhaps because that voice had been preserved in its intimate engagement with his friend Dulal while dictating?

She read the four brief and to-the-point sentences without any particular emotion. Their implications did not seem profound or problematic. They were, in fact, somewhat clerical, as if the work of a man used to keeping his reports short and unambiguous.

1. I appoint Mr Dulal Tarafdar to be my legal executor as certified by my signature below and notarised by the legal representative of the Christian Hospital Chandraghona and witnessed by the hospital's Director Dr. George Orissa Taylor.
2. All my personal possessions including furniture not the property of the Good Will Company I leave to Mr Dulal Tarafdar in recognition of his loyal service.
3. My personal cash reserves held at the National Bank of India Chittagong Branch I require Mr Tarafdar as my appointed executor to administer for the settlement of any outstanding debts, the balance to be retained by him, again in recognition of his loyal service and friendship.
4. My stock holdings in the Good Will Tea Company registered at the Central Exchange Bank of India, London, I leave to my sister Catharina von Welden of Wellington, New Zealand, to distribute to my family at her discretion.

There remained the other, larger manila envelope, also ambiguously opened or not on account of its loose flap, and of course what also remained was the duty of starting at the beginning. But no, she would not, or not now.

The letter and the expression of last wishes were not in any convincing sense the final word from Freddy, since they were, rather, postscripts to his narrative. And so, with a sense of trembling in her chest rather than in her fingers, she turned to the final entry in the 1937 diary of Frederick Wenczel of Waggachara Tea Estate, Rangamati, Bengal, and read his brief, erratic, barely comprehensible account in the second week of October of how

> When one first arrives at this place via the jetty on the other side of the river from the tea garden, where a busy little market thrives under many clustered bamboo shops designed to blow or be washed away and then rebuilt with little effort, one encounters what the new arrival cannot hope to find words to express, the smell of fish drying on racks in the sun combined with that of human excrement squirted out along the marge of the river, and the other ingredient, that of rotting fruits of which the ripe and fit to eat aroma is already of vomit. Already sick and weary from my long journey and its several mishaps, this welcome was enough to empty what remained of my desiccated reserves into the river that itself had the pallid appearance of a fever patient. But then, after several weeks, a strange and marvellous thing happened. I began to long for that mélange of smells and to relish it and even regard it as the emanation of an unforgiving but truthful and indeed loving divinity that knew the world and the creatures that lived upon it as the eflux of a great cosmic life-force,

indeed I am sure the very breath of the forces that we call the gods. And so after many years in the presence of this familiar atmosphere I have lived my last days in a state of bliss knowing that what I am breathing in will be what I enter into at the moment when I contribute my last breath to it. And so,

তুমি শান্তিতে থাক
Peace be with you.

Outside it was almost dark and she sat with the diary in her lap and listened to the small, settling-down sounds of the neighbourhood – intermittent traffic on the bypass road, some kids on scooters calling out shrilly from someone's driveway, clattering plates and the sound of hesitant piano scales from next door as early dinner was prepared, the young solo mum who had recently moved in there calling out almost unintelligibly above the clatter and the piano scales, something about Did you remember to? – the annoyed clang of a piano key and a girl's voice calling out, Oh shit, no, sorry Mum.

Wolf

Her body was smaller somehow like one of the poplars after the autumn gales had taken away its leaves, or the river when a summer drought exposed more of its stones than usual, or even like the sky when it was clear and simple and of course blue like Ma's eyes – he pressed their lids unwillingly shut with his thumb but could not quite close her poor mouth and then knelt by the bed with his head against her hard little shoulder. There was still just a very little warmth remaining in the bedclothes, he thought, he was almost sure, but not enough and no breath from her open mouth. Three great sobs entered him from across the river, they struck him below his ribs and then burst out of his mouth like shouts. It was still early and the grey warblers that Ma loved so much were trilling in the manuka he'd allowed to grow back along the riverbank over there below her open window, to hold the bank together but also for the blossom. Because it was early summer the manuka flowers that she also loved were still abundant and so were the bees that shared her affection for them. Few things had made her happy these past months but the warblers and the manuka flowers were among them and now there they were as was appropriate.

No more of the sobs struck his body below his lungs, winding him and demanding to be let out – he began to breathe slowly as if resting after a steep climb and after a time there was Ettie's hand on his shoulder but then she went away again and closed the door. He could hear them all being quiet on the other side of the door, and the careful clinking of cups being got ready. There was no need for him to go out there until he chose to and anyway Ma would have to be washed and dressed and her bed changed before anyone could visit her, she had always been particular. Her hair would have to be done neatly as she liked, it would have upset her to know she was being seen with it bedraggled out across the pillow. She always took particular care with her hair when Denis Badem was coming for his cup of tea and their chat on the veranda but of course that hadn't happened going on four years now. Was it about the time he died that she began to be a bit quieter?

Of course it was mostly after she heard from Catha about Freddy last year.

But there was the time back then a while ago when Ettie came in to where he was having his own cup of tea in the kitchen – she had her hand over her mouth but her grin escaped around it and crinkled up the corners of her eyes. His ma and that old rogue Denis Badem were making kissing shapes at each other with their lips stuck out, she said. No, he didn't believe it! Well then, go and have a look for yourself, said Ettie in a huff. He went out to the veranda pretending to ask if they wanted more tea but what he heard was the little experimental whistling sounds of their stuck-out lips trying to imitate the twitter of the little grey warblers that Ma loved.

Oh yes, Ma and Denis Badem were two little old lovebirds, was the joke he and Ettie shared for a while, they were two warblers in the bush! But then when he asked Ma to demonstrate the warbler twitter she and Denis had been practising out on the porch that time she said that no, it wasn't the bush warbler from round here they were trying to imitate because the ones from round here never left to go anywhere else! – no, they were birds called roar singer that lived in the reedy marshes near where she was born in the north of Germany.

A roar singer?

She made an impatient face and said the words slowly, roar *senger*, 'Auf Deutsch, nicht wahr?' They lived in the reeds down at the mouth of the river Schwentine, in English a reed warbler or something like that *nicht wahr* and when the weather began to get chilly in late autumn all the little birds would begin to gather in crowds and fly away as if they were testing their wings, and then one day they would all be gone. Her mutti had told her the roar sengers all flew away to somewhere warm and when she was a little girl she had always imagined that the warm place where they went had many sweet orange trees, because she had loved the special treat of oranges that sometimes came ashore from those warm places over there in the merchant ships at Kielerhafen. It was the twitter of the roar sengers that she and Denis had been trying to imitate because he remembered them and their song as well.

But how could that be, when he didn't come from that place she remembered?

Ma had a certain wicked look then as if she had won a victory, but what kind of victory would that be? She made her lips into the kissing shape and managed to do a little whistle-trill that did not really sound very much like the warblers down in the manuka by the river but also it did somewhat. But then she said that where Denis Badem came from at Iskenderun in the Levant the roar sengers were well known, they arrived in flocks every year, people said they came from where it was too cold for them at that time of year, and what was more, where Denis and his family came from there were many very old orange groves, he told her, his family had one, they ate the oranges all the time and also made sugared sweets out of the rinds, and orange blossom water to perfume certain kinds of food and refresh the air in a room. Women would also refresh their skin with the orange blossom water, and some people would sprinkle it on their pillows at night because it would help them to dream sweet dreams!

Ah, said Ma, how she would have liked to experience that, even putting the orange blossom water on her skin, but especially to sprinkle it on her pillow.

All her life she had believed this was the truth about the roar sengers and their journey away from the frozen marsh at the mouth of the Schwentine, but she had only now found out that it was true, what she had always believed was true, because Denis Badem was from that place and he had seen them arriving year after year after their long journey, those brave little birds that especially liked catching insects off the orange trees, and especially a certain beetle that would otherwise damage the trees, and so the little birds were always welcomed and it was forbidden he said to kill and eat them, unlike many other ones that boys would sell strings of on the roadsides, sparrows and suchlike that they trapped in nets, people liked to grill them on skewers, they were delicious he said.

He'd come out of Ma's room on the morning he found her dead and there were Ettie and Adam and Grace all looking at him as if they expected him to say that she was dead when they already knew she was. There was some tea ready on the table and it was as though they were waiting for him to just straight away sit down as if nothing had happened and have a nice cup of tea! Then Ettie put her arms around him and said sit down for a bit and we'll work out what to do next, but he already knew what he had to do next. Just leave her, leave Ma! he told them, he'd be back soon. Then he got his coat and hat on and went out and started the truck. Ettie was at the back door with her hand to her mouth. He remembered that sight of her for a long time afterwards and felt bad about it, but he knew what he had to do despite the memory of Ettie with her hand at her mouth. He was driving as though his body had taken over from his mind that was full of thoughts and images about Ma and not of how the road's twists and turns went, although he knew them all well. He swerved to miss a silly stray sheep that was panicking and running bleating in the road but it was just his body that did it, not his attention to the road.

When he got to the Badem house Asian came out and greeted him with a nice handshake and asked how was he? It was clear from his expression that he saw something was wrong and of course it was, but what could he say at that point apart from? – And so would he mind calling his dad, he told the serious young man whose eyebrows had almost closed his eyes with their weight of worry.

But of course, please come in. Please, Mister Wenczel! Please, Wolf!

No he preferred to wait because he was in a hurry.

And then when Omer soon came out with a worried look he just asked straight away did they still have any of that orange blossom water because his mother had died early that morning and one of her last wishes had been to have some of the special water to bathe her skin with, not that she had spoken about it in such a direct way. Then Omer shook his hand very firmly and held it tight while he shouted to Asian in Turk. Then Nehir was there with her hand to her mouth just like Ettie. Yes of course they had some of that orange flower water but now they made it themselves because they had those sweet orange trees growing out the back, she Nehir made it, her mother had taught her, it was the truthful water.

The orange blossom water Nehir brought out with trembling hands was in an old lemonade bottle with a sprung-wire porcelain stopper – Nehir put it in his hands and then held them for a moment with the cool bottle there between them. They were all trying to find the right words and shake his hand that wasn't holding the bottle against his chest but he didn't wait, he took the lemonade bottle of orange blossom water and drove back past the stray sheep making it run hopelessly bleating into a fence, and then he drove on to where Ettie and the two others were waiting and told them that now they should wash Ma and make her tidy, they should of course bathe her skin with this orange blossom water since that was what she had always wanted but perhaps had been too shy to ask Denis Badem for, but now that hardly mattered. And now he would rather just sit outside on the porch for a while if they didn't mind. So Ettie and Grace went in to the room where Ma was, and Adam came and sat with him on the porch.

After quite a while sitting there looking ahead in the direction of the river Adam said he remembered when Grandma first came to live with them, he'd have been about five or six, she used to sit out here and sew.

But how could he remember that, he'd have been too young.

But he did remember, because she had that old thing with pictures sewn on it, a little house and stuff like that. She told him stories, he used to like those stories.

Ah yes of course! – so then he got up and hurried back inside leaving Adam clambering to his feet in a what's-the-matter kind of way. Nothing was the matter, but he didn't have time to tell Adam it was just as well he'd reminded him about the old sampler because when he went into Ma's room where Ettie and Grace had drawn the covers away and were starting to take Ma's nightdress off he turned his face away and blurted where was the old sewing sampler thing of Ma's? – because they had to put that on top of the bed when they had finished making her tidy, and were they wiping her down with the orange blossom water?

Of course they were, they said even a little impatiently.

And so then he went hastily back out again to the porch where Ma had liked to sit and this time Adam put his big warm heavy arm across his shoulders so that he could feel the comforting warmth and substance in it and told him to take it easy, just sit still out here for a while, Dad, there was nothing more he could do. He Adam would telephone Henry, he could easy come down from Taumarunui with his wife and the kids, and the others too from wherever, it was simple. Aunty Cath was already on her way on the ferry from down there in Blenheim because he'd phoned her last week when Grandma stayed in bed. Henry could be here tomorrow and so could Greta on the train, probably with Aunty Cath. Josie and her husband would probably drive down from Auckland with their kids, they had that flash car now, a bloody Rover 14, they could give Peter a lift from St John's, they could be here day after tomorrow at the latest in time for the funeral.

Yes it was a pretty flash car all right that Rover, he said to Adam but as if the words coming out of his mouth were being said by someone else and he was hearing them not saying them. He was remembering that Ma went pretty quiet last year after hearing about Freddy. A few weeks later Josie and her lot visited in their flash new car and that was when out of the blue Ma said she wanted a couple of things buried with her when the time came, they were in the little top left-hand drawer of her tallboy in the bedroom. She said what she did about the things in the tallboy as though she'd been thinking about them for a while and had decided in her own Ma way that then was the best time to say something about it even though Josie was talking about her kids and their achievements. No one knew what to say at the time except Oh Ma! But back then and over the months after hearing about Freddy she was often quiet as though taking time to think about her life, though she never once talked about it.

He went to get up and go to the tallboy to see what was in the top left-hand drawer but Adam's big arm just stayed where it was across his shoulders.

Elke was mooching about down at the Smiths', said Adam, he could give her a ring in a bit. Just take it easy. They could all between them sort out what had to be done. Just sit tight for a while, Dad, there's no need to agitate yourself.

Agi-tate!

The word sounded so unlike anything Adam would ever say that he began to laugh. What did he mean, agitate?

You know – jump up and down all the time.

What, like a bloody spring lamb or something?

You know what I mean, Dad.

But of course come to think of it they would have to organise some food for everybody. Would Adam mind butchering one of the new-season hoggets?

The big arm lifting off his shoulders.

Come off it, Dad. Goodness sake.

Then Ettie came out on to the porch. He heard the sound of her, those quick movements, he knew them with his eyes shut, no one else moved quite like that, but there was a difference, it was the faint smell of orange flowers that he'd sniffed from the neck of Nehir's lemonade bottle before driving home from their place earlier.

He could come in and see his mum now, Ettie said. She put her hands against his cheeks from behind. They were warm and had that orange flower smell. And so he got up and went inside with her. The door to Ma's room was open, there was the faint smell of the orange flower water, and what he noticed at once was how dim it was in there and so the first thing he did was cross the room and open the curtains because that was what she had always liked to do in the mornings while the sun was still on her side of the house. And then there she was, very neat and tidy, with the broad stripe of sunshine across her on the sewing sampler thing. Ettie and Grace had closed her mouth with a nice blue scarf tied over her hair and fastened under her chin, she looked as though she was getting ready for an outing maybe a picnic down the river past Smithy's where there was that shingly shallow at the bend. Back in the day she'd even hopped in there herself sometimes, his little ma, she'd sit up to her waist in the water and wave her hands around in it because she thought that otherwise the eels might like to give her a nip. Not a lot of you for them to nip at Ma, he used to tease her, and it was true, the band of sunshine was lifted only slightly by the outline of her under the coverlet and the old sampler – the sunshine was flickering a little from the shaking leaves outside her window, it was like flickering water down there where they had their picnics.

'Not a lot of you for them to nibble on, Ma,' he said, and

then saw the horror on Ettie's and Grace's faces on the other side of the bed and the shock of that shoved aside something in his mind that had been getting in the way and there he was in the time of it, in the time of Ma there so neat and tidy just the way she always liked to be and with her hands folded on the sampler.

They'd had a good laugh about it finally after he explained that what he'd meant by the nibbling was the way Ma used to flap her hands in the water down at the bend, to keep the eels away, not . . . The laughter went on for a while with Ettie wiping her eyes and saying stop it! – but by the time the laughing did stop it had cleared a space around what had to be done so they could all just get on with the job. He could stop being so agitated like Adam reckoned he was and just move around his share of the work with time to think about it, in the time of what was happening there.

The poplar planks he and Adam had stacked to dry out in the shed six months ago were still a bit green but some could be mortised quickly enough, it would be good to put his mind to that work and make a proper job of it. Adam could help him when he had time but otherwise if Adam didn't mind he would prefer to be working by himself in the sunlight that came through the open doors of the shed, that was a good place to be at this time. He liked the way the pale straight-grained shavings curled down to the floor from his plane and the dust that floated in the sunshine inside the door. The warblers were down there in the bush by the river, he thought he could just hear them from time to time, and voices from the house.

He could tell that they were leaving him alone and he

didn't mind that. Grace brought him a cup of tea and a couple of cold-mutton sandwiches later on, so it had to be dinner time back over at the house with that leg of cold mutton left over from yesterday. She gave him a hug and said it looked lovely, Dad, what he was doing.

There was a spider that had stitched her web across the windowpane in the western wall, she was sitting off to one side of her web and was still there when the sun got round that way in the afternoon. 'Ah, so you're keeping an eye on me are you?' he said to her, glad that no one was there to hear him talking aloud to himself as if he thought that Ma was watching his work with that sharp look she had, but perhaps she was!

He heard the truck drive away a bit later but didn't bother to think about why, it would be Adam or Ettie on an errand. The three planed base-boards he'd fastened simply with short finishing nails from the forge, fastening batons across them for the inside and the side-boards likewise, they could be covered inside with some cloth later when the thing was finished, but now he could fasten the base-boards and the sides and the ends together with the mortises. They would make the thing neat and tidy the way Ma liked and people would see that care had been taken.

He was chiselling one of them out a bit too quickly but still carefully with his best narrow blade when he heard the truck return and then Catha calling out, 'Wolf! Wolf!' – and then Adam's voice rumbling quite loud but he couldn't hear what – but then there was his sis Catha in the doorway, the late sun made her fair, now nearly white hair glow around her face that he couldn't see clearly because of the light behind her, but he could see the dark shape of her open mouth that he then held against his chest feeling the warmth of her gasps, he held her there as if to capture the sounds that she was making and put them inside himself. Then she quickly stepped aside and put her hand lightly on the work he had done throughout the day and they went over to the house with that hand in his and Adam coming along behind with Catha's old carpetbag that had been their Ma's once. He remembered Catha wanting to keep it when Ma first came down the Kaitieke all those years ago, goodness knows why, 'that old thing' Ma used to call it and wanted to get rid of it. But it was the one she had brought all the way from Germany when Catha was just a little girl and perhaps that was what Catha wanted to keep, the journey, not just the old thing itself. Because she'd been there for the whole journey and used to say she remembered some of it, though no one believed her, especially Ma – but she always insisted that she did remember, with that stubborn shape to her mouth and her head held up, she remembered a lot, including when her little brother got born on the way, yes that was right, the same brother that had his papa's first name Wolf, yes this one!

That memory of hers reminded him.

There was something he wanted her to do.

Wanted? – Catha's eyebrow going up just like their Ma's used to.

There was something he would like her to do, something Ma had wanted. He would like her to do it.

But what?

Ma had asked for two things to be placed in her coffin when she died, they were in a drawer in her tallboy. He would rather Catha did that because she was the eldest and had been with Ma the longest. She might know what the things were and why they mattered, whereas he might not.

*

And so on the day there were a couple of dozen of them, family and friends, gathered at Ma's graveside up in the Raurimu cemetery, and when Omer lifted his hat and made it flap in a circle around his head a good six or eight of those at the graveside began to more or less whistle the little trill they had practised at his and Ettie's place that had also been Ma's for going on thirty years, and at the Badems' where Omer and Nehir and their oldest boy Asian and one of his kids knew the little trill because Ma's friend Denis had told them all about it when he was alive.

Then the neighbours and friends who didn't know what to make of the whistling heard Catha who was both laughing and crying say Auf wiedersehen und sichere Reise unsere liebe kleine Rohrsänger, that he could just catch the meaning of but that the neighbours and friends couldn't understand and most of the young family ones neither. So then Peter who was at St John's College in Auckland and a clever one with languages made a hemm in his throat and said, ahemm, Goodbye and safe travels our dear little, but then stopped, and Catha said, reed warbler, our dear little reed warbler, and then everybody including the neighbours and friends and even the pastor from Taumarunui all clapped.

And then for the rest of the day including at the afternoon tea back at the house people were talking about the twitter and the story of the brave little bird, and trying the twitter out with funny shapes to their lips. The sewing sampler was displayed in the front room and people were admiring it and touching the pictures on it with careful fingertips, but the things from the tallboy had been sealed in the coffin before it went up to the cemetery on the truck. Catha had not told him what the things were that Ma had wanted buried with her and he would not be asking. Ma had wanted them gone with her and that was how it should be as far as he was concerned.

Beth

A really good red wine seemed like the best idea, assuming Frank could still drink the stuff, so she got him a bottle of Te Mata Coleraine at the international Duty Free. A familiar crowd, at once avaricious and wistful, was wandering through the aisles past the luxury wristwatches and face creams. On the strength of its absurd label she bought herself an elegant container of very expensive Snowberry Intensive Renewal Face Serum. The label on its box promised that it contained a special ingredient, eProlex™, 'developed over several years of intensive skin science research by Snowberry at the University of Auckland'. The special ingredient was 'specifically designed to re-densify ageing skin as well as to help reduce lines and wrinkles'. She might apply some of it to her face after exposing herself to the fierce heat of the sun Frank had promised her at Dingo Beach along with the grilled prawns she might resemble after the sun, but she could also dab some on his leathery cheeks and provoke him with the word 're-densify', assuming he could still be provoked. And after she got back she'd be able to ask her pals at the Staff Club what they knew about their alma mater's intensive research into re-densification.

The rest of the international departure lounge was filled with a different but more familiar crowd, one she knew but was seeing afresh, as if her perceptions had themselves just then been re-densified. It was the crowd that didn't use the VIP lounges, all sorts and ages, some weary and others excited, keeping fractious children amused, huddled with the cabin baggage or eating cheap snacks, speaking many different languages – they were going somewhere new to find new lives for themselves, they were going somewhere that was warmer, or with more opportunity to *better* themselves – that word! – or they were returning to their homelands to visit their families, to a wedding, or a funeral, to see a new baby, or they were just heading off hoping something would happen to change their lives that had become too hard or too boring.

There was a large Indian family agitating around their aged matriarch as if she were a kind of magnetic force. The old woman had a fresh vermilion bindi dot above the long bridge of her nose and she looked piercingly at Beth past the dot and gave her a secretive smile as if to say, They all expect me to be paying attention but why should I? She gave the old woman a courteous smile back and got a knowing nod in return. The nod seemed to be saying, I know you. She had already seen the family at the check-in where a farewelling cadre had been clustered around those departing – there had been much mopping of tears and thrusting-forward of new babies for farewell kisses, and the elderly woman seemed to be the centre of attention.

She took the woman's unnerving nod with her to the juice bar and ordered a large freshly squeezed orange juice. Although she had only glimpsed Frank's granddaughter along with a dog in the background of the Skype call some weeks back, the young woman who served her the juice reminded her of Lizzie and so she found herself a table and sent Lizzie a text asking her how Frank was doing now? The answer came back quickly – Grandad Frank was doing okay though still couldn't speak very well, but she could tell he was really glad Beth was coming over. The message had a thumbs-up emoji at the end, which reminded her of the smiley-face one on the

Freddy archive box.

Joe went to Townsville with his girlfriend Sakura years ago on their zigzag route to Japan so she'd phoned to ask if he had any tips about the place. It was a way of letting him know she was going while at the same time involving him in her decision. But the silence before his reply said that he didn't much want to be reminded about that trip, and then he said he and Sakura had flown to Brisbane and hitched north to Townsville.

'Might not work for you, Ma.'

That was a little joke but also it wasn't, and then after a bit of awkward nothing-much chat he'd said he had to go, he had stuff to do, and he hoped she'd enjoy herself.

It was also hard to gauge the tone of Joe's hope that she'd enjoy herself and she couldn't really tell if he was pulling her leg or not. The hope soon ran pretty steeply against the dread she'd begun to feel not long after getting Lizzie's phone call about Frank. But the dread was as much about seeing Frank after his stroke as it was about how the poor bugger felt, and so spurred on by shame she set about organising her trip. The mental image of Frank with the winking galah head superimposed over his own lurked in her thoughts as she went about her work.

The best online deal was a seven-and-a-bit-hour flight to Townsville with a brief stop in Brisbane on the way and then another forty minutes or so by Uber from Townsville down to Cungulla. There was a crack-of-dawn flight and a late-afternoon one. If she got the later one she could cadge a lift to the airport with Joe and have a chance to chat. Maybe let him know she was sorry for reminding him about his trip with Sakura. But also she liked the idea of drawing breath before getting to Frank's place. Even allowing for the three-hour time difference, she couldn't expect to get there before nine at night if she took the later flight, so she'd booked into the Waters Edge near the Strand in Townsville. The place promised views to something called Magnetic Island which had some appeal as a vista to wake up with. Then she could go on down to Cungulla and get there late morning, having had time to rest.

Of course the Waters Edge recalled the countless times on their road trips that Noel had been seduced by motel names like Seaview where you were likely to be looking at a row of suburban bungalows or a laundromat across the road, but it was worth a try. And asking Lizzie for advice about where to stay before Cungulla would have sent a message that she was procrastinating, which she was.

But when she got there she went for a walk along the promised water's edge, had a dinner of crispy-skinned barramundi with chips and salad and a couple of glasses of fresh cold sauvignon blanc at the rowdy C-Bar, took a photo of her barramundi dinner and texted it to Joe, slept well and woke to a nice enough view of the sea across a strip of grass and past a palm tree. There was a narrow balcony outside the room with a metal table and a couple of chairs, so she rang for some breakfast and then sat out there for a while.

After leaning in to kiss her goodbye at Auckland airport, Joe had told her she looked freaked out and needed to chill. She should have a feed of barramundi with a nice cold beer in Townsville, go for a real good walk in the eucalypts, get into the sea, it wasn't all about bloody old Frank. So those had been some of his tips after all. The elderly Indian matriarch's knowing nod in the departure lounge had communicated something similar but without the tips.

It was going to be about a forty-minute drive down to

Cungulla. She went for a stroll along the Strand, then came back for a shower and checked out. She was going to visit an old mate, she told the Uber driver, and would he mind if she opened the window for some of that fresh air rather than have the aircon on? No worries lady, he said, and she leaned back in her seat thinking that's right, no worries.

Frank's place was on an unfenced residential street that ran along the beachfront at Cungulla. There was a dry expanse of grass with some skinny gums, then a strip of sand, then the sea with a patch of mangroves off to one side. The sea was very blue and still, with the pale shadows of clouds motionless on it. The dog spotted her first as she wheeled her bag around the side of the house past a fragrant frangipani tree and a bougainvillea that had sprawled across the corner of a wide open veranda. It ran at her yelping oddly as if it had a damaged throat. She gave it a scratch along its back and it trotted back the way it had come. The veranda faced the sea and Frank was sitting to one side of it in an old wicker chair. The dog had run to him as if to report her arrival, but then a young woman came out of the house towelling her hair.

Yes, she was Lizzie, sorry she couldn't get to the front door in time.

There was another old cane chair next to Frank, so she pulled it close to him and sat down. He reached over and took her hand, and yes the old Frank grin was there, though a bit lopsided. His left eyelid was halfway down. His legs sticking out of faded khaki shorts were skinny and sun-dark, and his big knobbly feet were crossed at the ankles. They stayed that way and he made no effort to get out of his chair or do more than grip her hand and grin.

But then she saw an effort pull at the muscles in his neck and cheek and he said, intelligibly, 'About bloody time.'

Lizzie brought some fresh lime juice and Frank sipped his through a straw. He could walk okay, she said, steadying the straw in his hand, but he had to take it slow and think about it a bit, and someone had to hold his arm.

John was at work and wee Frankie was having his nap. Later on they could have a barbie on the veranda, Grandad liked to do that. John could bring them back some prawns and stuff from town.

She'd made up the bed for Beth in Frankie's room, he could sleep in bed with John and her for a day or two.

She was glad Beth got the parcels of old papers okay. But the house was pretty much a museum even with them gone.

She had some study to do, she'd leave them to it.

Frank blew her a kiss off his fingertips as she went back inside.

'Clever,' he said. It came out clewer.

On impulse while packing her bag the day before she'd put in the larger of the two envelopes included with the Freddy papers that Lizzie had so neatly and professionally organised. She'd read its contents some days after her first foray.

Had he read any of the stuff that his clever granddaughter Lizzie had organised so beautifully, the family stuff that he'd told her his sister Ruth had been hoping to do something with, and their mother Greta before that?

He was looking out across the patchy yellowed grass at the glittering sea and just shook his head and made a little show of lifting her hand and dropping it. But she'd spotted the telescope on its stand in the front room and the shelves of books in the shadows further in and what she guessed were some of Helen's watercolour sketches of plants and trees on the walls – they were all prompts in their way, so she got up and went inside. Lizzie was sitting at the big table with a laptop and some folders.

Beth's room was just off this one and the toilet was down the passage.

Then she went back to her work.

There was a faded watercolour of a red bottlebrush flower next to the door to little Frank's room, its crazy punkish pistils with their white tips painted with neat precision. She guessed that Helen's granddaughter Lizzie might have got some of her scrupulous ways from that artist. Lizzie had parked her bag next to the bed, which had a neatly folded towel and a facecloth on it, also a bar of eucalyptus soap in a plain green paper wrapper. She took the towel and the soap along to the bathroom and had a pee and a quick wash, and then went back and got the Freddy envelope from her bag.

On the way back to the veranda she asked Lizzie where Dingo Beach was, where they had those extra-special prawns.

About two hundred and fifty-odd k down the coast, why, was Beth thinking of going down there?

'Thought this might interest you,' she said to Frank back on the veranda. 'You old bugger. You promised me prawns at Dingo Beach but it's halfway back to bloody Brisbane.'

She saw him preparing his face and mouth to say something.

'Next time.' *Neck sime.*

Then he nodded his head at the chair beside him.

Freddy, whose stuff Lizzie had packed up and sent to her, had telescopes where he lived on a tea plantation way the hell up a river near Assam, and he'd looked at the stars and written something. She thought Frank might be interested?

'He reminded me of you,' she said. 'Bit of a crazy.'

That wonky smile.

The sheets of paper were yellow, with faded blue typewriter text. The first sheet was headed up 'A New Theory of the Universe', and when she read that aloud Frank cackled with laughter. It was a sudden, surprising noise and concluded with a deep barking cough, at which the dog thumped its tail on the veranda. Frank was reaching for the box of tissues on the floor beside him, so she got one out and wiped his mouth and chin. Then she began to read aloud Freddy's 'New Theory of the Universe', which began with the statement that for many years he had liked to look at the stars through his telescope when the sky was clear and he now knew quite a lot about them, having had time at his disposal, but what had begun to interest him more than the celestial bodies themselves was the means by which their light was transmitted across such vast expanses of space.

Frank's lopsided smile had been replaced by a frown that almost shut his left, lidded eye. He waved 'Go on' with his good hand, the one from which he'd blown a kiss at Lizzie, the one that had held hers when she first arrived. The other one lay in his lap and it seemed he couldn't move it.

> Many years ago the English scientist, Dalton, gave the world of science the Atomic Theory, all chemical elements consisted of atoms the smallest particle of an element that could enter into chemical combination with atoms of other elements. With most elements the atoms combine together forming a molecule of two atoms.

Lizzie came out – she could make some lunch if they'd like? There were some just-ripe avocados, she could make a guacamole to put on that nice fresh bread?

Frank's hand that had waved her the kiss waved the

guacamole away. She came back with the jug of lime juice and put it down on the veranda next to them. Then she went back inside. The quick, faint clicking of her keyboard, a bit of a wheeze in Frank's breathing, the sporadic squawk of a bird down towards the sea.

'Want me to go on?'

'Freddy.' *Furdy.*

'Yes, Frank. Your Great-uncle Frederick Wenczel. The mystery man. Well, guess what, he's come to light after all these years. So to speak.'

She poured them each a refill of the lime juice and helped Frank with his straw. Then she read on.

> Our universe is an electric universe and where protons are found in this universe galaxies are in the process of formation, or have been formed in former eons of time. What exists between the galaxies, between the stars which form them and nebulae, masses of gasses which are seen in our own Milky Way.

She hesitated over Freddy's awkward sentence about the masses of gasses and looked up at Frank, but he was staring with that frown down towards the glitter of light that came between the eucalypt trunks from the sea. It seemed to her that what he was listening to and what he was seeing were connected – he was sitting very still as if concentrating on that connection.

'My hypothesis is this,' she read, and heard Frank's little laugh-cough and saw his face turn back towards her with his crooked smile back on it.

'Furdy's,' he began, but stopped.

'Yes, Freddy Wenczel's hypothesis.'

> My hypothesis is this; these enormous spaces are filled with electrons, negative particles of electricity which repel each other and by so doing in the vicinity of the solid or gaseous bodies like the sun and the planets are the cause of gravitation which these bodies seem to possess.

She took a quick peek at Frank – he was once again staring ahead and the forefinger of his functioning hand was tapping slowly on the arm of his wicker chair.

> Light from the farthest stars reaches us with the same speed as an electric current travels through a copper wire. The electron alone without the mass of a proton about which it revolves cannot reach a body consisting of elements, protons and electrons bound together by atomic force.

Another peek. Now Frank was looking at her with his grin that might have been or meant something not grin-like. Go on, went his hand.

> Thus the hypothetical 'Ether' of former scientists is nothing but a universal mass of electrons which pervades all space. Such is the medium which carries light throughout the universe.

Freddy Wenczel's 'New Hypothesis' text ended with the polite request to 'Please keep this paper it may be of interest sometime in the future.'

The cough of Frank's laugh.

'Not bad,' he said. *Nos pad.* His good hand clapping against the arm of his chair. *Nos pad, Furdy.*

*

Frank walked slowly and carefully with his good hand gripping her arm and got knee-deep in the sea. He reached his good hand down and scooped water over his face and head, soaking his shirt and shorts. Then she helped to lower him on to the sand with his feet in the sea while she paddled about with little Frankie. There were blushes on the wisps of cloud at the horizon and the trees in Frank's yard were shaking a little as the breeze got up. A raucous flock of cockatoos flew the length of the beach and Frank let go of her arm to give them a wave. She could smell the frangipani as they came back from the beach, and he made a show of snuffing up the fragrance.

Frankie's dadda John had already fired up the barbie and was lifting the prawns off it. He'd gone over the top and got a couple of whopping spanner crabs, did Beth like crab?

The crabs looked pretty serious, she reckoned, and she had something that might go well with them.

She fetched the bottle of Te Mata Coleraine from her bag and poured them all a glass. Frank wanted a proper glass as well and waved the straw away.

It was great to see her dear old cuzzie-mate again and she wished him a speedy recovery. Next time she came over the bugger had to take her down to Dingo Beach like he'd promised.

The rowdy cockatoos flew back again from wherever they'd gone. Frank seemed to be saluting them as he raised his glass and swivelled in his chair to watch them go.

Catharina

Of course even though she herself still thought of her mother as 'Mutti', she had long ago stopped calling her that in public, and even within the family 'Ma' as Wolf used it had become the usual way she referred to the neat little woman she had addressed in German at her graveside. There was no one there, or later on in Wolf's house for the afternoon tea, who bore him any ill will, let alone thought unkindly of his mother who was widely loved and respected in the community on account of her demeanour but also because of her skills as a seamstress, which were 'legendary', Greta said admiringly after listening to conversations at the tea – but even so word of German being spoken openly had got to the authorities, who came to see Wolf only a couple of days after the funeral.

She and Greta were still at the house helping with the tidy-up, although Greta was fretting to get back to her bellicose fiancé Albert who was dogmatic that there was going to be war and he damned well hoped so! The two policemen from Taumarunui were well known to Wolf and drank their cups of tea with him out on the porch. Afterwards they shook his hand, took polite farewell of Ettie and rather more formal leave of Greta and herself, and drove back the way they'd come up the road Wolf had surveyed and bridged long enough ago for almost everyone to have forgotten he'd done it, though at the time it had been a legendary feat or so Mutti had told her.

He was closing in on sixty, he said to Ettie, and his sister who had uttered the seditious words at their mother's graveside was somewhat older than him. His family had lived peacefully in the valley for a bit over thirty years, plenty of time to raise a secret army of toothless old enemy Huns hanging about somewhere in the bush down there towards the Wanganui who all whistled in a secret code.

Was that what he'd told them, Ettie wanted to know.

Yes, and also that his big boy Adam could easily pot a rabbit sticking its head up fifty yards away over the river. But don't worry, he hadn't reminded them that his sister's husband the professor of spying had been locked away on that island in Wellington harbour last time. Meanwhile the valley was short of patriots because the land wasn't that way inclined – half the sheep men had walked off when things got rough a few years ago, and poor old Smithy would be walking off his place any day now, no way he could skittle his loan and anyone could see that the dirt his grass was meant to grow on was so useless most of it had washed away down the river, same as it had with half the others. It was the elements that were traitors, not the local Krauts.

Then he'd gone out to get on with his day's work.

But what would become of Elke when Smithy went?

Elke might have to look after herself, said Ettie a little sharply, meaning perhaps that their granddaughter shouldn't take her and Wolf's house for granted, any more than she should dwell on the likelihood of her mother Aggie coming back to the valley any time in the near future.

And then after a couple more days she and Greta had been back on the train to Wellington, and she saw her clever daughter squeeze her eyes shut and make a phew shape with her lips when she thought her mother wasn't looking.

And perhaps Greta's phew was because back then in the days after Mutti's funeral a tension had grown up between her mother and Ettie, because Ettie knew that she, Catharina, had taken some things from the tallboy and put them in her mother's coffin before Wolf nailed the lid on. He'd run his finger around the edge of it and yes, it was a fine tight fit, said his nod and the set of his lips, but he'd been looking at her across it in the moment before he then tapped the first nail in. His look had said thank you, but also that he did not want to know what was in the two packets.

Ettie had been watching the nailing down and so she saw the two packets being placed on Ma's chest and also the look that Wolf gave his sister. What was that about, she asked later once the guests had gone – what were those things you put in the coffin, Catha? But she was half looking at Wolf as she asked, because the question was really for him, on account of the complicit look she had seen.

He didn't know and he didn't want to, he said, and that was why he'd asked Catha to do what their Ma had asked for, which was to bury those things with her. And so they were meant to go to the grave with her and as far as he was concerned all knowledge of them was meant to go there with her as well.

But Ettie's sharp glance at her had then clearly asked if she had seen what the things were, and so was she, Catharina, now the guardian of the secrets of them?

And yes, she had seen them, but was not going to tell Ettie or Wolf that she had unless they expressly asked her, because unlike Wolf she did not believe that Ma had forbidden anyone to look at them – she knew her little Mutti well and if she had wanted to forbid anyone to look at the special things she would have been very clear about it. Wolf was entitled to his view and she respected both his candour and his rectitude, but the alternative story and the one she herself preferred to believe with just as much candour and rectitude was that it could very well be that the objects were special ones that Mutti had wanted to take with her on her journey to the afterlife, however she characterised that in her beliefs, and why should her children and their children not know that part of their story? And it had seemed to her that her brother, with his usual way of speaking at once forthrightly and mysteriously, had not forbidden her on their mother's behalf to look at the special things in Mutti's tallboy – he had, rather, acknowledged by not mentioning it that his sister was entitled to her own view on their Ma's special things, and that was her business and none of his.

And yes, in the moment she had begun to open the small top left-hand drawer of the tallboy on the morning of the burial, she was quite sure she had not conveniently persuaded herself that what she planned to do was acceptable merely to disguise from herself the fact that she was just curious and what difference could it make?

Ach! – even so, she had hesitated for a moment, but then remembered the many times she had seen and heard her Mutti's bright sharp wit communicate clearly that yes, she had lived a life that would seem unusual or even scandalous in some respects in the eyes of more conventional members of the community, but they didn't need to know any more about her life than she chose to tell them, whereas her children and their children had every right to know if they wished.

She remembered very well Mutti's sharp riposte to poor Hugo when he had attempted to trump her account of life at the Bloch House and the conversations in which she had been included and encouraged to 'have a mind of her own'.

The objects were a letter envelope and a notebook in a

larger manila envelope. Both seemed quite old – the letter envelope yellowed and the notebook an old-fashioned one with Gothic lettering on the front. The address on the letter envelope was to Mrs Josephina Hansen, 4 Bute Street, Wellington, New Zealand, and inside were two pages of neat handwriting with a plain 'Theodora' signature at the end. The letter was dated 1908 and had a sender's address in Brisbane, Australia. She read the letter quickly and without surprise or dismay, remembering in ghostly fragments as she did so the dark-haired woman who had lived with them for a while in the little cottage in Bute Street. She was the sister of the man she knew to be Wolf's father but whom she remembered if at all as being oddly stooped like a goblin, as if her memory of him had been mixed up with an illustration in a children's book – he had died on the voyage from Germany to New Zealand when she was about four or five years old. Mutti had sometimes talked about him with sadness and love when she was older, but what she envisaged from Mutti's reminiscences were not memories.

Theodora Bloch's letter to Mutti was written in a firm, steady hand with the careful paragraphs of someone used to organising readable pages. Its tone was quite straightforward and almost curt except for a second-to-last paragraph about first encountering Mutti and herself when they went to see the sewing room in Hamburg. This she did not remember at all, although a horse was there that was much higher than her and the sensation of its vast warm flank under her hand was there as well. Perhaps the horse was connected to the scene described by Theodora's matter-of-fact poetry, or perhaps it was just one of the vague fragments that emerged when she tried to think about her childhood?

She was now just an old damned nuisance Quälgeist, as

she heard people saying pretty often, Theodora had written. She was the loving sister of the dear little man she believed Josephina had loved more than any other. She had had a life she was happy to look back on, much of it with the brother she had loved as had Josephina, and then with her comrades in the Social-Democratic Vanguard in Queensland, including her comrade Hugo Kunze in Brisbane. It had been her work for many years to write for the Vanguard and do office work for the Party. In recent years she had done less of that work and was now living more quietly and enjoying the company of her friends and especially the women who had come together to form the Women's Progressive Club. Perhaps the name Margaret Ogg had reached New Zealand?

Then came the second-to-last paragraph in which Theodora's matter-of-fact tone changed.

She wanted Josephina to know that for all the years leading up to her present circumstances she had never forgotten the sight of her standing in Herr Johannes Paul's sewing room in Hamburg with that beautiful child beside her. She remembered how the dusty light had lit their faces and the strands of fair hair that came out below their bonnets. She had fallen in love at that moment and had never ceased to love the woman she had seen for the first time in that sewing room even when it was clear her love would not be returned, and had continued to love her after she and Wolf became lovers at the Bloch House and then the mother and father of that boy child born on the voyage.

The last paragraph returned to the matter-of-fact tone of earlier ones, but the effect of the one before with its declaration of love seeped into it like the dusty light Theodora had described.

But now she, Theodora, had decided that after all these

years she could not go on without telling Josephina the truth. Josephina herself should know that she, Theodora, had led a life that had rewarded her in many ways, and not least with the enduring image of Josephina and her lovely child Catharina standing lit by those shafts of dusty sunlight in comrade Herr Paul's sewing room all those years ago.

'And so now goodbye my dear Josephina, and may your life be as rewarding as your nature deserves, and may your children have good lives lit by the warmth of their mother's love.'

She had quickly set aside an inappropriate sense of entitlement after reading Theodora's letter since, although she was mentioned in it, it had been for Mutti, and for Mutti to know about that dark-haired woman's feelings for her. She, the 'beautiful child' mentioned by Theodora, had been moved more by the letter's forthright tone than by its emotion, and she had put it back in its envelope wishing she had known that woman better and as an adult, not the child lit by dusty sunlight.

The journal in the larger manila envelope was obviously one of Wolf Bloch's – she could decipher that much from the Gothic inscription on its flyleaf, as well as the date, 1879. The journal was almost full. The first lengthy entry in it was dated 'Bloch House, Hamburg, April 20th, 1879', and the final brief entry in it was from 'December 20th, 1879'. This one recorded in scant detail the fact that Wolf Bloch was sick after eating something in the Cape Verde Islands. It was possibly the last thing he had written before his death. It, and the letter from his sister, though written some thirty years apart, seemed to be joined by a kind of invisible thread. She had replaced the journal in its envelope without reading further. It was easy to guess that it had been very precious to Mutti and it was with a sense of what was respectful that she had closed it. Perhaps Wolf Bloch had written about his and Mutti's relationship in earlier parts of the journal, and if so she preferred to consign it to the privacy of the grave – complying with her brother's preference or perhaps instinct by at least that much.

It was the vivid memory of Greta's covert phew as they left on the train some days after Mutti's funeral that had really cleared the path for the utter confusion of other memories around the events of the days at Wolf's place down the Kaitieke back then going on five years ago! – the sight of Mutti herself in her neat blue scarf, which she could not imagine ever forgetting, the special things in her little tallboy drawer likewise, but most of all the ragged whistling of the Rohrsänger's song by those around the grave and then her own voice saying those German words *Auf wiedersehen und sichere Reise unsere liebe kleine Rohrsänger*, words she had not even rehearsed to herself and might have thought unwise given time to think about them – and then a day or two later the polite handshakes of the policemen from Taumarunui.

The eldest of them was a man in his fifties, she judged, whose name was Thompson, Sergeant Thompson, with grey in his hair and moustache and a set of false teeth that she had noticed him push quickly in and out with his tongue before coming forward to shake her hand. Sergeant Thompson walked away afterwards with the slight hobble of someone with uncomfortable boots, perhaps because of bunions or corns. She had felt a pang of sympathy for him, a hobbled man consigned to the demeaning task of looking into potential enemy aliens among people he had probably known for years, while younger men with better teeth and feet were marching off to glory.

She saw the same Greta phew from five years ago but not a covert one this time as she took one of the twins from her, the thin leggy little boy called Frank, whom she tried to interest in the bottle of warm milk while he tore jerkily at his cheeks and neck and screamed until he turned crimson. His sister Ruth, meanwhile, was falling peacefully asleep with her bottle's teat slipping from the corner of her still weakly sucking mouth, while her poor mother likewise began to fall asleep.

Of course this exhausted woman was still her daughter Greta, the clever one who occupied an editor's desk at the *Evening Post*, or who believed she was expected to reoccupy that desk once her domestic situation permitted it, but for now the lank hair falling across her face was the sign of her utter surrender to exhaustion. And meanwhile she had assured her mother with that set of her jaw familiar from when she was still just a little girl proud of being able to read *The Swiss Family Robinson*, she and the twins would get along all right on the pension granted poor Albert.

'Poor Albert' the warmonger Greta had married when well into her thirties a week before he went off to camp as a volunteer, the 'poor Albert' who had blown one of his own legs off at training and been retired from active service six months after volunteering! Who without irony blamed his drinking on 'the enemy'!

She understood well that there was nothing to be gained by making her opinion of 'poor Albert' known, although of course it was, in her silence. And as if in reciprocal agreement, Greta no longer brought up what she had once referred to as her mother's 'unfortunate experiment' with Professor Hugo von Welden, the father she had revered as a martyr until he 'ran away'. Now it was clear between them that she knew better than to provoke her mother with anything more blatant than that tilt of her jaw that her mother called 'the look'. There was nothing to be gained from recriminations – they had agreed on that without actually doing so. A certain amount of levity seemed more reasonable under the circumstances, such as 'par for the course', Wolf's oddly inappropriate comment on 'poor Albert' since he, Wolf, had never played golf for goodness sake let alone met the man who had subsequently succeeded in fathering the twins while 'legless', Albert's own facetious term that now usually meant he was blind drunk.

Her phone calls with Wolf had not been helpful, and it was clear there was no possibility of his and Ettie's place being offered as a haven for Greta and the twins Frank and Ruth, any more than was her own modest cottage in Blenheim with its view of the plain yellow Wither Hills that she longed for quite unreasonably whenever she was away from them for more than a week.

She herself had looked after Wolf's odd granddaughter Elke for the summer holidays once or twice, and other wayward girls before Elke from time to time when she was still at the college. But now she preferred her own company and that of a few close friends nearby.

Albert Parks called himself the Parks Department as if the joke was fresh every time he told it, and did clumsy Oliver Hardy impersonations with a candle-black 'Adolf' moustache. Most of the time he just wasn't really there, said Greta, even though at least one of his legs was.

To her credit she seldom judged him even when she was angry but what she would not tolerate was him saying that he should have known better than to marry a bloody frooline and what about that bloody uncle of hers up country giving himself airs like landed gentry.

Uncle Wolf giving himself airs! At least she, Catharina, could have a laugh of sorts with Greta about the notion of Wolf 'giving himself airs'.

But the Wither Hills were like sleeping lions, she thought, though she had never seen one either awake or asleep, and when she had been away from the hills for a while she began to imagine their animal warmth and the peace of their long afternoon sleeps.

She needed to go home, she told her tired clever daughter Greta a few days later. She was after all just an old damned nuisance Quälgeist when all was said and done. She needed some time to herself, and to recover a sense that her life or what was left of it was her own. She was looking forward very much to the 'what was left'. She would get the ferry back to Picton in a week or two, once the twins had settled down a bit. It was little Frank that she worried about, he had a restless spirit that one, and not because he had a colicky tummy. His twin sister Ruth, on the other hand, might surprise them all one day. A child that appeared to sleep peacefully but with those agitations of her eyelids might be the one who would have a more thoughtful and troubling vision of how the world was.

But meanwhile her own perspective was not an especially long one, and she was almost content with her view of lion-coloured light on the Wither Hills towards the end of the day, and the peace of her solitude. If Greta needed her in an urgent way of some kind she could of course phone or send her a telegram, and the ferry boat to Wellington was not so far away after all.

It had been a calm crossing for once, and the unsteadiness of the current as the ferry went in through the narrow passage at the entry to the winding waterway into the Sound barely disturbed her where she stood in the salty breeze at the rail and watched the rough shoreline with its rim of white water slide away behind the ship.

She would have a nice boiled egg for supper and then go to bed with *Bovary*. She was up to the section in Part III, 'She Would and She Would Not', where Emma and Léon careen madly around Rouen in the horse-drawn cab with closed blinds. She always enjoyed getting to this part, where the coachman's comic frustration and despair as he is ordered to 'Go on!' mask but also mirror the concealed 'go on' passions of the couple within. 'At about six o'clock the carriage stopped in a back street of the Beauvoisine Quarter, and a woman got out, who walked with her veil down, and without turning her head.'

She could feel the shape of the smile on her face as she took her glasses off and put them on top of *Bovary* on the bedside cabinet, and then turned the light out and saw quite vividly the horse-drawn carriage tearing around the streets of the town with the sole purpose of prolonging what was concealed within it.

Afterword

This is a work of fiction. The characters and events in it are invented. However, the ghosts of historical events and of people whose stories are known to me haunt the fictions. My German great-grandmother Maria Josephine Catharina Reepen came to New Zealand from Haderslev in northern Denmark, although her German family had lived in Kiel in the north of Germany. She married my great-grandfather, Heinrich August Wedde, a runaway sailor, in Wellington in 1876. They had eight children, three of whom lived on Land Settlement farms in the Kaitīeke valley. One of them, Monty, stayed on after his brothers had walked off their land; he became a beekeeper and gave his name to a legendary apple, Monty's Surprise. He might have been surprised to find himself haunting the fictional character of Wolf Wenczel in this book.

My great-grandmother was buried in the Raurimu cemetery in 1927, and in 2016 I visited her grave with my second cousin Peter Wedde, after we had been at a family reunion in Wellington. It was about then, after the rich but confusing conversations of the reunion, looking down the long, twisty view-shaft of the Kaitīeke valley and the equally twisty view-shaft of family history, legend and forgetfulness, that I began to think about writing a fiction with that kind of twisty structure.

The crossovers between personal memory and official history are unstable, as are those between the purported disinterest of official, 'factual' history, and the self-interested biases of institutional and family histories. The kinds of time they occupy differ and dither, and the documents and mementos that vouch for them have unstable provenances. The past may be vividly present in personal memory, in that shifty time when we are remembering the past while attempting to be alert in the present.

What passes for personal memory may in fact consist of the stories we have been told about events and people that we almost believe we experienced. And then, little by little, over time, the attritions of personal and institutional forgetfulness begin to thin out the stories that once continued to occupy the present with their pasts and with the people whose pasts they were.

These ghostly presences and the unstable functions of memory and time constitute the slight, ghostly framework across which the fictional characters and events of this novel are deployed. However, I have had a photograph of my great-grandmother close by as I wrote this book, and it has been her firm gaze and wry lips that have watched me and reminded me that this story is not hers.

There are other hauntings. The fictional character of the Social Democrat Wolf Bloch with whom my character Josephina has a son (Wolf Wenczel) in 1880 while on board ship to New Zealand owes much to an historical person called Johannes Wedde (1843–1890), a remote relative whose memorial portrait is included on the Plakat Sozialistengesetz 1890, along with those of Karl Marx and other deceased comrades. Johannes Wedde was a prolific correspondent and writer and now mostly forgotten poet, and it is his lengthy and impassioned paean to the doomed Paris Commune of 1871, 'Zum Gedächtnis', that I have appropriated to my character Wolf Bloch, along with a couple of verses from Johannes Wedde's poem to his wife, 'An meine Frau' (Hamburg, 25 October 1883). The Wedde household in Hamburg also included his sister Theodora whose name I have appropriated to Wolf Bloch's sister in this fiction. She published a memoir of her brother, *Johannes Wedde: Gedenkblätter von seiner Schwester*, in 1891. The household was well known for its hospitality and as a meeting place for Social Democrats. I like to think the household would have extended its hospitality to my story, and included in that Gastfreundschaft some fragments of historical correspondence involving Friedrich Engels.

My character Theodora is credited with having written 'An

Appeal to Women' for the Brisbane-based Social-Democratic Vanguard. The tract was in fact written by the pseudonymous 'Comrade Mary', whose name was frequently associated with another Brisbane-based Social Democrat, codename 'Comrade Eznuk' – 'Eznuk' is 'Kunze' spelled backwards, and was the name of the German immigrant Hugo Kunze, like my character Wolf Bloch a refugee from the anti-socialist repressions of Chancellor Bismarck that began in 1878. I thank 'Comrade Mary' for providing Theodora Bloch with her Vanguard exhortation.

I have attributed some anonymous film reviews in the *Evening Post* from 1920 to my character Greta, the granddaughter of Josephina in my story. I thank the anonymous critic and hope that she or he would have wished Greta well in her career as a journalist.

A more egregious appropriation is the text, towards the end of this fiction, attributed to my character Freddy Wenczel. This is the 'New Theory of the Universe' that was in fact written by my great-grandmother's youngest child, Frederick Alexander 'Fritz' Wedde, the family's mystery man, who disappeared without trace for many years before emerging in Torreon, Mexico, in 1958, shortly before his death. I have appropriated a fragment of my own life story by relocating my fictional long-lost Freddy to a place where I lived as a child in the 1950s and revisited in 2005, the upper reaches of the Karnifuli River in what is now called Bangladesh. The historical Fritz is said to have built and lived in an observatory tower in Mexico from which he looked at the stars. I like to think that the historical Fritz would have been pleased to see his tract republished, since he ended it with the irresistible hope that 'it may be of interest sometime in the future'.

I could not have written this book without the generous support of Creative New Zealand grants. In addition, the Creative New Zealand Berlin Writer's Residency in 2015/16 allowed me to spend time in the Staatsbibliothek Berlin archives where I was able to read about Johannes Wedde and to access his poems and correspondence, and to understand the situation of Social Democrats through his eyes and those of his sister Theodora. The Residency also allowed me to visit Kiel in the north where my great-grandmother was born. It was through this visit that I understood the odd connection between that family and Kiel's poet, Klaus Groth, whose poem 'Wie traulich war das Fleckchen' ('How cosy was the little spot') became the book's meme for how memory both works and fails.

I acknowledge the critical sympathy of my wife Donna Malane, who read this book in instalments and always improved not only the part she had just read but also as a consequence what came next.

Finally, very grateful thanks to the book's marvellous editor, Jane Parkin; and to its publisher Fergus Barrowman for his invaluable encouragement.